"I've thought about things all night," Abby said at last. **"The only solution is for me to quit. You can hire someone else."**

"Who?" Caleb challenged. "Widows with infants aren't all that plentiful in Wolf Creek, and if I hired someone else it would just spark the same gossip we're dealing with."

Abby chewed on her lower lip. "I could take Betsy to my place," she offered.

He shook his head. "We've already discussed that. She belongs at home. Winter will be here before we know it, and getting back and forth will be a nightmare when the weather gets bad. Besides, I already know how hard it is for you to manage things at your place, and I don't think you can make it through the winter alone with three children."

She sat down in her chair and rested her elbows on the table, regarding him with tear-glazed eyes. "What other choice do we have, Caleb? I can't think of any other way."

The full force of his silvery gaze met hers, "The only way I can think of is for you to marry me."

Penny Richards

Wolf Creek Wedding
&
Wolf Creek Homecoming

LOVE INSPIRED
INSPIRATIONAL ROMANCE

LOVE INSPIRED®
INSPIRATIONAL ROMANCE

ISBN-13: 978-1-335-50826-3

Wolf Creek Wedding & Wolf Creek Homecoming

Copyright © 2020 by Harlequin Books S.A.

Wolf Creek Wedding
First published in 2013. This edition published in 2020.
Copyright © 2013 by Penny Richards

Wolf Creek Homecoming
First published in 2014. This edition published in 2020.
Copyright © 2014 by Penny Richards

This edition published by arrangement with Harlequin Books S.A.

For questions and comments about the quality of this book, please contact us at CustomerService@Harlequin.com.

Love Inspired
22 Adelaide St. West, 40th Floor
Toronto, Ontario M5H 4E3, Canada
www.Harlequin.com

Printed in U.S.A.

CONTENTS

Penny Richards has been publishing since 1983, writing mostly contemporary romances. She now happily pens inspirational historical romance and loves spending her days in the "past" when things were simpler and times were more innocent. She enjoys research, yard sales, flea markets, revamping old stuff and working in her flower gardens. A mother, grandmother and great-grandmother, she tries to spend as much time as possible with her family.

Books by Penny Richards

Love Inspired Historical

Wolf Creek Wedding
Wolf Creek Homecoming
Wolf Creek Father
Wolf Creek Widow
Wolf Creek Wife

Love Inspired

Unanswered Prayers

Visit the Author Profile page
at Harlequin.com for more titles.

WOLF CREEK WEDDING

For the unbelieving husband is sanctified by the wife.
—*1 Corinthians* 7:14

This book is for Mom, my biggest cheerleader.
I owe all my creativity—cooking, writing, art,
all of it—to you. You were a great example.
Wish you were here to help me in the garden.
I miss you.

ACKNOWLEDGMENTS

As always, thanks to LaRee and Sandy
for your input and encouragement.

Chapter One

Wolf Creek, Arkansas
October 1885

The faintest sound of a baby's crying was carried on the brisk October breeze. Dr. Rachel Stone's buggy pulled to a stop in front of a large, rambling farmhouse, which was located west of town, three miles down the road that led to Pisgah.

Forest-green shutters framed the front windows and contrasted with pristine white clapboards. A porch, complete with a green swing, spanned the front of the house. Autumn's chill was slow to arrive in southwest Arkansas. Blue morning glory climbed up posts toward the roof, and blankets of native clematis rambled onto the lawn, hundreds of tiny white flowers bobbing in the gentle breeze.

Abby Carter made a sound of disbelief, and her wide-eyed gaze found her friend's. On some level she'd known the Gentry family was one of the most affluent in Wolf Creek, but until now, she had never given it much thought.

Smiling at Abby's astonishment, Rachel climbed down and looped the reins over the hitching post. Rounding the carriage, she reached up to take baby Laura from Abby's arms.

"Mind your manners," Abby reminded six-year-old Ben as he scrambled down. Still wearing an expression of amazement, she jumped to the ground, and they all started up the broad steps of the porch.

They had barely reached the top when the front door crashed open. Abby's startled gaze flew to the face of the man who would be her new employer. Caleb Gentry. Wealthy gentleman farmer. Father of newly born Betsy. Widower, as of a few hours ago. He was a big man—tall, broad-shouldered and narrow-hipped, his features too chiseled and angular to be considered handsome. His clothes looked as if he'd slept in them—which he no doubt had, if he'd managed any sleep the previous night—and he was in dire need of a shave. His thick, coffee-brown hair stood on end, and there was a wild look in his steel-gray eyes.

He looked angry and unapproachable. Difficult. Abby's heart sank. What had she gotten into?

At the first sight of the quartet coming up the steps, Caleb flung open the door, relief sweeping through him. Their arrival offered welcome respite from the sickening churning of his stomach that had plagued him since Rachel emerged from his wife's room and informed him that Emily was dead. Stunning news to a man who had only recently come to terms with the idea of being a father.

Accustomed to dealing with the many unexpected problems that cropped up with the running of a successful farming operation and his most recent enterprise, a gravel business, Caleb felt that in general he handled his life with a certain competence. In the blink of an eye, though, he discovered things were going to be very different. When Rachel left him in charge of the baby while she went to talk to Abby Carter about becoming a wet nurse and to inform Emily's parents of her death, he'd known that he was not prepared to bear sole responsibility for every aspect of his daughter's welfare.

In fact, thus far, he'd done a miserable job of things.

The baby, whom he had named Betsy according to Emily's wishes, had spent more time crying than sleeping. Scared witless to hold her, he had nonetheless picked her up and patted, bounced and even tried singing to her. "Old Dan Tucker" vocalized in a gravelly baritone hadn't done a thing to still her wailing. He had drawn the line at diapering—she was just too little and it was too scary to handle her any more than necessary. No doubt she was wet as well as hungry, which is why he was so relieved to see the approaching foursome.

Rachel Stone led the way, carrying a baby who looked just under a year old. A boy of five or six followed her, and a slight blond-haired woman who must be Abby Carter brought up the rear.

"What the devil took you so long?" he growled, raking long fingers through hair that already stood on end.

"We got here as soon as we could," Rachel said in a conciliatory tone, ushering Ben ahead of her.

Betsy gave another ear-piercing wail. Without waiting for introductions, Caleb turned his wild-eyed gaze to the newcomer, grabbed her arm and hauled her through the doorway. "She's been screaming for hours," he snapped. "Do something."

Instead of answering, Abby Carter looked from the fingers gripping her upper arm into his eyes. Hers were calm, though he thought he detected a hint of reproach and maybe even irritation in their blue depths. He snatched his hand away, as if she were hot to the touch.

Without a word, Mrs. Carter crossed to the cradle sitting near the fireplace, where a small blaze kept the chill at bay. She took a diaper from a nearby stack and set about changing Betsy while murmuring whatever nonsensical things women say to children in need of comfort. Things that were missing from male vocabularies. Finished, she wrapped a flannel blanket around Betsy and looked at Rachel, a question in her eyes.

"The kitchen is through there," Rachel said, pointing. Without a word, Mrs. Carter disappeared through the doorway, bestowing the briefest glance on him as she passed.

Caleb planted his hands on his hips and dropped his head, silently berating himself for his impatience with the woman who had only come to help. From the kitchen, Betsy's crying stopped. Quiet, the first in hours, filled the room, bringing with it a calming peace that Caleb had sense enough to know was bound to be short-lived. He scrubbed a trembling hand down his face.

"I know it's nerve-racking," Rachel said. "You'll get used to it." Seeing the expression of panic return, she offered him a weary smile. "Abby can't fix everything, Caleb. Babies cry for lots of reasons, but everything is going to be fine. She's a good mother."

Caleb was not so sure about anything being fine ever again.

"Did the Emersons come while I was gone?" Rachel asked.

He nodded. "Your dad sent someone...for Emily. They're coming back later to see Betsy."

"Well, then," Rachel said, setting Mrs. Carter's baby on the floor, "I'll just take care of the birthing room, help get Abby settled and get back to town."

She gave Ben instructions to keep an eye on his sister, and disappeared into the room Emily had moved to early in her pregnancy because his "tossing and turning" kept her awake.

With silence reigning in the kitchen and the knowledge that Abby Carter was there to help smooth out this new wrinkle in his life, a sudden weariness overtook Caleb. Huffing out a deep sigh, he sank into a corner of the camelback sofa and re-visited the events that had changed his life forever.

More than four hours ago, the crying and plead-ing and screaming had stopped, replaced by the sudden, angry wail of a baby. The reprieve lasted only until Rachel stepped into the room carrying a small bundle in her arms and told him that he had a daughter and that Emily was dead. He was trying to assimilate that fact when Rachel informed him the baby would require a wet nurse and suggested recently widowed Abigail Carter. His head spin-ning with the gravity and magnitude of the events unfolding in his life, Caleb acquiesced and sent Ra-chel on her way.

A log fell in the fireplace, bringing him out of his drowsy trance. His glance wandered toward the kitchen. Thank goodness Rachel had been right about Mrs. Carter's willingness to help.

In the kitchen, Abby's tender gaze lingered on the face of the baby in her arms while her finger-tips skimmed the incomparable softness of Betsy's dark hair. Was there anything more precious than a new life or anything sadder than a child grow-ing up without the love and guidance of a parent? She was struck with a sudden pang of loss. Even now, eight months after William's death, she often experienced a stark reminder that he would not be there to share or to help with the joys and trials that cropped up daily with Ben and Laura. As difficult as it had been for her since he died, she knew life would be just as trying for Caleb Gentry, though in an entirely different way, something that she'd understood full well when Rachel had arrived earlier and told her the news of Emily Gentry's death.

"How awful!" Abby had said. "I can certainly sympathize with Mr. Gentry's loss." She'd never met Caleb Gentry, but she knew who he was, as did everyone in Pike County.

"Of everyone I know, I knew you'd understand," Rachel told her.

"You look worn out," Abby noted, ushering her friend inside. "Come on into the kitchen and rest a bit. I just took some cookies from the oven and I'm rewarming the breakfast coffee."

"Thanks, but I can't stay," Rachel told her. "Too many things to do. Before I drove out here, I had to go and tell the Emersons about Emily so that they could make arrangements for her body to be moved."

"They must be devastated," Abby said, unable to imagine losing either of her children. "What can I do to help? Make Mr. Gentry a meal?"

"Under different circumstances, I'm sure that would be appreciated, but that isn't why I'm here. To be blunt, little Betsy Gentry is in need of a wet nurse." Rachel hurried on before Abby could object. "I know things have been tight for you since William died, and I thought you might be glad of the extra money."

Abby stared into Rachel's dark eyes, her mind whirling with implications of the unexpected offer.

For months now, she had systematically, often tearfully, sold almost everything she owned of value, consoling herself with the maxim that her father's pocket watch and her mother's silver coffee service were just *things*. Things she did not *need*. She had juggled the meager funds and prayed for some sort of miracle to provide for her children. She'd even considered trying to teach again, but Wolf Creek was no different from other towns, which wanted only men or unmarried women instructing their young ones. Even if that were not the case, she wasn't sure how she'd manage a full-time job with two children of her own.

God will provide... He never shuts a door that He doesn't open a window...all things work for good.

Abby was familiar with all the platitudes, had even heard them coming from her own lips when the trials and losses were someone else's. She believed what the Bible said, and blamed the weakness of her faith that allowed worry to creep in, even though the Lord always came through.

Like now. Here was Rachel with the answer to her prayers, though the answer she offered in no way resembled anything Abby had considered during the long, worrisome nights. *Wet nurse!*

There was no one left to ask for help. Nathan Haversham at the bank had been more than understanding, but when she'd last spoken to him, he'd explained that he couldn't let his sympathy get in the way of the bank's business much longer, and just last week, she'd received a letter giving her a month to come up with the necessary funds or she would receive a notice of foreclosure.

She lifted a brimming blue gaze to Rachel's. When she spoke, her voice was as unsteady as her smile. "In truth, it's the answer to my prayers. When do I start?"

Rachel flipped open the cover of the gold watch that hung from a chain around her neck. "How about we gather up enough to tide you and the children over for a few days? I'll drive you to Caleb's, clean things up and help you get settled."

"Now?" Abby had asked, stunned.

Rachel had offered her a wan smile. "I imagine Miss Betsy Gentry is getting mighty hungry about now, and I'm sure her daddy is pacing the floor and tearing at his hair, wondering what in the world he's supposed to do about it."

Abby had gone about gathering up as much from her kitchen as she could on such short notice, and grabbing the clothes she and the children would need for the next couple of days.

Now, remembering the conversation, a smile claimed Abby's lips. Rachel's description of Caleb Gentry had been right on the mark. When she'd seen him framed in his doorway, he'd looked exactly as if he'd been tearing at his too-long hair.

She smiled down at the sleeping baby. Wealthy or not, Betsy Gentry's daddy could still get as ruffled as the next man. Somehow the thought made him a bit less intimidating.

The sound of something crashing to the floor

sent Abby's gaze flying to the kitchen door, her smile of contentment changing into a frown. She couldn't imagine what had happened, but suspected it had something to do with her children. There was nothing to do but go and see.

The sound of something breaking sent Caleb bolting up from the sofa. Realizing that he must have dozed, he rubbed at his gritty eyes and looked around to see what had caused the noise. It didn't take long to spot the shepherdess figurine that had belonged to his mother. Caleb had found it tucked away in one of his father's drawers after his death. Now the keepsake lay in dozens of broken fragments on the heart-pine floor. Abby Carter's son stood looking at him, guilt and fear stamped on his freckled face.

Caleb's lips tightened. The boy shouldn't have been snooping! He should have been sitting down minding his own business the way well-brought-up children should. So much for Abby Carter's mothering skills. Still, as furious, frustrated and exhausted as he was, he realized that he could not afford to fly off the handle, as he was prone to do. Not now. Instead, he stifled the words hovering on his lips, took a deep, calming breath and struggled to assess the situation with some sort of objectivity.

If he had to hazard a guess, he would say that the baby—a girl it seemed, from the lace adorning her smock—had been crawling around, doing some sort of infant reconnaissance while her brother followed her—though to what purpose Caleb could not fathom. Most likely the baby had bumped into the spindly legged table Emily had brought back from St. Louis when she'd gone to visit her sister, sending the porcelain shepherdess to her demise.

Caleb's gaze moved back to the boy, who regarded him with unconcealed apprehension. The baby had pushed to a sitting position amid the broken shards, poked two fingers into her mouth and regarded him with the same intensity as her brother. Then, in the span of a heartbeat, she plopped her plump palms to the floor and headed for a colorful, gilt-edged piece that snagged her interest.

Scowling with amazement at how fast she switched her focus, Caleb strode across the room and swung her up just as she was about to grab the jagged shard. To his surprise, she gave a gurgle of laughter. Marveling again at the quicksilver shifting of her attention, he turned her to face him, holding her out at arm's length. She rewarded his frown with a wide grin. Something about that sweet and innocent smile with its four gleaming teeth took the edge from his anger. Arms straight out, he carried the baby to the sofa and plunked her smack-dab in the middle of the cushions.

Sensitive to the situation he found himself in, and as uncertain how to deal with Abby Carter's offspring as he was his infant daughter, he wondered what to do next. Other than him and his brother *being* children many years ago, he had never been around the peculiar little creatures, and what he knew about how to deal with them could be put in a thimble with lots of room left over. From what he'd observed around town, many of them were meddlesome and troublesome, which the recent incident proved. His tired, troubled gaze returned to the child who stood gaping at him in fearful anxiety. He had to do *something*.

Caleb raked a hand through his tousled hair and pointed from the boy to the couch. "You," he said in a too-quiet tone. "Sit."

Wearing an anxious frown, Abby emerged from the kitchen holding a sleeping Betsy close. Just inside the doorway of the parlor, she stopped. Rachel was nowhere to be seen. Ben sat immobile on the sofa, looking as if he were afraid to even breathe. Laura, unaffected by the tension in the room, leaned against him, happily chewing on the hem of her dress. Caleb sat on the hearth, elbows on his knees, his chin resting on his folded hands, daring him to move. Abby's lingering gratification at having helped Betsy Gentry and her father vanished.

"Can we go home now?" Ben asked, both his voice and his lower lip trembling. "I don't like it here."

Abby's gaze swung from the fear on his face to Caleb Gentry, who sat watching the boy with the intensity of "a hawk watching a chicken," as her grandmother might have said. Her heart sank. Ben had done something wrong. Her frantic gaze raked the room for confirmation, lighting on the pieces of what looked like a broken figurine that lay scattered on the polished floorboards.

Rachel chose that moment to exit the bedroom, an armful of bedding clutched to her chest. "I'll just take these to the laundry in town and bring them back in a few d—" She stopped in her tracks and looked from Abby to Caleb and back again.

Sensing the tension in the room, Rachel said, "I'm sure the two of you have a lot to talk about. Just let me take these out to the carriage, and the children and I will go into the kitchen for some of those cookies you baked. You did bring them along, didn't you, Abby? Ben, take Laura into the kitchen. I'll be there in a minute."

It didn't escape either Caleb or Abby that even though Rachel spoke in her most professional tone, she was almost babbling, something the no-nonsense doctor just didn't do.

Abby nodded, watching as Ben hefted his baby sister onto his hip and left the room, his relief almost palpable. Caleb's frown grew even darker. When the children were gone, he made no move to address the disaster, other than to get up and begin picking up the bits of pottery. Watching him, Abby found herself torn between demanding to know what had happened and the urge to tell him that she would not be taking the job, after all. The memory of the bank's letter stopped her. She could not afford to reject this lifeline out of hand.

Why did you have to die on me, William? she thought angrily. Realizing how silly it was to be-rate her dead husband and knowing that even if he'd lived, she would still be in a pickle at the bank, she gave a deep sigh, placed the sleeping baby in her cradle and went to help clean up.

She and Caleb worked together side by side, neither speaking as they picked up pieces of his past. Finally, he stood, held out his hands and said, "It was my mother's."

Having been forced to part with several things that had once belonged to her own mother, Abby could imagine how he felt losing something dear to his heart just hours after losing his beloved wife. She straightened and placed the pieces she'd gathered into his big hands. The backs of her fingers brushed against his. Caleb stiffened. Abby stifled a small gasp and plunged her hands into the pockets of her skirt. Her confused gaze met his. The anger was gone, replaced by something akin to bewilderment.

"I'm sorry," she said.

"Yes, well, so am I." The strange moment passed, and once more his voice held a note of annoyance. "If the children had been seated as they should have been, it would never have happened."

Abby gasped, thoughts of foreclosure forgotten. Anger rose inside her like Wolf Creek floodwaters in the spring. How *dare* he say anything about her children! How *dare* he? From across the room, Betsy snuffled in her sleep. The slight sound was enough to remind Abby of the sorrow and strain the man standing before her must be feeling. Fear-

ing that her eyes still held the remnants of irritation, she lifted her gaze no higher than the second
button of his shirt.

"You're right," she said with a nod. "They should
have been seated." Then, feeling that her babies had
been unfairly judged, she couldn't help adding, "But
if you will recall, you were so anxious to see Betsy
calmed when I arrived, that we weren't even properly introduced."

Her meaning could not be clearer. Caleb had *demanded* that she do something to calm his daughter,
and in her hurry to do so, Ben and Laura had been
left in his and Rachel's charge. Abby gave a small
sigh. She probably shouldn't have mentioned that.
Being correct did not give one the right to say so.

Her cautious gaze climbed up the tanned column
of his throat to his rugged face. The red of either
embarrassment or anger tinged his sun-darkened
features. She stifled a groan and wished—as was
often the case—that she could call back her rash
statement. *Dear Lord, I try to bridle my tongue;
You know I do.*

Yes, He knew she fought a constant battle with
her stubbornness and her temper, which flared hotly
and died just as fast. Always had, and, she thought
with another sorrow-filled sigh, probably always
would. Her quick tongue had often landed her in
trouble as she'd grown up, but when she'd met William, she met a man who valued her opinions, one
who insisted that anyone as intelligent as she was
should speak her mind. Though the final decision

was always his, he had listened to her thoughts and ideas—an advantage she was aware that few wives were granted. As for her temper, more often than not, he just grabbed her in a big bear hug and held her until she quit struggling, laughing at her all the while, which quickly defused her ire and had her laughing with him.

But Caleb Gentry was nothing like her husband, she thought, staring up at features that might have been carved from unyielding Arkansas stone. How could they ever deal with each other in a practical way when, aside from her brief, annoyed outburst, the thought of just *speaking* to him turned her legs to jelly?

Before Caleb could say the words she knew were hovering on his lips, Rachel, the basket of cookies hooked over her wrist, returned, slanting Abby an uneasy look before disappearing into the kitchen. Abby stood, her chin high, all thought of retaliatory criticism dissolving as she realized that her brief spurt of provocation had probably jeopardized the job he offered.

Without speaking, Caleb tossed the breakage into the ash bucket that sat near the fireplace. Swiping his hands on the legs of his denim pants, he turned to face her with his arms crossed over his chest and an unreadable expression in his unusual gray eyes.

She was still trying to formulate an acceptable apology when he heaved a great sigh and asked, "Is Betsy all right, then?"

Surprised, both at the evenness of his voice and

the turn of the conversation, Abby stammered, "Y-Yes. Fine. She was just hungry."

That basic problem, indeed *the* problem, cleared up to his satisfaction—at least for the moment—they stood there, their mutual strain growing with every indrawn breath. Finally, she took her courage in hand. Knowing that even if she had messed up her chance to provide for her children, she could not leave without offering him what comfort she could for the days to come; she cleared her throat.

"Mr. Gentry," she said, lacing her hands together at her waist to still their trembling. "I want you to know that I am very sorry for your loss, and while I cannot know your exact feelings, I do know what it's like to lose a mate. My husband died eight months ago, shortly after Laura was born."

The expression in his eyes could only be described as bleak. "I had heard that." He cocked his head to the side, regarding her with a curious expression. "Tell me, Mrs. Carter, did you love your husband?"

Abby's eyes widened with surprise at the personal nature of the question. "Of course."

"Well, let me assure you that in no way could your feelings be compared to mine."

Her breath caught at the strength of his statement, and her twisting hands stilled. He must have loved Emily very much, though it was hard to imagine such a fierce, hard man ever feeling any emotion as tender as love.

Deciding to clear the air before she lost her

courage, she said, "There are some things that we should talk about before we make the decision as to whether or not I accept the position you're offering."

Surprise flickered in his eyes. He was not used to a woman taking the lead in the dialogue.

"I agree."

"First, I would like to apologize again for the destruction of the figurine. Since I wasn't here, I can't say for certain how it happened, but please believe me when I say that Ben is seldom meddlesome, though he is quite curious, as most children are. I will be glad to repay you for it." Nerves made her speech stilted and formal, and she had no idea how on earth she would make good on her promise if she did not land this job.

"I didn't see it happen, either, Mrs. Carter, and I concede that you were right in stating that I was anxious when you arrived and did not give you time to see that the children were properly settled. Most likely your baby—"

"Laura," she supplied.

"Laura. Laura probably bumped into the table and toppled the figurine. We can certainly ask, uh—"

"Ben."

"Yes, Ben." He cleared his throat, and his next words seemed to come only with the greatest effort. "I would venture to guess that it was just an unfortunate accident."

She nodded, sensing how hard the admission must have been. "You should know about all our warts," she said, determined to lay out possible problems beforehand. "Ben is very much a boy, and is often loud and rowdy, and Laura is just beginning to venture about and explore things...." Her voice trailed away on a sigh, and she lifted her shoulders in a slight shrug. Surely he could see where she was leading.

"They are good children, Mr. Gentry," she said, an earnest expression on her face, "and they are easily set to rights, but they are children, nonetheless."

Sensing that he was about to speak, she rushed on. "Another thing. Ben still misses his father very much, and that grief manifests itself in different ways—sometimes tears, sometimes misplaced mischief and even anger. If I were to take this position, I would appreciate your showing us as much patience as possible as we try to find our way in our new roles. Of course, knowing the suddenness and depth of your loss, we will extend you the same courtesy."

She was surprised that Caleb did not interrupt as many men would have. Again, she chided herself for speaking with such boldness and ruining all chance of employment, but as much as she needed the position, it was more important that her family be happy.

"I appreciate your honesty, Mrs. Carter," he said in a tone whose mocking edge caused her to doubt the sincerity of the statement. "And you should understand that I'm unfamiliar with children as well as being rather set in my ways. It will take some time for us all to adjust. As you say, there will have to be compromises on both sides."

Abby swallowed hard. "I would like to apologize for my rude outburst. My husband was a man who felt women are intelligent individuals and should voice their opinions, even when those attitudes may cause discord." She released a soft sigh of contrition and met his gaze with a stubborn determination. "I fear I have become used to doing just that. I realize that his attitude is not shared by other men and will do my best to bridle my tongue."

She couldn't read the expression in his eyes, but he nodded. "I'll keep that in mind."

He shifted his weight from one foot to the other. "One more thing."

Abby looked at him, wondering what else was on his mind.

"Since this will be your home for the next several months, I would appreciate it if you took on the responsibilities of cooking and cleaning. I will, of course, pay you extra for that."

Abby felt her mouth drop open in surprise. She snapped it shut, as her fair eyebrows puckered. "My home? I'm not sure I understand."

Another of those frowns drew his dark eyebrows together in an expression of surprise that mimicked hers. "Surely Rachel explained that you and the children would have to stay here for the next few months. At least until Betsy is of weaning age."

Chapter Two

Abby's eyes widened. "Do you mean *live* here?"

Caleb resisted the urge to sigh. Without a word, he went to the kitchen door and summoned Rachel, who left Ben and Laura eating cookies. She came into the parlor, a troubled expression in the dark eyes that moved from one friend to the other.

"I think you'd do a far better job than I in explaining to Mrs. Carter why it's necessary for her and the children to make this their home for the next few months."

Rachel nodded and turned to Abby. "I can't see any other way, can you?"

When Rachel suggested Abby become Betsy's wet nurse and told her to gather up enough things for a few days, Abby had been so eager to help and so thankful to see some ease from her financial problems that she hadn't given much thought as to *how* seeing to Betsy's needs would be accomplished or what it might entail.

"Couldn't I keep the baby at my place?"

Rachel looked to Caleb with raised eyebrows. After he'd vetoed the idea of Abby and her children moving in with him because they would be "disrupting his life, poking through his things, tracking in dirt and whining," Rachel had suggested that he allow Abby to take Betsy to her place until she was old enough to drink from a cup, at which time he could hire someone to care for her through the day, while he took the nights.

Caleb had nixed the notion outright, proving the inflexibility he was known for. "Betsy belongs here," he'd said. "Why can't Mrs. Carter come over a few times a day and uh…feed… Betsy and then go home, or maybe she could stay all day and go home at night?"

Clearly near the end of her rope with his stubbornness, Rachel had given him her most stern "doctor" look. "I understand how you feel, Caleb, but Abby lives almost two miles on the *other* side of town going toward Antoine. Around six miles from here. It would be impossible for her to traipse back and forth with two children in tow, especially with winter coming on. Besides, babies get hungry through the night, too, at least for a while. Caring for Betsy would be a full-time job. Still, she is your child, and it's your decision."

Setting his jaw, Caleb had stared down at the baby. Neither scenario suited him, but he felt his resolve eroding in the face of necessity. As usual, he'd been given little choice in what happened in his life. With a sigh of acquiescence, he had set aside his feelings and agreed to what was required.

"Betsy belongs here," he said now, repeating his earlier answer while staring implacably into Abby Carter's anxious eyes.

Abby chewed on her bottom lip, her practical side battling her tender heart, weighing the facts as if they were on scales. On one side was the letter from the bank; on the other was a baby who needed her. She sighed. It all boiled down to one thing. Did she believe what she professed? Did she really trust that God was in control and that He answered prayers?

She thought of her house situated a half mile off the road between Wolf Creek and Antoine, with its small, homey kitchen she'd made cheerful by the addition of yellow-print feed-sack curtains and the copper pots that once belonged to her mother— one of the few things she hadn't sold. Leaving the home she'd shared with William held little appeal, but with no other way to catch up on her missed note payments, there was no doubt in her mind that she would be leaving it sooner or later. One way or the other.

"How much are you willing to pay?" she asked, and gasped in surprise when she heard Caleb's generous offer.

"That would include your taking on the household chores and cooking that I mentioned earlier."

"I would be happy to take care of your household chores, since I'm not accustomed to idleness," she told him. A sudden thought struck her. She looked from Rachel to Caleb. "What about my animals? Who would take care of them?"

"I can make arrangements to move them here for the time being," her prospective employer offered.

Abby gave a helpless shrug. "It seems that between the two of you, you've thought of everything."

"Not everything, I'm sure," Rachel said. "The biggest obstacles, perhaps."

At long last, Caleb unfolded his arms and extended his hand. "It seems, Mrs. Carter, that we find ourselves in positions of mutual need. I will do my best to be patient with your children if you will take good care of my daughter. Do we have a deal?"

Weighing her children's requirements against the troublesome voice that whispered that she must be mad, she held out her own hand. Caleb Gentry's was warm and strong and rough with calluses. When he released his hold on her, she took a step back. It was too late to renege now.

"I hear Laura," Rachel said. "I'll go tend to her and Ben while you two work out a few details."

"Thank you."

Once Rachel disappeared into the kitchen, Abby and Caleb spent the next several moments discussing how she would pay for the things she needed to run the household, and she explained the number and kinds of animals he would be taking responsibility for. He specified what times he liked his meals, and Abby explained that she spent a portion of each morning in lessons with the children, and had Bible time before bedtime, assuring him that she would not let it get in the way of her care of Betsy.

"There is one more thing," she said, when it seemed they had most of the obvious wrinkles worked out.

"Yes?"

"Weather permitting, the children and I attend Wolf Creek Church every Sunday. I hope that won't be a problem. Of course, it's impossible to take Betsy out now, but I'll be glad to take her when she's old enough."

"I have no problem with that, but I will not be accompanying you." He excused himself, saying that he needed to unload her things from Rachel's buggy and speak to his hands about moving her animals.

When he left the room, Abby drew in a shaky breath. She and Caleb Gentry would do their best to deal equitably with each other the next few months, since each had something the other needed. Simply put, neither of them had much choice. No matter what happened in the coming weeks and months, they would grin and bear it.

More likely they would grit their teeth and bear it, she thought, recalling the look on his face when she'd entered the parlor after the figurine had been smashed. She remembered the expression on Ben's face when he'd said he didn't like it there. Well, life had a way of throwing a lot of things at you that you might not like, a lesson Ben ought to learn sooner than later.

Putting on a determined face, Abby headed to the kitchen to relieve Rachel of the children and see if she could get to the bottom of what had happened to the shattered shepherdess. She prayed she could find the words to tell Ben they wouldn't be going home for a while.

"Well?" Rachel said, when Abby entered the warmth of the kitchen.

Abby's gaze found her son, who was helping Laura drink from a cup, holding a dish towel beneath her chin to catch the drips. At the moment, he was not paying any attention to the adults in the room. "It seems I have a job. Thank you."

Abby leaned down and gave her friend a hug, then helped herself to a cookie and sat down across the table.

"I won't sugarcoat things," Rachel said with a grim smile and her customary honesty. "Caleb is a decent man, and I think folks who have business dealings with him would call him a fair man, but make no mistake, he is also a hard man and he doesn't suffer fools gladly. I'd be less than a friend if I told you the next few months will be easy…for either of you."

Abby broke off a piece of cookie, her lips curving in a wry smile. "Believe me, I know that."

She popped the piece of cookie into her mouth and Rachel sighed. "Somehow I feel guilty for putting you in this position, even though my intentions were the best."

Abby smiled. "I know that, too."

Once Rachel had gone back to town, Abby sat down on the bench next to her son, took Laura on her lap and handed Ben another cookie to help soften him up for the news she was about to impart. She decided to begin with the lesser of the two concerns. "The figurine that got broken belonged to Mr. Gentry's mother," she said. "It was very special to him. What happened, Ben?"

"It was an accident," he told her, his blue eyes earnest. "You told me to be good and mind my manners, and I was trying. Dr. Rachel put Laura on the floor and told me to keep an eye on her. I was afraid Laura would get into something she shouldn't, so I was trying to watch her." He took a huge bite of cookie, as if he needed to fortify himself.

Good intentions, then, Abby thought with a feeling of relief.

"She was crawling around, and then she sat up real fast, and when she did, she bumped the table and the next thing I knew we were in trouble."

"What did Mr. Gentry say?"

Ben shrugged. "Nothing much. He told me to sit down and then sat there just looking at me. I don't like him," Ben said. "I want to go home."

Abby uttered a silent prayer for guidance. "We need to talk about that, Ben." How did she explain the direness of their situation in a way he could understand without getting into past-due notes and bank foreclosures?

Loosing another sigh, she said, "I know you realize how hard it has been for us since your father died, and how I try to do not only my work but what I can of his, too. And you know how tired and cranky I've been sometimes."

Ben gave a solemn nod and finished off the last of his cookie.

"Before we came, I told you that Mr. Gentry's wife died today."

Another nod of understanding. "Well, Mr. Gentry is in the same position that I am in—needing to be both mother and father." How to explain in more detail? "Husbands and wives are partners."

"Partners are people who work together toward the same goal," Ben said.

"Yes." Abby smiled her approval. Every day, she tried to give him a new word definition and encouraged him to use the word as often as possible to build his vocabulary. *Partners* had been the word several weeks ago.

"In the case of marriage, that goal is to be a happy, healthy family who believes in truth and honesty and responsibility and hard work, one that puts God first. In most circumstances, the father is responsible for the hard, outside work like plowing and putting up hay and chopping firewood, as well as handling the money and seeing to the bills. The mother is responsible for taking care of the home and the children, the cooking and cleaning…that sort of thing. Though," she added, "in some cases, like ours and Mr. Gentry's, it becomes necessary for one parent to take on the duties of both parents, the way I've been trying to do."

Her faltering smile was sorrow-filled. How could she tell him that her present circumstance was due in part to William's inexperience, which had forced him to borrow from the bank? Or how she had sold almost everything she owned of value to try to satisfy the loan? She couldn't. Not now or ever. Ben had adored his father, and she would not be the one to say anything to lessen that feeling.

Her voice was thick with unshed tears when she spoke. "I've been having a hard time dealing with your father's responsibilities, Ben, and I'll be frank, I'm not doing a very good job."

"I think you're doing fine," he said. "I'll bet Mr. Gentry won't do nearly as good a job of being both parents as you do."

"Thank you, Ben. And that's the thing. Mr. Gentry already knows he can't do a good job as Betsy's mother." *Dear Lord, help me find the words.* "Men just aren't...equipped with the right...trappings... to be a mother. That's why Dr. Rachel came to me. Mr. Gentry would like for me—us—to stay here for a while so I can take care of Betsy."

Abby watched Ben's lower lip jut out and his eyes take on a familiar belligerence.

"It won't be forever," she hastened to say. "Just until Betsy gets a bit older, or until Mr. Gentry finds someone else. Until springtime, maybe. He and I will be partners, in a way. He will take care of our place and our animals, and I will take care of him and Betsy and the household chores. He will pay me a wage, just as if I had a job in town at the mercantile or the restaurant, and that money will help me take care of our obligations. That can be our word for the day.

"Obligations are things that are our responsibilities. Like what I was talking about when I described the duties of fathers and mothers. Parents have the obligation to bring up children to be good, God-fearing citizens. You are responsible for keeping your room clean and setting the table and feeding the animals and milking Nana. When I tell you to keep an eye on Laura, it is your obligation to see that she's safe. Sometimes, obligations involve money. Things we must pay for."

There! She had prepared him as best she could, though she felt she had done a poor job of it. To his credit, Ben did not spout off or throw a fit. Only the downward turn of his mouth and his refusal to meet her gaze spoke of his misery. Finally, he looked up at her.

"Like buying eggs when the hens stop laying and sugar and flour and coffee?" he asked.

"Yes." And shoes and shirts and medicine when your children get sick, Abby thought as she pulled him close to her side. "I have always been as truthful with you as I have felt you could understand, so I will not lie to you now. This will be hard on all of us."

Ben pulled away and regarded her with a solemn expression. "It won't be hard on Mr. Gentry. He doesn't have to live somewhere different."

"Actually, he does," Abby said with a gentle smile. "He won't be staying in his house while we're here. He'll be moving into the bunkhouse with his hired men. He will just take his meals here and use his office when necessary. That's quite a sacrifice for him, as well as having people he doesn't even know taking over his home. And we mustn't forget that his wife just died. I want you to think about how you felt when your father passed away. You were sad and angry with him and God for at least a month, and you took it out on your sister. Remember?"

Ben nodded.

Abby smiled and brushed back a lock of his fine blond hair. "Just remember that Mr. Gentry may be feeling the same way for a while, and try to be patient and forgiving. Can you do that?"

"I'll try."

"That's all I ask," Abby said.

She gave him a final hug and stood. As they were about to leave the kitchen, Caleb came through the door, looking rugged and unyielding, his arms laden with things she'd brought from her own kitchen. He set a loaf of bread wrapped in a clean dish towel onto the table next to the basket of cookies, and put a heavy cast-iron kettle of squirrel and dumplings on the stove.

"I've put your things in your room."

"Thank you," Abby said.

"Would you mind if Ben and Laura sleep with you for a day or two? I'll have to move some things from Emily's room into the attic for Ben to have his own room."

"That will be fine."

"I thought I'd put Betsy's cradle in your room, too, so you can be near both girls."

"Perfect."

"Let me show you around," he said, relieved that there were no objections.

He led the small procession down the hallway. The bedroom was furnished simply with a bed, an oak armoire and a highboy. Abby noted that he had built a small fire to combat the autumn chill, and warmth was already starting to spread throughout the area, which was far larger than any room at her home. As spacious as it was and even though she knew the furnishings were of good quality, the house seemed sterile somehow, as untouched as Caleb Gentry's heart. Shifting Laura on her hip, she ran her fingertip through the dust that had gathered on top of a chest of drawers. And it could use a thorough cleaning.

"I guess it needs a good cleaning," he said, echoing her thoughts.

The sound of his voice sent Abby's gaze winging to his, and she saw that the dull red of embarrassment had crept into the harsh sweep of his cheekbones. Too late, she realized what she had done. Oh, dear! Could she and the children do nothing right?

"Emily didn't have much energy the past few months, and I—"

"There's no need to apologize, Mr. Gentry," she rushed to assure him. "Any woman who has carried a child to term understands." She offered him a nonjudgmental smile. "It's a lovely home and it won't take much to get things in order."

"I suppose not." Clearly eager to be away from the house and all the turmoil and unhappiness in it, he said, "I need to get one of my hands to go over to your place and see to your animals tonight. We'll move them tomorrow."

"Thank you. I'm sorry to put you to the trouble."

"It's not a problem." She told him how to find her house and he gave a sharp nod. He looked as tense as she felt. It seemed as if they were both trying to outdo the other in civility.

She offered him a thin smile. "I'll just get our things put away and check on Betsy again."

"I have to go into town and make arrangements at the, uh—" he cleared his throat "—funeral home, so I can't stay to see that you get settled in. Feel free to just…look around if you need something. I'll be back by dusk for supper. Just fix whatever you want."

Laura muttered something that sounded remarkably like "supper" and offered Caleb one of her incredible smiles. Just as incredibly, the bleakness in his storm-gray eyes dimmed the tiniest bit. Though it in no way could be called a smile and was so fleeting that Abby was certain it must be a trick of the light, it seemed that just for a second, the un-yielding firmness of his mouth softened somewhat.

She gave her daughter a squeeze. It seemed that at least one of the Carters was not intimidated by the overwhelming presence of the man, and even seemed to be taken with him! Much to her own mortification considering the circumstances, Abby realized that in his own rough, brooding sort of way, Caleb Gentry was an attractive man.

Caleb rode his gelding into town, his body past weariness, sporadic images flitting through his weary mind like flashes of lighting against a sullen sky. Rachel coming from the room where a baby's crying was the only sound after Emily had gone suddenly quiet. His gaze straying to the bed, where a sheet covered Emily's face. His heart stumbling in his chest, and the resolute, relentless ticking of the clock, while his exhausted brain struggled to assimilate what his eyes were seeing. Rachel's voice, filled with weariness and regret. Emily was dead and his baby daughter needed someone to take care of her, to feed her. An overwhelming certainty that there must be something terribly wrong with him for his inability to feel anything over his wife's death but panic and fear....

The random images faded, and reason—of sorts—returned along with memories of the past couple of hours. He conceded that he had jumped to conclusions with Mrs. Carter's boy. It wasn't his fault his sister had broken the shepherdess, but with

Caleb's own emotions so raw, and his feelings of inadequacy at the surface, he had been eager to place blame. The truth was that his whole world was turned upside down. Nothing would ever be the same, so he might as well get used to the idea of Mrs. Carter and her children being around, at least for the foreseeable future.

Whether he liked it or not.

With a grunt of disgust, he guided the horse down Antioch Street, and took a right toward the railroad tracks. The house Rachel Stone shared with her father, which also housed her medical office, sat on a corner beyond the tracks that ran a block down from and parallel to Antioch. The funeral home was situated at the rear of the house, added a few years before, when Rachel's father, Dr. Edward Stone, had suffered a stroke that left him partially paralyzed.

Caleb rode around back, tied his horse to the hitching post and stepped through the doorway of the funeral parlor. Edward, who sat behind a gleaming desk, looked up when he heard the bell on the door ring, a solemn expression on his lined face. He rolled his wheelchair around to greet Caleb with his hand extended.

"I'm sorry, Caleb."

Caleb only nodded.

"Bart and Mary picked out a casket and brought her a dress. I didn't think you'd mind." When Caleb shook his head, the older man said, "She's ready, if you want to go on in."

Caleb nodded, though it was the last thing he

wanted to do. He entered the viewing room, where Emily lay dressed in a frilly gown of pale pink, her favorite color. Her dark lashes lay against the delicate paleness of her cheeks. If he didn't know better, he might think she was sleeping.

Dry-eyed, he stared down at the woman who had been a part of his life the past six years, waiting for the grief to overtake him and wondering if he should pray. But grief for losing a beloved wife did not come, and he had no idea what he could—or should—say to a God with whom he'd had so few dealings. The only sorrow he could define was sadness that Emily had been taken in her prime and would not be there for Betsy.

There was guilt aplenty.

Guilt aggravated by the nagging memory of the jolt that had passed through him when his fingers had touched those of Abby Carter. What kind of man was he to feel *anything* for any woman so soon after his wife's death?

The answer was clear. He was, perhaps, a man who hadn't tried hard enough to make his marriage a good one. A man who'd let someone else plan his marriage and shape his life…which might explain that unexpected awareness of Mrs. Carter but certainly did not excuse it.

He and Emily were both twenty-four when they married. Pretty enough, but thought to be a bit uppity, she was considered to be the town spinster. Caleb's father had instigated the notion of his marrying her. His father stated that since Gabe, whom Lucas

Gentry bitterly referred to as the "prodigal," had shown no signs of abandoning his wayward lifestyle to come home and share the burden of labor, it was past time for his elder son to choose a wife and sire a son to inherit the Gentry fortune.

Emily's parents had encouraged her to accept Caleb's offer—most probably her last. So they married and lived with Lucas in the house he had built for his own wife, Caleb and Gabe's mother, Libby.

Unfortunately, Lucas had died of a stroke three years ago, without seeing the birth of his grandchild. More regrettable perhaps was the fact that despite the tales Caleb had heard about love often following marriage, for him and Emily it had not.

Until now, he had never questioned why. They'd both been content to let the days slip by…sharing a house but not their lives, treating each other with respect but not love, neither of them caring enough to look for a spark of something that might be fanned into the flames of love. In retrospect, he found that troubling, but then, what did he know of love? He and Gabe had lost their mother to another man at a young age, and love was a sentiment foreign to their embittered father.

Father. *He* was a father now, and he hoped to be a better one than Lucas Gentry had been. He *would* be better. He might not know anything about loving his daughter, but he knew how to take care of her. Duty and obligation were things Caleb Gentry understood very well. And he would let her choose her husband when the time came.

Chapter Three

With a few free moments before starting the evening meal, Abby poured herself a cup of coffee and sank into a kitchen chair. Emily's funeral service had been held that morning, and Caleb had yet to return from town. Laura and Betsy were down for their afternoon naps, and Ben was taking advantage of the sunny afternoon, playing on the back porch with the wooden train set William had made him last Christmas.

The two days since she and the children had arrived at the Gentry farm had been somewhat stressful as they tried to adjust to their new home and responsibilities, but with the absence of any further mishaps or misunderstandings, Abby felt she was beginning to find her stride.

She took a sip of her coffee and contemplated what to fix for supper, which turned her thoughts to Caleb. In an effort to please her new employer, she had asked what he did and didn't like to eat, and he had informed her that not liking something was a luxury he and his brother had not been allowed. He ate everything, and she soon learned he ate a lot of it, tucking into a meal as if it might be his last. So much food might have made another man overweight, but Caleb was as fit any male she'd ever seen.

She'd learned a bit about him the past couple of days. His work ethic could not be faulted. The care he took with his animals and the upkeep of the farm spoke of concern, dedication and pride in his accomplishments, which was reflected by his affluence. In fact, he worked from sunrise until sunset with an intensity she understood too well, readying the farm for winter wheat planting between visits from the few neighbors who came to offer food and condolences.

Abby was a bit surprised that there were not as many visitors as she might have imagined considering the Gentry family's long standing presence in the community. She was also surprised at how uncomfortable he seemed with accepting their simple kindnesses.

She understood filling your days with work in an attempt to hold the pain of loss at bay, but she did not comprehend his awkwardness in accepting well-meaning compassion from people who wanted to show they cared. It was almost as if he didn't know how to deal with their kindness.

He seemed to be trying his best to make her job easier, always giving a polite answer to her questions about the workings of his household, and plenty of leeway to take care of Betsy in whatever way she thought was best. Still, in no way could his actions be interpreted as friendly. Sometimes she caught him looking at her with a strange expression that seemed to straddle the fence between skepticism and remorse.

She often caught him regarding the children with wary uncertainty, sometimes giving them looks that dared them to so much as breathe, but he also tried in a heavy-handed way to engage them in various ways. Despite how painful accepting their presence might be, Abby couldn't help feeling that he was doing his best, even though his best lacked enthusiasm or warmth and more often than not fell short.

There had been one sticky moment that first evening when he had started eating the squirrel and dumplings she had brought from home, only to be halted by Ben who regarded him in disbelief and said, "We didn't say the prayer."

Looking somewhat abashed, Caleb had stopped, bowed his head and listened while Ben gave thanks for the food. He had never forgotten after that. It was a small thing, but one for which Abby was grateful. She was also grateful that other than to show up for meals, she had seen little of him, which made everyone's life easier, especially the days she recalled the unexpected spark she'd felt when their fingers touched. Labeling it a figment of her imagination made it no less troubling.

The morning after her arrival, Caleb had taken

Frank, one of his two hired men and a wagon to her place where they'd rounded up her few remaining chickens, the rabbits and their cages, and Nana, one in a long string of goats she and William had purchased because Ben had not tolerated cow's milk well. They had tethered Shaggy Bear, her milk cow, to the wagon, loaded what feed she had and brought the whole kit and caboodle back to his place. When Caleb had come in for supper, she thought she'd heard him mumbling something about "milking goats" under his breath, but she could not be sure.

She was doing a top-to-bottom cleaning of the house and admitted that caring for it was much easier than caring for hers. While not a fancy place per se, the Gentry home was more than a simple farmhouse, designed not only for the convenience of a farming family, but also with an eye toward rustic charm. The house was the product of Gentry money, yet nowhere was there a hint of ostentation. The oak floors had been planed smooth and waxed to a satin sheen, as had the bookcases flanking the massive rock fireplace that was the hub of the parlor. The plaster walls throughout were painted in various colors, most of them too dark for Abby's taste, but classic colors that somehow suited Caleb.

Though blessed with a fine house, Emily Gentry seemed to have taken little interest in putting her stamp on it. Abby understood being so dragged down by pregnancy that regular cleaning became a chore, but where were the little touches that showed care and love? Other than a quilt or two and the occasional pastel drawing Emily had done, there were few of the personal touches Abby felt transformed lumber and nails from a house into a sanctuary away from the cares of the world.

If it were her home, she would paint the rooms light colors and swap the heavy drapes framing the windows for white muslin curtains, perhaps with a crochet-and-tassel edging to brighten things up.

Shame on you, Abby Carter! How dare you presume to redecorate a dead woman's house or think it lacked love?

Why, Caleb himself had indicated that even though Abby had lost her husband, she could have no idea how he felt at his own loss. A sudden wave of melancholy for the simple, love-filled house she and William had once shared swept through Abby, but she pushed it aside. Indulging in nostalgia for the past served as little purpose as speculating on Emily Gentry's personality and her relationship with her husband.

Caleb never so much as mentioned her name, and though Abby saw the grimness in his eyes as he approached each day with stubborn determination, she knew only too well what he must be going through.

Though she and William had not seen eye to eye the last months of their marriage, she had loved him, and it was weeks before anyone could mention his name without her tearing up. But as her preacher had counseled her, God made our wondrous bodies not only to heal themselves when overtaken with physical problems—if given care and time—He had done the same with our emotions. Time, he had told her, was the cure for her sorrow. He'd been right. There were still moments when thoughts of William brought tightness to her throat and tears to her eyes, but for the most part he had been relegated to a special place in her memories and her heart.

So, when things became tense and stilted between her and Caleb, she reminded herself of his recent loss and prayed that the sharpest edges of his pain would be smoothed over by God's grace.

And you still haven't decided what to fix for supper.

She was debating on whether to cook a pot of beans or fry some salt pork and potatoes and cook up the turnip and mustard greens Leo had picked for her that morning, when she heard footsteps on the front porch. Caleb must be back. Then, hearing a woman's voice and what had to be more than one person's footsteps, Abby leaped to her feet. It must be someone coming to pay his respects. She had been so careful not to overstep the boundaries of the duties Caleb had outlined that she wasn't sure if she should answer the door or not.

Then again, he wasn't here. Deciding that she should welcome his guests, she hurried through the kitchen, smoothing both her hair and her apron as she went. She was halfway to the front door when it was pushed open, and Caleb, accompanied by a rush of cool air and carrying a pot of something, stepped through the opening. His in-laws followed, each holding a wooden tray covered by a tea towel.

Their eyes were red-rimmed, but their wan faces wore resolute smiles.

Abby's questioning gaze flickered to Caleb. "The people from town fixed enough food for an army," he told her. "We brought what was left here."

"Indeed they did," Mary Emerson interjected, doing her best to summon a vestige of cheer. "There's no way Bart and I can eat it all before it goes bad, and I know Caleb eats like a horse, so we decided to share with you and the children this evening. I hope you haven't started supper."

"No. No, I haven't," Abby told her. "That's very kind of you."

"Besides," Mary added, with another smile, this one faint and sorrowful, "it seemed only right that we come spend some time with Betsy. Especially today."

Again, Abby's gaze sought Caleb's, hoping to gauge his reaction to the impromptu visit, but he had already disappeared through the kitchen door, and she could only nod.

"We'll just put it in the kitchen, then."

"That's fine," Abby said as the older woman followed her husband and Caleb through the house.

Not wanting her presence to remind the Emersons of their loss, Abby decided that she should stay out of sight and hopefully out of mind. She went to check on the babies and found them still sleeping. Letting herself out the front door, she rounded the house to the back porch to check on Ben. He was still playing with his train, the three open cars loaded down with green-and-black objects.

Abby's eyes widened when she recognized the cargo for what it was: onyx-and-jade chess pieces from the set displayed on the table next to the front window. A vivid recollection of the scene with Caleb and Ben she had interrupted mere days ago leaped into her mind. Her heart dropped to her toes and she sucked in a horrified breath. While she watched, he took the kings from their respective cars and began to have them "fight" each other. Her first instinct was to yell at him to put them down, but caution prevailed. If he dropped one of them and it broke, it would be total disaster!

Instead, she sauntered over to the steps. "Hi, sweetheart. Having fun?"

Ben's head snapped up and his wide eyes met hers. The guilt she saw there said without words that he knew he was in trouble. He swallowed and nodded.

"Aren't those Mr. Gentry's chessmen?"

He nodded again.

Abby sat down on the steps. "What are you doing with them?"

"Just playing sheriff and train robber," he said in a low voice.

"I see." She hoped her tone was reasonable. "Did Mr. Gentry give you permission to play with them?"

If possible, Ben's eyes grew even wider. "No, ma'am." His voice was the merest thread of sound.

"Hmm," she said with a nod. "You know full

well you are not to bother other peoples' belongings, don't you, Benjamin?"

"Yes, ma'am."

"Then why did you?"

Ben stared at the now-abandoned chess pieces. "I just needed something to haul in my train. I was being careful."

"I'm sure you meant no harm, and I'm sure you were being careful, but accidents happen. Remember Laura breaking the figurine? What if you'd broken one of Mr. Gentry's chess pieces? What do you think he would say?"

Ben looked up, his freckle-splashed face draining of color.

Abby sighed. "Well, no harm done. I don't think he knows they are missing yet. I'll put them back, and when Mr. and Mrs. Emerson leave, you will tell Mr. Gentry what you did and apologize."

Ben's face crumpled. "Do I have to?"

"You do." Abby reached out and took the chess pieces from the train, placing them in the pockets of her skirt. "Why don't you spend some time on your reading?"

"I'd rather go fishing," the boy said, a forlorn look in his eyes.

A sudden pain racked Abby's heart. Fishing was a venture Ben and his father had shared and something she knew Ben missed very much. She swallowed back the tightness in her throat and forced a smile. "It would be nice for you to get in one more good fishing session before it gets too cold," she agreed. "The next time we go into town, I'll ask Dr. Rachel if Danny can come out one day and fish. Frank says some mighty big crappie live in Wolf Creek."

"That would be fun," Ben said, his eyes brightening. Rachel's son, Daniel, was Ben's best friend. "Maybe we could take a picnic the way we used to when Dad…"

The sentence trailed away and his smile faded.

"A picnic is a definite possibility," Abby said, "if the wind isn't blowing too much for the baby. It's still pretty warm, and we could take a basket for her and a quilt for Laura, though I think she'll be walking before much longer."

Ben's wide grin made Abby's heart glad. "Yeah, she's pulling up to everything the past few days."

"If we had the picnic at midday, Mr. Gentry might like to join us," Abby suggested.

Ben's happy smile vanished. He looked up, his mouth already open to tell her that he didn't want Caleb to come along.

Abby tapped his mouth with a gentle finger "Matthew 7:12."

"Treat others the way you want to be treated," he said in a disgusted tone.

"Close enough," Abby said with a smile. "Now go find something to read for an hour or so. The Emersons have come to see Betsy and they brought supper, so there will be a lot of good things to choose from." She winked at him. "I even saw a chocolate cake."

Ben's blue eyes brightened at the mention of his favorite.

"This is a sad time for them, Ben, so be extra nice, all right?"

Ben nodded. Abby bent and pressed a kiss to his white-blond hair, then ushered him through the kitchen and into the parlor. To her surprise, he went straight to Mary Emerson and gave her a hug, following suit with Bart. Abby felt the sting of tears behind her eyelids. He *was* a sweet boy.

"Sorry," he mumbled, his gaze moving from one adult to the other and lingering on Caleb, whom he made no move to hug. Then without another word, he went to the room he shared with Abby.

She stifled a groan while fighting the conflicting urge to smile. The apology had not only been for Ben's sorrow about Emily. By snaring Caleb's eye, she somehow felt Ben had cleverly included his regret for playing with the chessmen without permission. Well, she might as well follow suit and take the coward's way out, too. There wasn't much Caleb could do or say with Emily's parents in the room. Straightening her shoulders, she crossed the room to the chess set, pulled the pieces from her pocket and placed them on the board. Heaven only knew if they belonged in a special spot. She was only thankful they were undamaged.

That done, she shot Caleb a quick glance. It was no surprise to see that his pewter-hued eyes had gone a stormy gray, like gloomy, rain-drenched clouds before a summer thunderstorm, one that would no doubt hit after the Emersons left.

Bart and Mary spent the remainder of the afternoon alternating between rocking Betsy and going through Emily's belongings, separating them into piles to keep, be given away or be tossed. Caleb had retreated to the fields, telling them to take whatever they wanted. Abby spent the afternoon taking care of the babies' needs, trying to be as unobtrusive as possible and biting her trembling bottom lip and blinking back her own tears when the sounds of sobbing escaped through the closed door.

By late afternoon, the chore was done, and everything was packed into two trunks and loaded onto Bart's wagon. Abby made sure that supper was warm when they finished, so that Mary, who must be emotionally exhausted, would not feel the need to offer her help.

The meal was over and they were almost finished washing the dishes when Mary said, "I understand from Rachel that you didn't bring much with you."

"No. We were in a bit of a hurry to get here."

"If you'd like, I can drive out early in the morning to watch the children while Caleb takes you to gather your things. I know you'd be more comfortable if Laura had her crib."

"I appreciate it, Mrs. Emerson, but I'm not sure that would be convenient for Caleb, and I don't want to make any more work on him than necessary."

"Please call me Mary," Emily's mother said.

"I've already talked to him, and he's fine with it, as long as you don't mind my watching Ben and Laura."

"Of course I don't mind."

Mary's eyes filled with tears, and she reached out and clasped one of Abby's hands. "Bart and I are so very glad that you're here for Betsy and Caleb, and we want to do everything we can so that you'll feel more at home."

Abby was overwhelmed by the heartfelt declaration. "Thank you, but I'm sure you'd have found someone, and actually, I'm the grateful one."

Mary and Bart left soon after the dishes were washed and put away. Just before stepping onto the front porch, a tearful Mary pulled Abby into a close embrace. "If you or the children ever need anything, please let either me or Bart know."

Abby promised she would and watched the carriage disappear down the lane. She drew a relieved breath at the older woman's glad acceptance of the situation. If only she could somehow bring some of that acceptance and just a smidgen of joy into Caleb's life, perhaps the next few months would be worth it.

Abby and Ben were in the parlor later, having their evening devotional, when Caleb came into the room. Abby looked up from the verse she was reading and found his gaze on Ben. She held her breath, hoping against hope that he would not fly off the handle.

"Ben."

"Sir?"

Abby heard the quaver in his voice.

"That chess set was a gift to me from Doc Stone," Caleb said in an even voice that somehow managed to fall just short of angry. "It isn't a toy, son, and it isn't to be played with unless you're playing an actual game of chess. If you want to learn—"

"Don't call me son!" Ben shouted, lifting his belligerent blue gaze to Caleb's.

"Benjamin!" Abby cried, leaping to her feet. She was stunned by Ben's sudden outburst, when Caleb had been trying to discuss the matter in a conciliatory tone. "You will apologize to Mr. Gentry at once."

"I won't!" he yelled, scrambling off the sofa and running to the bedroom. "I'm not his son!" The door slammed with a jarring thud.

Abby lifted her horrified gaze to Caleb's, wondering if he would tell her to start packing "I I'm so sorry," she said in a near whisper. "I don't know what got into him."

His silvery eyes held a weary sorrow. "I do. I understand exactly why he's upset. I've been where he is, remember?"

Abby recalled that he'd lost his mother when he was young. "You're being very decent about this."

"You told me yourself to expect that kind of outburst, and even though I may be short-tempered and stubborn, I like to think I am a decent man."

"I never meant to imply—"

A fleeting sorrowful smile lifted one corner of his mouth. "I know."

Abby regarded him thoughtfully and set out to try to make him understand. "Ben had no idea how expensive that chess set is, but that's neither here nor there. He knows better than to bother other people's things. I'm not trying to make excuses, but he just wanted something to haul in his train cars. He—"

"Leave it, Abby," Caleb said, but the weariness of his smile took the sting from the command. "I was going to offer to teach him how to play chess in the evenings, but I don't think he'd be very receptive to that just now."

Without another word, he crossed the room and began moving the chess pieces, presumably where they had been before Ben confiscated them. Caleb had made no mention of sending them packing, and she wasn't going to bring it up. She gave a rueful shake of her head, not fully understanding why he had not flown off the handle, but grateful that he had not. It was progress. Of sorts.

Bright and early the following morning, while dew still sparkled on the browning grass, Abby found herself seated in the wagon beside Caleb. Mary had arrived shortly after daybreak to take care of the children. She'd brought along a new-fangled bottle from the mercantile so that she could give Betsy a little sugar water if she grew fussy before Abby returned. Frank, the older of Caleb's two hired hands, followed the wagon on a bay gelding.

Caleb leaned forward, his elbows resting on his denim-clad knees, his tanned, callused hands holding the reins in a loose grasp. Completely and easily in control. Again, she thought that even though he was not what one might call handsome, there was something striking about him. It was no wonder that he'd once been the catch of Pike County, or little doubt that once a decent time of mourning had passed, he would be again.

It was only when it came to expressing the more tender emotions that Caleb Gentry seemed to be wanting. That and the lack of a relationship with God. She wondered why he had left no place in his life for a God who had been so generous to him, but she was far too cautious to ask. In truth, she spoke to him as little as possible, since she had the impression that he did not want anyone getting too close to him and seemed disinclined to get close to anyone, which was rather sad, even though it made her life easier.

She glanced again at his hands. They were strong hands, hands whose callused palms and scarred fingers spoke of hard work. She'd seen those hands move in unerring swiftness to soothe a nervous horse and calmly remove an adventurous kitten from the branches of an oak tree, proving he was capable of tenderness. Yet for some reason that kindheartedness was not extended to people—at least not that she had seen.

Well, that was not exactly true. Even in the few days she had been at the farm, she'd seen his softening toward Laura, who made a habit of pulling up to his legs and demanding that he hold her, something he did without hesitation or complaint. He even allowed her to explore his face, poking her tiny fingers into his ears and eyes, and once offering him a wet, openmouthed kiss. When he'd swiped a palm down his cheek and made a soft growling sound of disgust, Laura had laughed in delight, which only made his scowl grow fiercer. It was all Abby could do to keep from laughing herself, but she managed to stifle the urge, knowing it would not do at all.

She saw him growing more confident with Betsy, too, as he made time for her after the evening meal and before going to his study to work on his account ledgers. Abby wondered if he saw Emily's face when he looked down at their daughter's delicate features. Once, he ran a strong finger over the curve of Betsy's cheek, and remembering the little shock that had run through her when their hands touched, Abby experienced a brief, sudden stab of longing. It seemed like aeons since she had felt the tenderness of a man's touch. Would she ever again bask in the certainty that she was so cherished?

"Are you all right?"

The sound of his voice brought her wandering thoughts back to the present. Her gaze flew to his, which held a curious gleam. "Y-yes. Why do you ask?"

"You made a strange sound, and I thought something might be bothering you."

"Just thinking."

"About what?"

She slid him a sideways glance and said the first thing that came to mind. "No offense, Mr. Gentry, but you don't pay me enough to be privy to my thoughts." As soon as the words left her lips, she wished she could call them back. They were something she might have said to William. Almost... flirty, somehow. And totally inappropriate.

He regarded her for a moment, and then something bearing close kinship to a smile lifted one corner of his mouth for a heartbeat. "No offense taken, Mrs. Carter, and you're right. It's just that it's seldom you're so quiet. You're always talking to the children about something—even Laura and Betsy, who have no idea what you're saying."

"I was just respecting your privacy. You don't seem like the kind of man who indulges in idle chitchat."

"You're right," he said with a slow nod. "I have little use for chitchat and gossip, but I enjoy an intelligent discussion now and again."

Abby wasn't surprised that he valued intelligence. Chess was not a game for dummies, and no man who handled the myriad business responsibilities he did could be lacking in intelligence. If his impressive book collection was any indication, he was well read. The shelves on either side of the parlor fireplace were filled with titles that ranged from F. H. Bradley's *The Principles of Logic* to treatises on successful farming. There were many poetry and art-related books, no doubt Emily's. Abby tried to envision the creative Emily sharing her views on art and literature with her husband.

"I suppose you miss those discussions with Emily," Abby said, partly to keep the conversation going and partly because she was curious about his relationship with his dead wife.

"Emily and I had few common interests," he told her in a tone that said that line of conversation had ended.

"So," she asked after a few uncomfortable moments, "what shall we talk about?"

"You."

"Me?" She choked back a laugh. "There isn't much to tell, I assure you. You'd be very bored."

"That remains to be seen. From what you said the other day, your husband valued your comments and opinions, so I admit that I'm curious to hear some of them." He slanted a wry look her way and added, "A bit taken aback by your forwardness, but curious nonetheless. I'm also interested as to why you agreed to help me with Betsy."

"That's simple," she said with her customary bluntness. "Money."

He shot her a shocked look. "Rachel never led me to believe you were the avaricious type."

Again, Abby berated herself for speaking without thinking. This man was *not* William, and should not be answered with flippancy. "Oh, I'm not. Not really. I have little use for money for its sake, but we were forced to borrow against the farm, and the wages you've agreed to pay me will help me get caught up at the bank."

Caleb frowned. "I thought you bought your place outright."

She arched an eyebrow. "Ah. Gossip?" she challenged.

This time there was no denying his dry smile or the hint of color that crept into his lean cheeks. "The good old Wolf Creek grapevine," he acknowledged with a nod.

"The good old Wolf Creek grapevine had it right," she told him. "When my parents died, William and I used the money from the sale of their home to buy the farm and the equipment we'd need to farm it. And if you've heard that much gossip, you also know that he was a teacher, not a farmer. He had to borrow against the land."

"I know he took a job with the Southwestern Arkansas and Indian Territory Railroad Company."

"Yes," Abby said quietly. Neither mentioned that William Carter had been killed a short time after his daughter's birth while trying to connect two lumber-loaded railcars headed for an out-of-state market. Neither did Abby mention to Caleb that a few days before the accident, he had confided with an air of excitement that he had a potential buyer for the farm and he was thinking of taking the offer and moving them back to Springfield, Missouri, to be near his brother and his family.

Unfortunately, William was killed before anything could come of the deal, and Abby had no idea who the prospective buyer was.

"He should never have borrowed against the land," Caleb said into the gathering silence.

"That's an easy thing for someone like you to say," she told him, the memories bringing past heartache to the surface.

"Someone like me? What does that mean?" he asked, his tone mirroring his irritation.

"Someone who has money, has always had money and who never has to worry about how to buy feed for their livestock, or put food on the table or buy shoes for their children. Someone who has options."

Caleb didn't comment for long moments. When he turned his head to look at her, there was genuine concern in his eyes, but Abby, who was looking out over the dew-drenched fields, didn't see it. "So you did decide to take the job because of the money... because you had no other option."

Her gaze flew to his. "Oh! You make it sound so mercenary. Yes, I needed the money, but I wanted to help, too. Believe it or not, I do not pull wings off butterflies, nor am I greedy and avaricious."

Confusion filled his eyes. "I never thought you were. How have you managed these past months?"

Sensing that he was not angry, she gave a little shake of her head. "Though I hate to admit it, I've sold nearly everything I had that would bring a decent price." When he made no comment, she added, "Your offer was the answer to my prayers."

"Really?" he asked with an arched eyebrow of his own. "What took Him so long?"

"I beg your pardon," Abby said, not following or understanding the sarcasm in his voice.

"God. What took Him so long to answer your prayers? Why didn't He provide some sort of help sooner? Where was He when your husband died?"

Abby looked at him, taken aback. "It isn't for us to question His plan for us," she told him in an even tone. "Through faith, we believe that all will work out the way He wants it to, and for our benefit. And as for where He was when William died, I would imagine God was where He was when *His* son died."

Caleb had the grace to look bowled over by that answer. Though he wanted to ask if she dealt with William's loss by trusting that everything would come out all right and that something better was around the corner, he was silent.

"Surely you believe in God." The statement was simple and to the point.

"I suppose so," he said with a negligent lift of broad shoulders. "It's just that my brother and I were taught to rely on ourselves, so I haven't had many dealings with God."

"On the contrary," she argued, wondering how he'd lost his mother. "You deal with Him many times a day. Every day. Just look around you! It's beautiful!" Abby spread her arms wide, encouraging him to look at the world around him, to see and acknowledge the glory of it all.

But Caleb wasn't looking at the fallow fields or the red and gold of the changing leaves. He was looking at Abby. Bonnet-free, she had thrown back her head and lifted her face to the soft shine of the sun. A capricious breeze had tugged tendrils of blond hair from the coil at the nape of her neck and whipped delicate rose color into her cheeks. For the first time, he realized that Abigail Carter was a very pretty woman.

Caleb forced his eyes back to the road. "Yes. It is beautiful," he said in a husky voice.

Abby glanced at him, saw the set of his jaw and decided that she'd said enough on the subject for the moment. She knew from past experience that the best way to teach was by example. There would be plenty of time to show him in small ways that God was present and working in his life.

Almost a week had gone by since she and Caleb had made the trip to her place. The intervening days had passed quickly, and things had been going as well as could be expected. Abby's new routine had taken on a familiar rhythm as she grew accustomed to her new station in life and her new home. So far, neither Ben nor Laura had done anything else to antagonize the prickly Mr. Gentry.

As was her custom, Abby spent thirty minutes each night with Ben in Bible study. On two separate occasions, she had looked up and seen Caleb leaning against the doorjamb of his study, arms folded across his chest, listening as she read or questioned

Ben about certain verses. He never commented, and on both occasions, he had quickly shut the door, bade them good-night and headed for the bunk-house.

Today he was going into town for some feed and to pick up some pantry items Abby needed. When he came into the kitchen to tell her he was leaving, she said, "If you have time, I was wondering if you'd deliver a message for me."

His eyebrows lifted in surprise, but he only nodded. "I'd be glad to."

"I'm not used to dealing with this sort of thing, but I can. It's just that William always did, and you're familiar with business, so I thought…" She drew in another breath and rushed on. "I know it's an imposition, certainly beyond what most employers would do, but it will be so hard for me to get away with the babies, and—"

"Stop dithering, woman, and spit it out," Caleb said, scowling at her.

Abby's eyes widened and she bit back a sharp retort. *Dithering? Woman?* She lowered her gaze to his shirtfront and struggled to keep her tone pleasant. "It's just that…would you mind stopping at the bank to let Mr. Haversham know that I'm working for you now, and that I'll start making up the back payments as soon as possible?"

Some emotion she couldn't place flickered in Caleb's gray eyes. "I'd be glad to," he told her. "Anything else?"

"No. And thank you."

"You're welcome."

She watched the wagon disappear down the lane with a sigh of relief. He had agreed readily enough, and didn't seem to mind any inconvenience it might cause. But it *was* business, after all, and business was something he understood well.

"How are things, Caleb?" Emily's mother asked as he glanced over the list Abby had given him after making a thorough check of his pantry shelves.

What could he say to his dead wife's mother? He suspected that neither Mary nor Bart suspected the true circumstances of his marriage and how even though he had more money but was self-educated, he had always felt intellectually inferior to Emily, who had received her education at a fancy girls' school in St. Louis. He doubted they knew that Emily had taken far more joy from her drawing, reading and poetry writing than in making a home, or trying to build a marriage, so that when she had announced she was expecting a baby, it had come as a bit of a shock to them both.

Throughout the following months, her inability to come to terms with the whole idea of motherhood had left Caleb feeling as if he were solely to blame for her miserable pregnancy...and now her death. Thus the daily guilt he suffered.

Her dying had ended the steady ebb and flow of his life. Though Abby had a hot meal waiting for him when he returned to the house each evening, it was difficult for a man who liked the status quo to walk into the house and find strangers there. Being unable to enjoy the quiet peace and comfort of his home in the evenings made him nostalgic for the uncomplicated life he'd grown accustomed to during his marriage. Being with someone for six years forged habits and rituals that, when they ceased to exist, were missed nonetheless.

"I miss having her around," he told them truthfully.

The smile on Mary Emerson's face told him that his answer had pleased her, and that was all the thanks he needed.

Consulting Abby's list, Mary helped him select some just-picked apples and a small tin of cinnamon. He had a hankering for an apple pie, and so far, Abby hadn't balked at anything he'd suggested she fix, which, he had to admit, was a pleasant change.

"How is the arrangement with Abby Carter working out?" Bart Emerson asked, as if he could read his thoughts.

The troubled expression in the older man's eyes warned Caleb that something was wrong. "As well as can be expected, I suppose," he said, eyeing the older man thoughtfully. "What is it? I can tell something's wrong."

Bart cleared his throat. "I hate to mention it with everything you've been through lately, but you'll find out soon enough, I reckon."

"Spit it out," Caleb said, leaning against the counter.

"Well, uh, there are some folks in town making a terrible fuss about Mrs. Carter staying at your place."

Caleb's dark eyes narrowed. "What do you mean, fuss?"

"They don't think it's right, both of you being single and living under one roof."

Caleb swore beneath his breath. Though he was far from perfect and couldn't claim to be religious, the maliciousness of some so-called Christians never failed to astound him.

"Don't they know I just lost my wife, and I have a baby who needs to be fed every few hours?" he demanded. "Besides, Abby is newly widowed. And just for the record, I'm staying in the bunkhouse."

"I know, I know," Bart soothed. "You'd think they'd be more understanding what with Emily—" he cleared his throat "—and all. I'm thinking the problem is that Abby Carter is young and pretty. Maybe it would be different if she was old and ugly."

"And if she was old, I wouldn't need her, would I?" Caleb countered. He pinned Bart with a hard look. "Who exactly is 'they'?"

"Several in town," Bart hedged. "But the main one is Sarah VanSickle."

"The biggest gossip in three counties," Caleb muttered. He slapped his list onto the counter. "When I leave here, I have some business to see about for Abby, and then I'll go have a talk with Sarah."

"It won't do any good," Mary said. "She'd just make something of that. She's like a spoon, Caleb. She likes keeping things stirred up. The best thing to do is ignore it."

"Ignore it? That's easier said than done. I don't fancy being grist for the town's gossip mill, and I suspect Abby won't like it, either."

"I suppose not," Mary said, frowning. "Will you tell her?"

"No!" Caleb said in near panic. "She might decide to leave, and there's no way I could manage without her just now."

"I see your predicament, son, but you really ought to tell her before she finds out from someone else," Bart reasoned. "It's just a matter of time before Sarah's poison makes its way through the whole county."

Caleb hadn't thought of that, but knew Bart was right. He couldn't let Abby come to town and face the gossips without even preparing her, but how would he tell her? What would her reaction be? Furious and fearing he already knew the answer to that, he ground his teeth. Was anything in life ever easy?

It was almost dark when Caleb pulled the wagon to the rear of the house. The temperature was dropping since the sun had gone down, and he shivered, dreading the conversation to come. The feeling of trepidation vanished somewhat the moment he opened the back door and felt the tide of warm, cooking-scented air rush out to meet him. Breathing in the delicious aromas, he shifted the heavy sack of flour from his shoulder to the floor. Venison. Purple hull peas. Cornbread. Every night since Abby had come to stay he'd come in at suppertime to find something simmering on the back the stove.

Never much of a cook, Emily had stopped all attempts to do so when she'd announced her pregnancy, complaining of nausea, backaches and a general malaise. Soon she declared she was unable to do anything but knit and read, and in the subtle way she had, she made him feel like pond scum for putting her in her delicate condition. Rather than let the whole town know the situation, Caleb himself did what cooking and cleaning was to be done. Coming in and finding dinner waiting was nice, cooked by a stranger or not.

"How were the Emersons?" Abby said, setting the plates on the round oak table.

"Fine."

"Did you get the apples?"

He nodded. "Just picked."

"Wonderful." They sat down to eat, Ben said the prayer and after a few more questions that received short answers, Abby deduced that Caleb was not in the mood for any type of conversation and stopped talking except to ask if she could pass him any more food.

When the awkward meal was finished, she put Laura in the square, quilt-lined "pen" William had made for her and gave Ben a piece of butterscotch

Mary had thoughtfully sent. Abby told him to eat it on the porch and to get ready for bed as soon as he was finished. Caleb helped clear the table, something he'd gotten used to doing while fending for himself and continued to do for Abby.

He was setting a glass into the dishwater when she turned suddenly, a frown on her face. She was so close that he could see the almost-purple flecks in her blue eyes. So close he could smell the faint scent of the gardenia-scented soap she used for bathing. The sudden rush of awareness that jolted through him caught him off guard. Bart was right. Abby Carter was pretty. Very pretty. The revelation was swept away on another tidal wave of guilt. He took a sudden step back. What was the matter with him? His wife dead not two weeks, and he already found himself responding to the nearness of another woman!

"You seem distracted, Caleb. Is something wrong? Did Mr. Haversham refuse to discuss the farm?"

"No," Caleb said, thankful to turn his thoughts to something else. "As a matter of fact, he said he'd drop by on Sunday afternoon on his way back from his daughter's."

"Good," she said, but the worry stayed in her eyes. "Do you think he'll be open to what I have to say?"

Careful not to look at her, he wrapped the left-over cornbread in a flour-sack dish towel and lifted his wide shoulders in a shrug. "I didn't get into things with him, but Nate's a fair man, so I'm inclined to think he'll listen with an open mind."

"That's a relief." Neither spoke for several seconds.

"Abby, I—"

"Caleb, what—"

They both started to speak at once.

"Ladies first."

"It's just that something's wrong," she said, her blue eyes worry-filled. "I can tell. Did Ben—"

Caleb's first thought was that it was amazing that she could read his mood after less than two weeks, something Emily had never been able to do. "Ben's done nothing that I know about."

"Then what?"

He drew a deep breath, crossed his arms over his chest and plunged. "There's gossip in town."

"Gossip? About what?"

"Us. It seems Sarah VanSickle and some of the others in town think it's morally indecent for us to be living in the same house."

"But I go to church with Sarah," Abby said, as if the statement would negate the whole affair.

"If that old battle-ax is a Christian, I want no part of it."

"None of us is perfect, Caleb, and you'd do well to think twice about throwing out the baby with the bathwater."

Though she said the right thing, in her heart, she wanted to go to Sarah, confront her about her vicious character attacks and demand an accounting.

Had the spiteful woman given any serious thought to her actions? Did she have any idea of the harm she was causing two innocent people—even more if you considered the children? Abby blinked back the sting of tears. As much as she might want to confront her accuser, she knew she wouldn't.

A sudden thought occurred to her. "Caleb, we *aren't* living in the same house! If we make that clear, everyone will understand."

Caleb set the towel-wrapped bread in the pie safe, rested his elbow across its corner and regarded her with angry gray eyes. "Believe me, that was the first thing I pointed out to Mary and Bart, but they reminded me that a trifling thing like the truth does not matter one bit to Sarah. As a matter of fact, she's notorious about never letting facts get in the way of her maliciousness."

Abby cradled her hot cheeks in her palms. While the unwarranted accusations infuriated Caleb, the tears swimming in her eyes said she was more hurt and embarrassed than angry. He thrust his hands into his front pockets and stared out the window at the darkness, wondering what he could do to fix the mess they found themselves in.

"Do you think there are other people in town who feel the same way?" she asked.

He shot her a look that said he couldn't believe her naïveté. "Count on it."

"Well, then, I'll leave first thing in the morning," she said firmly, as if the decision would put an end to the whole matter.

"You will not!"

Shocked by his vehemence, she shook her head and said, "It's the only thing we can do. My reputation is at stake. So is yours."

"I'm not worried about my reputation," he said, a muscle in his lean jaw tightening. "People have been talking about the Gentrys for years. But I am concerned about you. And I'm very concerned about my daughter."

He took a breath and let it out slowly, as if he were trying to release the tension holding him. The fierce look in his eyes softened a bit as they met Abby's. "Look, we've already been through all this and decided this is the best way."

"But that was before Sarah's accusations."

"I understand, but we don't need to let her wreck a perfectly good partnership. Why don't we both sleep on it tonight. Things always look better in daylight. Maybe we'll dream up some way to resolve things that even Sarah VanSickle can't argue with."

Chapter Four

Abby lay quietly in her bed, the covers clutched in her fists, and tried to keep from flipping and flopping and waking Ben, who slept beside her. Though Sarah VanSickle's reputation as an inveterate gossip preceded her, the fact that Abby herself was now bearing the brunt of that hatefulness was a definite shock. The situation with Caleb was not what she would have chosen, but there was no denying that the opportunity to get her life in order had come along at a perfect time, and had seemed like the answer to her prayers. But if that were so, why was it being jeopardized by senseless gossip?

Dear God, what am I to do?

God was silent.

The faint fingers of dawn were poking through the window when she finally drifted off to sleep, tears of hopelessness drying on her cheeks as she faced the only moral decision possible. As much as Caleb might dislike her decision, as soon as she could gather her things, she was going back to her own farm.

With or without his daughter.

Being a man who preferred action, Caleb paced the path from the bunkhouse to the house over and over. He vacillated from self-pity over Emily's death and his current situation to fury at Sarah Van-Sickle for making an already bad situation worse. He wasn't sure why he was so surprised by the unexpected turn of events. Hadn't he always been the one saddled with the responsibility of doing the right thing?

As the older son of Lucas Gentry, it had fallen to Caleb to follow in his father's footsteps, while Gabe played the spoiled, pampered son. Though both boys were required to work the farm, more often than not, Gabe's contribution had been to keep everyone laughing at his jokes and antics, while Caleb was expected to toe the line and pick up the slack left by his younger brother. Caleb was the one who worked the longest hours and took the tongue-lashings and razor strap beatings, the one forced to learn farming from the ground up, including how to manage the soil and take care of the books. His father's demands left no time for fun, something Gabe enjoyed to the fullest.

Eight years ago, when Gabe was twenty and itching to experience more than Pike County had to offer, he'd gone to Lucas to ask for his inheritance, instead of waiting for his father to pass away.

To everyone's shock, Lucas had capitulated without argument, and Gabe had set out to see the world. Though there had been a few letters along the way, as far as Caleb knew, no one in Wolf Creek had seen his brother since he'd boarded the train for points east.

Rumors ran rampant. Word filtered back from friends of friends and even the pages of the big-city newspapers that were regularly shipped to Wolf Creek for the enlightenment of the few folks in town who liked to keep up with national happenings. Gabe's name had been linked to those of actresses, wealthy men's daughters and scandalous divorcées. He had a reputation of being a drinker, a gambler and a womanizer as he traveled California, New York, New Orleans, St. Louis and even Paris, London and Austria.

Five years after Gabe left to live the high life, and three years after Lucas browbeat Caleb into marrying Emily Emerson, Lucas died. Edward Stone claimed it was his heart. Caleb didn't doubt it. Gabe hadn't come home for the funeral; no one knew where or how to reach him.

And what did I get? A lifetime of work and responsibility, a wife I didn't love as I should have and now this. A baby to bring up alone. It wasn't fair, Caleb thought, feeling the rise of the anger that often simmered just beneath his calm exterior. But then, as Lucas had always declared when Caleb voiced that sentiment, life was many things, but it wasn't always fair.

Dwelling on past injustices would solve nothing, he thought now, gazing up at the wispy clouds trailing over the face of the moon. All he could do was deal with it in the best way possible. But what was that?

If he were a betting man, which he wasn't—he didn't work from dawn till dusk to fritter away his profits—he would say that Abby would once again suggest taking Betsy to her place, and if he didn't agree to that, she would quit. That meant that if he wanted to see his daughter, he would be running back and forth during the worst time of the year.

He wasn't sure just how the fatherhood thing worked, but he realized he was obligated to do his best by Betsy. His own upbringing had taught him the hard way that doing one's best involved being more than a tyrant who laid down the law and expected everyone to obey or suffer the consequences. He suspected that keeping a tight rein on his temper and being willing to listen to someone else's perspective was involved…the way Abby's husband had been willing to listen to her.

Caleb clenched his hands, and forced himself to consider every angle, something he did before making any major decisions. All right, beyond trips back and forth, what else would it mean if Abby left?

You'll come in from work to a cold, empty, unwelcoming house.

The notion held little appeal. He recalled the evening before when he'd stepped through the door and was greeted by the mouthwatering aromas of supper cooking on the big cast-iron woodstove. It had not escaped his notice that the dust and cobwebs that had collected the past several months had disappeared. The rugs had been taken out and whacked with a wire beater, and the wooden furniture gleamed with a combination of elbow grease, beeswax, turpentine and something that smelled of lemon.

If he refused to let Abby take the baby to her place and she quit, he would have to find a replacement, which, as he'd told Bart and Mary, would not alter his current situation one iota.

Which brought him back to the root of his quandary and kicked up his anger. Rumors and gossip. Why should he and Abby be concerned by the venomous ranting of a few small-minded, hypocritical folks? After all, they both knew there was nothing untoward going on between them.

He heaved a deep sigh. He also knew Abby was a decent, God-fearing woman who would never consent to remaining in a position that might damage her or her children—or him and Betsy, for that matter. Furthermore, what kind of cad would he be if he *let* her stay in a situation that would cause her reputation such damage? She'd have to leave the state to find another husband.

A terrifying thought slammed into his mind, stopping him dead in his tracks. A harsh, heartfelt "No!" shattered the silence of the moon-drenched night. Muttering about life's injustices, he stomped across the yard some more. Thought some more.

Weighed the good against the bad. Just before dawn, he gave a sigh of acceptance and made his peace with the inevitable.

When, weary and haggard, Caleb entered the kitchen from the barn the following morning, he saw that Ben was already seated, waiting for him. Though they were rarely seated before Caleb came in from his early chores, he'd told Abby he had no problem with her feeding the children before he got to the table. Abby had replied that unless it was some sort of emergency, she considered it the height of impoliteness to start a meal without the man of the house at the table.

Caleb's gaze roamed the room. Betsy was in her cradle near the fire, and Laura sat in the high chair he'd brought over from Abby's place, squishing a glob of sorghum and pancake into her mouth with the heel of her hand. A platter of sausage sat warming near the back of the stove, and Abby was busy taking buckwheat pancakes from a large cast-iron skillet.

It might have been a scene from a happy marriage, until you noticed the frown on Ben's face and the dejected slump of Abby's shoulders. He felt the almost overwhelming need to do something to improve the mood, but all he could manage was a terse "Good morning."

Abby sent him a quick glance over her shoulder. "Good morning."

She looked as tired as he felt. Dark smudges lay

beneath her red-rimmed blue eyes. Her nose was reddened, too, no doubt from crying. There was an unhappy droop to her lips, which some still-functioning part of his mind noted were very prettily shaped. From what he'd seen in the mirror when he'd shaved, he looked no better than she.

Caleb noticed the way Ben's gaze moved from his mother to Caleb, as if he somehow knew who was responsible for the unhappiness that seemed to roll from her in dark waves.

She set down the sausages, a platter of pancakes, a round of fresh-churned butter and a quart jar of sorghum molasses before returning to the stove for the coffeepot. After filling both their cups, she sat down to Caleb's right and Ben gave thanks for their food.

They ate in silence, much like other mornings, Caleb thought with unexpected depression. Much like the mornings he'd shared with his father. Even Gabe had known better than to cut up at the table, and Gentry meals had been reduced to cleaning their plates as fast as possible so they could escape to whatever backbreaking work Lucas had planned.

When they finished eating, Abby sent Ben out with the table scraps, and told him to milk the goat. When the door slammed shut behind him, Caleb picked up his coffee cup, wondering what to say. He'd fought with his decision and come to the only plausible conclusion, but he wasn't sure how to begin.

"I've thought about things all night," Abby said

at last, saving him the trouble. "The only solution is for me to quit. You can hire someone else."

"Who?" Caleb challenged as she poured more coffee into his cup. "Widows with infants aren't all that plentiful in Wolf Creek, and if I hired someone else it would just spark the same gossip we're dealing with."

Abby chewed on her lower lip. "I could take Betsy to my place," she offered again, as he'd known she would.

He shook his head. "We've already discussed that. She belongs at home. Winter will be here before we know it, and getting back and forth will be a nightmare when the weather gets bad. Seeing her the way I should would be a hardship, if not an impossibility. Besides, I already know how hard it is for you to manage things at your place, and I don't think you can make it through the winter alone with three children."

She plopped down in her chair and rested her elbows on the table, regarding him with tear-glazed eyes. "Then what other choice do we have, Caleb? I can't think of any other way."

The full force of his silvery gaze met hers. "The only way I can think of is for you to marry me."

Abby's eyes widened and her mouth fell open in shock. "Have you taken leave of your senses?" she asked when at last she was able to speak.

"I don't think so," Caleb replied in what he hoped was a measured, sensible tone. "I was up the whole night, too, trying to figure out what to do, and of everything I came up with, marriage makes the most sense."

"It makes no sense!" Abby cried, jumping up and pacing to the back door. "Never mind that we aren't in love! We hardly know each other."

"I know that you're a good person and a good mother, and it seems to me that love is highly overrated."

Her eyes widened and she looked at him as if he'd grown another head. "That's a cynical attitude, especially since you told me you loved Emily very much."

"When?" he asked, frowning.

"You asked me if I loved William, and I said that I had—very much. Then you said that I could have no idea how you felt when Emily died."

"I'm afraid you misunderstood. My marriage to Emily was not a love match."

"All the more reason I would think you'd put love at the top of the list when you look for another wife," she countered, taken aback by his admission.

"Actually, I had no clear idea whether or not I would ever marry again, and I confess that I haven't seen a whole lot of marriages that are based on love," he told her. "Besides, arranged marriages, mail-order brides—" he shrugged "—for the most part, those marriages work out just fine. Why wouldn't ours?"

His attitude went against everything Abby had been taught about love and marriage. His cold-hearted approach to one of God's most special institutions infuriated and saddened her. Shoving aside the pang of sorrow, she snapped, "Because it wouldn't, that's why."

Seeing the beginning of a storm gathering in his gray eyes, she softened her tone. "Marriage is sacred, Caleb, and I hope to find someone someday who will love me and my children, and despite your doubts, I'm sure that in time you'll find someone to love, too."

In a gesture fast becoming familiar, he raked a hand through his already-mussed hair. "Believe me, I gave that a lot of thought last night, too, but there's no woman in town—married or single— that I can ever imagine loving." Seeing her skepticism, he pushed his advantage. "You know as well as I do that the chance for either of us to find love in Wolf Creek is slim to none."

"I don't know that!"

He admitted a grudging admiration for the spark of irritation in her eyes. He didn't think he'd ever known Emily feeling strongly enough about a subject to defend it.

"Will you at least listen before you—" he offered her a brief, halfhearted smile and tossed her words back at her "—throw out the baby with the bathwater?"

She blinked, amazed by the change the wry quirking of his lips made in his craggy features. The notion that she found his smile fascinating triggered another stab of irritation. She did not want to find him attractive. She did not want to feel sorry for him, and she did *not* want to hear what he had to say. She crossed her arms over her chest. "Fine."

He looked at her, wondering again where to start. Telling her he was no happier about the idea than she was would not help his cause. He cleared his throat.

"First, I think we would both agree that fate and Sarah VanSickle's penchant for gossip have put us in a bad spot, and we have to figure out the best way to stop the rumors while still solving our mutual problems. After giving both sides careful consideration, I believe marriage is the best solution."

Abby pressed her lips together to keep from saying something inflammatory. She would hear him out.

He offered her another of those "almost" smiles. "I guess you've noticed that I'm not the most likable man in Wolf Creek, and the mirror tells me I'm not the most handsome."

Stunned at his brutal assessment of himself, she opened her mouth to offer a polite denial, but he held up a silencing palm. "Despite those drawbacks, I have it on the authority of several folks—including Emily's parents—that I am considered a good catch. If you consent to this marriage, I promise to take the best care I know how of you and your children. I realize that besides being your husband, I will be their father as well as Betsy's, which I confess frightens me more than I can say."

She couldn't picture Caleb Gentry being afraid

of anything, yet his whole attitude was one of vulnerability.

"I have no idea how to be a father to my own child, much less someone else's. I know I'll need to work on being more patient and realize that there will be other incidents like the shepherdess and the chessmen, but I also know there would have been those same sorts of incidents between your children and their real father. I doubt anyone short of a saint could refrain from losing his temper on occasion."

Impressed by the thought he'd given to their predicament, Abby nodded.

His mouth twisted into another of those mocking smiles. "As troubling as this shortcoming is, I am somewhat consoled by the fact that you, too, have a temper."

Abby felt a blush heat her cheeks.

All trace of sardonic humor vanished. "Sit down, Abby. Please." When she did his bidding, he continued. "If you marry me, I promise I'll try to do better, but you must understand that I won't always succeed."

He had given this a lot of thought, and really was as concerned about her and her children as he was his daughter.

"I know you're an educated woman and that you'll want more instruction for your children than is available here. When they get older, I'll pay for their schooling wherever you like."

Abby's eyes widened. "You'd do that? Why?"

"Because I know that sort of thing is important

to someone like you. Furthermore, I'll settle all your outstanding debts." He continued speaking over her indrawn breath. "If you're agreeable, I'll talk to Nathan Haversham about selling your farm. You can put the proceeds from the sale into a trust to secure your children's future—and yours, should anything happen to me."

Abby was surprised by the sudden sense of loss she felt at the thought of something happening to him. She sat, trying to absorb what he was saying. His offer was more than generous. And very tempting. To know she would never again have to worry about how to pay bills or feed her children. To feel secure in the knowledge that they would have every advantage the Gentry money could offer....

But things and advantages were no substitute for a father who would love them. Nor were they a suitable replacement for a husband who would care for her.

"You make it sound more like a business deal than a marriage."

"Maybe that's the best way to look at it. At least until we...come to know each other better." Abby blinked at the implication, and he cleared his throat. "There are some things you should know about me before you decide. I may not sit in a pew every Sunday, but I try to live a decent life."

Abby had never heard anything to the contrary.

"I don't gossip or stick my nose into anyone else's business, and while I drive a hard bargain, I believe anyone will tell you that I'm fair. To my knowledge I've never cheated anyone."

He sounded so perfect that Abby was beginning to wonder if she should offer him a laundry list of her own qualities—good and bad. With a breathless burst of self-conscious laughter, she said as much.

"I think I know the most important things about you, and it will be an adventure of sorts to uncover the others through the years. Just for the record, like you, I believe in the sanctity of marriage, and I take any commitment I make seriously, including marriage vows."

Abby regarded him, her brow furrowed in question. "Those vows speak of love, Caleb. What about that?" It seemed they had come full circle. She longed to experience that emotion again; he doubted its existence. How could a marriage between them ever work?

He spread his hands in a helpless gesture. "I don't know, Abby. But if love really exists, perhaps it will find us."

She wanted to ask what would happen if it didn't find them, but was unable to phrase the question for the thoughts swirling through her mind. She recalled one of William's favorite sayings: "An open heart will find love." Would he think her mad to contemplate such a thing, or would he think she was wise for doing what she must for the sake of the children? Was it possible that in time, if she kept an open mind, she would grow to love Caleb Gentry? And what of him? Would his heart open enough to let love in? Love not only for her and the children, but a love of God and His word?

The preposterous idea seemed unseemly, somehow, and yet Caleb had a point. People did enter loveless marriages every day and for less pressing reasons than finding a mother for a child. Betsy would need a caring mother as she grew up.

And what about her own prayers? *Lord, is this the answer I prayed for? Is this what You would have me do?* She wished she had time to consider it more fully, but in the end, would it matter? The problems and choices would stay the same.

"I don't know what to say," she whispered in a tormented voice.

"Say yes, Abby," Caleb urged, his deep voice soft, pleading. "Say yes."

Abby still couldn't believe she'd agreed to Caleb's unexpected proposal. Once she yielded, they'd called Ben in to tell them the news. Abby settled him on the sofa and took the chair facing him.

"You know that Mr. Gentry's wife died," she began.

Ben gave a solemn nod.

"And you know how hard it has been for us since your father died." Another nod. "Well, since we're living here already, Caleb has asked me to marry him, so that we can make a new family, all of us. You and Laura and Betsy will be brother and sisters and Caleb will be your stepfather."

"Do you have to marry him, Mama?" Ben asked.

Abby sneaked a peek at Caleb, whose face had turned a dull red. "Yes, Ben, for the good of us all, it seems I do."

"Well, he's not my father," Ben shouted, jumping up and glaring at her. "And I won't call him that."

"Benjamin Aaron—" Abby began, only to be stopped by Caleb's hand on her shoulder.

"It's all right, Abby." To Ben, he said, "You don't have to call me Papa, Ben. Call me Caleb."

"But he can't!" Abby cried. "That's disrespectful."

"Not if I give him permission," Caleb countered. "I can't have him calling me Mr. Gentry for the rest of his life."

The rest of his life. The words sank into her mind, and a queasy feeling settled in her stomach as she faced head-on the seriousness of her bargain. "No," she whispered. "I suppose not."

"Ben," Caleb said, "I know I've been short with you sometimes, but you need to understand that I've never had children before Betsy, and I'm not used to them or the things they do."

Ben refused to lift his head and meet Caleb's gaze.

"I know it's been hard for you since your father died, and that it was hard for you to leave your home and come to a place that's unfamiliar and where there are new rules. It's hard for me and your mother, too. She says it will take time for us to get used to each other, and I think she's right."

Ben stared at the toes of his scuffed boots. When

he didn't reply, Caleb asked, "Ben, did your father ever get angry with you?"

Ben nodded, still refusing to look up.

"And I imagine that sometimes you were mad at him, too. But you got over it, and you still cared for him, didn't you?" Without waiting for Ben to answer, Caleb added, "I suspect we will be no different. You're right. I'm not your father, but I hope the time will come when you will at least count me as a friend if you can't think of me as a father."

Leaving Ben with that to ponder, Caleb gave Abby's shoulder a gentle squeeze and left her alone with her son.

When he was gone, Abby went to Ben and drew him close. He buried his face against her as he seldom did since he'd turned six, and she thought she heard him snuffling. "I know this is hard for you, but it is necessary, Ben. I can't tell you all the reasons why, because they're grown up reasons, and even if I did, you wouldn't understand. You must trust me when I tell you that the decision Caleb and I have made is for the good of us all."

Stepping back, she tilted up his freckled face and offered him a sorrowful smile. "I can't change the way you feel, Ben, but I need you to try to understand. We don't know what happened to Caleb that has made him—" *Harsh. Distant. Detached.* "—the way he is, but we need to try to get along. I know he wants things to be better. Rachel says he's a good man, and I don't think she would say that if it weren't the truth. We just have to give him a chance, the way he has to give us a chance. Will you try?"

Tears filled Ben's blue eyes and he nodded.

"We need to pray about it, too. We need to believe that we are where God wants us, even though we don't understand why. One day we will."

Ben nodded, swiped at his eyes and drew his shirt sleeve across his runny nose. *Snail trails.* She smiled.

Ben gave her a hard hug and left Abby wondering, despite their limited choices and her guarantees to her son, if she and Caleb really were doing the right thing for everyone involved.

Chapter Five

While Abby had her talk with Ben, Caleb went out to get his hands started on a final late hay-cutting. Then he and Abby spent the better part of an hour discussing their decision at length. If things went according to plan, the ceremony would be held in three days, on a Saturday afternoon at the house, since they both felt Betsy was too little to be taken out and about.

Shortly after the noon meal, Caleb headed to town to make the necessary arrangements for the wedding. He didn't relish the next couple of hours and kept the horse to a slow walk for most of the three-plus miles. He had agreed to take care of the legalities, including telling Emily's parents of the decision before doing anything else. He hoped they understood. At Abby's insistence that he take care of all the legalities, he would speak with Nathan Haversham at the bank about setting up a power of attorney and then selling Abby's farm and investing the proceeds for her children's future. Last, Caleb would approach Abby's minister about performing the wedding ceremony.

He did not feel like a potential bridegroom.

Ever since she had agreed to his preposterous proposal, his feelings had vacillated between those of a shipwrecked sailor who spies land on the horizon and a man condemned to walk the plank. He was not happy about entering another marriage; contrarily, he was relieved that things would soon be resolved. There was even a small kernel of conviction that the decision was the best choice for everyone concerned.

Without a doubt there were those in town, such as Sarah VanSickle and her ilk, who would judge them as harshly for marrying so soon after Emily's death as they were for Abby staying at his house without a ring on her finger. His jaw tightened. There was just no pleasing some folks.

"Why so glum, young fella?" Frank asked, spying Ben sitting on an overturned bucket, his chin in his palms, his elbows resting on his patched, denim-clad knees.

"Nuthin'."

"Nuthin' doesn't make a fella look like he's lost his last friend. Come on, boy, tell me what's wrong, and maybe I can help."

Heaving a sigh, Ben looked up at the hired hand. "She's gonna marry him. He's gonna be my stepfather."

"Whoa, Nellie!" Franks said. "Are you sayin' your mama and Caleb are getting hitched?"

Ben nodded.

Frank took off his dirty felt hat, slapped it against his scrawny thigh, scratched his head and replaced the hat on his uncombed hair. "Well, if that don't beat all!" he said, flipping over another bucket and plopping down. "I take it you ain't too pleased about it."

Defiance darkened Ben's eyes. "I don't like him."

"Can't imagine why not," Frank said. "He's a right good man once you get to know him. Course I been knowin' him ever since he was a little guy like you, so maybe I'm a tad partial."

Ben frowned. "You knew Caleb when he was a kid?"

"Yep."

"What was he like?"

"A real hard worker. His daddy was a hard taskmaster. Seen to it that Caleb did more'n his share of chores around here."

"I do chores."

"I know you do, and it's good for you. A man's gotta work to be able to provide for his family."

"My father worked for the railroad," Ben said. "He got killed."

"I heard that, and I'm real sorry." They sat in silence for a moment and then Frank said, "Your mama lost her husband and Caleb lost his wife. Seems like a right smart thing to do to get hitched up so as they can help each other."

Ben thought back to what his mother had said about both her and Caleb needing something the other had. Sighed.

"Don't give up on Caleb before you ever get started," Frank said, slanting a serious look at Ben. "He's got his faults, but he's got a lotta good in him, too, and he can teach you things most boys don't know about."

"Like what?"

"Like runnin' a farm, and gravel business. Huntin'. He knows a lot about book learnin', too. He even taught me to read and write a bit. Smart man, Caleb Gentry."

A slight smile curved the old man's mouth. Smart enough to grab up a good woman when he had the chance, whether or not he realized yet that it was a good thing.

While Betsy slept in her cradle and Ben went to "help" Frank and Leo, Laura sat in Abby's lap gnawing on a hard crust of bread while she stared at a page of her mama's handwritten recipe book. With the wheels set into motion by Caleb's trip to town, her doubts had once again begun to creep in. She was trying hard to make herself believe the things she'd told her son, especially about trusting God that this marriage was the best solution for all involved—indeed the only solution.

Even though she'd only been at the Gentry farm a few days, she knew that one thing she'd said was true: Caleb was a decent and good man, as his generosity proved. If he was also a hard man, well, no one was perfect, as he had pointed out by reminding her of her own quick temper and the conjecture that things had not always been idyllic between William and the children—or her and William for that matter. Though it chafed to hear it, it was true.

At Caleb's suggestion, she'd spent the morning hand-writing invitations to a few of her closest friends from church, asking them to come and witness the ceremony and to stay for some refreshment afterward. He'd promised to deliver the requests when he went to town. He also told her to make up a list of whatever she might need from the mercantile for the occasion, and he would go back for it the following day.

His unexpected thoughtfulness had come as a bit of a surprise. She knew his offer meant more time away from the farm, and she appreciated his wanting to make the wedding something more than a quick, secretive affair done solely to satisfy the gossipmongers. With the town rife with rumor and a few of the people in her own church in the middle of it, Abby wasn't sure how her invitations would be received. She was so hurt by the unexpected scandal that she was no longer sure who her friends were, or which ones were nothing more than pew warmers.

Well, there was no sense fretting over it, she thought, putting Laura in her playpen. In a demonstration of rare wastefulness, telling herself she deserved a treat, Abby dumped out the bit of leftover breakfast coffee and set a fresh pot on the stovetop to brew.

Resolutely, and with a deep sigh, she turned her mind back to the recipes. There was much to do and only a short time to do it. Since apples were in abundance, she would bake a fresh apple cake. She'd have Ben pick up some of the pecans from beneath the tree that grew out near the edge of the woods. Frank and Leo could shell them. She'd be making goat cheese tomorrow, which would go well with some of her muscadine jelly on fresh crackers she'd have Caleb pick up at the mercantile. She could make some small venison pastries....

The sound of someone knocking on the door disrupted her thoughts. Getting to her feet, she headed for the parlor and opened the door to see Rachel framed in the doorway, the wide smile on her face mirroring the one in her dark eyes.

"What can I do?"

Abby stared at her friend in disbelief. "About what?"

Rachel laughed. "The wedding, goose!" she said, stepping inside.

"How on earth did you hear about it so quickly?" Abby asked, closing the door behind her friend.

Rachel went straight to the fireplace. Though it was a glorious autumn day, there was a nip in the air. "I was on my way to the Donnellys' and passed Caleb on the road. He gave me the highlights, so when I finished there, I came on over."

Still stunned by how fast news traveled, Abby

gave a weak smile. "Did he tell you why we're doing this?"

"Of course he did. I've been hearing rumblings the past few days, and if it's any consolation, I've been doing my best to stamp out the lies whenever I get a chance."

"Thank you. And thank you for coming. I'm feeling a bit overwhelmed."

"I'm sure you are."

"Come on into the kitchen. I just put on some fresh coffee, and I've been trying to figure out what sort of refreshments to fix. I don't have much time, so it can't be anything too elaborate—not that it should be too fancy considering the circumstances. I just felt I should offer something for those who accept my invitation…assuming anyone does."

"What do you mean? Of course they will," Rachel said, following Abby into the kitchen.

Abby set the coffeepot to a cooler part of the stove and turned toward her friend. "Thank you, Rachel, but even though they aren't true, and you're trying to stop them, it doesn't change the fact that gossips are bandying lies all over town, and plenty of people will judge me and Caleb because of it."

She turned away to fetch the cups and saucers to hide a sudden rush of tears, but she could not hide the tremor in her voice. "It's beyond me how something that started out as a mission of mercy and a way for me to provide for my children wound up as fodder for the gossip mill and a marriage between two people who'd rather be snakebit!"

"Trust me, marriage—even to Caleb Gentry—is a much better fate than being snakebit," the always-serious doctor said.

The fact that the words were spoken without an iota of humor struck Abby as comical, no doubt because her nerves were shaky. A reluctant smile tugged at her mouth. "Maybe you're right."

She filled the cups, set the sugar bowl on the table, punched a couple of holes in a can of condensed milk and set it next to the sugar. "Sorry," she said. "I don't have anything sweet. Caleb inhales anything and everything I bake."

Rachel groaned. "I don't need a thing! I had a slice of pie at Millie's." She picked up the can of milk. "My, aren't we uptown?" she said with a lift of her dark eyebrows. "I'm not sure when I last had this in my coffee. It's a little pricy for a mere physician."

Abby knew that Rachel often went without pay or traded for her services. "Then by all means, enjoy. Compliments of Caleb Gentry." She sighed. "I'm pretty sure he has no problem paying for it."

"Probably not," Rachel said, stirring some of the thick, sweet milk into the fragrant coffee. She swallowed a healthy swig and shoved the sugar bowl away.

"What?" Abby teased. "No two spoons full of sugar today?"

Rachel's gaze met Abby's. "If I added sugar, it would be so sweet that even I couldn't stand it," she said with a dry solemnity that brought a burst of laughter to Abby's lips. Rachel's love of anything sweet was well known.

"Thanks, Rachel, I needed to laugh."

Rachel smiled back. "I aim to please." She took another sip of coffee. "So tell me how it all came about."

Abby spent the next few moments relating the gist of her conversations with Caleb. "So, here we are. As you know, he's on his way to see if the preacher can come out Saturday afternoon, and I sent invitations to a few people I thought might come. I was just looking through some recipes when you knocked."

"Tell me what you're planning. I'll be glad to bring something."

They spent the next half hour discussing things to serve. After decisions were made and Rachel volunteered to bring some serving pieces of her mother's for the event, the hint of animation in Abby's eyes dimmed.

"Why the frown?"

Abby cut a wry glance at her friend. "Oh, I don't know. Maybe the fact that I'm marrying a stranger, or maybe because both our reputations are in ruins."

"'This too shall pass,'" Rachel said. "Look, this will be the prime topic of conversation until something juicier comes along. Trust me, Abby, I know. Besides, Caleb's family is no stranger to controversy."

"What do you mean?"

"Evidently when he and his brother were small, Libby Gentry left them for another man."

Abby couldn't hide her shock. "B-But I thought she died. There's a marker under the magnolia tree out back. I assumed her remains were buried there."

"I've heard that Lucas forbade either of them to ever mention her name again," Rachel said. "He emptied the house of everything that was hers, set fire to it and buried what wouldn't burn. I guess in a way it *is* her remains."

Abby thought of the broken shepherdess and wondered how it had escaped Lucas Gentry's cruel hand.

"And then there's Gabe," Rachel said, averting her gaze.

The animosity in her voice drew Abby's attention back to the conversation. There was a grim expression on Rachel's face that was totally foreign to the woman Abby had grown so fond of.

"His younger brother," she said, remembering Caleb mentioning him as he'd tried to explain the lack of love in his life.

"Yes, Gabe. Gabriel. Though he bears absolutely no resemblance to anything angelic. More like Wolf Creek's very own black sheep." She gave a little shiver, as if shaking off a chill or a bad memory, and offered Abby a forced smile.

"As for marrying a stranger, I wonder if we ever really know someone until we share their life."

It took Abby a few seconds to realize Rachel had switched topics. "I've thought of that, but I'm not sure I understand how strangers…" The words dried on her lips, the same way her mouth dried up when she thought of the deeper implications of the course she had willingly chosen for herself. She tried to imagine a future with Caleb as father to a child of hers and felt a blush spread over her face. "It's just…there should be…love."

Rachel nodded. "I know you loved William."

Abby nodded. "I did. He was a dreamer and a romantic and good to the bone. He was handsome and joyful and filled with ideas. Most of them were pie-in-the-sky aspirations, but he had a knack for getting so caught up in his dreams that he could light that same kind of fire in me—at least in the beginning. And I supported him because I loved him, and as his wife, that was part of my job."

"A wife's support is always important," Rachel said.

"I know, and I was glad to do so, at least in those early years." Abby gave a short little laugh and met her friend's troubled gaze. "In all honesty, I didn't want to leave Springfield and come here. My inheritance wasn't large, but it would have given us a more-than-comfortable lifestyle while we both taught. But he'd read an article in the *St. Louis Post Dispatch* touting the fulfillment of farming. He said he was tired of academia and wanted to work with his hands, so I agreed and we came to Wolf Creek."

She did not say that she had awakened one day to the bitter reality that not only was the money gone, but William's dreams and aspirations had vanished, as well. They'd been replaced by doubts and growing depression.

"Before he was killed, I often wished he were stronger-willed and a better manager. Looking back, it's scary how tight money has been the past couple of years."

"Yet you've always survived."

"Yes."

"And you didn't stop loving him."

Abby was thoughtful as she chewed on her thumbnail a moment before answering. "No."

She did not tell Rachel that even though she sometimes missed him so much she ached inside, she had come to realize that her feelings had always been those of a young girl caught up in the fantasy and romance of love, a love that sometimes faltered when tempered in the fires of reality.

"Even though you and Caleb don't love each other, you can still have a good life together. If you ask me, there may not be any better two things to build a relationship on than mutual respect and trust."

Abby noted that the cynicism was back. Was Rachel referring to her relationship with her son Daniel's father? Abby knew there was no man in Rachel's life, and since she had offered no insight, and Abby was unwilling to ask someone and be guilty of being nosy herself, she had no idea what the situation was.

"I pray you're right." She lifted her head, met Rachel's concerned gaze and blurted, "Do you think

I'm being mercenary for agreeing to marry a man who's promised to fix all my financial woes, feed and clothe me and my children, and be a husband and father to us for the rest of our lives?"

Rachel stared at her for a moment in stunned disbelief, and then burst out laughing. After a few seconds she grew serious and reached out to take Abby's hand.

"Oh, Abby! If you and Caleb *were* in love and he asked you to marry him, he would be doing the same thing. Besides, it isn't as if you're coming empty-handed into this marriage, you know. Besides working alongside him every day you're bringing warmth and love into the home and the life of a man who needs it desperately. Never, never feel as if Caleb is the one doing all the giving."

After Rachel left, Abby thought long about what she'd said. She had to admit that Rachel's perspective had taken the edge off her own anxiety. She *was* bringing something to the marriage. And, as hard and unapproachable as he might be, she did respect Caleb. More importantly, she trusted him. That trust engendered a feeling of safety she hadn't experienced in a long time.

Caleb would not be intimidated by what he confronted in life. He would look difficulties in the eye, size them up and proceed with determination and hard work to fix them, whatever they might be, just as he had when confronted with news of the scandal attached to both their names.

It gave her some consolation that he would do

no less in their marriage. Whatever problems might arise between them, she felt he would somehow do his best to fix them.

The next morning, Abby was washing the breakfast dishes, and Caleb had once again gone to town to get the items she needed for the wedding refreshments. Though she still had doubts and fears, her heart had been somewhat lighter since Rachel's visit the day before. What concerns Abby could not banish, she managed to push aside with a flurry of housecleaning.

She had just set the cast-iron skillet on the back of the stove when she heard Ben yell, "It's Mr. Teasdale, Mama!"

There was no denying the excitement in his voice. Ben was always thrilled to see what new treasures the peddler might have tucked away in his satchels and crates.

Truth be told, Abby was glad to see him, too. A wee sprite of a man with a broad smile and false teeth far too big for his face, Simon Teasdale made a pass through the area every few months, bringing shoes, guns and knives for the menfolk; pots and pans, spices, perfumes, bolts of fabric and other frippery for the ladies.

Abby sneaked a peek at Betsy, who was asleep in her cradle, snatched up Laura and hurried to the door. Maybe he would have something suitable for her wedding, since all her dresses—including her better ones—were not only out of style, but a bit worse for the wear.

She flung open the door. "Mr. Teasdale! It's good to see you. Come in!"

"Don't mind if I do," he said with a toothy smile. "Hello there, Ben. I believe you've grown a foot since I last saw you!" he said, hanging his hat on the coatrack and shrugging out of his coat. Ben grinned, anticipation glowing in his eyes. As expected, the peddler pulled two peppermint sticks from his coat pocket and handed one to Ben and one to Laura, who was still on her mother's hip.

With the children satisfied for the moment, Simon backed up to the small fire burning in the grate. "I didn't know what to think when I went by your place and it was shut up tighter'n a drum. Then I went on into town and heard what happened to Mrs. Gentry." He shook his balding head. "A pity. She always did seem such a frail sort. I always figured she was just here for a short time."

Abby didn't know how to respond to that. Simon brightened suddenly. "Well, now, there's no sense dwelling on sad things when I hear congratulations are in order."

Abby blushed.

"I saw Doc Rachel in town, and as soon as I heard the news I hightailed it out here to see if I might have some female trifle you might have need of for the big day. I didn't figure you could head off to town with two little ones in tow."

"It really isn't going to be a big day, Mr. Teasdale. Just a few friends here at the house with a little refreshment afterward."

"Well, I have some nice cider that would be fine drinking with some cinnamon sticks and whole cloves simmered in it. The weather is perfect for something warm." He winked. "I even have some oranges and lemons you might add."

"That sounds wonderful, but what I could really use is a dress."

"A dress, hmm?" The little man cocked his head and looked her up and down. Coming from any other man, it might have been insulting, but Abby knew he was only trying to judge her size. "I'm sure we can find something that will be just the thing," he told her, heading back out to his wagon.

Abby passed on the gowns with bustles, declaring that they were too fancy for Wolf Creek and she'd get little use of them. Instead, she chose a simple dress of gold-hued velvet with a plain round neck, long sleeves and a fitted bodice with tiny abalone buttons marching down the front. The skirt flared gently toward the floor with no need for a multitude of petticoats. It was quietly elegant, and would be suitable for church.

She emerged from the bedroom fifteen minutes later and whirled around for Simon's inspection.

"You'll make a beautiful bride, my dear," he said. "Caleb will be as pleased as punch."

Abby didn't have the heart to contradict him. "I don't have much money right now," she said. "Will you take something in trade?"

"Please. Let it be my wedding gift to you," Simon said.

"Oh, I couldn't possibly!" Abby objected. "Wait here." She went back into her room and emerged in a moment with a lovely cameo brooch encircled with fine gold filigree. "This was my mother's. Would you take it in exchange for the gown?"

Simon looked as torn as Abby. "It's a lovely piece and worth far more than the dress. I hate to see you part with it. Perhaps—"

"Please," Abby coaxed, pressing the brooch into his bony hands even though she hated losing one of her last links to her mother. "I wouldn't feel right otherwise." Though neither of them was happy about the upcoming nuptials, she *was* marrying the wealthiest man in the county, and she would not have Caleb ashamed of her. "If it will make you feel better, you can throw in the cider, oranges and spices."

In the end, Simon added a shirt and some new Sunday trousers for Ben, who had taken a growth spurt the past couple of months, and a pair of dark gold shoes of the softest leather that matched Abby's dress. When he left, her heart was a bit lighter. Simon Teasdale was a good man who always brought a spot of sunshine when he came.

By Friday afternoon Abby wondered if she'd be able to get everything done in the next twenty-four hours. The children's clothes were ready and the house was spotless, but Betsy hadn't slept well the night before, and the usually sweet-tempered Laura was teething and whiny. Miserable, Ben slunk around like someone who'd lost his last friend, despite Abby giving him the piece of licorice Simon had left as a surprise.

Abby was weary from being up with Betsy, and Ben still needed a haircut and the cake needed to be baked. She would get up early in the morning to finish the last-minute details before the guests arrived.

Caleb must have sensed that she was feeling pressure, because he'd asked Ben to go with him to help Frank and Leo look for pine knots. Ben had declined at first, but Caleb had bent to whisper something in his ear, and Ben had given a reluctant nod.

Abby had just put both girls down for a nap and was mixing up the apple cake when she heard someone at the door. She opened it to find Rachel along with four other friends standing there, laden down with various items, their faces wreathed in wide smiles. Emily's mother stood at the rear of the group.

"Congratulations!" they chorused as one, breezing into the house.

"What's going on?"

"We've come to help with the wedding preparations," Allison Granger, a short, plump, redheaded schoolteacher, said. She swept past Abby and set a pair of silver candlesticks and two tall white tapers on the dining room table. Ellie Carpenter, who owned the café, uncovered three small cut-glass plates wrapped in dish towels. Rachel brought a tall cut-crystal vase that had belonged to her mother. Gracie Morrison offered a fine white damask table-cloth for the dining room table, and Lydia North's contribution was a silver charger piled high with delicate cookies laced with finely chopped pecans. Mary Emerson carried a large crystal punch bowl with matching cups that she announced had belonged to her grandmama. When she saw the tears in Abby's eyes, she took her hands and squeezed tightly. "Bless you, child," she whispered.

Then, amid a cacophony of chatter and laughter, Rachel shooed Abby back to the kitchen to finish the cake, while they finished "fixing things up." As Abby added the flour to the already blended sugar, butter, eggs and chopped apple, she could hear snippets of their conversations and their happy laughter. She wasn't aware of the smile that claimed her lips, but she was aware that her friends' appearance had restored her flagging faith in the goodness of the townsfolk.

When the cake was in the oven, she reentered the parlor. Her shocked gaze moved around the room and to the adjoining dining room in amazement. Both were transformed with English ivy and branches of French mulberry laden with clusters of fuchsia berries.

"What do you think?" Rachel asked.

Abby felt the sting of tears again. She did have friends who cared. "I think it's beautiful and that you are all wonderful, wonderful friends."

"Well, thanks. We love you, too," Allison said

with a saucy grin. "We aren't finished yet. Rachel and I will be out in the morning to finish up."

"It couldn't look any better."

"Just wait until you see it tomorrow."

While Abby's friends were helping her with the wedding preparations, Caleb was sitting beside the boy who, come the following day, would be his stepson. Ben was stubborn, hardheaded and inquisitive, but thanks to his mother, he was mannerly. It hit Caleb like a freight train that he would be responsible, at least in part, for shaping Ben into the man he would one day be. It was a daunting realization. He hadn't the slightest notion of how to break through the child's animosity, much less make him a good man, but he had to do something, start somewhere. Bart Emerson had been adamant that Caleb try to get on a better footing with the boy.

"Thanks for coming with me, Ben," Caleb said, his mouth as dry as the desert. "Dr. Rachel and some of your mother's friends had a surprise for her, and I thought you might want to be with the men rather than a bunch of nattering women."

Ben's sullen expression vanished, and he slanted Caleb a questioning look. "What's nattering?"

"A lot of talking, which from what I've been told, is often about nothing in particular and everything in general, especially when ladies are involved. I understand the conversation usually centers around cooking and children and husbands and is accompanied by tea or coffee and a lot of laughter." Which didn't, he thought in amazement, sound too bad at all. "In this case, your mother's friends wanted to come help her with the last-minute preparations for tomorrow."

"A hen party," Ben said. "Danny says that's what he and his granddad call it when Doc Rachel's friends come over."

"Yes, I've heard it called that, too."

Ben didn't speak for a moment, and then said, almost conversationally, "I don't really want you to be my stepfather."

Caleb was taken aback by Ben's forthrightness, even while he admired his courage. It couldn't be easy for a child to speak his mind to an adult.

"I understand that," Caleb said, striving to make his tone calm and polite. "I'm sure your mother has told you that this... marriage is something that neither of us would have chosen, but sometimes circumstances force us to make difficult choices."

"Mama told me that you needed her for Betsy and she needed you to help with the farm and stuff. She said you were like partners."

He might have known Abby would do a far better job of explaining things than he could ever hope to do. "That's right. I know you had a very good father and that I can't hope to replace him in your life. I wouldn't want to, Ben."

A picture flashed in his mind, one of him and Abby and the three children around the dinner table, laughing. It was a pleasant image but pretty far-fetched. But was it? Surely they would find some closeness in the future.

"I do hope in time that we'll become a real family, even though our new family will be different from what we had before."

"Mama says different isn't bad, it's just a change."

"She's right. Are you looking forward to tomorrow?" Caleb asked as the wagon bounced down the rutted road.

"Not really," Ben said, his gaze focused on the trees in the distance.

"I thought you might be looking forward to all the good things to eat and seeing your friends."

Ben slanted him a glance. "What kind of good things?"

"Well, I know for a fact that someone brought some cookies, and your mother is making a cake with some apples and the nuts you picked up. I'm sure there will be lots of other good things."

Ben sat straighter and Caleb thought he saw a hint of a smile teasing the corner of his mouth.

"And your friends will be there."

"Really?" he said, showing the first animation since they'd left the house. "Daniel's coming?"

"Daniel and Toby and Sam are coming for sure. I'm not sure who else. And while the girls are having their hen party and nattering, we men will play horseshoes and sit out on the porch and chew the fat."

"I don't want to chew on any fat," Ben said, his eyebrows drawing together in a scowl. "I don't like fat."

Caleb couldn't help the laughter that erupted at

Ben's lack of understanding. His eyes were still smiling they met Ben's narrowed gaze. "Chewing the fat is a bunch of men sitting around talking about fishing, or hunting or trapping, or their businesses."

"Sounds like a hen party to me," Ben said.

Caleb thought about that a moment, then smiled. "Exactly."

Chapter Six

Friends and well-wishers sat or stood around the large parlor whose wide aperture opened into the dining room, where the overflow crowd stood. All eyes were on the couple in front of the rock fireplace. A tall vase of wild grasses resembling horses' tails and turning a lovely autumn purple sat in the center of the mantel, which was laden with English ivy. More French mulberry was tucked among the feathery lengths along with stems of native sunflower. Deep burgundy grosgrain ribbon from the mercantile provided by Mary was wound cleverly throughout the ivy.

Mary cradled baby Betsy in her arms, and Laura sat on Rachel's lap, chewing on the yellow ribbon that graced the front of her smocked gingham dress. Rachel was flanked on either side by her seven-year-old son, Daniel, and Ben. Edward Stone sat in his wheelchair, and Bart Emerson stood sentinel next to him, ready to give assistance with the boys if it became necessary. The only guests representing Caleb were Frank and Leo, Nathan Haversham and his wife, and a lawyer from town whom Abby recognized but had not met.

She clutched her trembling hands around a bouquet of ivy and the perky yellow flowers that grew in abundance along roadsides and fields, their yellow faces appearing to float on the autumn breeze, looking almost stemless. The past couple of days, Abby had felt as disconnected as the flowers looked. She'd done what was necessary, moving through the days without conscious thought or effort.

It seemed she had prayed nonstop since agreeing to Caleb's proposal. First she'd prayed that some other way to fix the muddle would come to mind, only to realize time and again that there was no other avenue that would work for everyone concerned. When she'd reached a tentative peace with that, she asked for courage and wisdom to be the wife and mother Caleb and Betsy needed. Still, doubts ambushed her fragile peace when she least expected them—like now. Was she doing the right thing?

Right or wrong, she stood beside Caleb, clad in her new wedding finery, uttering her vows in a soft, almost inaudible voice, while random memories of her first wedding stole through into her mind.

She and William had said their vows in a church in front of dozens of friends and family. Abby's parents had thrown a lavish garden party afterward. Sunshine poured through the lacy leaves of the trees, and birds sang sweet summer songs, promising more sunny days ahead. She and William had been so young, so inexperienced, so much in love. Never once did they consider all the things that could go wrong in a marriage, or in a life. Ignorance truly had been bliss.

She and Caleb were going into this union with no illusions of love or dreams of happily ever after. They knew exactly where they stood. They were two people with different needs, and this marriage was the best way for them to have those needs met.

Lost in her troubled thoughts, Abby's only link to the reality of the moment was the strong hand that clasped hers. Caleb's hand was as warm as hers was cold. She sneaked a glance upward from beneath her lashes. He had never seemed so tall, never looked so stern and unapproachable. Then, suddenly, the preacher reached the part of the ceremony where she promised to love and cherish Caleb for the rest of her life. She repeated the words because it was expected of her, feeling like the world's worst fraud.

Somehow she got through her part of the ceremony, and then it was Caleb's turn. Unlike her, he spoke his vows in a firm, almost determined voice, as if he were daring anyone to stop him. Finally, he placed a plain gold band on her finger, and seconds later, she felt the slightest tug on her hand and realized that he was pulling her closer and lowering his lips to hers in the traditional, expected, end-of-ceremony kiss. A brief gesture meant to seal the promises they'd just made.

Abby's eyelids drifted shut of their own accord. Though the touch of his lips was whisper-soft, she experienced an unexpected jolt of awareness, not unlike that she'd felt when their fingers brushed the first day they'd met. He raised his head suddenly, and her eyes flew open in surprise. That same expression was mirrored in his eyes. Awareness, and something else she couldn't put her finger on. Confusion? Thoughtfulness?

He released her hand and moved to her side while the minister prayed, asking for God's blessing on the new marriage and encouraging Caleb and Abby to put their trust in Him. After blessing the food they were about to enjoy, he announced that refreshments awaited everyone in the dining room.

The sound of Caleb clearing his throat once again made them the room's focus. "Abby and I would like to thank you all for your friendship and understanding, for your hard work in making everything look so special and for helping with the refreshments. We appreciate it." He followed the short speech with one of his rare smiles.

Abby's breath hung in her throat. She was always astounded at how the smile transformed his harsh features, bracketing his hard mouth with attractive grooves and deepening the network of tiny lines at the corners of his eyes, changing him from stern to handsome. Both the unexpected kindness and the smile caused her pulse to quicken in a way that was somehow both confusing and distressing. Then he took her hand, and together they preceded the guests into the dining room. Abby surveyed her friends' handiwork and her heart swelled with a feeling of love and gratitude.

True to their word, Rachel and Allison had driven out earlier to finalize the decorations. Vases of yellow flowers interspersed with branches of French mulberry were scattered throughout both rooms. Centered on the pristine whiteness of the borrowed tablecloth and encircled by more ivy sat Abby's cake on the silver platter, flanked by the silver candlesticks and white tapers.

Mary's punch bowl sat at one end of the table, surrounded by its matching cups. The cider had been heated to marry the flavor of the spices, and the faint scent of cinnamon, cloves and nutmeg wafted through the air. Flickering candle flames shimmered, reflecting the hue of the cider and flinging the amber glow from each crystal facet of the antique punch bowl.

There were two kinds of cookies beside the cake. A haunch of beef brought by Mary and Bart waited to be carved and placed on fresh-baked bread with freshly churned butter or soft herbed goat cheese. Abby's venison pastries, plump with meat and vegetables, were piled atop a footed plate. It was a lovely table, and she would be eternally thankful to the friends who had done so much to make her day memorable.

"You've done a fine job," Caleb said in a low

voice, a look of appreciation in his eyes as he took in the room's simple elegance. It was his first comment to her as her husband, and his obvious satisfaction was a balm to her troubled heart.

"I had a lot of help from friends."

"It seems you have very good friends," he told her, almost as if the very notion was a foreign one.

"Yes," she replied, "I do."

He looked down at her, and something in his eyes told her he would like to say more, but just then Nathan Haversham came up and slapped him on the back before extending his hand in congratulations to them both. The next several minutes were spent accepting well wishes from those in attendance.

Since opportunities for fun were rare to the hard-working people in the community, the wedding guests used the next couple of hours to indulge in food and conversation. Thankfully, the autumn day was warm enough that those who wanted could sit outside. Caleb's chess set had been set up on the porch, and Edward Stone challenged Nathan Haversham to a game. The children were playing tag, and true to his word, Caleb had set up horseshoes for those who wanted to play. Inevitably, the men and women drifted into groups.

Finally, Rachel and the others began to clear away the dishes and the remaining food. Both babies were being taken care of, and Abby, who wasn't used to idleness, stood on the porch watching the guests and wondering, with a churning stomach, what would happen when they all left. It was something she and Caleb, who stood beneath the sheltering branches of a huge black gum tree talking to Emily's father, had not discussed.

"Abby?"

She recognized Mary Emerson's voice and turned with a tentative smile on her face, clasping her trembling hands together, her fingers coming into contact with the ring Caleb had placed on her finger. Though Mary and Bart Emerson had been very supportive, Abby wondered how they really felt about this marriage coming so soon on the heels of their daughter's death.

"I want to thank you for everything, Mrs. Emerson," she said, before the older woman could speak. "I truly appreciate all you and Mr. Emerson have done."

"We were glad to help," Mary said. "And please call me Mary."

Abby nodded. "I'm sorry all this happened," she said, her voice a thread of sound. "Neither Caleb nor I intended for things to end up this way."

"End up?" Mary said, reaching out and taking both of Abby's cold hands in hers. "My dear, things have not *ended up*. They are only beginning for you and Caleb, and I know full well that you both had only the best in mind for Betsy when Rachel brought you here."

Abby blinked back the sudden rush of tears. "It's hard to believe people can be so mean-spirited." She met Mary's gaze with customary directness. "I've never been anything but kind to Sarah VanSickle and her friends."

"I'm sure that's true, and I know how disheartening it can be when things like this happen, but I'm convinced there will always be people who love making others miserable. I've never been sure *why,* but I suspect it may be because they are so unhappy themselves."

Abby gave a short laugh. "What does Sarah VanSickle have to be miserable about? She's one of the most prominent women in Wolf Creek."

"Unfortunately, things and position don't guarantee happiness. I can't say for certain, but I do know that Sarah set her cap for Lucas Gentry back when she was just a girl, and when he chose Libby, she never really got over it. Or forgave him," Mary said in an attempt to explain the woman's mindset.

Abby did her best to dredge up some compassion for Sarah's plight, but it was hard when she had tried so hard to wreck both Abby's and Caleb's reputations.

"We have no control over things that happen in our lives, but we can control how we react. Sarah chose to be miserable instead of embracing the man and the life she has now. Which is what I want you to do."

"I'm not sure I understand."

"Both you and Caleb have been put in a bad situation. You've both lost spouses and you both need something the other has." Seeing surprise on Abby's face, Mary offered her a gentle smile. "It's no secret in town that you've been struggling, Abby, or that you were struggling before your husband was killed. When Emily died, you and Caleb were brought together, and Sarah VanSickle's lies have more or less forced you into a marriage I'm sure neither of you wanted. I know that because Caleb wasn't too overjoyed when he and Emily married."

Though Caleb had told her as much, Abby was surprised to realize that Mary knew the truth. "And you knew it from the start?"

"Oh, yes. Actually, Emily wasn't too thrilled about marrying Caleb, either."

Abby shook her head in disbelief. "Yet they both agreed to a loveless marriage."

"Loveless?" Mary seemed to consider that as if it had never before occurred to her. "Yes, I suppose you're right." Wryness edged her voice. "Oh, Emily wanted to *get* married, but the eligible men in Wolf Creek were too rough around the edges to suit her. She'd gone to school in St. Louis to study art—though she never finished—and she spoke of going back east to Boston or some such place, marrying some starving artist and living in genteel poverty on wine and cheese or something."

"Why didn't she?"

"She was very shy and not cut out for life in the big city," Mary said in a reminiscent tone. "Which is why she came home before finishing her studies. Also, I'm afraid Bart and I indulged her more than we should have. She was spoiled. There's no way she was going to strike out on her own. Time passed and before we realized it, she was twenty-four and considered a spinster."

"How did the marriage come about?" Abby asked.

"Lucas Gentry wanted grandchildren," she said bluntly, "and since it didn't look as if Gabe was ever going to come home and settle down, Caleb was the one expected to come up to scratch. He was always the one who tried to smooth things over when he and Gabe were children, and Lucas had come to expect it.

"If you think Caleb is hard, you should have met his father," Mary told Abby with a lift of her dark eyebrows. "Lucas Gentry was a despot if ever one breathed. He was always difficult, but when Libby went to Boston and he was left with the boys, he lost what little kindness he had. He always expected everything and more that Caleb could give him and the farm, and even more so after Gabe took off."

"Rachel told me a little about that. Has he ever been back?"

Mary shook her head. "Not to my knowledge, though we've heard plenty of rumors, none of them good."

"It's a wonder Caleb didn't grow up to be just like his father."

"In many ways he did, but thankfully, mostly the good ways. For all his bitterness and his toughness when it came to business dealings, no one can say Lucas Gentry was anything but honest. Sometimes ruthless, but honest. Caleb's just like him when it comes to that."

They didn't speak for a few moments, and finally Abby asked, "It didn't bother you that Caleb and Emily's marriage wasn't a love match, then?"

Mary laughed. "Oh, you young people and your romantic notions! The truth is that people marry for many reasons, but a scant few of them marry for love. Caleb and Emily had known each other all their lives, and they were fond enough of each other, and that was good enough for me and Bart. We knew Caleb possessed a strong sense of duty and that he would take good care of her, and I suppose we pressed her more than we should have. We wanted to see her settled in case something happened to us, and like Lucas, we wanted grandchildren nearby. Our other daughter and her family live in St. Louis, and it's too far to go unless you have more than a few days to stay. Unfortunately, Emily was never able to conceive until Betsy."

Abby was fascinated by Mary's willingness to share so much of her daughter's past, but still didn't know exactly *why* Mary was doing so. "What do Sarah's choices and Caleb and Emily's marriage have to do with me and Caleb?" Abby asked at last.

Mary offered her a sheepish smile. "I'm sorry. I do get to rambling, don't I? What I'm trying to say is that fate or circumstance or perhaps God has brought you and Caleb to this place in your life. You both took vows that bind you until death. You're both young and healthy, and God willing will have many years together and children of your own. I just don't want either of you to do what Sarah has done and dwell on the past, whether it's William's death or Emily's or what might have been. Do you see what I'm getting at?"

Abby gave a tentative nod. "I think you're saying to let go of the past and look to the future." Though Mary hinted that Emily had not made Caleb happy, Abby couldn't find the courage to have that confirmed. "So you and Mr. Emerson don't mind that Caleb and I have married so soon after Emily's death?"

Mary shook her head. "Not at all. In fact, we're thrilled that you'll be Betsy's mother, because we believe you'll be a good one." She squeezed Abby's hands again and her eyes filled with tears. "We loved our daughter, but we were not ignorant of her faults and weaknesses. She wasn't the right woman for a man like Caleb. I pray you are. Embrace this marriage and this new life as best you can. Caleb needs someone who can see the man he truly is. He needs someone who can bring joy into his life, Abby. Believe me when I say he's had little enough of it."

With a brief hug, Mary left Abby standing there with much to think about. After hearing what she had about Caleb's past from Rachel and now more from Mary, Abby was beginning to have a clearer picture of the man she had married. She understood now why there was so little softness in him, so little tolerance. He'd been duty bound and forced to take responsibility since childhood. Under the circumstances, he was accepting the invasion of his house by three strangers better than she would have done. It was a miracle he'd turned out as well as he had. It would behoove her to remember that when things between them grew rough.

Mary and Bart left soon afterward, and shortly after that Rachel and the other women trooped out of the house, announcing that things were back in order and both weary babies were asleep. Ben was going home with Daniel for a couple of days so that they could go fishing with the father of one of Daniel's friends before the weather turned too cold.

After giving Ben a goodbye hug, Abby stood next to Caleb watching the buggy pull down the lane and disappear around a curve. An uncomfortable silence stretched between them. It wouldn't be long until sundown. A slight breeze and the shade beneath the porch hinted of colder weather that would soon descend. Abby gave an involuntary shiver.

Without a word, Caleb shrugged out of his suit jacket and draped it around her shoulders. The warmth from his body and the woodsy scent of his soap permeated the fabric. Abby tipped her head back to look up at him, suppressing another tremor, one she suspected had nothing to do with the chill of the late afternoon and everything to do with the nearness of the man standing so close to her.

"Everything went better than I expected," he said, taking a step back and running his fingers through his hair in a gesture that spoke volumes about his real state of mind. He needed a haircut, she thought again, making her first wifely observation. And his lean cheeks were already shadowed with end-of-day growth.

Focusing her attention on the tree with its shedding crimson leaves, she said, "I thought it was very nice considering the time we had to get things together," she agreed in a voice that held an unnatural primness.

Wearing a solemn expression, Caleb held out his hand and cocked his head toward two rocking chairs that sat in front of the parlor window. "Let's sit for a while if it isn't too cool for you. I'm so stuffed I don't need any dinner, and hopefully the girls will sleep for a bit."

With a bit of reluctance, Abby placed her hand in his and let him guide her to one of the chairs. As before, his touch produced that peculiar tingling that sizzled throughout her body. Grudgingly, almost fearfully, she accepted the significance of the feeling. Not only did she find the irascible man she was now married to attractive, she was attracted *to* him. Her husband. Her reaction was unnerving and unacceptable. She and Caleb had a business arrangement, nothing more.

He released his hold on her, and they sat, both of them beginning to rock as they gazed out over the front lawn. Still somewhat befuddled by her reaction to his touch, she could not think of a single intelligent topic of conversation.

"You look very pretty," he said at last, turning to look at her. "Like newly minted gold."

"Th-Thank you," she stammered, surprised to find that her voice still worked. "You look very handsome yourself."

Though brief, his laughter was rich and throaty, and that unexpected, arresting smile was back. "Handsome? I don't think so," he said with a shake of his dark, shaggy head.

"You need a haircut," she said without thinking, She looked away, stifling a groan. No telling *how* he'd react to that! He had not married her to be inflicted with her wifely judgments. How long his hair grew was none of her business. She waited for his response, her spine straight, her body racked with tension.

"Yeah," he said, scraping back his hair again. "I know. But I wasn't around the afternoon you cut Ben's, and we've all been so busy the past few days I didn't want to put anything more on you. I'm sorry if I embarrassed you."

"I wasn't embarrassed!" she said, aghast at the thought. "I was just—" she gave a helpless shrug "—making conversation." Actually, she found his slightly unkempt look appealing.

For long moments, the only sounds to be heard were the sassy solo of a nearby mockingbird and the squeaking of the rocker runners on the porch.

"What is it, Abby?" he asked.

She stopped rocking and turned his direction, without actually meeting his gaze. "I guess I'm wondering what happens next."

Her meaning could not be clearer, and he considered her question with care. "Well, I'm going to get up from here—preferably before it gets dark—take off this suit and put on my everyday stuff. Since Ben's not here, I'm going to milk your cow and that blasted goat while Frank and Leo feed."

"Oh." She was unable to deny either the relief that swept through her, or the tiniest pang of regret.

"I'd planned on moving my things back into the house, if you have no objections, but it's getting a little late for that."

Her eyes met his. Abby couldn't breathe…or think. "You don't have to ask my permission," she said. "It's your house."

"No, Abby. It's our house. Our home. It would make things easier if I moved back in, and there's no reason not to now, but if you'd be more comfortable with my staying at the bunkhouse, that's what I'll do. I thought I'd take the room with all the junk in it. It was my dad's."

It went without saying that she would be more comfortable the less she saw him, the less she had to deal with him, but that was not the issue here. No matter what he said, it *was* his house and he had a right to live in it, especially since no one in the community could possibly object after today.

"That's fine," she said. "I'll put clean linens on the bed for you."

"I can do that. I'm used to it."

"Absolutely not!" Her mother would roll over in her grave at the idea of any daughter of hers allowing a man to do her chores.

He nodded, and she imagined she saw the corners of his mouth turn up just a bit. The expression in his eyes looked very much like wry humor.

"As for what happens next... I think it's called getting on with our lives, whatever that involves. We just go on doing what we've been doing. A few words and a piece of paper haven't changed anything except that now we don't have to feel guilty about our arrangement."

"Can it really be that easy?" she asked, letting her eyes meet his at last.

"Easy?" He seemed to consider the situation. "Let's see. We have two people forced into a marriage, one of them a man who isn't used to kids and is suddenly accountable for three—one of whom can hardly tolerate him." His tone was pseudo-serious. "We also have a man and a woman who both have hair-trigger tempers living under the same roof." He shook his head. "Easy? Hardly. But I've never had too many things come easy in my life, and I think I'm up to the challenge."

Challenge? Yes, that's what it would be, just as her life the past few years had been a challenge. Only the kinds of trials this new life presented would be far different from those she shared with William.

"Reach into the left inside pocket of my coat," he said.

Abby gave him a questioning look and did as he asked, her fingers encountering a small package. She pulled out a small gift wrapped in a piece of crisp tissue paper and tied with a length of red ribbon.

"What's this?" she asked, turning it over in her hands. It felt like something metal.

"It's for you. Consider it a wedding gift."

The unexpected gesture caught her off guard. "It never occurred to me… I don't have anything for you. I'm sorry."

He waved aside her apology. "Go ahead. Open it."

Abby untied the ribbon, wondering if she imagined the expression of anticipation in his eyes. Sliding the thin strip of satin from around the package, she spread aside the paper. When she saw what was inside, her eyes filled with tears and she choked back a sob of disbelief. Lying in the nest of tissue paper lay the cameo brooch she'd traded for her wedding dress. She lifted her stunned, tear-filled gaze to his. "How…?"

"Simon waved me down when I went into town the other day. He knew I'd want you to have it back."

"I can never repay you," she said, rising and clasping the precious pin to her chest.

"You repay me every day," he told her, getting to his feet. "By cooking and making this house a pleasant place to come to at night. By taking good care of Betsy. I'm the one in your debt."

"But you've had to take on people and responsibilities that—" He reached out and placed his fingertips against her lips to silence her. His touch almost stopped her heart.

"As far as I'm concerned, the responsibilities are equal on both sides, and I'm perfectly happy with our deal. How about you?"

Her gaze, still blurry with tears, clung to his. "I think so, yes," she whispered.

"Good." Then, without a word, he strode past her and down the steps, leaving her emotions in more turmoil than they had been before he subjected her to his unexpected gentleness…or his touch.

Caleb went to the bunkhouse and changed into clean work clothes, then set about doing his evening chores, his mind filled with memories of the day.

He thought of how he had fumed for days before the wedding about the unfairness of being tied to a family he didn't want and needed less. He'd even let God know how unhappy he was about it, but Bart had assured him earlier that God knew what He was doing, even if Caleb and Abby didn't.

When she'd stepped through the bedroom door, looking like a ray of autumn sunshine in a dress of rich gold, his fury vanished. Her blond hair was caught up atop her head. Curly wisps teased the nape of her neck and small sprigs of ivy and yellow flowers were nestled in an artful jumble of curls.

His heart seemed to stumble, and he'd swallowed hard. Then she'd spied him from across the room and headed in his direction, pausing to speak to people she knew along the way. When she stopped in front of him, the sweet scent of gardenia made a soothing assault on his senses. Funny, he'd never realized that she barely came to his shoulder. She'd looked up and attempted a smile that fell far short.

He'd wished he knew what to do to erase the anxiety from her eyes, wished that haunted look was not working its way into his heart and causing it to ache for something he couldn't put a name to and understood less. He'd stared down into her eyes. Large, bewildered and no less blue than the brilliant autumn sky, they were surrounded by thick dark lashes, totally at odds with her fair hair. He'd had to fight the urge to pull her into his arms and promise her that everything would be all right, that they would work through their uncertain future. Together.

Then someone had called his name and he'd snapped out of his crazy imaginings. His gaze had roamed the room, settling on Betsy, asleep in her grandmother's arms, and then moved to Laura sitting in total contentment on Rachel's lap, and finally to Ben who, standing alongside Daniel Stone, was poking a little girl standing in front of them with a stick they'd smuggled inside. The girl gave a whimper of frustration. Ben looked toward Caleb, the expression in his eyes daring him to say anything in a room full of guests.

Reality had kicked in with a vengeance. So much for the progress he thought they'd made. Nothing had changed. Ben did not like him or the idea of Caleb becoming a father figure. Abby still loved her husband. She didn't want this marriage of convenience any more than he did. As consoling as it might be to imagine a happily ever after, common sense told him it would be folly to even contemplate such a future.

Chapter Seven

It wasn't working, Caleb thought, standing another piece of firewood in place and swinging the ax downward. The piece of oak split beneath the satisfying show of strength. He'd been married to Abby for three weeks now, and November was more than a week old, but the tactics he'd decided to utilize in his marriage weren't working out as planned, or as he'd expected.

After realizing there was no real future for him and Abby, he'd decided to go about his life as he always had and treat her and her children as he had Emily—with polite civility. He'd count on them to hold up their side of the bargain while he did the same. That was the plan, but somehow it wasn't working out as he'd imagined.

They'd fallen into a routine, and inevitably, as he should have known it would, he saw their lives meshing in dozens of ways that demanded personal interaction.

Abby kept the house clean and tidy. She cooked the meals and cared for the children, teaching Ben spelling and numbers and reading. Though he usually escaped to his study after dinner, more than once, Caleb had heard her reading to Ben from books on history and farming principles and then explaining what she read. She continued the word of the day and the nightly devotionals. Several times, he'd come to get a book from the shelf and caught himself listening with more interest than he would admit as she explained certain Bible verses to Ben. Caleb was amazed at her ability to reduce the most complicated passages into something a six-year-old could understand.

Her smile intrigued him, as did the lilting laughter in her voice as she played with Laura. Ah, Laura! He was finding it impossible to resist Abby's baby girl, who offered him a smile when he came through the door in the evenings, and tugged on his pants legs and jabbered until he reached down and picked her up.

He marveled at Abby's patience as she walked the floor with Betsy when she had a belly ache. A time or two, he'd even taken a turn himself, rocking and walking so that Abby could snatch a couple of hours' sleep. There was no denying that he was fascinated and amazed by his new bride, or that he found a certain enjoyment at seeing the fire in her eyes when she was angry. No doubt about it, the keep-them-at-arm's-length approach to marriage was far easier to assume than execute.

Except with Ben.

So far, nothing Caleb had done had made any real inroads with the obstinate boy who resisted any and all overtures of friendship. But he kept trying, giving Ben light chores to get him out of the house and also so that he could spend time with the men and his new stepfather. Though he'd missed a lot by not having a mother's influence, Caleb reasoned that no boy should spend all of every day with females. Still, Ben was proving to be a hard nut to crack. Caleb set up another log and gave it a satisfying *whack*. Like the other one, it split down the middle. It would take time, but he was determined to get on an easier footing with the boy.

That evening after their Bible study, Abby tucked Ben in and checked on the girls. When she closed the bedroom door behind her she found Caleb sitting in front of the fireplace, his long legs stretched out and crossed at the ankles. It was a purely masculine pose, one she'd seen often in the years of her marriage to William.

She was surprised to see Caleb sitting there, since he usually went to his office to do bookwork after helping her in the kitchen, something he still insisted on, though she'd told him it was not necessary. It had become a comfortable routine, one that seldom varied.

"No bookwork?" she asked, turning toward the veritable smorgasbord of literary offerings lining the floor-to-ceiling shelves on either side of the fire-place.

"Nothing that won't wait until tomorrow," he said. He held up a new volume. "I was anxious to get started on my new Henry James book."

"The American?" she asked.

"Yes. You've heard of it?"

"A bit. You have a wonderful collection," she said on a sigh.

"Necessity."

She shot him a questioning glance over her shoulder. "Necessity?"

Caleb shrugged. "Lucas expected me to learn how to run things, so there was no way I could go away to school. I had to educate myself the best way I could."

Abby didn't miss the tightening of his jaw when he mentioned his late father.

"Well, you have a very eclectic collection," she said. Besides *The Sketch-Book of Geoffrey Crayon* and *Narrative of the Life of Frederick Douglass, an American Slave,* there were books on gold mining, meteorology, manners and birding. The shelves also held dozens of novels as well as several issues of popular magazines, including sporting journals and ladies' publications.

He gave a negligent shrug. "Lots of things interest me, so I send for whatever books are available." His tone was desert-dry, and he lifted one eyebrow and a corner of his mouth in a sardonic expression. "It's one of the advantages of having a lot of money."

Abby chose to ignore both. Ignoring the utterly masculine picture he made sprawled in the chair was not so easy. "You have quite a collection of fiction, as well," she said, appalled at how breathless she sounded.

His mockery was replaced by a fleeting, guilty smile. "It's one of my many failings. I'm quite a fan of fiction, and I even admit to enjoying a rip-roaring dime novel, as well. I'm a huge Allan Pinkerton admirer."

"Really?" she said, wide-eyed. "I like him, too." Then with an arch look, she pulled a volume from the shelf and said in a pseudo-serious tone, "I particularly like Alcott, Brontë and Stowe, as it seems you do."

"Those are Emily's," he said with a wounded expression.

"You haven't read them, then?" she asked. "Not manly enough for you?"

"Hardly."

"Well, perhaps you should read some of them. I'm a firm believer that all men should read some women's fiction."

"And why is that?" he asked, his rare foray into lightheartedness giving way to sudden gravity.

"So that they might gain a better perspective into the ways and thoughts of women, of course."

"And you think it's important for a man to understand women?"

"Not only do I think it's important, I think it's imperative if the two sexes even hope to live together in a semblance of harmony."

He frowned.

She laughed. "If it will soothe your ruffled masculine feathers, I believe it's equally important for women to attempt to understand the men in their life."

"Attempt?"

"Well, you are strange creatures," she said with raised eyebrows and a slight shrug.

"And women aren't?"

"Why, no," she told him with artificial sincerity. "Women are the soul of kindness, thrift, honor and decency."

Coldness molded his rugged features. "Begging your pardon, ma'am, but that has not always been my experience. I offer Sarah VanSickle as an example."

"Oh. Well, I think most people would agree that Sarah is in a class all her own. But don't you find that I exhibit those qualities?" she asked with mock-innocence.

"Well, you... I mean that... I didn't mean that you..."

"Yes?" she asked with another lift of her fair eyebrows, her eyes alight with suppressed laughter.

"You're—you're teasing me!" He leaped to his feet, his tone disbelieving, shocked, even.

"I am," she admitted, straight-faced.

Caleb didn't recall anyone teasing him since he

was a youngster and the brunt of jokes about his height. "I've not been teased as an adult," he told her.

"You and Emily didn't joke with each other?"

"No."

Abby stared at him for a moment, trying to digest what he'd said and put it into perspective with what she knew about his past. Her heart broke a tiny bit.

"Well, that's just…sad."

She saw him stiffen, recognized the familiar chill in his eyes. "I don't need or want your pity," he snapped.

"And you don't have it!" she shot back, frustrated with his unyielding attitude. "What you have is genuine sorrow that you've been deprived of so much joy in your life."

"Which equates to pity," he retorted. "I won't have it, Abby. Especially not from you."

Annoyance and futility washed over her. Was there no reaching the man? "If you don't want my empathy, what do you want from me, Caleb? What will you have?" she cried, tilting her head back to look up at him.

They stood there staring at each other, both breathing heavily, both angry, both hurt and wondering how such an innocent conversation could have turned into something so painful.

Everything. I want everything from you that you have to give.

The realization slammed into him with the force of a kicking mule, robbing him of speech. What were these unsettling emotions he felt for her? He had no yardstick with which to measure these new feelings. He only knew he had never experienced anything like it before, nor had he expected to. What he did know was that he didn't like feeling vulnerable and not in control, and he liked less the fact that he didn't know what to do about it.

Close on the heels of admitting that he was feeling things for her—things he had no right to feel with Emily hardly cold in her grave—came a rush of that ever-present guilt. Never mind that Abby was legally his wife. He turned away and headed for the door, needing to put some space between him and this woman, this stranger who had come into his life and taken over his home. The woman who threatened to take over his heart.

His hand was on the doorknob when her voice stopped him. He didn't turn, but stood stiff and unyielding. He heard her footfalls on the floor and felt her hand on his back, warm through the fabric of his shirt.

"I'm sorry," she said, her voice an anguished murmur.

He imagined he felt her forehead lean against his back, a whisper-soft touch that spoke of regret and thickened his throat with tears.

"I never meant to hurt you, and you're very wrong if you think what I feel for you is pity."

He wanted to ask her what she did feel for him, but was too afraid of her answer, just as he was too terrified to speak of how he felt and what he wanted from her.

Abby was a warm and caring woman who knew how to laugh, how to make a house into a home. A woman who knew how to make a man feel wanted and welcome when he stepped through the door at the end of the day. She was accustomed to a man loving her and being unafraid to show that love. A man who knew how and when to *tease* her.

She certainly wasn't used to someone who had no knowledge of how to care for another person, and even less idea how to show that caring. He told himself it wasn't fair to saddle her with his shortcomings, that it was best if he kept things on an impersonal level as he'd planned to from the first, yet for a brief, heart-stopping instant he toyed with the urge to beg her to help bring him out of the shadows of mere existence and into a world of life and love.

Common sense stopped him. She still loved her William, and Caleb was not handsome, not funny and he didn't know how to tease. He was a man who knew only duty and the weight of responsibility. He might be considered the best catch of the county, but he was not the sort of man a woman like Abby could ever love. Accepting their impasse, Caleb felt his anger melt away to be replaced with an aching, unfamiliar remorse.

Steeling himself against the gentleness he knew he would see in her eyes, he turned to face her. Her hand dropped away. The loss of her touch left him feeling empty and alone. He stared down at her, fighting the urge to pull her into his arms and try to absorb her sweetness into his very soul, but he knew it was crucial that whatever it was he was feeling be nipped in the bud before it had a chance to grow into something he instinctively knew held the potential to hurt him far worse than his mother's leaving or Emily's death.

He took an involuntary step backward, needing to put some space between them before he lost his head and his control. Then, deliberately, like a scalpel-wielding surgeon excising something harmful, he clenched his jaw and closed his heart to the tender feelings threatening to overwhelm him.

"What I want is for you to take care of my house and my daughter."

He imagined he saw the sheen of tears in her eyes before she lowered her gaze and gave a single nod. Her voice was a mere thread of sound as she said simply, "I see."

Then without another word he turned, wrenched open the door and stalked onto the porch. The cold darkness enveloped him. He was at the bottom of the steps when he heard the door click quietly shut. He walked away, his masculine pride intact and an empty void where his heart had been.

Her mother was right, Abby thought as she set the table for the evening meal. Life did go on, even when your pride had been trampled in the dust, your heart had been torn to shreds and your only defense was to fortify that bruised heart with an all-consuming anger. She blinked back the hot sting of tears that had been her constant companion ever since her altercation with Caleb.

How had it come to this? Was it possible that she had fallen in love with her new husband in such a short span of time? Guilt surged through her. How could she betray everything she had felt for William—a man of goodness and kindness—by falling for a man whose heart was as hard as the rocks that were so prevalent throughout the pastureland at her old home? A man who hadn't the slightest notion how to love.

Ever since their argument three days ago, they had both maintained a polite stoicism that bordered on the ridiculous. There were times she would have laughed had she not been afraid her laughter would turn to tears. If possible, Caleb had grown more silent, more unapproachable, working from sunup until sundown, pushing Frank and Leo past any reasonable limits, and piling chores on Ben that she deemed far too heavy for a child his age.

Beyond starting all-out war, her only recourse was to do her housework and take care of Betsy with the same attention as before. She slammed down an ironstone plate and slapped down a handful of silverware next to it. It was not the innocent baby's fault her father was a stubborn, pigheaded, mulish…idiot!

Like Abby, Caleb not only embraced his anger, he looked for ways to fuel it. Determined to live up to his reputation, he doubled down on the outside work, which brought about a lot of muttering and cussing from Frank and Leo. When they finished with one chore, he found something else to keep them all busy. Anything to keep from going into the house until darkness and his growling stomach forced him inside. Anything to keep him away from a woman whose only transgression was kindness and two little girls who were working their way into his heart.

The morning following his altercation with Abby, Ben had cornered him in the barn, his fists clenched at his sides, his freckled face wearing a pugnacious expression that said without words that he wished he were ten years older and a hundred pounds heavier.

"You leave my mother alone," he ground out from between clenched teeth.

Caleb's first reaction was to give the boy a piece of his mind. He couldn't believe Ben had the audacity to talk to him like that—or any adult for that matter. Then he remembered wishing he had the guts to confront his own father when Lucas had jumped on Libby about something. He also realized he was dealing with Abby's son. Evidently she had passed down the impertinence gene to her son.

"Whatever is between me and your mother is our business, not yours."

"She's my *mother!*" Ben shouted.

"And she's my wife," Caleb said, struggling to maintain his authority without becoming argumentative. "Don't you remember how we talked about how it was going to take time for us to all learn to get along and how we would have times when things didn't go exactly right?"

Some of the anger left Ben's face at the reminder.

"This was one of those times. Now I want you to go milk Nana, and then I'll show you how to milk Shaggy Bear."

"It's cold."

At the plaintive note in the boy's voice Caleb surrendered his anger. "I know that, but you know they have to be milked twice a day, cold or not. Owning livestock means they have to be taken care of no matter what."

When Abby found out Caleb had turned over both the morning and evening milking to Ben, she cast her husband a look that would have made a lesser man quake in his boots. He heard her muttering under her breath about it being too hard.

When he had Ben stack the firewood as it was split and added keeping the fireplace boxes filled with wood and kindling to his list of chores, she adopted an overly polite demeanor that warned Caleb a storm was brewing. He bit back a grim smile. It was only a matter of time before her temper got the best of her, and with his own bad humor festering like a sore tooth, he relished the notion of their clashing of wills. Anything was preferable to their cold truce.

"It's too much," Abby said later that evening as she indicated for Caleb to take the chair that sat in the middle of the parlor. Furious with him or not, he was weeks past needing a haircut. He'd passed the attractive shaggy stage soon after the wedding and had now reached the point of embarrassment. She couldn't have him going to town looking like a hobo off a train. When she'd told him as much after putting the children to bed, he'd snapped, "Fine. Get the scissors."

So here he sat with a sheet draped around his shoulders while Abby combed and snipped and heaved deep sighs of annoyance. Caleb turned with a frown, almost causing her to cut out a chunk of hair over his ear.

"Spit it out," he said with his customary brusqueness.

"Hold still." She took hands full of his hair and jerked his head back where she wanted it.

A muscle in his jaw tightened.

"It's too much."

"What's too much?" he asked, noting the closeness of the scissors to his face from the corner of his eye.

"All the work you've given to Ben. He was already milking the goat and feeding the chickens and dogs, and now you've added milking the cow and carrying in big chunks of firewood."

"I don't hear Ben complaining."

"He's afraid to complain. You frighten him."

That bit of information set Caleb back on his heels. He didn't reply for a long time, and finally said, "I'm going to tell you what I told Ben when he jumped me about yelling at you."

Abby moved around to stand next to his jean-clad thighs. Her eyes held disbelief as she stared into his. "He heard us arguing?"

Caleb held her gaze. "Evidently. I told him that what happened between you and me was none of his business. Now I'm telling you that what happens between me and Ben is none of *your* business. I've given you free rein with Betsy. You're the only mother she'll ever know. For all intents and purposes, I'm now Ben's father, and I deserve to bring him up as I see fit."

"I don't yell at Betsy," Abby said, sifting the front of his tobacco-brown hair through her fingers, looking for stray long strands. His hair was soft and thick and clean, and as he did, smelled like something woodsy and masculine.

A biting smile lifted one corner of Caleb's mouth. "Give it time. She's not grown yet."

Abby stared at him, her hands stilling in his hair.

"What?" he asked, seeing the look of wonder in her eyes.

"I… I think you were… Were you just teasing me?"

Caleb thought about it a moment but had no answer. Had he been teasing her? Was it really such a simple thing?

Abby felt some of her anger dissolve and heaved another sigh. Could he disarm her so easily? "I don't want Ben to grow up with nothing but rules and work and demands."

Caleb thought about his own raising and how his father's never ending orders had chafed. He would never be that unreasonable with Ben. There had to be a compromise. "He needs to learn a good work ethic and how to be responsible."

"He's just six years old," she reminded.

"Old enough to start learning. What he's doing won't hurt him."

She breathed another grudging sigh. "Probably not."

Reluctantly, she conceded that part of her anger was based on the knowledge that by Caleb taking more of a role in Ben's life, she was losing some of her own influence. She felt the sting of tears in her eyes. "I want him to know he's loved."

"He knows you love him."

"Yes, but fathers are to love their children, too, Caleb, and as you pointed out, you're the one who has taken over William's place. Being a father is more than laying down the law and doling out chores. The Bible says that fathers shouldn't provoke their children to wrath."

"And what does that mean, exactly?"

"I've always thought it meant to be consistent and fair in your treatment of all your children. To not be overly harsh with one or the other, and not to show favoritism. Like you do with the girls. You show them much more positive attention than you do Ben."

His lips tightened. "At everyone's insistence, I'm trying to get to know my daughter, and as for Laura..." He paused, then continued. "Much like her mother, she refuses to take no for an answer when I try to discourage her." Though heaven only knew why, the way he tried to keep her at arm's length.

"She likes you," Abby told him, combing his forelock back to blend into the rest of his newly cut hair. "She gets so excited when she hears your voice and your boots stomping on the back porch at night."

Abby did not notice the strange longing in her voice, and Caleb had no comeback.

"So you think I need to show Ben more positive attention."

"Yes. Balance work with fun things."

"Fun?" He said the word as if it were foreign to him.

"Yes, fun. What did you like to do for fun when you were a boy?"

"I didn't do anything for fun," he told her in all seriousness.

She stared down at him, wide-eyed. "Nothing? Surely you went fishing or hunting."

He shook his head. "Gabe was the one who had fun. I worked. If I hunted or fished it was to bring food home for the table."

"And laughter?"

He gave a snort of something that might have passed for a scornful laugh. "Not after my mother left. If we laughed about anything, we took a tongue-lashing for slacking off."

Abby tried to grasp what he was saying and failed. How could any child grow up without laughter? How could any child grow up the way Caleb had?

"Would William have listened to you if you two were having this conversation?" he asked, the change in conversation catching her off guard. "Would he have backed off on Ben if you begged him with tears in your eyes?"

She summoned a wobbly smile. "William would not have known how to instill a good work ethic— not that he was afraid of work," she hastened to clarify. "But he was too much inclined to let himself be sidetracked by other things that interested him more than daily chores. He was not as…disciplined as you are."

"And by so doing, put you in the bad financial position you found yourself in."

"Yes. God forgive me, but I pray Ben did not inherit an overabundance of that particular trait from his father."

"So it's possible that maybe I'm saving some other young woman that fate, if Ben listens and learns from me."

"Maybe," she admitted. "I've thought many times since coming here how wonderful it would be if Ben had a father with your work ethic and William's ability to find the fun in life."

"*Finding* the fun?"

"Oh, yes! Fun doesn't always just rush out and meet you. Sometimes you find it in something as simple as skipping rocks on the creek, or playing a game of patty-cake or peekaboo. But it's there."

Another silenced stretched between them as they both mulled over their conversation. Abby realized with something of a start that somehow, when she'd finished cutting Caleb's hair, she had placed her hands on his shoulders. Embarrassment swept through her, and she began to brush at the hair lying there.

Filling her voice with lightness she did not feel, she took a step back. "All done. And mighty handsome you look, too, if I may say so."

He gave a derisive grunt of laughter.

Abby fought against tears and the rush of the empathy he wanted no part of. She ached to take away his pain, to see the harsh slash of his mouth curved in laughter, his eyes filled with contentment.... Silently, she vowed to never let her temper get the best of her again. She would not be the one to deal him any more grief. Heaven knew he'd suffered enough of that in his lifetime. But even as she made the promise to herself, she knew that somewhere, someday, probably sooner than later, she would fail to keep it.

She snuffled and brushed at his shoulders with more vigor. "You are a very attractive man," she told him. "I can't imagine why you think otherwise."

"Maybe because I look at my face in the mirror

every morning when I shave," he suggested with a touch of that unexpected, infrequent irony.

"While no one would say you are a conventionally handsome man, I think almost every woman in Wolf Creek would admit that your face is very intriguing. Women are easy targets for a man with a dangerous look about him."

"Dangerous?" he mocked.

"Mmm," she said, nodding. "Especially with that end-of-day beard. I imagine it's safe to say I'm the most envied woman in Wolf Creek for landing you."

Reaching up, he manacled her wrists with his callused fingers. Though purely innocent, she was suddenly aware of leaning against his thigh. His gaze meshed with hers.

"And what about you, Abby? Are you a sucker for a dangerous-looking man?"

"I don't know." She looked and sounded thoughtful. "It depends, I suppose."

"On?"

"On the man, and whatever other qualities he might have."

Caleb exerted the slightest pressure on her wrists, forcing her to lean over until her face was mere inches from his. Drawing a decent breath became very, very tricky. Finally, she had to shut her eyes; the intensity in his was too much to understand...or to bear.

At that precise moment his lips touched hers. All sorts of alarms rang in her head, and a scorching heat swept through her while a tiny voice whispered that she must be out of her mind to let him....

He's your husband. He has every right.

Long before she was ready, he ended the kiss. Trembling the slightest bit, Abby straightened. Pulling her hands from his grasp, she pressed her fingertips to her throbbing lips. His eyes revealed a compelling thoughtfulness that set her heart to racing. In that moment, she knew she had done a very foolish thing. For better or worse, she had fallen in love with Caleb Gentry.

"Oh. My."

The two words were the height of inadequacy and in no way expressed the host of feelings coursing through her. Astonishment. Dismay. Guilt. Hopelessness. She wanted to cry. To hide somewhere and examine the amazing feelings bubbling up inside her. Wished she could tell someone about that kiss. Wondered how she could hide this tender, burgeoning feeling from a man who, so bereft of sentiment himself, seldom missed any nuance of emotional change in others.

"Careful there. You'll turn my head." The words were spoken in a low, husky voice.

Despite the emotional turbulence tumbling through her, she grasped his meaning. "You're getting pretty good at that."

"What?"

"Teasing."

One corner of his mouth hiked in a sardonic smile. "I thought I was being sarcastic. Ironic."

She sighed. "With you, it seems to be the same thing, which makes you even more dangerous."

"The only thing dangerous in this room is you wielding those scissors. I'm surprised you haven't used them on me."

"Why would I do that?" she asked.

"For taking advantage."

"But you didn't. You have every right."

For long moments the words and all their implications hung suspended in the quiet of the room. When he made no move to answer, she pulled free the sheet she'd draped over him and shook the hair onto the floor to be swept up. Hoping to ease the tension, she said briskly, "At any rate, you're all respectable-looking again."

He stood and turned to face her. "Thank you."

"My pleasure."

"Mine, too."

Without another word, he turned and left her standing in the middle of the room, wondering what—if anything—she was to make of *that* comment.

Chapter Eight

I love him.

Lying in bed, the back of her wrist resting against her forehead, Abby stared into the room's darkness and pondered the disturbing revelation. Surely this couldn't have happened! *How* had it happened?

For weeks now she'd experienced a feeling of pleasure when he came through the door and a sense of satisfaction when she saw him growing closer to the children. She'd liked knowing he was there and that she could count on him. She had admitted long ago that he was an attractive man, if you liked the rugged, rough-hewn type...which she obviously did, but one did not fall in love with a person for that reason...especially when said person resembled a prickly cactus in most other respects!

Neither did one fall in love with someone because the mere touch of his lips on yours sent your senses head over heels! That feeling was a vital part of love—indeed was often mistaken for love—but

alone it was a mere shadow of that precious emotion. No, what she felt for Caleb was much more
complicated than what she felt when he kissed her.

Abby made a mental list of all the reasons this
new state of affairs was impossible. First, he was
very intelligent, but he had no idea what spontaneity
was and she doubted he had ever done anything on
the spur of the moment. He was impatient, stubborn
and even ruthless in many ways. He was unyielding
and measured in his approach to everything he did,
and even in the short time she'd lived beneath his
roof, she'd realized that once he set his mind on a
course, he was not apt to deviate from it.

She liked impromptu events, whether it was carrying supper out onto the lawn in the spring or taking that extra loaf of bread to some housebound
friend. Caleb's notion of impulsiveness was to decide there was still enough daylight to fell another
tree or plow another field.

Second, she definitely had a mind of her own,
as well as her own views on how things should—
or could—be done. She was accustomed to voicing
those opinions. From the expression on his face the
few times she had spoken her mind, her new husband found the notion of women being outspoken
outrageous at the very least. She doubted he could
learn to tolerate that trait in a wife.

Third, she loved children and had chosen teaching because of that love. At best Caleb tolerated
them. No, that wasn't exactly correct. It was not
fair for her to fault him for not understanding how

to deal with children when he had been shown so little love himself. In truth, he was beginning to be much more at ease both with Betsy and Laura, thanks in part to Laura's unflagging determination that Caleb pay attention to her whether he wanted to or not. Abby had even heard him laugh when Laura grabbed his ears and planted a sloppy kiss on his nose, and there had been many times in the past few weeks she had seen his eyes light up when Betsy gave him a sleepy smile.

He can learn to love, a small voice whispered. *He is learning to love.*

Even though she had been unable to attend church services since coming to live in Caleb's house, her relationship with her Lord was a vital part of her life. Caleb barely acknowledged His existence. Her and William's mutual love of God had been the cement that kept their love alive and gave her the strength to stand by him when he made bad decisions, lost both his smile and his self-worth, and sank deeper and deeper into debt and depression. Those were the times she clung to God's promise that they would not be brought to any ordeal that they could not overcome with His help.

Caleb knew little of the strength that came from God, and even less about the comfort to be found as a child of His. He was the sort of man more accustomed to relying on his own strengths than trusting in anything or anyone he could not see and did not understand.

She gave a deep sigh and felt tears trickle from

the corners of her eyes. *Time to face the truth, Abby.*
The truth was that even though Caleb might be
drawn to her in some physical way—after all, he
had kissed her—and since they had little in common except hot tempers and a love of reading, there
was scant chance of a marriage between them sur-
viving.

*Marriages between vastly different people sur-
vive all the time.* True enough. Without love, they
might not thrive and grow, but they could and did
survive. The problem was that she wanted more.
Even though her marriage to William had been less
than perfect at the end, they had gone into it with
a genuine love for each other, and though that love
might have changed somewhat with their problems,
it had never died.

What next?

She knew she had to change her attitude. It was
not all about her, after all. Instead of taking refuge in anger and dwelling on their differences, she
should consider all the good things that had come
into her life because of her unexpected and incon-
venient husband.

First and foremost, her future and the future of
her children were secure. No one knew better than
she that possessions were not the important things
of life, yet she slept better knowing that Ben and
Laura did not have to worry about a roof over their
heads or food to eat through the coming winter.
Because of Caleb, all her old debt was wiped clean.

Then there was Betsy, the reason for everything

that had transpired the past few weeks. Abby was now mother to a precious baby girl who had already carved out a special place in Abby's heart.

She lived in a beautiful house that she would gradually make her own. She was married to a man any woman in the county would be proud to call husband. Even though he had a reputation as a hard, unyielding man, Abby knew better. He was a man who, despite having a hard-as-nails father and a mother who had left him as a child, had somehow grown into a decent person. He was fair, worked hard and gave impeccable attention to anything left in his care, whether it was a field, a child or a wife.

So where did that leave her?

Whether or not she wanted it to be, it seemed she was in love with her husband. Though she felt a twinge of guilt for betraying what she and William had shared, she knew he would want her and the children to be happy and taken care of. God wanted that, too, and He had brought her to this place. So the question remained, did she really want things to change between her and Caleb? If so, what could she do to change them?

"When you don't know where to go or what to do, go to God." The words her mother had often spoken drifted through Abby's troubled mind, stilling the turbulence and settling like a balm on her heavy heart.

Realizing how wrong she had been to try to "do it herself" and knowing she did want theirs to be a real marriage, Abby prayed with a heart of thankfulness instead of one of bitterness and rebellion. She thanked God for bringing Caleb into her life and providing for her and her children. She prayed that somehow, someway, some little everyday thing would touch his heart and help him to see just how much he needed God in his life. And she prayed that one day theirs would be a marriage where love, not necessity, bound them.

By the time she whispered "amen," Abby knew without a doubt that what she'd told Ben was true. Nothing that had happened to her or Caleb was by chance. They were exactly where they were supposed to be, exactly where God wanted them. It was up to her to teach him about love—all kinds of love. It was up to her to guide him to the place God wanted him to be.

To be the man God wanted him to be.

Caleb stared at the mirror that reflected back bloodshot eyes and scraped off twenty-four hours' worth of whiskers. He'd tossed and turned much of the night, torn among a dozen uncertainties, and recriminations for giving in to impulse and kissing Abby. He had betrayed not only Emily's memory but his own planned course of action. After giving careful consideration to the dozens of reasons a deeper relationship between him and Abby wouldn't work, he had let the memory of her tear-drenched eyes and the heart-wrenching quaver in her voice penetrate the wall he'd erected around his heart after his mother left. Sad eyes and a soft smile and a single kiss.

The memory caused his razor to slip. He jerked at the sudden sting, and stared at the thin trail of blood trickling down his chin. Dabbing at the cut with the corner of a towel, he acknowledged that he was in big trouble and had no idea what to do about it.

His approach to dealing with her and her children was not working at all. Polite civility didn't stand a chance against Abby's inherent goodness or the dozens of ways she was insinuating herself and her traditions into his life. Overt acts and an attempt to penetrate Ben's antagonism had not brought him and the boy any closer. Cool neutrality certainly hadn't put off Laura, who simply ran roughshod over his intentions to remain detached by simply granting him one of her radiant smiles. The child would be a heartbreaker in a few years, he thought, and felt a rush of panic when he realized that he would be the one responsible for keeping all prospective beaux at bay.

Muttering under his breath, he squeezed the excess hot water from a towel and pressed it to his face, knowing he had just about used up his excuses not to go in to breakfast.

He put off hurrying to the kitchen because it was what he wanted to do so badly.

Definitely in trouble.

He shuffled down the hallway in his stocking feet, both dreading and anticipating what the day might bring. Having no idea what to expect from one day to the next was itself something to look forward to.

He heard Betsy crying in the kitchen and figured right away that his morning was not off to the start he'd imagined. He pushed through the swinging door and surveyed Abby's usually peaceful domain. The unmistakable smell of bacon burning assailed his nostrils. Not only was Betsy crying, but Ben, who was usually waiting for his arrival, was nowhere to be seen. Abby, whose hair was twisted into a haphazard knot atop her head, put the baby down, then rushed from the cradle near the fireplace to the stove, grabbing up a meat fork and scooping the charred meat from the smoking grease.

The only semblance of normality was Laura. As usual, she greeted him with a wide grin and an unintelligible but heartfelt greeting. The sight of her smile lifted his heart. She *did* like him! The pleasing notion settled over his heart like a benediction.

Without thinking of his actions, he crossed the room, bent down and pressed a kiss to her blond curls. She reciprocated by reaching up and patting his cheeks with oatmeal-coated hands, while bombarding him with more baby gibberish, some of which sounded very much like "Dada."

Caleb was in the process of wiping the mess from his face when he heard Abby give a cry of pain. He whirled toward the stove and saw her pressing her palm to her mouth. He also saw the dark circles beneath her eyes.

"What happened?" he asked over the sound of Betsy's continued wailing.

"I was trying to move the skillet to a cooler part of the stove and picked up the handle with a damp towel."

Caleb moved closer, grasped her hand and turned it palm-up. An angry red weal streaked her hand. "I'll go out to the barn and get the bag balm."

"It'll be fine," Abby assured him. "It's a long way from my heart."

One corner of his mouth hiked upward in a half smile. The statement was one his father had always quoted to him and Gabe when they got hurt as boys—Lucas Gentry's way of telling his sons to take it like a man. Coming from someone as decidedly feminine as Abby, the saying seemed out of place.

"But you *can* help."

He regarded her with lifted eyebrows.

"You can either fry your own eggs, or you can try to calm Betsy down, which is usually Ben's job."

"I always break the yolks," he said, going to the cradle and picking up his baby girl. He nestled her against his shoulder, splaying one big hand on her back and cupping the other beneath her bottom. He began to bounce and pat. "Where's Ben?"

"In the barn, and thank you. Choice number two. You can either have no bacon or burned bacon." Without giving him time to answer, she said, "He decided to take advantage of the break in the rain and get the milking over with before it started up again."

Caleb was impressed with the child's fore-thought. "No bacon. What's wrong with Betsy?" She was usually a contented baby.

Abby shot him a look he couldn't quite decipher and reached for a couple of large brown eggs. "I overslept, and got behind with breakfast. I imagine she's starving."

All his plans to stay emotionally detached faded as Caleb wondered if the memory of their kiss had kept her awake and led to her oversleeping, as it had him.

A particularly ear-splitting scream from Betsy brought him back to earth in a hurry. Bouncing and patting wasn't working. Betsy was hungry, and he had no idea what to do. "Hold up on the eggs," he said, as Abby was about to crack the first one into the skillet.

She looked up at him, frowning.

"It's a miserable day. There's nothing I can do outside right now, so there's no hurry for breakfast. I'll go out and help Ben with his chores while you feed Betsy. We can start over on breakfast later."

Usually unflappable, Abby looked as if she were about to burst into grateful tears. "That would be a tremendous help. Thank you."

She placed the eggs back into the crockery bowl and reached for the baby, cradling her in one arm. Without thinking, she reached out her free hand and pushed an unruly lock of damp hair off Caleb's forehead. Then, as if she realized what she was doing, she jerked away. "I really appreciate this, and I know Ben will."

Wearing a frown of his own, Caleb said, "Between us, we'll make short work of things."

He grabbed his coat from the hook just inside the kitchen door and stepped out onto the porch, wondering what had just transpired in his kitchen. Burned meat. Burned hand. Crying baby. Happy baby. Two parallel conversations going on at once and he had somehow, miraculously, managed to follow both. A far cry from breakfast when he was married to Emily and had done most of the cooking himself. An even further cry from life as he'd known it in the past.

For the first time in his life, he was beginning to understand that marriage was a partnership, and how that partnership worked. It was two people with vastly disparate jobs working together and helping each other as needed. It was sharing not only happiness but problems, large and small.

He slipped his arms into his coat and snatched up the milk bucket. It was an interesting concept, one that held infinite possibilities.

Caleb found Ben in the barn, milking Nana, who was happily munching on some hay. He was as surprised to see Caleb as Caleb had been to know that Ben had taken it on himself to start his chores before breakfast.

"How are you doing?"

"Fine." The milk hit the bucket with a hiss.

"Have you milked Shaggy Bear yet?"

"No, sir."

"I'll do it, and we can get back inside where it's warm faster," Caleb offered.

Ben cast him a questioning, sideways look.

Caleb cleared his throat. "I appreciate you getting started with this. It was a smart decision."

Ben frowned. "I don't know how smart it was, but I couldn't take any more of Betsy's crying. It gets pretty bad between her and Laura some days."

Ah, Caleb thought, smothering a grin behind a sudden bout of coughing. A man after his own heart.

"Why do you think I told your mom I'd come and help you?" he said, settling on the three-legged milking stool. "It was a madhouse in there. Abby burned the bacon, and her hand, and—"

"Is she okay?" Ben interrupted.

Ben's obvious concern for his mother's welfare was touching. He'd always heard boys had a special relationship with their mothers, but he and Gabe had been deprived of that. Suddenly Caleb wondered if he would have had a good relationship with his mother if she'd stayed, and he wondered if her leaving had somehow been at the root of all Gabe's problems.

"It'll be fine," he told Ben. "I'll take the bag balm in when we go back inside."

"I hate when she burns the bacon," Ben said on a sigh.

"Me, too." Caleb relaxed into the rhythm of

milking. "I told her I'd come help you while she took care of the babies and then we'd start breakfast from scratch. Once we get the animals fed, there isn't much we can do, so it looks as if we'll be spending another day inside."

Ben heaved another sigh. "I'm tired of being inside."

"I know." As they milked, the barn was filled with the first companionable silence they'd shared. Civility hadn't worked; maybe companionship would ease the tensions between him and Ben. Caleb struggled to find another topic of conversation that might prolong the tentative peace.

Holidays! he thought at last. Kids loved holidays.

"Thanksgiving is coming up next week. Does your family do anything special?"

"We usually go to Doc Stone's and spend the day, so Mom and Doctor Rachel can drink coffee and have a hen party after we eat." He shot Caleb a quick, conspiratorial grin at mention of the hen party, obviously remembering their earlier conversation on the subject. "On Christmas, they come to our house. My dad and Doc Edward used to play pinochle and dominoes, and Danny and I play something outdoors if the weather is okay."

"Sounds like fun." Fun. As he'd told Abby, he had no idea what comprised fun, although Ben's description did sound like a pleasant way to spend the day. As he'd grown up, one day was pretty much like the other, holiday or not. He wondered if Abby would want to keep up with the tradition, and wondered what his reaction would be if she asked him about going. Whatever happened, Caleb knew Abby's family would celebrate all the good things of life in one way or the other.

"I thought I'd go turkey hunting when it gets closer to time and see if I can get one. Would you like to go?"

Ben looked at him, his eyes filled with cautious eagerness. "I'd like to, since I've never been hunting before, but I don't have a gun. My dad didn't hunt," he added as an afterthought.

Caleb, who'd grown up with a rifle and shotgun in his hands, couldn't hide his genuine shock. If William Carter had bought every bite of meat his family put in their mouths, no wonder he had financial woes.

"High time you went, then. I have a shotgun you can use." Caleb found the idea of passing down his first gun to his new stepson a pleasing one.

"I doubt Mom will let me. She says I'm too young."

Caleb offered what he hoped was a conspiratorial look. "Moms are too protective sometimes," he lamented with a shake of his head. "Most women are. I got my first shotgun when I was about your age. In fact, it's the one I'll let you borrow. I think she'll change her mind if she knows I'll teach you how to be really safe with it."

"You'd let me use your shotgun?"

"Sure. Why not?"

Ben turned back to his milking, but not before Caleb saw the wide smile that spread across his face.

"Absolutely not!" Abby raged when Caleb broached the subject over breakfast some thirty minutes later. "He's too young for that sort of responsibility! Firearms are dangerous."

Ben looked from his mother to Caleb, his head swiveling from one adult to the other as he monitored the heated conversation.

"I disagree," Caleb said in a calm, rational tone. "Firearms aren't dangerous if you're taught to use them correctly and respect what they're capable of doing. Ben needs to learn to use a weapon, both for food and for protection. There are still a lot of nasty critters out there, both four-and two-legged. Shooting is an important skill for a man."

"Exactly. A man. Ben is six years old."

Abby, whose hair had come loose even more, paced the room in long, angry strides, waving her arms in agitation and pointing her finger at Caleb when she wanted to make a point.

Caleb set his napkin aside and leaned back in his chair, crossing his arms over his chest. He knew in the end he would win the battle, but for the moment, he was relishing the vision of his wife in the glory of her motherly protectiveness. Pretty enough, but in no way beautiful, Abby was magnificent when she was angry. Her creamy cheeks were flushed with the heat of battle; she tipped back her head and looked down her straight little nose at him as if she were a queen and he nothing but a lowly subject. Disapproval turned her blue gaze to ice, and her eyes glittered like sunshine splintering off the frozen surface of the pond in winter.

He could not recall a single argument between himself and Emily. They had been too disengaged to trouble themselves with forcing an opposing opinion on the other.

"Abby."

She stopped stalking around the room, put her fists on her hips and glared at him. "Yes?" she replied in an imperious tone.

"I've listened to your opinions and your arguments, since you've made it clear that you've been accustomed to expressing yourself in the past." His voice was calm, his demeanor unthreatening.

Wariness crept into her eyes.

"Now, as I also understand is customary, I, as your husband, will make the final decision."

Her mouth dropped open in surprise, then snapped shut when she had no ready comeback. Her eyes flashed, and polite civility aside, Caleb realized that he wanted very much to kiss her again.

"Ben will be going hunting with me. He will be carrying a gun. A shotgun, to be exact. He will be taught to use it responsibly and safely." He turned to Ben. "If you've finished your breakfast, come with me. We can have our first lesson right now."

Eagerness in every line of his body, Ben jumped up from the table—without pausing to ask permission—and followed Caleb to the kitchen door. An enraged breath hissed from Abby's lips, but she did not say another word.

He turned in the aperture. "By the way, I'll be teaching our girls how to shoot as soon as they're old enough."

He could have sworn he heard an actual growl of anger.

He offered her a benign smile that failed to reach his eyes. "As a matter of fact, wife, come spring, I'll be teaching you, as well."

He turned and left the room, but not before he saw her slam the dishrag she was using into the pan of hot soapy water, or before he saw that water splash up into her startled face. He didn't laugh, but the pleased smile on his face was every bit as broad as Ben's.

Halfway down the hall, he stopped in his tracks. In his own way, he'd been teasing Abby, knowing that she had talked herself into a corner—so to speak—by telling him that so long as she got to voice her opinion, William had made the final decision.

When she'd first gotten so riled about the hunting trip, Caleb had quickly seen the advantage of letting her use her own position on the husband-wife relationship to his advantage and had turned the tables on her to get the result he wanted. He did chuckle then, but not so loud that she'd hear him. He doubted she would see the humor in the situation.

Hoisted by her own petard!

Recalling how easily he had turned her sanctimonious speech about William listening to her views right back on her, Abby's face flushed with sudden heat. Caleb had entered the discussion knowing full well how she felt and with full intention of using her own position against her. If his smug attitude was anything to go by, he had enjoyed every minute of it!

Still seething, she set the clean cast-iron skillet on the stove with a satisfying clang, and then shot a look toward the playpen where Laura grasped the edge of the railing and stared at her with a serious expression on her usually smiling face.

"Mamamamama," she said, holding out her arms.

Her sweet entreaty dissolved the lingering traces of Abby's anger. "Hey there, little girl," she cooed. "Do you need a dry diaper?"

She did. Abby carried her into the bedroom, changed her and spent the next several minutes playing peekaboo and blowing air bubbles against Laura's bare tummy, which sent the little one into gales of giggles. Every time she stopped, Laura lifted the hem of her dress for Abby to do it again.

"What's Laura laughing about?" Ben said from the doorway.

"I'm blowing on her belly, and she loves it, and so did you when you were a baby."

"Let me try," Ben said with a wide grin. As soon as he took Abby's place, Laura began to fuss and try to get away from him, doing her best to roll over onto her stomach and crawl away.

"I guess she's tired of that game," Abby said. "Or she doesn't like you doing it."

Ben's bottom lip stuck out in a pout.

"No sulking, young man," she ordered, riffling his hair with her fingers. She set Laura on the floor, where she clung to the quilt hanging over the edge of the bed and took off around its corner.

"She's probably getting sleepy. It's about time for her morning nap." Injecting what she hoped was nonchalance into her tone, she asked, "Where's Caleb?"

"In his office. He said he had some figures to go over, and then he might teach me how to play dominoes."

"Oh." Abby felt her eyebrows lift in surprise. First Caleb offered to help with the milking, and then insisted on teaching Ben how to hunt, and now he planned on giving her son a lesson in dominoes. What was going on? Could Caleb's sudden interest in Ben be God's way of answering her prayers?

"Did he teach you about the rifle?"

"It's a shotgun, Mom," Ben said in a self-important tone. "There is a difference."

"Oh. I wasn't aware of that."

"Well, there is. Shotguns are described by 'gauge' and rifles by 'caliber.' There's a lot of other stuff I don't understand yet about how many lead balls are in a shell—they're real small for birds— but Caleb says it won't take me long to learn. He showed me how to load it and everything, and he says I should always have it on 'safe,' never to point it at anyone and don't put my finger on the trigger until I'm ready to shoot."

Abby had to admit she was impressed with what Ben had learned in such a short time and the care Caleb was taking with his teaching.

"He said we'd practice when it dries up some."

"That sounds…nice," she said.

"I'm tired of all my toys," Ben said, leaning against her in an increasingly rare show of dependence.

"Well," she said, smoothing his hair, "I suppose you could read *Swiss Family Robinson* until Caleb finishes, or you can come and scrape carrots for a stew I'm going to make."

"Do you mean you're actually going to let him use a sharp knife?"

The irony-laced question brought up Abby's head. Caleb stood in the doorway, hands braced over his head on either side, regarding her with the merest hint of a mockery lighting his eyes. He was so tall and his shoulders were so broad…and he looked so steady and safe somehow. *And you, Abigail Gentry, are in deep, deep trouble.*

She pressed her lips together in a prim line. Why, he was actually baiting her! She'd encouraged him to loosen up, but she hadn't meant for him to find his pleasure in mocking her. Or had she? Abby let out a slow breath and took a firm grasp on her temper.

"I believe he'll be fine with adult supervision," she said in her best schoolmarm voice.

"I believe you're right," he said with equal stuffiness.

"Dadadada!"

Laura had spied him in the doorway and let go of the quilt. To Abby's surprise, she reached out with her chubby hands and took two toddling steps toward him and stood there, swaying like a drunk on Saturday night. When she realized what she was doing, her smile faded.

More to Abby's surprise, Caleb squatted down, holding out his arms to her. "Come on, baby girl," he said, motioning for her to keep coming. "Come see Daddy."

The encouragement was all Laura needed. Abby watched in stunned bemusement as, with her solemn expression mirroring the concentration of Caleb's, Laura took another tottering step and then two more before losing her balance a scant yard from him and plopping onto her bottom. She promptly burst into tears while Abby fought back tears of her own.

An instant later, Caleb had scooped her up into his arms and was planting quick, light kisses on her chubby, tear-streaked cheeks, crooning to her that it was all right, that she was a really big girl, and she'd done a good job. Laura stopped crying and nestled her face against his shoulder.

Caleb's wide-eyed gaze sought Abby's. "She's walking!" Then, seeing the shimmer of tears in her eyes, he said, "I'm sorry." The stiffness was back in his tone.

"You have nothing to be sorry for," she said, wiping her damp cheeks with her fingertips.

"But her first steps were to me, not you."

"No, it's fine. Really."

He seemed to be thinking over the past few moments to try to figure out what else might have caused her tears. "I'm sorry," he said again, his eyes dark with contrition. "I called myself Daddy."

"But you *are,*" Abby told him. "You are her father. For the rest of her life."

"Then what is it?" he demanded. "Why are you crying?"

She sniffed back more tears. "Because it is very clear to me that whether or not you know it, whether or not you like it, she loves you and you love her."

Caleb shifted from one foot to the other, uncomfortable with the thought of love. "She's an easy child to be with."

The answer wasn't what Abby hoped for, but she should have known better than for him to admit to loving anything or anyone, at least not so soon. She had never doubted that God would respond in some way to her prayer, but she had not known what form His answers would take. What she had just witnessed between her daughter and her new husband was an amazing step in the right direction.

Chapter Nine

As expected, the Stones issued their usual Thanksgiving invitation, this time via Caleb when he went into town for oats. There had been no major problems the past few days, and he and Abby went about each day much as they had the one before, which made the decision of when to approach her about the invitation much easier. He would wait until after their evening Bible study and the children were in bed, since he was uncertain how the conversation might go. Instead of spending Bible time in his office pouring over bookwork, he decided to read his new farming journal in the parlor.

They were studying the parable of the seeds. Caleb admired how Abby not only related the different soils with the conditions of peoples' hearts but also how she wove it into their own planting of crops in the upcoming spring. Caleb tried to focus on the pages of the magazine but couldn't keep his gaze from straying to her any more than he could keep from remembering the way her lips felt beneath his. Several times during the lesson, she looked up and caught him watching her. To his surprise, she looked uncomfortable with his presence, but was trying her best not to let it show.

He wondered at the new demeanor, one he'd seen more and more often lately. She'd seldom been this uneasy with him. In fact, he didn't think she had been since those early days, and it wasn't like her. He liked the fiery Abby who talked back, who challenged everything about him from his attitudes to how he expressed himself. He liked the gentle Abby, too. The one who patiently explained things to Ben, who sang to Betsy and Laura and smiled at him when he stepped through the kitchen door at night. He didn't like the wariness or the fact that ever since he'd kissed her, she'd seemed...

The kiss! She'd been acting funny ever since he'd kissed her. Caleb considered his own actions. If his goal was to hold Abby at arm's length as he had Emily, he'd done a bang-up job—except for the kiss.

A sudden thought held him stock-still. He and Emily had liked each other well enough when they married, but that relationship had deteriorated through the years until they might as well have been strangers living beneath the same roof. Was it possible that his detachment and cool behavior toward her lay at the root of their inability to connect in any meaningful way, or had his behavior come about because of her own standoffishness? He supposed he would never know.

What he did know was that he had no idea of how to be tender, how to accept or demonstrate simple acts of kindness, something that had hit home when his neighbors had come with condolences after Emily's death. He had no idea how to love or be loved. Lucas had done a remarkable job of teaching him and Gabe that any show of gentleness made you less a man. For the first time in his life, Caleb wondered if his dad had always so inflexible, or if the high walls around Lucas's heart had been erected after his wife's desertion.

Another thing Caleb would never know.

Caleb faced the fact that despite his determination to keep his heart free from any entanglements, he was being inexorably drawn into Abby's web of goodness. *So what's wrong with that? What can it hurt to embrace all the good things she could bring to his life? Why not welcome and enjoy Laura's undeniable adoration? Why shouldn't I accept the challenge of becoming a real father figure to Ben?*

"Is everything all right?"

The sound of Abby's voice brought him back to the present with a jolt. Though he'd done nothing to clarify his thoughts, he was glad to leave his uncertainty behind for a while. He looked around the room and saw that Ben was nowhere in sight, the Bible was put away and Abby stood in the doorway of Ben's room, staring at him with concern in her blue eyes. She must have finished her lesson, checked on the babies and put Ben to bed while he was woolgathering.

"I'm fine. Why?"

"Well, you don't often sit out here in the evenings, and you seem distracted."

"I suppose I am," he said, laying the publication aside. "I need to talk to you about something."

"Is it life or death?" she quipped with a hint of her usual spunk.

"Of course not," he said. "Why?"

Her shoulders rose in a slight shrug. "You have a very grim expression on your face."

"Oh. Actually, it's nothing grim at all. I saw Rachel when I was in town and she asked us to join them for Thanksgiving."

She looked surprised. "Oh. We've joined them every Thanksgiving since we came from Missouri, but I wasn't sure she'd ask this year, with William..." Her voice trailed away.

"Ben told me that's how you usually spend the day," Caleb confessed.

"He did?"

He gave a slow nod. "The day we did the milking together, and I told him we'd go turkey hunting. Would you like to go?" He heard the wariness in his voice and sensed they were both feeling their way through the conversation...as if they were walking through a swamp with dangerous quicksand pits.

"What did you and Emily do?"

"After my dad died, we went to her family. Before that, I usually dropped her off and came home. It was just another day."

The flicker of shock that crossed her features

was so fleeting he might have imagined it. "Eating with the Stones would certainly be a nice change of pace since I haven't been anywhere since Betsy was born," she said, a thoughtful expression on her face.

"Of course you should go, then."

She looked into his eyes for several uncomfortable seconds, as if she were trying to see into his very soul. Then she smiled, the simple action stealing Caleb's breath. "As much as I might like to get out, this will be the first holiday season for both of us without—" she paused "—without Emily and William. I'm thinking it might be a bit uncomfortable for us both. Besides, I think Betsy is too little to be taken out yet, especially with the weather so nasty. So if it's all the same to you, I'd like very much to stay at home and start our own Thanksgiving tradition."

Caleb slowly released a strangled breath. "That's fine. I'd like that," he said and realized as he spoke that it was the truth. "Ben and I will go out tomorrow and see if we can get a turkey."

"I have every confidence in you," Abby told him, her blue eyes alight with a teasing humor, "but just in case you come home empty-handed, we can have one of those beautiful hams you smoked."

"Great." Why did he sound so stiff? Why couldn't he show an enthusiasm to match hers?

"The Stones usually come to us for Christmas," Abby said, "but again, I'm not sure that would be a good idea. I think we both need some time to get accustomed to our new life and each other, don't you?"

"I do," he said. "But if you change your mind, if

we're a bit more settled as a family in a month, we could rethink it."

"That sounds like a good plan," she said, attempting a smile that fell a bit short of the mark. "Will you let them know our decision the next time you go into town?"

"I'd be glad to. Is there anything I can bring you from the mercantile?"

"Bring me?"

"Whatever else you might need for the meal."

She narrowed her eyes in thought and tapped her forefinger against her lips, drawing Caleb's attention to their soft fullness. "Let me think on it a bit. I know you eat everything, but is there anything you'd especially like me to fix?"

"I don't expect you to cook anything special for me," he told her, actually taken aback by the offer.

She fisted her hands on her hips. "Of course I'll fix whatever you want. We're starting a new Gentry holiday tradition. Funds permitting, I always make some sort of fruit salad for me, and Ben wants sweet potatoes with lots of butter, brown sugar and pecans on top."

Caleb's mouth began to water. "I'd love some sweet potatoes," he confessed. "My dad hated them."

He offered no further information; the simple statement said it all. "Then you will have sweet potatoes. Anything else?"

"Do you know how to make pecan pie? My mother used to make it, but the only time I get it now is if I happen to stop by the café when Ellie's made one."

"Not only do I make the best pecan pie in town, I'll match my crust to anyone's in the state."

Caleb was unable to stop the quick smile that quirked his lips. "Pretty boastful, aren't you?"

"It isn't boasting if it's the truth, is it?"

"Well, we'll see, won't we?" Caleb wondered if the question was his way of teasing.

"We will," she said with a saucy lift of her chin. "If you think of anything else, let me know. This is the one holiday I go a little crazy in the kitchen. Christmas is a bit lower key so that we can enjoy the day, our gifts and each other."

Enjoy the day. The concept was foreign, as was the idea of just spending time enjoying gifts and each other. Gifts! Though he'd always picked up something for Emily at the mercantile, usually something her mother said she'd like, Caleb had never bought Christmas gifts for anyone before. This year he would need not only something for Abby, but Ben and Laura, as well. He raked his hand through his hair, a bit overwhelmed by the whole idea. Well, he had almost a whole month to deal with that!

"That sounds...nice," he told her, realizing that the comment was unsatisfactory but unable to think of another. "If you think of anything you want or need, just let me know."

Caleb picked up the farming quarterly, effectively ending their conversation, which Abby thought was a shame. She'd enjoyed learning more about him and his likes, and the bit of sparring they'd engaged in about the pie had been stimulating after so many days of dealing with each other by saying and doing only the appropriate thing.

A time or two, she'd thought they were making a bit of progress, but the truth was that Caleb hadn't been the same since the night she'd cut his hair and he'd kissed her. Knowing the kind of man he was, she imagined he was berating himself for the momentary lack of control, since Emily had been gone such a short time. But since he'd confessed the true circumstances of his marriage, Abby wasn't sure she understood his guilt. Common sense told her that she should be satisfied with her life, and in many ways she was, but she'd be a lot happier sparring with him from time to time rather than dealing with a polite stranger. Like Laura, Abby knew she should be happy with baby steps.

Something positive had been accomplished through their decision to stay at home for Thanksgiving, though. As much as she might have liked to spend the day with Rachel and Edward, the things she'd told Caleb were true. She did feel it would be uncomfortable for them both to spend the day with friends, even though those friends were much loved, and she would enjoy beginning a new tradition that was centered on their new family. A baby step, but a strong one.

Abby was shelling pecans for Caleb's pie in front of the kitchen fireplace when the back door was flung open and Ben poked in his head.

"Mom, come see!" he yelled, his smile so broad it looked as if his cheeks should hurt.

"Shush! You'll wake the babies," she cautioned, casting a cautious glance toward the playpen and cradle. Seeing that neither little girl was stirring, Abby set the bowls onto the table and shook out her apron in the ash bucket.

"Does all this excitement mean you got us a turkey for tomorrow?" she asked.

He nodded vigorously. "I got a big old tom. He's got a beard and everything."

Grabbing a shawl from the hook next to the back door and draping it around her shoulders, Abby followed him onto the porch. "And are you sure it was you who shot him?"

"Positive!" he cried, racing down the steps and across the yard.

In typical mother fashion, she was torn between pride and a hint of sorrow that her little boy had taken one more step toward manhood. "Where is he? I can't be gone from inside but a minute."

"Out by the woodpile. Caleb said you should see him before he chops off his head."

Abby grimaced. William had never hunted, but with the help of neighbors they'd slaughtered pigs, goats and even a calf or two. He had always been careful to shield her from the grisly side of putting food on the table, just as she had been shielded from the financial ugliness that had hit her with such brutal force when he died. Deciding that she would rather know what to expect than not, she gamely followed her son out near the henhouse, where Caleb was building a fire beneath a huge cast-iron cauldron.

He looked up when he heard them approach, an expression of satisfaction in his eyes.

"Mom's shelling pecans for your pie!" Ben announced, skittering to a halt in front of Caleb.

"That's good."

"He shot this all by himself?" Abby asked with a dubious lift of her eyebrows.

Caleb nodded. "I called him up, and Ben blasted him."

"Caleb's gonna teach me how to call them up, too," Ben boasted.

"What's the fire for?" Abby asked.

It was Caleb's turn to look disbelieving. "You've never pulled feathers from a chicken?"

"No. We always bought ours from a neighbor, already dressed."

"You're kidding."

"No."

"All right. Here's what happens, and you need to pay attention, since you'll be killing and dressing chickens often in the future."

Abby's stomach churned at the thought.

"I'm going to chop off his head and gut him, and then we're going to dip him in scalding water so the feathers will pull out easier."

"Can't we just pull off the whole skin, like you do a rabbit or a squirrel?"

"Nooo," Caleb drawled in a measured tone,

clearly holding some emotion in check. "If we skin him, he'll dry out something fierce in the oven. With the skin on, he'll get nice toasty brown and juicy."

"Oh," she said with a reluctant nod. "I suppose gutting is a man's work and plucking is a woman's."

"In most cases, yes. Today, I'll be glad to do it since you're shelling pecans for my pie." She thought she saw a twinkle of pleasure in his gray eyes. "Also, it's pretty cold out here, and you have two sleeping babies that neither Ben nor I are in condition to watch since we're not fit to be inside until we clean up. Besides, you look all nice and fresh."

A gentle rush of pleasure spread throughout her. Somehow the simple statement felt like a compliment, whether or not he meant it as one. "Should I stay and watch so I'll know what to do next time?"

"Your nose is already getting red. We've got it, don't we, Ben?"

"Yes, sir." He looked at Abby, his eyes glowing with pleasure, something she hadn't seen in a long time. "Hey, Mom, do you have any cocoa?"

"Yes."

"Do you think Caleb and I could have a cup of hot chocolate when we finish here?"

"I think for a couple of men who've provided Thanksgiving turkey, anything might be possible, including sugar cookies with raisins." She was talking to Ben, but her eyes were on Caleb.

"We'll see you inside in a bit, then," he said with a slow smile.

Abby turned and crossed the yard, her heart filled with lightness. There was no mistaking the new camaraderie between Ben and Caleb. She smiled. *Thank You, God.*

The changes since she'd altered her attitude and her prayers were just short of miraculous. She wondered how many other things she might have accomplished sooner if she'd just gotten out of the way and let God do what He did best.

An hour later, the big bird had been plucked and all its pinfeathers singed off. Since the weather was so cold, Caleb had hung it in the smokehouse overnight. Since Abby liked Thanksgiving dinner to be served at exactly noon, he would fetch it for her early in the morning.

She was stirring together a slurry of cocoa powder, sugar and a bit of milk when Ben and Caleb came into the kitchen, leaving their coats and muddy boots inside the back door. Their faces were red with cold, and their eyes alight with anticipation.

Ben headed straight to the table where a platter of fresh-baked sugar cookies sat waiting. The moment Laura saw Caleb she squealed "Dada" and held out her arms to be picked up. Caleb went straight to her, and then crossed to the cradle where Betsy was waving her arms around and staring at something mesmerizing on the ceiling. Balancing Laura on one hip, he reached down and put one big hand on Betsy's tummy, asking her if she'd had a good nap, almost as if he expected her to supply an answer. She kicked harder, which drew an unexpected chuckle from Caleb. Laura, who wanted to be the center of his attention, grabbed his face and forced him to look at her.

"That situation is going to get sticky in a few years," Abby told him.

"What's that?" he asked, crossing to the stove and peering over her shoulder.

Abby drew in a shaky breath at his nearness. He smelled of wood smoke and cold and the spicy masculine soap she associated with him. "Both of the girls vying for your attention."

"Why would they do that?"

"Because that's what girls do," Abby said, looking up at him from over her shoulder. "Big or small, they all want to be Daddy's girl."

"What does Daddy do in a case like that?"

It sounded like a teasing question, but the alarm on his face and the anxiety in his voice told Abby he was concerned. And why not? The man had never been around children, which, even to her, were sometimes strange little beings. She couldn't help the laughter that spilled from her lips. "If Daddy is as smart as I believe you are, he will be very careful to treat them the same and not show any favoritism."

He gave a purely masculine sound, something between a grunt and a growl. "Sounds impossible."

"It is. My dad always said he just muddled through as best he could."

"What's that stuff?" Caleb asked.

"Cocoa powder, sugar and a little milk," she explained. "Cocoa won't mix into milk if you just dump it in. You a have to make a syrup of sorts and then pour it in the hot milk. I like to add a dash of cinnamon and a teaspoon of vanilla if I have it."

"It smells delicious. I can't wait to try it."

Abby stirred in the cocoa mixture and swirled the wooden spoon around in the pan of hot milk. "Surely you've had hot chocolate before."

"Back before my mother left, but I barely remember it."

Abby stared up at Caleb in disbelief, again struck by the unfairness of his upbringing and the sadness she felt every time she thought of all the things he'd never experienced and those he had because of his parents' actions. Caleb had a long way to go, but like him, she had never shirked a challenge. She would take one day at a time, deal with one thing at a time, and put her trust in God, who could make anything happen.

Caleb went to bed filled with a satisfaction he could not remember ever experiencing. Furnishing the family with the main part of the holiday dinner was something he wouldn't soon forget. It had been a satisfying day in many respects. Ben had listened to Caleb's instructions from the moment they'd left the house until he came back the hero. The two of them had not only gotten along, the boy had actually seemed to have...fun. Caleb smiled into the darkness. If easy companionship and pleasure at seeing someone else's eyes light up with enjoyment was the definition of fun, then he'd had fun, too. When Ben took aim and shot the turkey, Caleb had felt his heart swell with something that superseded satisfaction and felt a lot like pride.

Other than work, he couldn't remember doing anything with his own dad. Lucas had never taught him or Gabe to fish; that had been left up to Frank. Caleb wondered if his life might have been different if his mother had stuck around, but knowing his father, the best she might have done was soften the most painful moments of his childhood.

His childhood. That was a hoot. He'd never had a childhood. But Betsy would, and so would Ben and Laura and any other children he and Abby might have. He stopped breathing momentarily. The notion of having a baby with Abby brought a feeling of contentment that warred with a sudden panic reminiscent of that which he'd felt during Emily's labor. He wasn't sure he could survive a second round of the terror he'd suffered in the hours before Betsy's birth. The thought of losing Abby in the same manner left him feeling empty inside. He couldn't deny his growing feelings for her any longer. He could tell himself he was only being drawn into her circle of caring kindness, that he was becoming attached to Laura and forging a better relationship with Ben, and he could admit he was attracted to Abby physically. He could even let himself believe that it was okay for all these things to happen, that it would only make things better for all concerned.

So why didn't he embrace this new life and all its good things?

Fear.

He was afraid. Maybe the anxiety was a result of his mother's abandonment, or maybe it was just an innate part of his personality, but he always liked controlling a situation, afraid to trust anyone, especially where his feelings were concerned. On the other side of that coin, in spite of his successes, he had never felt he measured up to Emily, who he knew wanted someone more polished and outgoing than a farmer from Wolf Creek, or to his father, who always found fault, always made Caleb feel as if he came up short. He'd often wondered if he'd worked harder or pushed himself more if he might have received a few simple words of praise for a job well done.

Caleb prided himself on his honesty. He worried that if he had not been enough, done enough for his dad or Emily, those shortcomings might cause whatever tentative feelings Abby might have for him to wither and die. The bottom line was that he was afraid that if he allowed himself to care she would leave him as his mother had, and if that were to happen, he knew the pain would be more devastating than anything he'd ever experienced.

Thanksgiving dawned cold, cloudy and damp, and when Caleb brought the turkey inside before daybreak, he declared it would snow before evening.

"Snow! Isn't it early for snow?" Abby asked,

placing the bird into a blue granite roasting pan with white speckles.

"It is, and we don't usually see much if any, since the winters are comparatively mild to other parts of the country, but I've seen it snow in November a couple of times. What are you doing?" he asked as she smeared her hands with butter and began rubbing it over the carcass.

"Putting butter on so it will get golden-brown."

Finished greasing the bird, she plopped on the lid, and then washed her hands in a pan of soapy water. She was reaching to open the oven when Caleb held out a restraining arm.

"I'll get that."

She watched as he lifted the bird, which must have weighed at least fourteen pounds, slid it onto the bottom rack and closed the oven door.

"What next?"

"Nothing for now. I'll get the sweet potatoes ready in a bit and peel the others to mash. Then I'll get the green beans simmering with some ham, open a jar of corn and make the fruit salad. By the way, thank you so much for getting the ingredients for me. I didn't get any last year."

"You're very welcome."

Much to her astonishment, he had come home from town two days before with ingredients for her fruit salad. There had been oranges, some canned pineapple and even some grapes that had been shipped from California along with some bananas, a dear item for folks in Wolf Creek. When

Caleb had seen the joy on her face, the cost had been worth every penny.

"So you don't have anything to do for a little while. Sit." He placed a hand on her shoulder and guided her toward a chair. "You've been going strong ever since your feet hit the floor. In fact, it makes me tired just watching you."

"But I have to fix breakfast."

"No buts. The kids won't be up for at least a couple of hours. The coffee is ready. Sit down and have a cup with me."

The request was unexpected and thoughtful. The idea of sitting down and sharing a cup of coffee and a few moments without three children afoot was deliciously pleasing. And a bit scary. It was seldom they talked without children around as buffers, and when they did, they generally wound up arguing.

Or kissing.

The wayward thought sent a frisson of nervous awareness shivering through her. To hide it, Abby tucked a strand of hair up into the knot at the top of her head. She started to sit, then bolted upright, only to feel Caleb's hand on her shoulder, forcing her back down.

"What's the matter now?"

"I have to pour the coffee."

There was a considering look in his eyes. "Believe it or not, Mrs. Gentry, I can pour a cup of coffee for myself and for you, too."

"But—"

"I said no buts. I doubt my manly ego will be more than slightly bruised."

Abby didn't say anything, but she'd noticed that more and more often lately, his sarcastic comments could be construed as poking fun at himself or even teasing. Another change that had happened since her prayer.

Abby watched Caleb pour himself a mug of coffee and then reach for the pretty floral cup that had belonged to her mother. Funny that he would remember that she liked drinking her coffee from the delicate china cup instead of a thick mug. It was one of her quirks, one she was surprised he'd noticed. Surprised, but pleased.

She was also pleased with the unrelenting masculine portrait he exhibited. Work-hardened muscles rippling beneath the fabric of his shirt, strong, yet gentle hands doing the things she usually did, and doing them with care and efficiency. Abby thought his hands were one of the things she most loved about him.

With a sigh, she accepted the cup he offered and helped herself to the thick cream he'd set before her.

"I don't suppose you'd let me have a slice of that pecan pie for breakfast." It was a statement.

"What pecan pie?" she asked, unable to stop herself from casting a flirtatious glance at him.

Caleb's eyes narrowed in mock ferocity. "The pie you hid in the pie safe," he said, once again surprising her with his teasing comeback.

She rested her elbows on the table and propped

her chin in her hands. "The pie I hid? I thought that's what a pie safe was for," she countered. "To put pie in to keep it…safe."

"Until you came the only thing it kept safe was extra bullets."

"I'm glad I could make proper use of it, then," she told him. She pushed away from the table with a smile. "Of course you can have pie for breakfast. You brought home a turkey and cleaned it for me. Pie for breakfast seems a pretty fair trade."

"Thank you, but sit down. I can get it. I'm not used to having a woman wait on me the way you do."

Abby sat. "And I'm not used to not waiting on a man."

Caleb took the pie from the cabinet and reached for a saucer on the shelf. "Want some?" he asked, taking a large butcher knife from a wooden container.

"No, thank you. I can't do the sweet thing this early."

"I can do the sweet thing any time," he said, cutting a slice that was almost a quarter of the pie.

"I've noticed," she said, tongue-in-cheek.

Abby was afraid to consider the easy tone of their conversation overmuch. She didn't want to dwell on what had brought it about or if it might last. All she wanted to do was enjoy it while it did.

"I want to thank you for taking Ben hunting," she said, hoping to keep the mood alive.

Caleb took a seat across from her and reached for his mug. "I thought you were against the idea."

"I was," she told him with a nod, "but I'm not the kind of person who can't admit to being wrong. I could tell from the look on his face and the way he interacted with you that he enjoyed himself, and he was really proud. I think it was a step in the right direction for the two of you."

Caleb nodded. "He did a good job. He listens and does what he's told. He'll make a good hunter eventually."

"I'm glad he's learning to be more comfortable with outdoor pursuits. William wasn't. He was better at figuring out how things worked and working with wood. He made Ben's train that last Christmas."

"All I can do with wood is cut and split it," Caleb said. He lifted a forkful of pie to his mouth.

Abby didn't miss the humorous glint in his eyes as he chewed and swallowed. "You are definitely becoming adept with the teasing…or the sarcasm, whichever you want to call it."

"I take it that's good."

"I like it." She took a swallow of coffee and decided to push a bit. The man was floundering in an uncharted sea of children and anchored down with an unwanted wife, yet he was staying afloat better than she'd expected. Maybe he needed a little assurance that he was doing okay. "You're very good with Laura."

He looked embarrassed by the praise. "All I do

is pick her up when she wants me to." He flashed one of his rare, quicksilver grins. "Let me clarify that. When she *demands* it."

"She is a bit pushy, isn't she?" Abby said, smiling back. "All in all, Caleb Gentry, for a man with little to no experience, you're doing very well with your unwanted family."

Clearly surprised, he dropped his gaze to his uneaten pie. He didn't speak for long seconds. Finally he looked up at her, an unexpected intensity in his eyes. "Thank you for saying that. As for you all being an unwanted family...that might have been true at the beginning, but we are a family. I know too well that I'm not William, but I am trying."

Her heart breaking the tiniest bit, she said, "You aren't William and you never will be."

Caleb looked as if she'd slapped him.

Furious at herself for not saying the right thing, she leaped to her feet and leaned across the table. "I'm sorry. That didn't come out the way I meant it to," she said, earnest entreaty in her blue eyes. "What I meant to say is that you aren't William and I don't want you to be. I want you to be you. He was a good man, and you're a good man, too. But you're different, and that's the way it should be."

She straightened and whirled away from him. As usual when she was upset, she began to pace. "I know you're trying very hard, but I don't want us to always be the unwanted family. I don't want us to be a burden you have to bear for the rest of your life so that you spend every day trying to do what's right.

"I want you to do things with Ben that you both like to do. I want you to teach him all about farming and hunting, and the satisfaction that comes with a hard day's work. I don't want you to mimic what William and Ben had, I want you to build your own relationship with him, just as you're starting to do.

"I want you to help me in the kitchen, but only if you want to be here. I want you to keep on loving Laura and I want you to become comfortable with us in your life. I want to see you smile more, to hear you laugh."

She paused and looked at him. Her eyes filled with tears, but she didn't try to hide them. "What I want, Caleb Gentry, is for you to be h-happy." The last word was choked out on a sob.

Before she realized what he was about, Caleb had risen and crossed the room to her, blocking her path. She stopped but refused to look up. To her dismay, he lifted her chin, forcing her to meet his gaze. "Pity, Abby?"

"No!" she said with controlled vehemence. "Not pity, Caleb."

Tension vibrated from his big body as he searched her tear-drenched eyes for long, tense moments. Finally, the breath he'd been holding hissed out in a long sigh. Then without another word, he turned and strode for the doorway, nabbing his coat from the hook as he went.

Oh, why, why couldn't she learn to leave things

alone? Why must she always have to open her mouth? Now, he probably suspected that she cared and he would not like that one little bit. "Caleb, wh—"

He turned abruptly. "Shh," he commanded softly, holding up a silencing finger.

He didn't look angry, she thought. He looked perplexed, or... Oh, she didn't know how he looked! "Where are you going?"

"To do the milking. It's a holiday, so I'll give Ben the day off. I won't be long." He took the lantern and a box of matches from a nearby shelf, opened the door, and let himself out.

It was only after he'd gone that Abby noticed that he hadn't finished his pie. Reaching for his fork, she cut an oversized bite for herself and chewed on it while her tears flowed down her cheeks. She took a sip of her coffee only to find that it had grown tepid. Feeling as if she were recovering from a bad bout of influenza, she rose, refilled her cup and fed another log to the fire, praying that her impulsiveness had not ruined the progress they'd made. Praying that she had not ruined his mood or the day.

Then she sat down and finished his pie.

She had shed tears for him.

Caleb milked the goat and thought about what a difference a day could make in someone's life. His fear aside, Abby was different from any woman he'd ever known. He couldn't pretend as he had the day before that he was attracted to her or that she and the children were working their way into his life. The truth was they had worked their way into his heart, and he loved her. Loved her as he had never loved Emily, as he had never expected to love anyone. Loved her as he had never imagined he could love.

He wanted to keep her from ever hurting again, wanted to lavish her with everything his money could buy. Wanted to look up in ten or twenty or fifty years and see her sitting across the room from him, and know he was the reason for the smile on her face. He wanted Ben to look at him and feel the same love and respect he'd felt for William. He wanted Laura to look at him and see the kind of man she could use as a measuring stick when she sought her own husband. *Dear God, I want them all to love me.*

The problem was that with that love came an overwhelming responsibility. It wasn't just a feeling, it was action, and Caleb wasn't sure how to make his prayer come true.

Prayer? Had he just prayed? He didn't think so, wasn't sure. Maybe, though, he had let God know his feelings. What next? If he knew what to do to become a better husband and father, would it make a difference? Were there any guarantees that his feelings would be reciprocated?

He thought Abby felt something for him, but was her desire to see him happy just her natural longing for things to be right for everyone, or were the tears she shed for him based on something more? How could he know?

Caleb had no illusions about his past. He did not condone his mother's actions, but if Libby Gentry had sought love somewhere else, it was only because Lucas had driven her away with his inflexibility, his disagreeable attitude and his acerbic tongue. Caleb had lots of memories of his soft-spoken mother crying tears of hurt and humiliation.

This marriage was no business deal as he'd alleged when he'd proposed marriage to Abby. This was the lives of five people. It all boiled down to whether or not he was willing to risk opening himself up to change, to try to become the man Abby deserved.

What if you do something to hurt them without meaning to? What if you can't be all she wants in a husband?

There was no way of knowing how it would end, but one thing was certain. He had come a long way in a short time. He wasn't going anywhere, and neither was Abby. The best tactic was to take one day at a time and try to build on their shaky foundation. It was all he could do.

Abby was opening a particularly stubborn jar of green beans when he came back inside. One look at his rugged face told her that she needn't have worried. Whatever he thought of what she'd said, whatever he felt about it, he was in perfect control, and she saw no animosity in his demeanor or his eyes.

"No one's up yet?"

"No. Thank goodness." She grabbed a dish towel

and looped it over the top of the jar for a better grip. "I'd like to get things under control before I'm inundated with little people."

"I'll get that," he said, walking over and taking the can from her and giving the top a hard twist. "I'd open another if I were you. Frank and Leo have pretty good appetites, and it isn't often they get to eat someone's cooking other than their own."

"You're right. I'm not used to cooking for three big men."

"You'll never guess what I found in the barn," Caleb said, opening the pie safe.

"Probably not," Abby agreed, dumping the beans into a pan and heading for the pantry for another.

"Traps."

She turned. "Traps?"

"Animal traps," he said, with a nod. "What happened to my pie?"

She changed the subject to hide her guilt. "Animal traps? For what?"

"For Ben. I'll teach him to trap and tan the hides and he can make himself a little money. I used to love to trap when I was a kid."

Abby looked at him with raised eyebrows.

"Yeah. I know I said I didn't do anything for fun, but I started thinking about it and I realized I did enjoy trapping, although it was primarily a way to earn some spending money, since my father was such a skinflint."

"And you think Ben will like it?"

"I think Ben likes anything outside—even milking that ornery goat."

"Okay. Hunting and trapping." Abby sighed. What next?

Caleb placed his hands on his hips. "What did you say you did with my pie?"

Abby blushed. "I'm sorry. I ate it."

The Thanksgiving meal was far different from those she'd shared with her friends and William, but it was enjoyable just the same. Abby had managed to get Betsy fed before the men came in, and thankfully she had fallen asleep. Laura's chair sat next to Abby's so that she could dole out spoons full of potatoes and fists full of green beans as the meal progressed.

Ben gave thanks for the meal, while Frank and Leo sat with bowed heads, their eagerness to get at the food almost palpable. The older men ate with gusto, and though their manners left much to be desired, their lavish compliments on Abby's culinary skills far outweighed her dismay. Still she barely suppressed a shudder when Frank reached out with his fork to stab another slice of turkey and Leo gave a loud belch after the meal. When she sneaked a glance at Caleb she saw amusement in his eyes. She also knew somehow that he would deal with the situation after the meal.

One step at a time, she thought. At least the two men were entertaining. Frank regaled her with tales from Caleb and Gabe's youth, though Abby saw the darkness gathering on her husband's face whenever his brother's name was mentioned.

As had been a practice in the past, Abby asked that everyone at the table tell one thing for which they were thankful.

Ben started. "I'm thankful for killing a turkey and for my new traps."

Abby smiled. "Leo?" she urged.

"I'm thankful for this here fine food. It was truly delicious, Missus Gentry."

"Thank you, Leo," Abby said, knowing the praise came from his heart. "Frank."

The older man sat there a moment, a thoughtful expression on his face. "I'm thankful that you've come here, Mrs. Gentry. For the first time in many a year—maybe since Miz Libby left—this old farm has a good feeling about it."

Abby wondered if she could speak for the tears she felt tightening her throat. "Thank you, Frank. That's very sweet." Blinking hard, Abby's gaze moved to the next person, who happened to be Laura. "Laura, love, what are you thankful for?" Abby asked.

The baby, who had been chattering throughout the meal, and periodically trying to tempt Caleb with various squished food, smiled broadly, held out a handful of sweet potato and said as if she understood the question perfectly, "Dada."

Everyone at the table laughed, including Caleb. Sensing she was the center of everyone's attention, Laura's grin widened, and she smacked both hands down into the food smeared on her tray. "Dada," she chortled again, as if to prolong her moment of recognition.

Caleb was next. "I'm thankful for Laura, of course," he said with a quick grin, "and for everyone else here at the table. Leo, you and Frank make my workload lighter, and Abby, you and the children have indeed made this house feel like home."

Abby swallowed and blinked hard and fast to hold back the incipient tears.

"Mom, it's your turn," Ben prompted. "What are you thankful for?"

Knowing she was the focus of everyone's attention, Abby stared at her plate and tried to gather her thoughts. She was thankful for so much she hardly knew where to begin. Finally, she said just that.

"But to be more specific," she continued, looking at each of them, "I'm thankful that God brought me here when I was at such a low point in my life, and I'm thankful for each and every one of you."

Her gaze, filled with the love she could not speak aloud, rested on Caleb. "To second Laura, I'm thankful for Caleb. I'm very blessed."

Chapter Ten

The cold two weeks following Thanksgiving raced by in a tumble of windswept leaves and dreary days of rain and fog. Considering the year had started out with such tragedy, it promised to end on a positive note. As usual, Caleb was unfailingly polite and helpful, but it seemed that he smiled more, and there was a relaxed, almost contented air about him that had not been present when she'd first come to his aid.

With things going fairly well between Abby and Caleb, and a bit fearful the lingering grief over William's and Emily's deaths would cast a pall over the day, especially for Ben, Abby had decided to change tactics and ask both the Stones and the Emersons to Christmas dinner, reasoning that Daniel's presence might make the day easier for Ben and that Bart and Mary might like spending the day with their baby granddaughter. At the very least, company might provide at least some distraction from everyone's grief.

Except for the day she and Caleb had gone to fetch her things from her old house, Abby had not been away from the house since she'd come to the Gentry farm. She longed for an afternoon free from the demands of children to be by herself and do some Christmas shopping, since for the first time she could remember, she had money enough to buy gifts without feeling guilty, thanks to Caleb's generous household allowance. The problem was that she wasn't certain how a shopping expedition could be accomplished short of leaving the children in Caleb's care for an afternoon. He would balk, she knew, but the weather had been too miserable to get the girls out, which left no choice but to ask him.

She waited until all the children were down for the night before she broached the subject.

"I'd like to ask a favor," she said.

"If I can, certainly," he replied, but there was a wary expression in his eyes.

"Christmas will be here before we know it," she said. "If it's all right with you, I'd like to have both the Stones and the Emersons for dinner. Company might make the day less difficult for us all, and with Danny here, Ben's day might go easier."

"That sounds like a good idea," Caleb agreed. "I'll ask them the next time I'm in town."

Abby laced her fingers together. "I wanted to talk to you about that, too."

He hiked one dark eyebrow in question.

"Except to get the last of our things from the farm, I haven't been anywhere since Betsy was born." She didn't miss the stricken look on his face, as if he'd never realized that fact before.

"I'm sorry. I never thought— I mean…"

"I didn't mention it to make you feel guilty, Caleb. It's no one's fault, but I was wondering if you would mind watching the children one afternoon so that I can buy a few gifts. It's next to impossible to browse with three little ones—not to mention the surprise element. And the babies don't really need to be out in this damp cold."

"You want me to watch them? Here? Alone?" There was no mistaking the panic in his voice.

"It would only be for a few hours."

"But how will I handle the girls?"

"Laura drinks from a cup and can eat almost anything soft. I'll feed Betsy before I go, and if she begins to fret, you can give her some warm cow's milk in the bottle Mary brought. As you said, we're a family. What if something happened to me?"

All the color drained from his face. "Nothing's going to happen to you!" He bit out the words with chilling intensity, as if by doing so he could actually prevent it from happening.

Abby understood that the burst of anger stemmed from his fear that history would repeat itself with her. "I'm sure you're right, but nevertheless, you'll never learn how to deal with them all if you don't start somewhere," she told him, her voice patient, but firm.

"What if something happens to one of them while you're gone?"

"Nothing will happen."

He swallowed hard. "How can you be sure?"

"Do you want me to yell it like you did?" she asked with a ghost of a smile. "Just to make sure?"

He offered her a sheepish half smile. "I'm being foolish, aren't I?"

"Just a bit."

He blew out a deep breath. "I'm afraid I'll do something wrong and hurt one of them…or something."

"Don't you think that I'm afraid that something will happen every day?" Abby asked in a gentle voice. "Just because I care for them day after day does not mean I don't do things that are wrong, and even potentially harmful."

"But you'd never hurt one of them," he argued.

"Neither would you."

"All right. All right." The expression of panic in his eyes matched the shaky tone of his voice. "Only for a few hours. And it may as well be tomorrow, so we can get it over with."

"I'll leave as soon as we have an early lunch and be back by dark," she promised.

"I want to go!" Ben cried when he found out she was going to town.

"Not this time, Ben. I'm going to buy Christmas gifts, and I can't buy yours if you're along."

"But Caleb doesn't know what to do if the babies start crying."

"You can help him. You're very good with them both."

Knowing he was fighting a losing battle, Ben sighed. "Me and Caleb can't stand too much of that squalling. It gets on our nerves."

"Caleb and I," Abby corrected, trying her best to suppress a smile. She leaned down. "Guess what?" she whispered conspiratorially. "It gets on my nerves, too, sometimes."

"Really?"

"Really."

"It will be fine, Ben," she said, pressing a kiss to the tip of his nose. "I promise."

After the noon meal, Caleb hitched up the buggy and helped Abby climb in, and after giving last-minute instructions on what to do, she headed toward town.

Caleb watched her go with a feeling of doom closing in on him. He knew she was right, but how would he survive the next few hours with three demanding children when he had no clue what he was doing?

Thankfully, once Laura's belly was full, the heat from the fireplace soon made her eyelids droop, and she fell asleep in the pen contraption.

Caleb decided to try his luck at rocking Betsy to sleep while Ben got out his train and stacked some wooden blocks in it for freight.

Abby's quest for gifts started Caleb thinking about Christmas presents of his own. Though he'd picked up a trinket for Emily each year, there had been no thought put into it since Mary always told him what Emily wanted. He had no clue what Abby might like, and he'd never bought anything for a child before. A fresh dousing of reality rushed through him. There was more to this husband and parenting thing than he'd ever imagined—if you wanted to do it right.

That realization made him feeling a little sorry for himself. Laura slept in the pen William built and Ben was playing with the train his father had crafted. As Caleb had told Abby, he was no good with woodworking. He couldn't make a rocking horse for Laura or Betsy, or fashion a dollhouse when they grew older.

Wearing a brooding expression, he was watching Ben stack the blocks in the train cars when he recalled the day he'd "borrowed" his chessmen to haul around. Sudden inspiration struck. Toy soldiers! He could buy Ben some toy soldiers to play with. And maybe a book about trapping and tanning hides. Betsy was so little that a dress from the mercantile would suffice, and Laura would likely be tickled with a rag doll of some sort. Surely Mary would have something in stock for everyone.

But what about Abby? Other than books, he didn't know what she liked. Did she knit? Crochet? What? All he'd seen her do since she'd lived under his roof was cook and clean and wash clothes and take care of little ones.

A now-familiar rush of guilt swept through him. As much as it galled him to admit it, Abby was the one doing most of the giving around the Gentry household. He hadn't meant it to be that way, but it was, which just proved that he was no better at the husband thing than he was the father thing.

She needed something special, something just for her—but what? He had no idea what kind of clothes she liked, and had no one to ask. He doubted Mary knew anything about her likes and dislikes. Maybe Rachel...

Suddenly, he remembered her wistfully mention how nice it would be to have a slipper-shaped bath-tub to relax in after a long day. Though he already owned the biggest oval-shaped trough the mercantile carried, he knew first hand that it was not long enough to stretch out in. Maybe she'd like a new tub. He thought he'd seen one at the mercantile a while back. Maybe he'd run the idea past Mary the next time he went to town.

Feeling pleased with himself, he looked down at the baby sleeping in his arms. Moving slowly, to keep from waking her, he rose and put her in her cradle, covering her with a small colorful quilt. Feeling sleepy himself, he settled into a corner of the sofa and stared at the mesmerizing dance of the flames. Betsy gave a soft snuffle, and the muffled whistling wind sent some lingering leaves clattering against the house. The crackling, hissing and pop of the burning logs sent his eyelids downward....

The sound of a log falling jerked him to wake-fulness with an undignified snort. Straightening, Caleb wiped a hand over his face and stole a glance at the babies, who still slept soundly. Ben sat staring at him, amusement in the blue eyes so like his mother's.

"How long did I sleep?" he asked.

"Not long."

"Bored?"

Ben nodded.

Caleb recalled Abby telling him you had to look for the fun times, that they were where you least expected them. After a moment's thought, he disappeared into the bedroom and began rummaging around in the bureau drawers, soon finding what he was looking for.

"Come here, Ben," Caleb said, entering the parlor. Curious, Ben crossed to him. "These were Emily's," Caleb said, holding out a drawing tablet and a box of pastel crayons.

He walked over and took an autumn landscape with mountains and a lake from the wall. Done in an impressionistic style, there was little detail in the picture, and he thought Ben might be able to make a credible replica of the piece.

"I thought you might like to try your hand at drawing. Look at this and see if you can copy it."

"Drawing's for girls," Ben said with typical masculine disdain.

"Actually, most of the famous artists are men," Caleb said, searching his mind for some other activity the boy might enjoy. "But if you don't want to try, how about a game of chess?"

"I don't know how to play chess."

Well, it wasn't a no, Caleb thought. "Then it's

high time you learned. Why don't I make us a cup of hot chocolate, and I'll teach you?"

"You don't know how to make hot chocolate."

"Sure I do," he said with a confidence he was far from feeling. "Your mom told me how."

"Abby! What are you doing in town?" Mary Emerson asked when Abby stepped through the door of the mercantile.

"I escaped for the afternoon," Abby said, unwinding the woolen scarf from around her neck and tugging off her gloves. The warmth from the potbelly stove in the center of the room felt wonderful against her chilled face.

"Where are the children?"

"Would you believe Caleb is watching them?"

Mary's eyes widened and she burst out laughing. "Caleb? All of them?"

Abby's smile could only be described as mischievous. "All of them. I told him he needed to learn to take care of them and that I needed to get away for a few hours to do some Christmas shopping. I left him instructions on what to do with Laura and Betsy, and here I am."

"Will wonders never cease," Mary said, her eyes still glittering with mirth. She came around the counter and gave Abby a hug. "It's so good to see you. How is Betsy?"

"Growing like a weed," Abby said, shrugging out of her coat.

"We've been meaning to drive out, but the

weather has been so nasty, and it's almost dark by the time we close, that we just haven't made it. How are things with you and Caleb?"

"All of us still walk around on eggshells from time to time, but we're doing well enough, I think."

"Be patient, Abby," Mary told her. "Things will work out."

"I pray you're right."

Abby extended the invitation for Christmas dinner and was assured that, like the Stones, the Emersons would be there "with bells on." She knew she was blessed to have the Emersons' support and wondered if Bart and Mary would be so generous with their approval if they suspected that Abby had fallen love with their son-in-law, even though they knew Caleb and Emily had not loved each other.

Abby pushed away the troubling thought and wandered through the store, taking time to look at everything that caught her interest. Mary pointed out some soft yarn hats with earflaps and mittens to match, and Abby bought one each for Laura and Betsy. She also bought them each a rag doll—Laura's with blond braids, Betsy's with brown. It was a foolish purchase, since it would be spring before Betsy could even hold hers, but it still gave Abby a great deal of pleasure. She bought Ben a pair of new boots, a game of checkers and a book about horses.

Choosing a gift for Caleb was harder. She knew so little about him, and he could buy himself whatever he wanted—not that he did. In the end, she chose three dime novels, a soft flannel shirt and a pocket knife with a scrimshaw handle. She splurged on oranges and chocolate and licorice for Ben's stocking.

She was almost finished with her shopping when Mary carried a small wooden crate from the storeroom. "I want you to have this," she said, placing it on the counter.

"What is it?"

"It's a china nativity set Emily bought while she was away at school. She always put it on the mantel at Christmas. I brought it here because I thought it might make me feel closer to her at this time of year, but when I took it out, I only felt sad. I'll understand if you feel uncomfortable using it, but please take it. It should be Betsy's one day."

"Of course I'll take it," Abby said. "And I'm sure I'll use it." She smiled gently at the woman who had the power to make her life miserable, and had instead been one of her most loyal champions. "And you can be sure that Betsy will be told about it when she's old enough."

"Thank you, Abby," Mary said, enfolding her in a close embrace. "You're a blessing."

Abby hugged her back. "So are you."

After telling Mary she would load her parcels later, Abby bade the older woman goodbye and picked her way across the still-muddy street to the café, where she was meeting Rachel.

"Did you get your shopping done?" Rachel asked as they took off their coats and scarves and hung them on the pegs near the door.

"I did, and it was nice not having to worry about how much money I was spending."

"I know," Rachel said. "Not everyone in town is so fortunate."

Ellie, tall, blond and curvaceous, waved them to a table, took their order and soon set slices of caramel apple pie and mugs of fragrant coffee in front of them. To Abby, her friend looked more like she belonged in the pages of *Godey's Lady's Book* than she did running a small-town café.

"Who's having a hard time?" Ellie asked, joining them at the table.

"The Thomersons," Rachel said. The expression on her face looked as if she'd taken a bite of a green persimmon. "Elton got into the hooch last night and knocked Meg around again. Our new sheriff put him in jail for a few days to let him think about it, but he won't be there long—unfortunately."

"How badly did he hurt her?" Abby asked.

"He broke her arm, so she won't be taking in any laundry for a while. Her parents can help with the kids, but he'll tell her he's sorry and she'll go back to him, and it will be the same thing a few weeks or months from now."

"What can we do?" Abby asked.

"Not much," Rachel said with a sigh. "The truth of the matter is that nothing will change until she decides she's had enough and leaves him."

Blowing out a frustrated breath, Rachel forced a smile, picked up her fork and said with forced gaiety, "Well, enough of that! I came here to enjoy some time with my friends."

Abby savored every bite of Ellie's luscious pie and the precious time with her friends even more. As she expected it would, the talk turned to her and Caleb.

"So how is Caleb Gentry as a husband?" Ellie asked, her brown eyes sparkling with curiosity. "Brooding? Frightening? What?"

Abby laughed. "Brooding? Yes, sometimes. Frightening, never. Well," she amended, "not after I lost my temper that first time."

"You lost your temper with Caleb Gentry?" Ellie breathed, leaning her elbows on the table and leaning forward.

"I did," Abby said. "And lived to tell about it." Seeing the horrified expression on Ellie's face, she said, "I'm only joking, Ellie. I have lost my temper with him, more than once actually, but he takes it in stride pretty well."

Abby grew thoughtful. "In fact, the last time we argued was before Thanksgiving. He wanted to give Ben a shotgun and take him hunting. As you can imagine, I was furious, and then I looked over and saw him leaning back in his chair with his arms crossed over his chest watching me rave and rant with this sort of…almost a *pleased* smile in his eyes. If it weren't crazy I'd say the wretch was enjoying every minute of it."

"That's strange," Ellie said.

"Our whole marriage is strange," Abby replied,

taking a sip of her coffee. "But it's not bad," she hastened to add. "In fact, on the whole, he's been very good to me and more accommodating than I would have imagined from our first meeting."

She flashed a smile between Rachel and Ellie. "He likes to read, so we talk about that. And I see a lot of changes in him already, and he's solid and dependable..."

Lost in her thoughts, Abby didn't see the look that passed between her friends. "And he's really attractive if you like rugged-looking men."

"Oh, dear!" Ellie said, her eyes wide.

"Oh, dear what?"

"You're falling for him."

Horrified that her feelings were so obvious, Abby flashed a flustered look from Ellie to Rachel, who was regarding her with a considering expression.

"Don't be ridiculous!" Abby bristled. She made her tone cool and impersonal. "I think Caleb is a good man, but most people don't realize it because he'd not very social and because of his father's reputation. He's treated me and my children well, that's all."

Wearing a delighted smile, Ellie got to her feet and swept up the two mugs for a refill. "Pull the other one, honey," she said, tossing a teasing smile over her shoulder. "It's got bells on it."

Thirty minutes later, Abby gave Rachel some money to help out Meg Thomerson, and said good-bye to her friends. It was almost dark when Abby pulled the buggy into the front yard. Happy at having the afternoon to herself, and filled with the joy of the season, she'd stopped on the way home and plucked an armful of pine and holly branches to make a wreath for the front door. It was only when she saw the lights of the house in the distance and allowed herself to contemplate the disaster that might be awaiting her that her happiness started to dissipate.

Laden with packages, she was halfway up the front steps when she heard what sounded like a crow of laughter from Caleb. Surprised, a bit wary, she stopped in her tracks. What on earth?

Balancing her parcels, she turned the doorknob and stepped inside, stunned at the scene before her. Caleb and Ben were seated at the game table, the chess set in front of them. Laura sat in the crook of Caleb's arm, gnawing on a crust of stale bread. The cradle sat near Caleb's elbow, and she watched as he gave it a gentle push.

Hearing the door open, Ben cried, "Hey, Caleb! Mom's home."

Abby's gaze met her husband's. He looked exhausted but oddly content and achingly appealing. His hair looked as if he'd run his hand through it several times—a gesture that was becoming endearingly familiar. A streak of some indeterminate substance that was most likely wet, mushy bread was smeared across his cheek. His end-of-day beard gave him a beguiling but dangerous look that set Abby's heart to racing. She felt her heart swell with love.

For the first time since she'd stepped into the Gentry house with Rachel, it felt like home.

The weeks leading to Christmas were the most pleasant Abby had experienced in years. With her help, Caleb had fashioned the pine boughs into a wreath and wired pine cones to it. She'd cut strips from one of his seen-better-days red flannel shirts and sewn the strips together, fashioning a bow at the bottom for a splash of color. When they'd finished, he'd smiled at her, a smile so stunning she'd dared to hope his feelings toward her were changing.

Two days before Christmas, Abby was baking star-shaped sugar cookies when a beaming Ben bounded through the back door. Laura, who was sitting in her chair munching on a cookie, waved her sweet at him and said what sounded very much like "Ben."

"Mama! Come see what we brought you," he shouted.

"Shh," she cautioned, holding a silencing finger to her lips. "You'll wake Betsy."

"Okay," he said in a loud whisper. "But you gotta come see what Caleb and I found."

Drying her hands on her apron, Abby grabbed a shawl and threw it around her shoulders. Then she settled Laura on her hip and wrapped the heavy wool around them both.

The wagon sat near the back porch, and lying in the bed was a cedar tree. Caleb stood near the rear of the wagon, an expression of anticipation on his cold-reddened face. "Ben said you liked to have a tree," he said, almost as if he were asking if he'd done the right thing.

"I love a tree, don't you?"

He lifted his shoulders in a shrug. "I don't know. I don't recall ever having one, though we might have when my mother was still here. It's really nicely shaped," he added.

"It's wonderful. Thank you for going to the trouble."

"It wasn't any trouble. I'll make a stand and Ben and I will put it in the parlor. Where do you want it?"

"Mm, somewhere away from the heat of the fireplace. Maybe in front of the window to the left of the door. I can slide the chair over a bit."

"That's where we'll put it, then."

As it turned out, the tree was much more than just nicely shaped. It was perfect. When the girls were down for the night and the Bible lesson was over, Abby popped popcorn, which both she Ben both insisted that Caleb help string for a garland.

Mumbling that he "didn't sew," Caleb nonetheless took the piece of thread Abby handed him and proceeded to work the popcorn along its length.

"Caleb Gentry, stop that!"

His gaze flew to hers and he spoke around a mouthful of popcorn. "Stop what?"

"Stop eating the popcorn. I've been watching you and Ben both, and you're eating more than you're stringing.

"Doesn't the Bible say something about a man not eating if he doesn't work?"

"Yes."

"Then since I'm working, I thought I'd earned the right to eat," he said his expression one of false sincerity.

"And I think that's what's meant by twisting the scriptures," she told him in a prim tone as she tore more narrow strips from the cast-off shirt to use as bows on the tips of the branches. Neither Caleb nor Ben missed the way she pressed her lips together to keep from smiling, and they both broke out into soft laughter.

Perfectionist that he was, Caleb made certain that the popcorn garland was draped just so, then looked the tree over and announced that it was lacking something.

"A little sparkle would be nice," Abby said after a moment. "Something to catch the lamplight. I have some silver stars William cut from the bottoms of cans, if you don't mind us using them.

"That sounds like just what we need."

Then she remembered the crate Mary had sent. "I don't know if you'll feel comfortable with it, but Mary sent some things that belonged to Emily. A nativity set and some ornaments, I think."

"I don't mind using them. What about you? This is your house to decorate as you will, Abby."

"Thank you, but if it's all the same to you, I'd like to use them. Emily will always be a part of Betsy, and

I think we should do everything we can to give her a sense of who her mother was, don't you?"

Caleb looked a bit taken aback by her unselfish attitude. "Of course. You're right."

When everything was hung on the tree, they all stood back and surveyed their handiwork. "It's beautiful," Abby said.

"The best ever," Ben said, nodding.

"I agree, Ben," Caleb added, a look of almost childlike wonder on his face. It might have been a trick of the light, but Abby thought she saw a suspicious sparkle in his eyes. Once again, her heart ached for the little boy who'd never had a chance to be. She vowed that if he would let her she would try to make up for all the experiences he'd been denied by his mother's leaving and his father's heavy hand.

By Christmas Eve, Caleb felt like a child living in some faraway, make-believe land. The house was redolent with the scents and sounds of the season: pine and cedar, cinnamon and cloves, roasting chestnuts. Abby seemed determined to make this the best Christmas he'd ever experienced, which wouldn't have taken nearly as much work as she insisted on doing. She'd baked all sorts of goodies and placed boughs and berries in every nook and cranny, insisting that they sing carols and other Christmas songs as they worked, including her favorite, "Jolly Old St. Nicholas."

Caleb somewhat recalled the song and joined in

with his pleasing baritone when the words came to mind.

Since he'd never had gingerbread men that he could recall, Abby baked some and gave them raisin eyes. The crispy gents rested on a platter next to crunchy crystal-dusted sugar cookies, waiting to become a bedtime snack along with a cup of hot chocolate.

Before she would let them indulge in the sweet treats, Abby took her Bible, settled Laura in her lap and began to read the story of Jesus's birth. Caleb had given up retiring to his office weeks ago, and as he did every night, he listened as she answered Ben's questions with enviable patience. When the child's curiosity was satisfied, they bowed their heads and Abby began to pray.

"Father in Heaven, we come to You with grateful hearts. We are so blessed, not only this holiday season but every day. We're thankful for the beautiful world You made and for creating us with all of our senses so that we can enjoy its riches. We ask for Your continued blessings as we end one year and move into another. May the coming days and weeks be happy and peaceful. I'm particularly thankful, Father, for all You have given me. A wonderful home, three precious children to love and a husband who has been a blessing in so many ways…"

For a second, Caleb could have sworn that his heart stopped. He never heard her end the prayer, but when she looked up at him, the warmth of her smile felt like a benediction. Without waiting for him to respond, she got to her feet and held Laura out for him to take while she went to get the pot of chocolate that had been warming on the back of the stove.

When the cookies had been passed out and their hands were wrapped around steaming mugs of cocoa, they sang Christmas carols until their voices grew hoarse. Then, just before sending Ben off to bed, she read *A Visit From St. Nicholas*. By that time, Ben's eyes were growing heavy and he was ready to go to bed and sleep so Santa could come.

Caleb followed Abby into Ben's room to tuck him in, something he'd started doing a few days before. Ben seemed to like it, and it was an easy enough thing to do. Caleb stood watching Abby brush a tender kiss to her son's forehead. He was torn between an almost overwhelming feeling of humbleness that she was actually thankful for him and wishing he could share in the love and closeness she felt for her family. What would it be like to have that every day for the rest of his life?

Wonderful.

It would be the most perfect life he could imagine, one he did not dare to hope was within his grasp. How could he ever fit into Abby's perfect world where people worked together and sang while they worked…where they made things and did things for one another just because they got joy from doing so?

Though the night was as close to perfect as Caleb ever hoped to experience, he went to bed certain he had never felt more alone in his life.

Chapter Eleven

Christmas morning dawned cold and windy. With a sigh, Caleb padded out of his room in sock feet, lit the lamp and began to stoke the fire, something he did throughout the night so the house would be warm when Abby and the children got up. Going to the kitchen, he did the same, and then filled the coffeepot, set it back on the stove and returned to the parlor and lit another lamp.

A quick glance at the mantel clock told him it was more than an hour until dawn. Since he didn't recall having a traditional Christmas, he was uncertain whether or not he should wake everyone or wait for them to get up on their own. He admitted to feeling eager—and anxious—to see how his gifts were received.

Before he could make a decision, he heard Ben's bedroom door open and saw a tousled blond head poke out. "Is it time?" he asked, his sleep-roughened voice holding suppressed excitement.

Caleb shrugged. "I don't know. Shouldn't your mother be up first?"

"She's up," Abby said, stepping into the room and covering a wide yawn. Closing the bedroom door behind her so they wouldn't wake the babies, she crossed over to warm her hands at the fireplace. A plaid robe of red wool covered her long flannel gown and was belted around her slim waist. A long blond braid hung over her shoulder. Thick wool socks covered her feet.

She cast Caleb a hopeful look. "I don't suppose the coffee is ready yet." It was more statement than question.

"I don't think so, but I did start it."

Her eyes closed in appreciation and a soft smile curved her lips. "You're a good man, Caleb Gentry."

The heartfelt compliment filled him with inexplicable pleasure.

"Can we open our gifts now, Mama?"

Abby gave in with a sigh. "I suppose so, but we'll take turns just as we always have." She looked at Caleb and explained. "We'll each open one gift in turn. That way we can not only enjoy our gifts but take pleasure in watching everyone else." She cast Caleb a wry look. "Otherwise, Christmas would be over in about two minutes." Turning her attention to Ben, she reminded, "Stockings first."

Brought up as he had been, Caleb knew nothing about building anticipation.

Ben passed out the stockings. When he handed Caleb one of his wool socks, he shot Abby a surprised look. Her answer was a gentle smile. Caleb dumped the stocking's contents, wondering what unexpected delights it might hold. He vaguely remembered having a stocking when he was very small, no doubt before his mother left. This year, Santa had filled his sock with an orange, an apple, a tangerine, a handful of exotic-looking nuts, licorice, a new shaving brush, a box of .22 bullets, a stick of taffy and the biggest peppermint stick he'd ever seen.

He looked up to thank Abby and caught the excitement on Ben's face when he shoved his arm into his sock up to the elbow and pulled a yo-yo. Once Ben had looked over those goodies, Abby let him choose another gift to unwrap. Ben chose a small leather bag.

"Marbles!" he cried. "Wow!"

"Those are from Caleb," Abby told him. "Just be careful that you don't leave any lying around for the little ones to put in their mouths," Abby cautioned. "They might choke."

"I won't," Ben promised.

"Abby, you go next," Caleb said. "You'll have to go into the kitchen to see one of your presents."

Her blue eyes narrowed in mock consternation, but Caleb didn't miss the curiosity in their depths. "What have you done, Caleb Gentry?"

"Go look in the kitchen. Take the lamp."

Rising, Abby grabbed the lamp and gave him a sidelong look in passing. Ben, wearing a conspiratorial smile since he was in on the whole thing, was close on her heels.

Her squeal of pleasure just seconds after she entered the kitchen said without words that she was thrilled with her new slipper tub and a smile of satisfaction curved Caleb's mouth. Abby came back to the parlor, almost in a run, pleasure shining in her eyes. "I love it! I can stretch out, but oh, Caleb you shouldn't have."

"Why not?"

"It's too much."

"Not if you let us all use it."

"Oh. I see," she told him with a knowing nod. "It's my gift, but I have to share."

"Something like that. You don't have to share the French gardenia bath salts and hand cream I left in the bottom, though." He winked at Ben. "I don't think Ben and I would smell too manly if we used that."

"Deal," Abby said. "Thank you very much. I'm sure that I—we—will enjoy it very much. Now you open one."

The request took Caleb aback. The truth was that he didn't recall ever receiving a present from anyone before. He felt his throat tighten, and a strange ache squeezed his heart. He heard the quaver in his voice when he said, "You weren't supposed to get me anything."

"Why? You bought all of us gifts, didn't you?"

"Yes, but—"

"No buts," she said holding up a silencing finger.

Admittedly curious as to what the package might hold, he pushed the tissue paper aside to reveal Allan Pinkerton's latest publication. "Dime novels! Three of them."

"I thought books were a pretty safe bet, and since I haven't read any of them, I thought they'd be perfect."

"Oh," he said, taking care to keep his expression neutral. "I see how this works. You give me the present," he parodied, "but I have to share."

Abby looked shocked for an instant, and then broke into a giggle. "Touché. I do hope you'll enjoy them."

"I know I—we—will," he deadpanned.

The next half hour was one of the most enjoyable times Caleb ever recalled. He loved seeing the happiness on Ben's and Abby's faces as they opened the gifts he'd selected in such high hopes of pleasing them. Ben was thrilled with his boots, book and checkers game Abby bought him, but when he opened the larger package from Caleb, he gasped in amazement. Exquisitely detailed tin soldiers of the North and the South, including Grant and Lee astride their horses. He lifted a glowing gaze to Caleb, speechless for once.

"You can haul them in your train," he said, "since you're now using the chessmen for their intended purpose."

"They're really, really nice, Caleb. Thank you."

Caleb was as humbled by Ben's gratitude as he was the thought that had gone into the gifts his new family had chosen for him, especially since they were his first.

Besides her tub, Abby unwrapped a new Sunday dress of sky-blue trimmed with a white collar and cuffs that Caleb knew would be a perfect match for her eyes, and an ivory-handled mirror, comb and brush set. There was an everyday skirt and blouse from "Ben, Laura and Betsy." Caleb had let Ben look over everything he'd bought and pick which outfit he wanted to give his mother from him and his sisters.

When he opened the shirt given to him by "the children," Abby smiled. "It seemed a fair trade since I ripped up one of yours to use for bows."

"I like it a lot, Ben. It looks very warm. Thank you."

When he opened the knife and saw the intricate scrimshaw working on the handle, he said, "You've done too much."

"No," she told him, her blue eyes dark with sincerity. "It really isn't enough considering all you've done for me, and besides, I could only do it because of your generosity."

Caleb cleared his throat, and uneasy with the unexpected praise, asked Ben if he was ready for breakfast yet.

Later, wearing her new dress with her mother's brooch pinned at her throat, Abby played hostess for the first time as Mrs. Caleb Gentry. Since Caleb's shirt was too short in the sleeves, he said he'd send it back with Mary and Bart and pick up another the next time he went to Wolf Creek.

Frank had accepted an invitation to eat with a family in town, and Leo was having Christmas dinner with the Widow Lambert. Caught up in her own feelings for Caleb, Abby wondered if there might be a romance brewing between the middle-aged couple.

The Emersons and Stones arrived in plenty of time for Rachel to help with the meal, while Mary kept the girls entertained. The boys played with their new toys, and Edward and Caleb discussed the almanac's predictions for the winter and whether or not the summer would be as mild as the previous one.

The Christmas meal was filled with laughter and stories of past Christmases, though Abby noticed that Caleb was more of an observer than a participant in that particular venture. A couple of times she'd caught an expression that could only be described as bewilderment in his eyes. The afternoon was spent playing chess and checkers, and once the babies were put down for afternoon naps, the three women sat at the kitchen table and had a "hen party."

Finally, in midafternoon, Edward declared he was ready for a nap, and the gathering broke up. As Abby straightened the kitchen and put the worn-out children down for naps, Caleb and Ben changed out of their holiday clothes and went to set the traps Caleb had found.

Propped against the corner of the sofa with one of Caleb's new books, and covered with an afghan, Abby let her mind drift back to past holidays with William. She thought of them lovingly, a bit longingly and with more than a hint of sorrow. Then she tucked the bittersweet memories away until the next year. Those days were gone. She had a new husband now, a new family, and so far, though they had miles to go, things were better than she had dared to hope.

To Abby, the week following Christmas was always a bit of a letdown after the building anticipation that accompanied the holiday. Nevertheless, the day after Christmas they got back to their routine. She tried to get Ben involved with learning the state capitals, but her son, in a dejected mood of his own, was being uncooperative and whiny about the slightest thing. Though he was still enthralled by his gifts, he was tired of being inside. Mostly he wanted Caleb to take him to check the traps they'd set after their company left the day before.

Abby felt in limbo herself, as if the old year was gasping out its last dying breath, and hope, in the guise of a new year, was not yet born. She felt unsettled and just a bit depressed for no reason she could put her finger on. The knock at the door promised respite from her feelings, as it must have Ben, who jumped up from his chair and raced to the window.

"It's Mrs. VanSickle, Mama," he said, wrinkling his nose in disgust. Though Abby was always careful not to talk about people in front of him, he was a smart child who had an uncanny ability to pick up on nuances of people's character.

Abby felt her heart sink and her stomach tightened with anxiety. Why on earth had Sarah Van-Sickle come to call? What new gossip could she possibly have that she felt might interest Abby? For a heartbeat, she considered not answering the summons, but knowing Sarah, she would start yelling for entrance next.

With dread in her heart and a false smile of welcome on her lips, Abby opened the door to the woman whose personal goal seemed to be causing misery for others.

The fiftysomething woman was dressed in an eggplant-hued morning gown trimmed with black velvet. A bulky overcoat and the stylish shelf bustle of her dress did nothing for her portly figure. Jet earrings dangled at her ears, and a jaunty hat of black velvet with two pheasant feathers and a veil sat atop a jumble of sausage-like curls, a style that would have been far more appropriate for a younger woman.

Her eyes, so dark they looked as black as the dress's trim, snapped with some sort of energy that seemed to radiate from her in waves. Struck by the notion that nothing good could possibly come from this visit, Abby tried to brace herself for whatever was to transpire.

"Aren't you going to ask me in?" Sarah said, her voice as crisp as the winter air.

"Certainly," Abby said, her manners returning along with a semblance of composure. "Please, come in."

Huffing out her displeasure, Sarah stepped inside and began to shrug out of her coat, while Abby instructed Ben to get his own jacket and go outside to help Caleb with whatever he was doing.

After glancing around the room with an air of disdain, Sarah hung her coat on the oak and brass hall tree next to the door and began pulling off her soft kid gloves, which she tucked into the reticule hanging from her wrist.

"Please sit down," Abby said, gesturing toward the sofa.

Sarah sat, smoothed her dress over her knees and stared at Abby, who perched on the edge of a wing-back chair, facing her unwanted guest.

"I must say, you're very looking well. Marriage seems to agree with you."

Abby ignored the implications of her statement and offered a halfhearted smile. "Yes, well, it has been something of an adjustment for us all, but we're doing well." Not for all the tea in China would Abby let the detestable woman know that her forced marriage was anything other than perfect.

"What do you think William would say to your being widowed less than a year before taking a new husband?" Sarah asked with a scornful lift of her dark eyebrows.

Lacing her fingers together in her lap, Abby struggled to rein in her temper and choose her words with care. "I think he would understand that sometimes we are required to do things we would rather not, for the sake of the better good."

Her meaning could not have been clearer, yet Sarah didn't have the grace to even blush. Abby wondered a bit uncharitably if her guest had brains enough to realize what she'd done. Then, seeing the undeniable glimmer of satisfaction in Sarah's coal-black eyes, Abby realized she knew exactly what she was about.

"I haven't seen you at church in a long while," the busybody said after a moment.

From anyone else Abby might have taken the words as a statement of concern; from Sarah it was an indictment.

"I know," Abby said, striving to make her reply pleasant. "I miss going very much, but with this cold, wet weather setting in so early, it seemed unwise to take the baby out. We plan on getting back when she's a bit older or we get a break in the weather."

"I don't suppose I can see the child? I vow, she's all Mary and Bart can talk about."

"I'm afraid she's asleep. Perhaps another time." Abby, who was barely controlling her irritation, took perverse pleasure in the refusal, as petty as it was.

"Hmm." Sarah tapped an impatient foot. "Aren't you going to offer me any refreshment?" she asked, making Abby's purposeful lapse in protocol sound like the gravest affront to etiquette.

Abby should have known not to twist the lion's tail, but she was so furious over the woman's gall at coming under the pretense of friendship, that all she could think of was getting rid of her. Instead of answering, Abby met the older woman's gaze with a steady one of her own. Her meaning was very clear. "Was there any particular reason you stopped by, Sarah?"

In the blink of her dark eyes, Sarah's veneer of civility vanished. She regarded Abby in a considering manner. "You've heard of Caleb's newest enterprise, I suppose?"

Taken aback by the sudden shift in the conversation, Abby said, "I'm afraid my hands are a bit full with taking care of the children to take much interest in Caleb's business dealings."

"A pity."

"And why is that?"

"If you paid more attention to the kind of man you married, you'd realize that Caleb Gentry is a manipulator just like his father. Surely you're smart enough to know he only married you to get his hands on your farm."

Abby couldn't be more confused, though she did realize two things: Saran VanSickle was indeed a vicious person, and she was taking a great deal of pleasure from whatever bit of information she was about to impart.

"And why would he want my farm, Sarah? It isn't even a good farm. It's nothing but a pile of rocks, actually."

Sarah laughed. "Which is precisely why he wanted it, my dear. Lucas started a gravel business, which Caleb inherited when his father died. Viola Haversham told me last winter that Lucas had his eye on your property, and then within weeks of each other, both he and your husband died. I can only imagine that Caleb was thrilled to snatch up the property by marrying you."

Abby's heart thundered in her chest. Lucas Gentry had been the person William had said was interested in their land! But that had nothing to do with her and Caleb. Certainly not with their marriage. Did it?

"Actually, Sarah, the land has been sold. The papers were signed just over a week ago."

Sarah laughed, an unpleasant sound that held unmistakable satisfaction. "Oh, so he told you he bought it, did he? I do hope you actually saw the bank draft."

Abby's stomach tightened in sudden nausea, even as her mind struggled to digest Sarah's statement. Her meaning could not be clearer. She was saying that Caleb had not sold the land. Saying in effect that he had not even bought the land himself, but had lied about it selling at all. She was telling Abby that he had taken advantage of her self-acknowledged ignorance of business affairs to steal the farm from her.

Ridiculous! Or was it? Could there be any truth to Sarah's claim? The banker's wife would know what was going on, wouldn't she? Isn't that what pillow talk was all about?

Abby's mind whispered that Caleb wouldn't do something like that. He was too principled, and she trusted him. She had to trust him, or her whole world would fall apart…again.

"The farm did sell, but Caleb didn't buy it," she said in a firm voice, while some contrary part of her mind argued that she had no way of knowing whether he had or not since she had given him her power of attorney.

Sarah rearranged her sharp features into feigned regret. "Oh, well, forgive me for even mentioning it, then. I'm sure Vi must have misunderstood, but I'm sure you understand that I only wanted to make certain that you knew what kind of man you've married."

Getting to her feet, Abby crossed to the hall tree, took down Sarah's coat and held it out toward her, her whole body trembling with fury. "And why did I marry him, Sarah?" Abby said, her temper and her voice spiking in spite of her attempts to control them. "If it weren't for you and your need to hurt people, Caleb and I wouldn't be in a marriage we neither one wanted."

"Why I'm sure I just—"

"Not another word, you venomous biddy! Take your coat and get out of here."

Both Abby and Sarah gasped and whirled toward the door leading to the kitchen. The quiet command had come from Caleb, who was striding across the room.

Sarah's face paled, and with a little squeak of fear, she rushed to Abby and jerked the coat from her hands. In her hurry to get away from the man bearing down on her like an avenging angel, she didn't even bother putting it on, but grabbed the doorknob and hauled open the door.

"Sarah."

Caleb's voice was deceptively quiet.

She turned, her eyes wide with alarm.

"I'm sure you'll understand if I tell you that I never want to see you on this place again. And be assured that if I ever hear of you saying anything hurtful about me or my wife, I will go to your husband and see to it that he knows what kind of person he's married to. Assuming there's a remote possibility he has any doubts."

Without granting him an answer, Sarah rushed through the open door and slammed it behind her. The sound of her shoes clattering down the steps was loud in the stillness of the room.

Caleb and Abby stared at each other across the expanse of the room, across a sea of uncertainty and doubt. Caleb felt his whole world crumbling for the second time, but all Abby saw in his eyes was a wary stiffness.

"Hey, Caleb!" Ben came running into the room by way of the kitchen. "Are you ready to go?"

Caleb's gaze never left Abby's. "Not now, Ben."

"But you said we could—"

"Not now, Ben!" Caleb said in a tone so harsh that Ben visibly flinched.

From the corner of her eye, Abby saw her son turn and run from the room, but her gaze never faltered from her husband's.

"It's true, isn't it?"

Caleb's mouth twisted into a humorless smile. "What? That I married you to get your land? I think you know why we entered this marriage we neither one want to be in."

Hearing him repeat almost verbatim the words she'd spoken to Sarah, sent a searing pain through Abby's heart. It was clear that they'd wounded Caleb, too. While it was true that she hadn't wanted the marriage, it was also true that now she did. Very much.

"Was your father interested in the farm back before William died?" she asked, a wary challenge in her voice.

"Yes, though I didn't know anything about it until I talked to Nate about selling it for you. He told me that my father was considering offering for the place and suggested I do just what Sarah said. I was marrying you, so why not just consider it mine once we tied the knot? I told him I couldn't do that. I wouldn't." Breaking eye contact, he strode to the fireplace and stood staring at the flames.

"So you really did sell it," she said, moving to stand behind him.

He scraped a hand through his tousled hair. "Yes."

"To whom'?" she demanded, wanting, no, *needing* to know the truth, to prove Sarah a liar.

Placing a booted foot on the hearth, he rested his forearm on the mantel and shot her an insolent look over his shoulder. "Me. All the gravel on it makes it worth a great deal of money, and I am in the gravel business." His tone was mocking, bitter.

"I see."

He whirled suddenly. "Do you?"

"I see that you kept something very important from me," she cried. "Something that affects my children's future."

He actually jerked his head back as if she'd struck him. She saw his eyes go from silver to stormy gray as distress and uncertainty mutated to cold anger. Too late, she realized she'd made an unforgivable lapse in judgment.

In a voice as frigid as the winter day, he said, "Let me be very clear, madam. Your children's future is well provided for. I did not marry you for your farm. We both know the reasons we married. I said I would find a buyer for you, and I did. I told you that I would set aside the money for your children's future. I did."

Abby had never seen him so angry. She hardly knew the man looking at her with such harsh arrogance. She sucked in a breath, realizing with a dreadful certainty that she was losing him—probably had lost him—and all because for a few tormented minutes, she had bought into Sarah Van-Sickle's lies.

"Why didn't you tell me you were the buyer?" she asked pleadingly, wanting to understand, hoping to appease his anger. "Why didn't you at least discuss it with me?"

Caleb threw back his head and stared at the ceiling for a moment before pinning her with a contemptuous look. "Ah, yes, you are an intelligent woman who is accustomed to having her say, therefore I should have talked it over with you. After all, that's what you and William would have done."

"Yes, we—"

"I am *not* William Carter, Abby," he told her with a quietness that was far more devastating than yelling would be. "I am not used to asking for anyone's opinion when I enter a business arrangement. I'm certainly not used to consulting my wife!"

No, he was not William, and though Caleb had done remarkably well adapting to their marriage, he would never be like the easygoing William—in any way. Caleb was a proud, difficult man whose integrity she had cast doubt on. She wasn't sure he could ever forgive her for that. Her remorseful, aching heart broke a bit more.

"Couldn't you have at least *told* me?" she asked, her voice a soft tremble.

"I suppose I could have," he said, his tone softer now, too, "but I didn't because you're going at a dead run from daylight until dark, and because you told me you had no understanding of such matters. When you gave me your power of attorney, I assumed you trusted me. I didn't think it mattered who bought the farm, as long as I kept my end of the bargain."

Though Sarah's poison might have caused Abby to question Caleb for a brief moment, she knew beyond doubt he was telling the truth. He would never lie to her about something like this. He would never lie about anything. She felt the hot scald of threatening tears and wondered if he could ever forgive her.

"If there is any question in your mind about my cheating you," he added, "rest assured, I did not. I paid you far above market value. If you don't believe me, feel free to ask Nate."

"I don't need to ask Nate," she whispered brokenly. "I do believe you."

He didn't bother to answer. Turning, he left her standing beside the fireplace, her heart and her hopes for the future shattered like the china figurine of his mother's. All by one moment's carelessness.

Chapter Twelve

Abby hadn't wept this deeply since the first weeks following William's death, but she did after Caleb left her alone in the parlor with nothing but the ticking clock for company. Drawing a shuddering breath, she berated herself for her suspicions. How could she have doubted him even for even a second when he had proved over and over that he was honorable?

He had come so far the past few weeks in the way he related to all of them. There were moments she'd felt they were starting to build something that held the potential for a lifetime of love. Now she had ruined everything by questioning his integrity. He'd been angry when he left. Furious. Fresh tears streamed down her cheeks. Could he ever forgive her? Would he?

Caleb stormed out of the house, his long strides eating up the distance to the barn while despair gnawed at his heart and sickness clawed at his stomach. He scraped back his hair with both hands and gave a throaty snarl of fury.

He should have known better than to let any woman work her way beneath his guard and his skin! Hadn't his mother's desertion taught him that much? He must have been a fool to feel guilty about his growing feelings for Abby, when it was clear now that nothing he'd done or tried to do to make things better between them had made a nickel's worth of difference. In retrospect, there was a lot to be said for loveless marriages, like the one he had shared with Emily.

The thought had no sooner entered his mind than he knew he was lying to himself. As devastated as he was by Abby's distrust, he knew his life with Emily had been a shadow life compared to the past few weeks. The problem with feeling too much was that it opened you up not just to the good things, but the bad. Mutual caring was part and parcel with the ability to inflict not just joy, but pain, intentional or not.

On some level he'd known that, but experiencing it firsthand was far different. He'd also known his growing feelings for Abby were dangerous, but he had no more been able to stop them than he'd been able to stop the sun from rising each morning. Now he was paying the price.

He relived the scene with Abby, hearing again her accusing voice demanding to know the details about the sale of her farm, demanding to know why he had not talked to her, had not told her about his plans. He felt the prickle of tears beneath his eyelids. It hurt. Dear sweet Heaven, it hurt.

But no more. The price of loving was just too high.

He was mucking out the horse's stall thirty minutes later when he heard Abby calling for Ben. He hardened his heart against the sound of her voice and the mental image that accompanied it, and kept scattering fresh hay around the cubicle. After a while, she called again.

He was just closing the door to the stall when the barn door was flung against the wall and Abby rushed in. He couldn't ignore her. They were married. He braced himself and turned to face her.

Her hair was coming loose and the expression in her eyes bordered on panic. His heart tightened in pain and he fought the urge to go to her and pull her into his arms. Instead, he stood there leaning against the pitchfork, regarding her with what he hoped was a neutral expression.

"Caleb," she said, breathing hard, the heat of her breath creating a fog in the cold air. "Is Ben with you?"

"No."

"I've looked the house over, and he's nowhere inside. I've called and I've called, but he doesn't come and doesn't answer. That isn't like him."

A memory flashed through Caleb's mind. Ben coming into the parlor wanting to go check his traps as Caleb had promised him they would. A promise he'd made before he'd known that Sarah Van-Sickle's spite was about to send his whole world crashing down.

"Not now, Ben."

He'd told him no twice. And not kindly.

"Go back to the house, Abby," Caleb told her. "I'll find him."

She made a little whimpering sound and looked as if she might burst into tears. "How can you possibly know where he's gone?"

"He wanted to go check his traps and I told him no, so I imagine he took off to do it by himself."

Caleb didn't tell her how dangerous that seemingly easy task could be. Who knew what might be caught in the traps? Critters like coyotes and bobcats and the like had to be shot in the head before you could remove them from the traps. Caleb's blood ran cold. Ben didn't have a gun—did he?

Leaning the pitchfork against the wall, Caleb grasped Abby's elbow and guided her toward the door, pulling her outside into the overcast, foggy day. "I need to get my .22," he told her, "and see if Ben took the shotgun."

Abby gasped. "He knows he's not supposed to have it unless you're along."

"I know, but he's a boy, and boys are not noted for doing what they're supposed to." The words were accompanied by a grim smile. "He'll be somewhere along the creek."

"How do you know?" she asked, trotting along beside him.

"Because everything has to have water, so you look for different animal trails along the creek and set your traps accordingly."

Caleb hauled her up the back porch steps and they stepped into the warmth of the kitchen. Abby stayed near the door, her arms crossed as if to ward off a chill, while he went to fetch his gun.

"The shotgun's where it should be," he said, grabbing a felt hat from the rack to protect his bare head from the rain.

"Thank God," Abby murmured.

Resting the rifle on his shoulder, he reached for the doorknob, troubled by a growing sense of alarm. The temperature was dropping every hour, and with the light drizzle, Ben might lose his way. Unfamiliar panic rushed through Caleb's body. Panic and that too-familiar guilt.

"Caleb."

He turned. Abby stood before him, her face pale, blue eyes awash with tears she somehow held at bay. She reached out, as if to lay her palm against his chest, and then caught herself, clenched her hand into a fist and let her arm fall to her side.

"I'm sorry."

There was no need for her to say more.

Face grim, eyes as hard as steel, he said, "So am I."

It took every ounce of willpower to turn and walk away from her when all he wanted was to cradle her close and tell her that he would make things right somehow, if only he knew how.

Caleb made his way across the barren, fallow fields to the tree line, his booted feet squelching through the mud as he headed toward the big pine that marked the spot where they usually went into the woods. Entering the copse of trees was like stepping into another world. The fog was denser beneath the shelter of the trees, as if their overarching branches held it close to the earth. Seeing beyond a few yards was all but impossible. Silence ruled the gray day; all the forest critters must be snug in their nests. The misty rain had become a light drizzle that dripped from pine needles, bare tree limbs and the brim of his hat, the only sound to be heard besides his ragged breathing and the soft soughing of the rising wind.

Caleb picked up his already-hurried pace, refusing to let himself think of what might happen if Ben was not found soon. Picking his way through the sodden ground cover, stepping around muscadine vines and over moss-covered trees and lichen-scaled rocks, Caleb moved closer to the spot along the creek where he and Ben had placed their first trap the day before. The creek was bordered by banks so steep they were almost vertical in some places, dangerous on a good day. Now, slick with rain and fallen leaves, the softened edges prone to crumble, they were downright treacherous. Swollen from all the rain they'd received recently, the water of the usually placid brook rushed headlong to the

Little Missouri. Thank goodness all the traps were set on high ground.

Caleb located the animal trail and the trap, saw that it was empty and scanned the area for sign of Ben's blue plaid coat. Nothing. He did see leaves that had looked as if they'd been scuffled through and followed the trail to the next spot.

No sign of a trapped animal, no sign of Ben.

Caleb trudged on, filled with a sense of urgency and that nagging, growing guilt.

Ben opened his eyes slowly and blinked against the rain falling into his face. He was cold. Freezing. And his leg hurt like the very dickens. He'd lost his cap somewhere. Rain plastered his hair to his head and ran in icy rivulets down his neck. With his teeth chattering like the Morse code the telegraph man sent through the lines, he lifted his upper body to his elbows to see what was wrong with his leg. His stomach roiled, and he lost his breakfast. Broken, he reckoned, from the look and feel of it.

When the queasiness passed, he lifted his head again to look around. He lay at the bottom of the gorge where he'd tumbled after slipping on a pile of slick leaves. Water raced pell-mell over rocks and boulders just feet from where he lay. He realized his shoulder ached, and his head. He reached up to check his forehead and found a big goose egg. Drawing back his hand, he saw that his fingers were covered with blood.

He had to get home. His mom would be worried sick, as she always said. He could stand the pain… Caleb said men had to be tough, and blood had never bothered Ben, so he had to try to get home. Gritting his teeth, he tried to get up, but realized pretty fast that even if got to his feet, which he didn't think he could do, there was no way he could climb up the steep bank.

A wave of worry and self-pity settled over him. No one knew where he was. The realization was soon followed by a reassuring thought. As soon as his mother realized he was gone, she'd send Caleb to find him. He was good at tracking. He was good at a lot of things. Course his father had been good at a lot of things, too, Ben thought loyally. Just different things.

Though he'd tried not to, Ben liked Caleb more all the time. He'd felt ashamed at first, but Caleb had been right. Even though his father would always be his father, he and Caleb could be friends. He thought his mama was starting to like Caleb, too, but something had set her off today. Probably something Mrs. VanSickle said. Caleb hadn't looked too happy, either. He hated when his parents argued, hated that his mom and Caleb were at odds.

Ben gave a violent shiver. He was so cold, and it was raining right into his face. He tried to turn onto his side and cried out in pain, but managed to turn just a bit. His hands felt like ice. He blew on them and then tucked them beneath his armpits, the only halfway dry place on his coat.

A new worry surfaced. What if his mother

didn't tell Caleb? What if they were too mad to talk to each other? What if no one came looking for him? How long until dark? A rush of panic sent him scrambling backward, and loosed a scream of agony. Grinding his teeth together, he tried to curl into a ball, and the tears started up again. He didn't think he was brave enough to stay here all night by himself.

Only two more places to check. If there was no sign of Ben, he'd gotten off the trail in the fog and was lost. Caleb's jaw tightened. Trudging through the woods, he'd called out for Ben periodically, but heard no answer. Once, he caught himself mumbling beneath his breath, and when he'd realized what he was doing, he'd stopped dead in his tracks. Praying? Had he really been praying to find Ben? Well, why not? There was no doubt that Abby was calling on God for help and strength. And it couldn't hurt.

A sound, the first he'd heard since stepping into the foggy emptiness of the forest, stopped Caleb midstride. What was that? An animal of some sort? Ben calling out? Caleb cocked his head, listening for the slightest sound.

An agonized cry sent his head up, like a hound catching scent of its prey.

"Ben!" he cried, running farther along the ridge of the creek. "Ben! Where are you?"

"Caleb!" a muffled voice shouted. "Over here!"

Holding the .22 rifle at his side, Caleb slogged

over the mushy leaf-strewn ground toward the sound of Ben's voice. "Ben!" he called again.

"I'm down here, at the bottom of the gully. I slipped and fell."

Caleb located Ben a minute later. He was lying flat of his back no more than five feet from the rushing waters of the creek, and it was clear from the pain lingering in his eyes that he was hurt. The expression of joy that flashed on Ben's face when he saw Caleb almost broke his heart. "Where are you hurt?" he asked, scanning the sheer embankment for the safest, fastest way to descend.

"I'm pretty sure I broke my leg."

Caleb didn't miss the slight catch in the boy's voice.

"Hang on. I'll be right there." He leaned the rifle against a nearby tree and edged sideways down the sharp incline, grabbing small saplings and bushes for handholds. He was soon squatting next to Ben, who reached up and flung his arms around Caleb's neck. A feeling of love so intense he could barely breathe surged through him. He closed his eyes and hugged Ben close. "What happened, bud?" he asked, hearing a catch in his own voice.

Ben pulled back to look into Caleb's eyes. "I was checking the traps and slipped. You told me we could come and check them and then you and Mama were arguing, and…" His voice trailed away, and his eyes grew wide with apprehension. "Is she mad?"

"No," Caleb said, pushing a lock of wet hair

from Ben's eyes. "She's not mad. She's worried. You shouldn't have come out here alone. Not in this weather."

"I know." He looked toward the top of the ravine. "How are we gonna get back to the top?"

"I'm going to carry you."

"Is it gonna hurt?"

"I'm not going to lie to you, Ben. I'll try to be easy, but when I pick you up, it will probably hurt pretty bad. If you feeling like yelling, yell."

He did. Loudly.

A baby in each arm, Abby looked at the clock. Almost two hours since Caleb had disappeared into the darkness of the woods beyond the cornfield. She pressed her lips together and blinked fast to hold back the tears. Where could they be? To make matters worse, both babies seemed acutely attuned to her mood. She fed Betsy, who was usually content once her tummy was full, but not today, and sunny Laura refused to play in her pen and wanted every bit of Abby's attention, which was impossible with Betsy in her arms.

She felt another tear slide down her cheek when she heard someone at the back door. Setting Laura into her playpen despite her angry protests, and laying Betsy in her cradle, Abby ran to the kitchen.

Caleb stood in the doorway, rain dripping off the brim of his felt hat, holding Ben in his arms. Both were sopping wet and shivering. Ben's eyes were closed; Caleb's were haunted.

"What's wrong?" Abby wailed. "Is he all right?"

"He'll be fine. I think he fainted, which is probably the best thing he could have done."

"Fainted? What happened?"

"He slipped down the creek embankment and broke his leg," Caleb told her. "He's got a giant bump and a cut on his head, but he isn't talking crazy. Right now he's chilled to the bone."

"Bring him to his room. I'll get him stripped down and under the covers, so he'll warm up."

"While you're doing that, I'll ride into town for Rachel."

"Change into something dry before you go," Abby told him, wifely concern in her voice. "I don't need you sick, too."

She hurried ahead of him down the hall to turn back the blankets on Ben's bed. "Your rain gear is on a peg in the pantry," she said over her shoulder.

She rushed into the room ahead of Caleb. "Just put him on top of the quilts until I can get him out of these wet things. That way, he won't get the sheets wet."

Caleb did as she instructed, and Abby made fast work of cutting Ben out of his pants and his other wet clothes and then Caleb eased Ben beneath the blankets and left the room while Abby was still fussing over him.

Assured by Rachel that Ben would most likely sleep through the night, Abby had been persuaded to go to bed in her room to be near the girls if they needed her.

Tormented by the day's events, more specifically his part in them, Caleb was unable to sleep. The house was silent except for the chiming of the clock in the next room and the hiss and *clunk* of the wood burning in the fireplace. He sat in the rocking chair next to Ben's bed, his elbows resting on his knees, his clasped hands dangling between his thighs, his weary gaze focused blindly on the rag rug beneath his feet.

Rachel had come and gone, working her healing power with bandages and splints and pain medication. Ben had cried out once, probably when she'd set the leg. Caleb wasn't sure there was a medicine on earth that would help his pain; as far as he knew, there was no cure for guilt.

He'd made a mess of everything—his marriage to Abby, his feeble attempts at learning to be a father...all of it. Ben's accident was his fault. Caleb should not have let the boy see the anger directed at his mother, and Ben should not have been sent away as he had been. Not when Caleb had made a promise.

Beyond that, he never should have let Sarah VanSickle coerce him and Abby into marriage. He should never have become entangled in Abby's and her children's lives. He'd had no experience with children to fall back on, and even though he and Emily were married for six years, he had scant knowledge of how marriages worked. He was not good husband material. He was definitely not father material. He'd let Ben down, let himself down. Caleb dug the heels of his hands into his eye sockets, pressing hard to try to drive away the pain. He didn't remember being so miserable in his entire life.

"I'm sorry, Ben," he choked out in a low, emotion-clogged voice. "I never meant to hurt you or for you to get hurt. I never meant to hurt anyone."

He rested his forehead on the edge of the bed, and sobbed, huge gulping sobs…the first time he remembered crying since the afternoon he and Gabe had come home from school and were told their mother had gone to live in Boston, that she hadn't cared enough for either of them to take them with her.

The first thing Abby did when she woke up was check on Ben. He was sleeping deeply, no doubt due to the pain medication Rachel had given him. After laying the back of her hand against his forehead to check for fever, Abby headed for the kitchen. She rubbed at her gritty eyes and prayed Caleb had made the coffee as he usually did before she woke up.

She smiled when she saw the coffeepot sitting at the back of the stove. Her gaze drifted to the door. His coat was gone. He was probably doing not only his chores, but Ben's this morning.

Abby poured herself a cup of coffee and sat down at the table, resting her chin in her hands. How could she approach Caleb about their argument the day before? What could she ever say to make him realize that she must have temporarily taken leave of her senses?

Even knowing the horrible woman had come to stir up some kind of trouble, Abby had fallen for her lies—hook, line and sinker. Well, it hadn't exactly been a lie, but she had manipulated the truth enough to make it sound plausible…like saying that Lucas wanted the property, a statement that meshed perfectly with Abby's knowledge that someone had been interested in it before William died. Adding that Viola Haversham had been told the truth by her husband seemed likely, too; otherwise how could Sarah have found out?

Stating that she should have checked on the sale also made sense—most people would—except that as Caleb reminded her, she had given him her power of attorney and therefore she'd felt no need to check on the sale. Which brought her back to the certainty that Caleb would never have cheated her in any way. Yet she'd all but come out and accused him of just that.

Even her argument that he should have talked it over with her held no real weight, because she had trusted him with the task. Once again, she'd let her quick temper put her in an awful spot. All the time Caleb had been looking for Ben she had prayed that he would be found, that he would be all right, and for God to give her the right words to fix the mess she'd made of things. But morning had arrived and her mind was still a blank. She wasn't sure she could talk herself out of this one, but she had to try.

How would Caleb act this morning? Would he still be angry? Cold and distant? Or, like her, would he feel remorse and a soul-deep need to make things right again?

As if thinking of him conjured him up, she heard his step on the porch. She sat very still, her gaze focused on the doorway, barely breathing. He strode into the room, bringing in cold air and vitality and a quiet strength. Blinking back tears, she wondered why she had fought her feelings for him for so long and knew that she had never loved him more than she did at that moment. She watched as he hung his coat on the hook and then turned to look at her, his gray eyes devoid of emotion. "How's Ben?"

So, she thought, his attitude was to be the polite cordiality he'd displayed during the first days of their marriage. Fine. She could deal with that until she had the opportunity to change it.

"He's resting well and doesn't seem to have any fever. Would you like a cup of coffee?"

"I'll get it."

She watched the play of muscles across his shoulders as he reached for the cup he must have used earlier. She noticed that his hair was already brushing his collar. She sighed. He would need another haircut soon. Filling his mug, he sat down across from her.

"Caleb, I don't know how to say this, but—"

"Then don't." He words were hard. Harsh. Like the expression in his eyes.

"But I said things to hurt you, and I didn't—"

"You said what you felt," he said. "There's no need to apologize for your feelings. Ever. It probably happened for the best."

"How can you say that?" she asked, frowning. "I know you would never do the terrible things I all but accused you of, but Sarah made it all sound so…so logical, and I…" She stopped, drew a breath and took another tack. "And you're perfectly within your rights to refuse to discuss your business with me. I had no right to expect you to, just because William did."

"It won't work, Abby."

"What?" She blinked in surprise. Was he going to refuse to accept her apology then?

"This marriage."

"What?" she said again, unable—or unwilling—to believe what she thought he was saying. Their marriage wouldn't work? But it *was* working.

He shook his head. "It won't work, and we knew it wouldn't, but we let Sarah VanSickle manipulate the situation. Face it, Abby. I'm not husband material, and God knows I'm not father material, as I'm sure Ben will tell you."

Was he saying what she thought he was? Abby felt as if her whole existence were in jeopardy, as if her world were about to collapse and there was nothing she could do about it.

"Actually, I think you're adapting to fatherhood

very well." Her voice shook as she tried to make her argument. "You and Ben have been getting along so well and Laura…"

"Loves me. I know." He gave a bitter laugh. "And what about me as a husband? If I'm adapting so well, why is it that we quarrel so much?"

"But we don't. Not really. Not any more than any husband and wife."

"I like peace and quiet," he said brusquely. "I'm not used to being in the midst of chaos."

She felt the blood drain from her face. He was saying that he didn't like the confusion and disorder that was their family dynamic. Had all the changes she thought she'd seen in him been an act, then?

"What are you trying to tell me, Caleb?" she asked, her troubled gaze probing his, as if she could find the answers she sought there. "Just spit it out," she commanded, not realizing she had stolen one of his favorite phrases.

"I've been planning on making a trip to Fort Worth to see about buying some new equipment. I'd planned on leaving after the first of the year, but I've decided to leave this afternoon."

Abby opened her mouth to tell him that he'd never mentioned that he was planning to go anywhere, that she had no idea he was even thinking of buying more equipment, but then she remembered that he was not William, that he felt no need to confide in her, or talk over his plans…or his dreams. Her mouth snapped shut and she pressed her lips together to keep them from trembling. She imagined she saw a sardonic smile in the calm depths of his eyes. Something in that look told her that the conversation was over, that there was nothing more to be said, nothing to gain by saying anything.

"I see," she said in a low voice. She pushed away from the table and stood, hoping he did not see the shaking of her hands. "I'll get your clothes ready. Will you need your suit?"

"Don't bother."

The coldness of the two words snatched away her breath.

"I can get my things together," he said. "I've been doing for myself for a long time."

Yes, she knew he had. Knowing how much of himself he put into his work and those who worked for him, it had given her much pleasure to do for him for a change.

"How long will you be gone?"

His gaze shifted from hers and he spoke to the doorway behind her. "Possibly a week."

He drew in a deep breath, and Abby had the distinct impression that he was trying to fortify himself for something. Finally, he brought his gaze back to her. "I want you and the children to be gone when I get back. It shouldn't be too painful for Ben to travel in a few days."

A pain so sharp that she actually felt as if she'd been struck in the solar plexus knocked the air from Abby's lungs. The room began to spin. She swayed and pressed her palms hard against the tabletop. She would not faint. She had never fainted in her life.

If he noticed her distress, he never let on. "I'll buy your train tickets to anywhere you like. Don't you have a brother in Springfield?"

She nodded. She wanted to tell him she would buy her own tickets but it was hard to talk when you couldn't even breathe.

"When you get settled, you can let Nate know where you are, and he can transfer the money from the sale of your farm and what I've put into savings for the children to a bank of your choice."

There were so many questions churning around in her head that Abby could not seem to grab hold of any coherent thought.

"Betsy?" she managed to squeak out.

Caleb rose and set his coffee cup on the counter. He leaned back against it, crossing his arms over his chest in a gesture of finality. "I'll have Mary come and get her. She'll just have to get used to the bottle."

"I see you've thought of everything," she said.

The words hung in the air between them, the same words she'd spoken the day Rachel had explained why taking Betsy to her place would not work. She could see that he remembered by the stiffening of his shoulders.

"I hope so."

She drew herself up straighter and lifted her chin. "What about the children? What about Ben?"

For the first time, Abby thought she saw a softening in his attitude. Imagined she saw a glimmer of pain in his eyes.

When he spoke, his voice was huskier than it had been. "Tell him the truth. That I would not make him a good father. He got over losing William, and he'll forget me soon enough. It isn't as if we were close."

But you were! Abby wanted to scream. She could *see* the closeness growing between them every day. Despite her breaking heart and an aching sense of loss, Abby felt the first stirring of anger.

"I won't do it."

"I beg your pardon."

The tears she'd kept at bay spilled over her lashes and down her cheeks. "I will not do your dirty work for you, Caleb Gentry," she spat out, swiping at the tears with her fingertips.

"What?"

"You heard me! I've thought you many things these past weeks—stubborn, hard, fair, even kind and gentle, but I never thought you were a coward. I will not have you do to Ben what your mother did to you. You will tell him goodbye, and why you're forcing us to leave here."

There was no compromise in her voice, or the gemlike hardness in her blue eyes. "I mean it, Caleb. Either tell him yourself, or be man enough to stay."

He left on the afternoon train as planned, but as per Abby's demands, he had told Ben himself that he was going. Caleb had not known what to expect from Ben, but the boy had listened to what Caleb had to say, and then nodded and turned his head away. There had been no reproach in his eyes, no discernible emotion. Unlike his mother, Ben had not argued that they were growing closer, and he had not cried or begged him to stay, as Caleb expected. Hoped? Feeling a bit let down by Ben's lack of emotion, Caleb considered the possibility that the medicine Rachel was giving Ben for the pain must have dulled his senses.

Caleb left the room feeling as if he had just lost something irreplaceable. When he'd carried his bags to the wagon where Frank waited to drive him to town, he'd had to pass through the parlor. Laura was in her pen. Abby was holding Betsy at her shoulder, her face buried against his daughter's soft dark hair. She didn't look up as he passed, but Laura called to him. He didn't stop. Didn't even look at her. Couldn't. He had to let them go. For their sake and for his.

"You're a dad-blamed fool, is what you are, Caleb Gentry," Frank said.

"I didn't ask your opinion, Frank."

"Well, you're gettin' it, anyway!"

Caleb cast him a sideways look. "You might remember who you're talking to, old man," he growled.

"You don't scare me none. And maybe you should remember that I tanned your hide many a time when you were a snot-nosed whippersnapper and did something stupid." He slowed the wagon a bit to go around a pothole. "And tellin' Abby and the kids to leave is about the most dim-witted thing you've ever done."

Caleb had had no choice but to tell Frank and Leo what was going on, since he would be leaving Abby's and the children's departure in their capable hands.

"Frank..." Caleb warned.

Frank was wound up. "You need that woman and those kids like roses need sunshine. Lord knows I thought the world of Emily, strange as she was, and I was more'n sorry she died. But she did, and ain't nothin' we can do about that. Sarah VanSickle aside, Abby Carter and her younguns are the best thing that ever happened to you."

Frank wasn't telling Caleb anything he didn't know, but that didn't mean he wanted to hear it.

"You're crazy about Laura, and you and Ben have got about as close as dirt to a fence post since you started teachin' him about the woods and all." Frank cut a sly look at Caleb. "And unless these old eyes are worse off than I think they are, you're sweet on that wife of yours, too."

"I do care for them," Caleb said on a sigh, giving his longtime friend that much. "But all that aside, it's better for everyone this way. Better to send Abby away now before she gets fed up with me the way my mother got sick of Lucas. I don't want to come home one day five or six years from now and see that she's packed up and took off to—to Springfield. I don't think I could stand that, Frank.

I don't want Betsy to have to go through what Gabe and I went through."

Frank scowled. "And why would she do that?"

"Because I'm just like my father."

Frank croaked a hoarse laugh. "You're *nothing* like Lucas Gentry," he said, "but at least we're gettin' somewhere—I think." He looked at Caleb across his shoulder. "Let me see if I got this straight. You sent her away, even though it's tearin' you apart, just so you won't fall for her any harder and have it tear you apart later?"

Caleb nodded.

"Like I said, son, this is one of the most brainless things I've ever known you to do. And what did you mean about not wanting Betsy to go through what you and Gabe did?"

"No child should come home and be told that their mother didn't care enough for them to take them with her when she walked away."

A frown furrowed Frank's wrinkled forehead. "And where did you hear that load of nonsense?"

"From my father," Caleb said bitterly.

"I always knew Libby's leavin' hurt Lucas to the bone, and I always knew he was a ruthless son of a gun. Never knew him to be a liar until now, though."

"What are you talking about?"

"Libby got a hankerin' to go back east for a few months," Frank said thoughtfully, "seein' as it had been years since she'd gone for a visit. Said she wanted to take you boys to visit your grandparents, since they'd never set eyes on either one of you. Lucas said no. Maybe he was scared that if she took you boys with her, she'd never come back."

"So she left without us."

"Nope. She didn't go." Frank took off his hat and scratched his grizzled head. "That next spring, her brother, Tad, and his wife, Ada, came and brought Ada's brother with them. Do you remember your mama, Caleb?"

Caleb shook his head. "Not much."

"She was a looker, Libby Gentry was, and I knew she was really unhappy, but even so, I never knew her to look twice at another man, least not until then. Long story short, your daddy claimed he caught them together in what they call a 'compromising situation.'"

"Go on," Caleb said in a voice that sounded like he was talking around ground glass.

"Lucas beat Ada's brother, Sam, to within an inch of his life. Edward Stone can vouch for that. Lucas told her to pack up and go back east. Said he'd handle the divorce."

"Divorce?"

"Yep. Pike County scandal of the year. Libby denied everything and tried to talk him around, but you know how ornery yer daddy could be. She and Gabe were up front, and the wagon was loaded, ready to head out—we were supposed to pick you up at school, Caleb, and then put you on the train—and your daddy, he walks out of the house as calm as you please, smokin' one of them cheroots he was so fond of and tells me and Micah—" he shot Caleb a questioning glance "—you remember Micah?"

Caleb nodded.

"Well Lucas tells Micah to unload the trunks with your and Gabe's stuff in 'em, and told me to get Gabe down 'cause she ain't takin either one of you nowhere."

"What!"

"It was a dad-blamed mess, let me tell you. Your mama is a-cryin' and screamin' and Lucas just takes Gabe and turns around and starts back to the house, lookin' all pleased with hisself. Your mama jumps down and starts trying to get me and Micah to reload the trunks, but Lucas says that if we do he'll see that we never work in these parts again, so we did what he said.

"Then she goes and grabs your daddy's arm and starts screamin' at him that she can't leave you boys— she won't. He just takes hold of her hand, moves it off his arm, all the while he's callin' her a few choice names. Then he sets Gabe down, slings Libby over his shoulder, dumps her back in the wagon and tells her to never show her face back here again, or he'll see to it that her family loses everything they have."

"Could he do that?" Caleb asked, shocked to his soul by what he'd just heard.

"Probably."

Abby spent the next four days packing the bare minimum of what she and the children would need in Springfield. Let Caleb do what he would with what she left behind. Her emotions ranged from fury to a sadness that eclipsed what she'd felt when William died. Was it because she and William shared a loving relationship, and even after his death she'd been sustained by memories and the children they'd had together? Did her suffering seem more acute because she felt as if she'd failed Caleb and this marriage somehow?

Prayer brought no answers or peace. Convinced always that God was in control, she had no idea why He would bring her and Caleb together only to rip them apart.

She couldn't eat, couldn't sleep. The only decent rest she'd had since the afternoon he'd left was the day she'd climbed into his bed and breathed in his familiar, beloved scent. Ben was surly; Laura was whiny and seemed to watch the back door for Caleb's return. The essence of him haunted the house, bombarding her with dozens of recollections of him throughout the day. Cutting his hair. Him kissing her. Seeing his dry sarcasm slowly become teasing. When she forced the memories away, tangible reminders of him tormented her: his rain gear hanging in the pantry. His coat hanging near the back door. The smell of his woodsy soap that clung to the clothes and sheets.

On the second day of his absence, she decided that she was going crazy worrying. There had been no compromise in Caleb, and unable to bear the idea of never seeing him again, of never having the hope of him loving her and feeling his arms around her, she knew there was no sense putting off the inevitable. She'd packed in a frenzy. There were still three days until Caleb's week was up and he came home, but they would be long gone when he did. They were leaving this afternoon, with Abby praying she could run far enough away to forget. Knowing it was impossible.

"Are we going back to our old house?"

Ben was propped up in bed where he'd been reading his new horse book. Abby was scurrying around the room, stacking his clothes so she could pack them in the trunk Frank and Leo had brought down from the attic.

"No. Someone else…owns it now. We're going to see Uncle Phillip and Aunt Zoe in Springfield. You'll like it there."

"Can I hunt and trap there?"

"Oh, no," Abby said, keeping her voice deliberately light. "Uncle Phil lives in the city. There are other things to do there. Theater, and museums, and libraries, and parks with lots of trees where you can run and play."

"If I can't hunt, I don't want to go." His voice was firm and his lower lip stuck out in an all-too-familiar pout, something she'd not seen much of the past couple of months but that had made regular appearances since Caleb had left.

Abby saw one of his stubborn spells on the horizon. "We have to go, Ben."

"Why?"

"Remember when you were so unhappy about living here and I told you it was only until Caleb could find someone else to take care of Betsy, or she got a little older?"

Ben nodded.

"Well, Betsy's grandmother and another lady in Wolf Creek will be taking care of Betsy from now on, so there's no reason for us to stay." She could not tell him that Caleb had demanded that they be gone when he returned. It would break his heart.

"Why would he do that when he said..."

Hearing his hesitation, Abby paused and turned to look at him. "What did he say, Ben?"

"That he loves us."

Abby kept her silence. Where on earth had Ben gotten such an idea? If Caleb loved them, he had a strange way of showing it.

"Benjamin Aaron, you know what happens when you tell a lie."

"Yes, ma'am."

"Tell me the truth now. Did Caleb really tell you he loved us?"

Ben's fair eyebrows drew together in a frown. "Not in those words, but that's what he meant."

"And when did you have this conversation with him?"

"The night I got hurt. I woke up and he was sitting beside my bed."

Abby's heart stumbled. She'd had no idea that after sending her to bed, Caleb had sat up with Ben in case he needed something. "Exactly what did he say?" she asked, her voice a thread of sound.

"That he was sorry. That he didn't mean to hurt us, or for me to get hurt."

No surprise there. Abby knew Caleb was not a monster. "That's all?"

Ben looked as if he were about to burst into tears. "He said he couldn't stand it if we left him, but he had to let us go because it was the best thing to do."

Abby felt the prickle of tears beneath her own eyelids. "And what did you say?"

"Nothing. He didn't know I was awake."

"I see."

"He was crying, Mama," Ben said, and burst into tears himself.

Abby went to the bed and gathered him close. If what Ben said was true, Caleb no more wanted them to go than she wanted to leave him. She recalled him telling her that he wasn't good husband or father material. By some twisted reasoning that only a man like her husband could concoct, he'd convinced himself that he was undeserving, that it would be better to end things before… What? His inexperience hurt one of them? Or was it because he was falling in love with all of them and feared that he would somehow lose them?

Trying to control another sob, Abby wiped at the tears running down her cheeks. Oh, what a muddle they were in!

Ben drew a shuddering breath and sobbed, "We can't leave, Mama. We can't."

Abby placed her hands on his cheeks and tipped his head back to look into his eyes. "Darling, we have to. It's what Caleb wants."

"It's *not* what he wants, and besides, when you guys got married, you said it was until death do you part. You promised. Both of you promised in front of God."

Being reminded of that sacred vow by a six-year-old drew Abby up short. Out of the mouths of babes...

Abby kissed away his tears and gave him a brief, hard hug.

"You're right, Ben," she said offering him a shaky smile. "We did."

It was just getting light the following day when Caleb guided the rig he'd rented in Gurdon down the lane toward home. He'd gone to Fort Worth and bought his equipment, but his heart and mind were in Wolf Creek. He'd spent the four days he'd been gone thinking about what Frank had told him. When he'd asked the older man why he'd never said anything before, Frank told him that Lucas had forbidden anyone to talk about it and that Caleb had never asked.

Caleb had no reason to doubt the story, and Frank was right, he had not asked, and he had not talked about his mother because Lucas had forbidden him and Gabe to even mention her name. With no one to offer the other side of the story, it had been easy for Lucas to poison their malleable minds against the woman he and Gabe had both adored.

Having misjudged his mother set Caleb to thinking about some of the things Abby said about God and letting Him become a part of life. His thoughts drifted back to his sixteenth summer when he'd gone to town for a night of revelry with his friends and found that Wolf Creek Church was holding a revival.

Caught up by the size of the crowd, he'd wandered over in time to hear the preacher talk about Jesus's sacrifice on the cross. Caleb realized his life wasn't what it should be, and along with many others had been immersed in the nearby creek. He remembered how good he'd felt when he'd come up out of the water, how clean.

Then he'd gone home and told Lucas what he'd done. It hadn't taken his father's ridicule long to shatter Caleb's newfound peace and joy. He'd tried to stay faithful for a while, but gradually, he'd slipped back into his old ways.

Now, thinking about the parable of the seeds and Abby's explanation of them, he knew he'd received the message with gladness, but his new and fragile faith had no time to take root before Lucas's taunts had ripped it away.

Caleb had thought a lot about his life and God as he'd driven through the night, and he'd decided that with Abby and God on his side, there was hope that he could become a better man.

Unable to wait until morning to catch the next

train to Wolf Creek, he'd paid an exorbitant price to rent the buggy and had driven all night.

The nearer he got to the house the better he could see. No one was outside doing chores. The house was dark and uninviting. There was no smoke coming from the chimneys, and there would be no mouthwatering scent of bacon frying when he stepped through the back door. No Abby bustling around. No Ben waiting patiently to start eating. No Betsy sleeping in her cradle and no Laura waiting with a wide smile.

He was too late.

Pulling the wagon to a stop near the back porch, he jumped down, looped the reins over the hitching post and trudged up the back steps, his jaw set and his heart like a stone in his chest.

He'd see how things were with Frank and Leo, and then he'd go back into town, check on Betsy and then go and buy a ticket to Springfield. When he found Abby, he'd tell her that he was a fool, that he loved her, that he'd try harder to be what she and the children needed. He'd get down on his knees and beg her to come back, if that's what it took. After all, he was the one who'd said he believed in the sanctity of marriage.

When he opened the door, the first thing he saw was Laura's empty chair. He could picture her smile with her little nose wrinkled up as she held up her arms for him to hold her. Caleb blinked hard and let his gaze roam the cold, spotless room. He should have known Abby would leave things clean and tidy.

There was no fire in the fireplace, and with a sigh, he reached for the shovel and bucket to clean out the ashes. The first scoop revealed red-hot coals. They hadn't been gone all that long then. Late yesterday, maybe. He was reaching for some slivers of pine knot when he heard a sound behind him and bolted to his feet.

Abby stood in the doorway wearing the ratty red plaid robe and a pair of his wool socks. Wavy blond hair had escaped her braid and straggled around her pale face. There were purple smudges beneath her eyes from lack of sleep.

She was the most beautiful thing he had ever seen.

"You're still here." An absurd thing to say, but a ridiculous joy was filling his heart.

"And where else would I be?" she asked, launching herself across the room. For an instant, Caleb thought she was running into his arms. Then he realized that it was not welcome he saw in her eyes. It was fury.

Before he could more than register that fact, she flung herself at him.

"Don't you ever, *ever* send me away again!" she cried, anger bracing her voice while her small fists beat feebly at his chest, punctuating every word.

Of all the things he'd expected, this was not it. He circled her wrists with his fingers in an instinctive gesture of self-protection.

"Calm down, Abby," he said, holding her at arm's length and frowning down at her.

"I won't calm down!" she choked out, tears streaming down her cheeks as she struggled to free herself. "I won't leave, and I won't let you leave, either. If you do, I'll hunt you down."

A curious peace began to steal through him as she spoke. All the pain from the previous days evaporated like a mist burned away by the sun.

"Why would you do that, Abby?" he asked softly, gentling his hold.

She glared at him and even stomped her foot. Laughter of pure joy welled up inside him and spilled into the room. She was really something when she was mad.

"Because I love you, you big thickheaded lout! And don't you dare laugh at me! We promised before God that we would stay together until we die and I promised to love you but I didn't and I felt guilty because I was lying to God but the children loved you and then suddenly I did, too, and you promised to love me, Caleb, you promised, and you *will* love me, I'll make you love me if it's the last thing I do!"

The words came out in a rush, one long meandering statement that could be summed up in six words. He was a very lucky man.

"You'd do that?" he asked, releasing his hold on her and reaching out to push a wayward lock of hair out of her eyes. She trembled at his touch. "You'd really hunt me down?"

Suddenly all the starch went out of her and she collapsed against him, burying her face against his chest. "If I had to I would." She looked up at him with troubled eyes. "Will I have to?"

He smiled then, and knew his world was all right once again, maybe for the first time in his life. "No, Abby. You won't have to hunt me down, and you can't make me love you, because I already do."

With a little cry, she wound her arms around his neck and pressed her lips to his.

Finally, he pulled away, a smile on his lips. "I forgot to tell you that I've finally found something fun. Something I like."

Wearing a bemused expression, Abby ran a fingertip over one of his dark eyebrows. "You did? What?"

"Seeing you mad. It's fantastic."

"Seeing me…" she began heatedly, and then stopped when she realized he was teasing her. "And why do you like making me mad?"

"Because your eyes light up with fire, and… I don't know, you're just amazing when you're angry."

"You are a strange man, Caleb Gentry," she said with a shake of her head.

"But you love me."

"I do."

He kissed her again, kissed her the way he'd wanted to for weeks, the way he would kiss her for the rest of their lives.

Chapter Thirteen

One year later

"Whas that, Mama?" almost two-year-old Laura asked, pointing out the window.

Abby rose from the rocking chair near the fire, where she'd been sewing a patch on Ben's denim overalls, and went to look out the window.

"That's snow. Isn't it pretty?" she said, her heart filling with wonder at how the pristine blanket of white covered the dreary winter landscape, capping the barn roof and fence tops with white and leaving a glittering layer on the pine boughs and bare branches of the trees. It looked as if they'd been dressed up especially for Christmas, which was just two days away. The timing couldn't be better.

"See the snow, Betsy?" Abby said, pulling the little girl close and pointing to the flurry of flakes falling outside the window.

"See," one-year-old Betsy chimed in, copying her mother.

"It's pretty," Laura repeated with a smile.

"If there's enough on the ground, by morning, you and Ben can go outside and make a snowman," Abby told her.

"Snowman?"

Abby laughed and drew her other daughter close. "I'll just have to show you. And if it's deep enough to be clean, I'll make snow ice cream."

Laura's eyes, the same brilliant blue as her mother's, lit with delight. She knew all about ice cream. "Mmm. Like ice cream."

"Speaking of *mmm,* would you like me to make you some hot chocolate while we're waiting for your dad and brother to get back?"

"Hot choc'late!" Laura cried, turning to skip toward the kitchen. Betsy, who had been walking for only a month, fell in her haste to follow her sister. With a laugh, Abby picked her up, though with the size of her tummy, it was getting harder and harder to carry her for very long.

As she went about settling the little ones in their high chairs, adding a couple of logs to the fire blazing in the fireplace and making the hot cocoa, Abby couldn't help comparing this Christmas with the previous one. A year ago, she'd been in a hopeless situation, newly married to a man she didn't even know, just to provide a home for her two children and a wet nurse for his child.

This year everything had changed. She was Betsy's only mother, just as Caleb was Laura's only father. Though Ben and Caleb would always butt heads from time to time, probably because Ben was as argumentative as his outspoken mother, they had grown as close as any father and son. Ben was teaching Caleb how to enjoy boyish pursuits, and Caleb was leading Ben toward manhood one step at a time.

Abby grew to love Caleb more every day. She could not bear to think what her life might have been like if she hadn't listened to Ben's insistence that they stay despite what Caleb had ordered her to do. She was expecting his son or daughter any time now.

The day she'd told him she was having his baby he'd turned as pale as a ghost, turned away without a word and disappeared for hours. Worried that he was unhappy about adding another child to the three they already shared, Abby found him down by the creek Ben had almost fallen into the day he went missing. Caleb was sitting on a big rock near the edge of the creek, staring at the rain-swollen water, as if he might find answers there.

She'd approached him with more trepidation than she'd felt with him for months. When he heard her footsteps, he'd looked up for just a second and then turned away. In that moment, no more than a heartbeat, she'd seen the torment in his eyes. Of all the things she'd imagined him feeling, she had not expected his reaction to be anguish.

Sudden understanding snatched away her breath.

Kneeling behind him, she slid her arms around his waist, resting her cheek against the work-hardened muscles of his back. He stiffened at her touch, and then she felt the tension holding him ease a bit. She let their breathing and their heartbeats meld into one while she struggled to find the words to ease his torment.

"It will be all right, Caleb," she said at last. "Nothing will happen to me."

"Can you promise me that, Abby?" He jerked free and stood so suddenly that she had to catch herself with her palms. Contrition replaced the despair in his eyes. He bent and helped her to her feet, but released her as soon as she was steady.

"I thought you might want us to have a child together."

His answer was to throw back his head and laugh, a bitter, hopeless sort of laugh. When he lowered his gaze to hers, his silver eyes were glazed with tears. Finally, he reached for her, pulling her so close she thought he would crush her. Instead of pulling away, she pressed even closer, willing her strength and certainty to permeate every atom of his being so that he could face his wrenching fear.

"Heaven only knows there's nothing I'd like more, but not at the risk of losing you." He whispered the words into her hair.

"You won't lose me," she said again.

"How can you be so sure?" he asked, gripping her shoulders and holding her at arm's length. "Why should God give me anything when I've done so little for Him? I try to pray, and I go to church with you, and I try to be a decent person, but I wake up every day wondering if this is the day He'll decide I've had enough happiness and take it all away."

"Oh, Caleb," she said, lifting a hand to cradle it against his stubble on his cheek. "What a terrible way to live! We're supposed to wake up each day and rejoice in it. Good or bad may come, but even if it does, He'll help us through it the same way He did when He brought us together last fall."

"God working in His mysterious ways?" he said with a dubious lift of his dark eyebrows.

She nodded and watched his eyes, imagining she saw a lessening of the desolation reflected there. Hoping to lighten his mood even more, she gave a slight lift of her shoulders. "We can't undo it, you know. And even if we could, I don't want to."

"You're happy, then?"

She spoke with no hesitation. "Happier than I can say."

"But you'll have three babies to care for."

She gave him a stern look and raised her eyebrows. "I intend for you to help, Mr. Gentry."

He shook his head. "A year ago, I had one child I didn't know what to do with. Soon I'll have four."

"But you do know what to do with them," she'd told him.

"I do?"

She'd nodded. "Give them a firm, steady hand and do it with love."

"That simple, huh?" he'd said, finally smiling a bit.

"Well, no. But it's a good starting place." She'd grasped his hands with hers and tugged gently. "Come home, Caleb," she'd urged. "It's almost dinnertime, and I left Frank and Leo watching the children."

He did smile then, and slipped his arm around her shoulders. "Now that's a scary thought."

The sound of feet stomping off snow sounded on the back porch and brought Abby's thoughts back to the present. Caleb and Ben burst through the door, accompanied by a blast of frigid air.

"I smell hot chocolate!" Ben cried.

"Me, too," Caleb said. "I hope you made enough for us men." Abby didn't fail to notice the way Ben's chest swelled with importance at being called a man.

"As a matter of fact, I did. I thought we could warm it up later."

"We didn't tarry in town. Just got our supplies and—" he winked at Ben, and swung Laura up in one arm, Betsy in the other "—did our Christmas shopping and got on our way. It's really getting cold out there. I'd guess the snow's already four or five inches deep. By the way, Mary and Bart sent their gifts, just in case they can't make it on Christmas."

Quite a speech for a man who had trouble expressing his feelings just over a year ago, Abby thought. "Surely it won't get that bad," she said, "but if it does, I suppose it's a good thing we're ready."

"Dad says you can never tell about this Arkansas weather," Ben said, taking the cup she offered him. With a soft smile, Abby handed a second cup to her husband. This time it was Caleb's turn to puff out his chest a bit.

Seeing the growing closeness between the two men in her life was as perfect an ending as Abby could want for a cold snowy day.

The mantel clock chimed 3:00 a.m. Abby had risen an hour earlier to pace the parlor floor. The evening had gone downhill ever since dinner, when her lower back had begun to ache. The baby, who'd been doing somersaults the past day or so, lay heavy inside her. Symptoms she knew well. She hoped she could hold off sending Caleb for Rachel until daylight. From what she could tell, the snow was still falling.

Without warning, a pain struck, robbing her of breath and sending her to her knees. When it passed, she clung to the wing chair and heaved herself to her feet. Like her others, this baby looked to be anxious to be born.

"Abby?"

The sound of Caleb's voice sent her gaze flying to the bedroom doorway.

"What are you doing up?" she asked as he crossed the space separating them and took her in his arms.

"I heard you cry out," he said. "The baby?"

She nodded against his chest. "I wanted to wait until morning to send you for Rachel, but my babies come fast, and something tells me this one is impatient to get here."

"Go back to bed. I'll get ready and—" His horrified voice came to a sudden halt as Abby doubled over in his arms.

When the pain passed, she grabbed double handfuls of his shirt and gave him an angry shake. "Listen to me, Caleb! You won't have *time* to go for Rachel!" she almost snarled. "I've had two very strong pains in a matter of minutes."

He paled before her eyes. "Surely you aren't implying that you want *me* to help with the delivery."

Realizing that she was not behaving in a rational manner, she released her hold on his shirt and smoothed it with gentle, deliberate hands. It was hard to act reasonable when you felt as if you were being torn apart, but there was no time to plead her case. Things had to be done, and soon.

Trying to maintain her composure, she looked up at him and said in a serene tone, "I'm trying to be sensible, Caleb, but if you do not want me to have a conniption fit, you will stop wallowing in self-pity and do what needs to be done."

Even though her demeanor was tranquil, the fury in her eyes would have left a lesser man quaking. His eyes narrowed in response. "Now is not the time for one of your tantrums, woman."

Abby remembered her mother telling her that

when men encountered a situation that scared the living daylights out of them, they resorted to temper. She smiled, her own anger gone as quickly as it had come.

"I'm glad you finally realize that," she said in a voice dripping sarcasm just before she doubled over with another pain.

Caleb held her until it passed and spoke against her hair. "I adore the ground you walk on, Abby, but I don't think I can do this."

He sounded broken. Panting, she straightened and looked at him. Panic had gathered like storm clouds in his gray eyes. At least he'd gone from not being able to do it to not *thinking* he could. Everything with Caleb was baby steps, but this time there was no time to take things slow.

"I don't have any idea what to do," he told her in a shaking voice.

"The main thing to remember is that this is not about you. It's about our son or daughter. Just do what I tell you to, and everything will be fine. I have faith in you."

"I don't know why," he muttered.

"Because you've never let me down, and you never will." Caleb was done arguing. He leaned over, planted a hard kiss to her lips, swung her up into his arms and carried her to the bedroom.

With trembling hands, he stoked the stove and started water to boiling. Abby was gathering cloths and getting the bed ready. Occasionally, the sound of a stifled cry filtered through the dark house to the kitchen, and Caleb's heart tightened in a painful spasm. The soft cries resurrected memories he thought he'd forgotten. Pictures and sounds echoed through his mind. Emily's endless screams and moans. The soft soothing sound of Rachel's voice.

This wasn't about him. It wasn't about Emily, he thought as he sterilized the knife and scissors and washed his hands thoroughly. When he carried everything into the bedroom, Abby was there, propped up in bed, sweat beading her brow, a soft smile of encouragement on her face, her eyes alight with love.

"I love you, Caleb."

He gave her a sour look. "Don't try to butter me up."

Surprisingly, she laughed. "Everything will be fine," she said, clutching his hand as another pain snatched at her breath.

When it passed, she said, "Where is your faith? Do you truly believe God brought us through all the trials of these past months to not give us a healthy baby?"

"I don't know what He intends. You're the expert on that. All I know is that I'm worried about you, and with good reason."

"There's no time to worry anymore," she said, gritting her teeth against an onslaught of pain. "Your son or daughter is eager to make an appearance."

Within minutes of her announcement, Elijah David Gentry made his entrance into the world screaming his little lungs out. Caleb stared down into the face of his son and felt like crying himself.

"Give him to me," Abby said. She took the precious gift and saw the look of awe on her husband's face. "Isn't it amazing?" she said, pulling a flannel blanket over the baby, who calmed almost as soon as she took him.

Swaying a bit, he nodded.

"You aren't going to faint, are you?" she asked, her eyes growing wide.

The perceived slur to his manhood stiffened his spine and brought a hint of irritation to his eyes. "Is it so terrible that I was worried about you to the point of total terror?"

"Come here, Caleb."

Obediently, he sat down on the edge of the bed, and she reached up and caressed his bristly cheek. "It isn't terrible at all. Knowing how much you love me is the most wonderful thing I've ever experienced, and I thank God every day for bringing you into my life. I'm very grateful."

"I'm the one who's grateful," he told her.

And he was. He was doubly grateful to God for sending him a woman as wonderful as Abby. He knew he had much to learn about wives and children and God and that it would be a lifetime of learning. He did know that God indeed worked in mysterious ways. Without Emily's death and the problems it brought him, he might never have known real love, might never have known true forgiveness.

The past year had taught him that God truly was in control, that He had a plan and that love did indeed cover a multitude of sins. Caleb knew that if he held on to those truths, that even if there were moments of pain and doubt in the days, weeks and years ahead, life would still be full, complete and sweet.

* * * * *

WOLF CREEK
HOMECOMING

For all have sinned and fall short of the glory of God, and all are justified freely by his grace through the redemption that came by Christ Jesus.
—*Romans* 3:23–24

For LaRee and Sandy—friends, confidantes, mentors, brainstorming partners, critique group and travelin' buds who listen, help, inspire, set me straight and pick me up, dust me off and tell me I can. Whoever would have thought we'd be here when we met at a writer's conference almost thirty years ago?

Prologue

"Hey there, Rachel Stone!"

Weighted down with loneliness and bone tired, Rachel was mounting the steps of her boarding-house when she heard the greeting. The familiar, husky voice stopped her in her tracks and caused her heart to stumble. There was no way it could be who it sounded like, she thought, turning. But it was. Her mouth fell open in surprise.

Gabe Gentry, the handsome, younger Gentry son, was standing there. The same son who, if the rumors could be believed, had asked for his inheritance prior to his father's death and left their hometown of Wolf Creek two years ago. If the gossipmongers were correct, he was busily running through the funds, chasing every good time he could find.

But Rachel believed that gossip was just bits and

pieces of the truth often distorted and exaggerated as the tattletales passed the story around. She had a hard time believing he was as bad as everyone claimed, since her own experiences with him had been good ones.

He was attractive, friendly, fun loving and always pleasant, and she'd liked being around him. Of course, that might be because she had always had a bit of a "thing" for him, even though she was the elder by two years. Guilty or not, his reputation made him the kind of male who inhabited a young woman's daydreams, and the kind parents prayed would give their daughters a wide berth.

While she was woolgathering, he stopped less than two feet from her and reached out to tap her chin with a gentle finger. Her mouth snapped shut.

"Cat got your tongue?" he asked, favoring her with a mischievous half smile.

Rachel stared into his dark blue eyes, willing steadiness to her trembling voice. "Gabe?" she said at last. "What are you doing here, and how did you find me?" she asked, still trying to come to terms with the fact that the man who had been the subject of too many of her youthful fantasies was standing on her doorstep.

He laughed, thrusting his hands into the pockets of his stylish trousers. "It really is a small world. Would you believe I ran into Buck Hargrove coming out of a restaurant last night? He's here on some sort of railroad business, and while we were catching up on what's been going on back home, he mentioned you were here studying to be a doctor. Since I don't see too many folks from home traveling around the way I do, I thought I'd look you up." He smiled, a rueful twist of his lips. "Never thought I'd admit it, but I'm a little homesick for Wolf Creek."

"You could go back for a visit sometime, you know."

Was it her imagination, or did a shadow cross his attractive face? "Yeah," he said with a bright smile. "Maybe I'll do that."

He seemed uncomfortable for a moment then rallied. "So are you really going to be a doctor?"

"That's the plan."

"That's unbelievable."

"Why is it unbelievable? I thought everyone knew I wanted to follow in my father's footsteps."

"Yeah, but saying something like that and actually doing it… Maybe it's so incredible because everyone thinks of medicine as a man's line of work."

She loved talking about her chosen field but felt strange trying to justify her decision standing in front of her rented rooms. "Would you like to come inside? Mrs. Abernathy usually has lemonade made, and I don't think she'll object if we sit in the parlor awhile."

He looked indecisive for just a second, but then smiled and said, "I'd like that very much."

Inside, Rachel fetched the beverage and some cookies, and they sat in the shabby parlor. Gabe looked out of place in his fine, tailor-made clothing, sitting among her landlady's simple, worn furnishings.

Settled in a threadbare armchair, a glass of lemonade in hand, she asked, "Where were we?"

"You were about to tell me the woes of women entering medicine."

"Oh, yes. The annoying part is the arrogance of the male students and even some of the professors. They make no secret that they think it's utter folly for a woman to even think of entering their elite ranks."

Her face took on a pompous expression. "Women are not mentally equipped to grasp the intricacies of the circulatory, lymphatic and muscular systems and they are *far* too delicate to deal with the sight of blood and innards," she intoned.

Gabe threw back his head and roared with laughter. "They actually said that?" he asked when he'd regained his composure.

"Among other things."

"And how are you doing with the blood and guts?"

"Actually very well. I have yet to faint at anything we've dealt with in the lab, which not all of them can say."

"They don't know you grew up around that sort of thing. I remember that you rescued every injured critter you came across."

He remembered that? So did she. One time in particular came to mind. She'd been around fourteen and Gabe had helped carry home a dog that Luther Thomerson had beaten with his buggy whip.

"So tell me your plans," he urged, leaning forward and resting his elbows on his knees. All of his attention was focused on her. "Will you set up practice here in St. Louis?"

"Oh, no! I'd never be happy in a place so big and impersonal. I intend to help my father."

"And waste your skills on folks who probably can't pay for them?" he scoffed. "You could make a lot of money in a big city."

"There's more to life than money," she told him, her expression earnest. "Those people need medical attention, too. My father gets a great deal of satisfaction helping those who need it."

"You can't live on satisfaction."

Her passionate gaze sought his. "Perhaps not, but if we put God first, He'll see to it we have what we need. I know it's a cliché, but money really can't buy happiness." She placed a palm against her chest. "That comes from inside us. From knowing who we are, and what we stand for."

"You really believe that, don't you?" he said, his eyes filled with wonder.

"I know it's true."

He laughed again. "Well, money may not buy happiness," he quipped, clearly uncomfortable, "but it certainly does a fine job of mimicking it." He pulled the gold watch from his pocket. "I should be going. I don't want to wear out my welcome."

"Of course." She stood, clasping her hands together, both sorry and relieved that he was going. As wonderful as it was to see him, he made her very uncomfortable. Rising, he set his glass on a nearby table. She followed him to the door and opened it, realizing that when he left he wouldn't be back.

They stepped out onto the stoop, and Rachel extended her hand. His fingers curled warmly, excitingly around hers. Urging a smile, she said, "Thank you for stopping by. Like you, I miss seeing people from home."

"I've enjoyed it, too." He turned to go, but at the top of the steps, he came back, his eyes filled with indecision. "Would you like to have dinner tomorrow evening?"

For a heartbeat, Rachel wasn't certain she'd heard correctly. She knew she should say no, but for the life of her could not bring to mind a good reason why. It was doubtless that she would see him after tomorrow, and she would at least have one brilliant memory to see her through the lonely months ahead. "I'd love to."

He looked pleased, relieved. "About seven?"

"Fine."

Before she realized what he meant to do, he brushed a kiss to her cheek and then ran lightly down the steps. Stunned by the unexpected gesture, she reached up and touched the place with her fingertips, wondering what it would be like to feel his lips touch hers.

Chapter One

❧

Wolf Creek, Arkansas, 1886

Rachel stepped inside the medical office that was situated in the rear of the house she'd shared with her father and son since receiving her medical degree.

The rush of warm air from the fireplace was welcome after a cold drive in from the country. In a capricious mood, Mother Nature had dumped more than a foot of snow the night before, something rare in the southwestern part of the state.

She'd just come from the Gentry farm, where she had given Abby Gentry and her newborn son, Eli, a thorough examination. Baby Eli had been so eager to enter the world, there had been no time for his father to fetch help, forcing Caleb to help birth his son. Thankfully, mother and baby had come through the delivery with flying colors. Father was fine, too, but still a little shaky.

Breathing a weary sigh of satisfaction, Rachel set her medical bag on a nearby table and placed the quilt she'd used for added warmth on the seat of a straight-backed chair. She unwound the scarf from around her head and neck and shrugged out of her coat. Tossing them both over the back of the chair, she headed for the kitchen, where her son, Danny, and her father sat at the table near a rip-roaring fire, playing Chinese checkers.

"How are Abby and the baby?" Edward asked, with a smile of welcome.

"Just dandy," Rachel assured him as she leaned down to give her son a welcoming hug. She was about to launch into the story of Caleb delivering the baby when a loud pounding came from the direction of her office. She gave a little groan. "I should have known better than to think I could spend the rest of the day baking cookies for Santa."

"It's part of the job," Edward called as she retraced her steps to the office.

Danny, who followed her out of curiosity, pushed aside the lace curtains and peered out the window. "It's Mr. Teasdale!" he cried, recognizing the peddler's wagon. He brushed past Rachel to the door.

No doubt Simon was making a final tour of customers before Christmas to make sure they had everything they needed for the holiday. She wondered why he had come to the office entrance instead of the front and stood back while Danny flung open the door. Simon, whose fist was raised for another round of pounding, jumped.

"Simon," she said, seeing the panic in his eyes, "what is it?"

"Oh, Doc," he squeaked, his high-pitched voice quavering with emotion, "I was coming in from Antoine when I come upon this fella by the side of the road. His wallet was a few feet away, and it was empty. Looked like he'd been beat within an inch of his life. I was afraid to move him, but I wasn't sure how long he'd been there, and I was more scared he'd freeze to death if I came to town for help, so I loaded him up." The words tripped over themselves in their hurry to get out.

With no knowledge of how badly the victim was hurt, Rachel could only hope that Simon hadn't done any additional damage by moving him.

"You did right, Simon," she said, putting on her coat and following him to the back of the cart.

"Run get Roland," she told Danny, who lost no time hurrying toward a small house down the way.

"I like to have never got him in the wagon," Simon was saying. "And it took me more than two hours to get here. My Addie Sue is plumb wore down slogging through all that snow." He unlatched the rear door and threw it open.

The man lay in the makeshift bed where Simon slept when it was impossible to make the next town at day's end. The shadowy interior made it difficult to tell anything about the stranger except that he was big and tall.

"I'll get the stretcher while we're waiting for Danny," she said.

In a matter of moments, Danny was back with Roland, the brawny teen who helped Rachel whenever and however she needed. "Let's see if we can get him inside, so I can take a look at him."

Working together, they carefully transferred the injured man onto the gurney and into the morning sunlight, where Rachel gave the stranger a quick once-over. Young. Strong. Bloody knuckles. He'd fought back. Good.

Her gaze moved to his face, and it suddenly became impossible to draw in a decent lungful of air. Every molecule of oxygen seemed to have been sucked into a vast void somewhere. Her head began to spin, and her heart began to race.

Despite the multiple bruises and the swelling and the blood still seeping from the jagged cut angling from his forehead through his left eyebrow and across his temple to just below his ear, and despite the fact that she had not seen him in more than nine years, she had no problem recognizing him.

It was none other than Gabe Gentry. Simon squeaked out his name in a shocked voice.

Gabe. As handsome as ever. She had traced those heavy brows and the bow of his top lip with her fingertips. She had felt the rasp of his whiskers against her cheek. Had…

Stop it!

Common sense returned, and a rush of fury and self-loathing banished the beguiling memories that jeopardized her hard-won detachment. Rachel's jaw tightened and she felt the bite of her fingernails into her palms. She would have liked nothing more than to load Gabriel Gentry back into Simon's wagon and order him to take the blackguard elsewhere, but she had taken an oath to heal, and as wretched as this man was, she was bound by her promise as a physician to do her best by him.

More to the point, and her consternation, it was her God-given duty as a Christian to do so.

Once she and Roland had transferred Gabe to the examination table, Simon said his goodbyes and went to see that his horse got a generous ration of oats while he went to Ellie's café to see about getting some hot food in his belly. Roland stayed to help move Gabe to a proper bed after Rachel finished tending him.

She was alone with her patient when her father rolled his wheelchair into the room. The fact that he was using it, instead of the two canes he used to get around since the stroke, told her he'd done too much during the day.

"Good grief!" Edward murmured, rolling closer. "Unless I'm mistaken, that's Gabe Gentry."

"It is," she said, pleased that her anger was manifested by nothing but the brusque reply.

"Do you need any help?" Edward asked.

"I will in a moment," she told him.

Wielding the scissors with a rough carelessness, she cut away Gabe's expensive coat and shirt. Deep purple bruises covered his chest. Her fingers began a gentle probing.

"Ouch!" Edward said, leaning in for a better

look. "That's going to be painful when he wakes up. Any broken ribs?"

"Two, at least," she said, finishing her careful examination of his torso. "And his left arm, obviously." Both of Gabe's eyes were black. His perfect, straight nose was broken. When the dirt and blood were washed away, she straightened his nose and taped it into place.

"Who would do something like this to another human?"

"From what I've heard about his escapades since he left here, I imagine he's made his share of enemies," Rachel observed, as she began to cut away his trousers to check his lower body for injuries. They were minimal, just several nasty bruises.

"Boots?" Edward asked.

"I'd say so," she concurred, thoughtfully. "That's probably how the ribs were broken. He'll spend a miserable few weeks," she stated and felt a sudden rush of shame for the jolt of satisfaction that accompanied the thought. Her father's puzzled expression told her that he, too, was wondering at the root of her animosity. Well, let him wonder. She had no intention of enlightening him. Not now. Not ever.

"Was he robbed?" Edward asked.

"Apparently. Simon said his empty wallet was lying a few feet from him."

"Wasn't there another robbery near Antoine a couple of months ago?"

"Yes," she said, pulling a sheet over his lower body. "Can you reach the bandages?"

"Sure."

"I'll lift him upright if you can stand long enough to wrap him up."

"I can," Edward said, and they proceeded to bind the broken ribs.

"Do you think it was the same bunch, since Sheriff Garrett never caught the culprits?" he asked, as he tied off the ends of the bandage.

"Probably."

"Do you need any help with the arm?"

"I can get it, thanks." She splinted the arm and then poured a basin of water and began to wash the congealed blood from the gash on his face. It would leave an ugly scar.

"He's going to need stitches," she noted, staring dispassionately at the jagged wound, possibly made with a knife.

And how will your lady friends like that? I wonder.

Her teeth clamped down on her lower lip, and shame again swept through her at her uncharacteristic spitefulness. She felt angry and sick to her stomach and oddly depleted.

"Too bad," Edward said. "He's always been such a good-looking guy."

Gabe was starting to move around by the time she finished stitching him up, so she gave him a draft of laudanum to help him sleep. Once she finished treating him, she and Roland settled Gabe in the downstairs bedroom she reserved for the occasional overnight patient.

"Do you know him?" Roland asked.

"It's Gabe Gentry," she said, pulling the quilts up to his chin.

"I sort of remember him from when I was a little kid. Didn't he take off to see the world several years ago?"

"Yes."

"I heard he made a name for himself with the ladies," Roland said with a sly smile.

"So they say."

Not really wanting to talk about Gabe's past, whatever it might or might not include, she thanked Roland, paid him for his time and wished him a merry Christmas.

She was cleaning up the examination room when her father rolled to the doorway, where he sat watching her with an unreadable expression in his eyes. "Did I miss anything?"

"You did a splendid job, Rachel. You should know by now that you're a fine doctor, and I'm very proud of you."

Proud of her. She turned away so he wouldn't see the tears that sprang into her eyes. How could he be proud of her after the humiliation and disgrace she'd brought to him and to the family name?

"Thank you," she murmured, knowing she had to reply. With her emotions and her features under control, she said, "He should sleep for a while. If you don't mind keeping an eye on him for an hour or so, I think I'll try to do the same."

Edward nodded. "If he needs you, I'll call."

"He won't," she retorted. "People like him don't need anyone."

* * *

Lying in her tousled bed, her forearm covering her eyes in a futile attempt to block the memories sweeping over her, Rachel gave a soft groan of anguish. She hadn't expected to see Gabe in Simon's wagon.

Indeed, since he hadn't been back to Wolf Creek since leaving, she'd begun to think she'd never again set eyes on him. Being confronted with his very real presence had rekindled the feelings she'd experienced when he'd walked away from her without a second thought.

Shame suffused her. Because she'd been fool enough to discount the stories she'd heard about him, because he'd been sweet and made her laugh, and *listened* to her, she had made the biggest mistake of her life.

She was a self-sufficient woman who had gone alone to a big city and challenged tradition by daring to go into in a field dominated by men. She came from a loving home and had a solid Christian background. She should have known better than to let him into her heart, but she had been so lonely and homesick, and he brought back memories of easier, happier times. He made her feel smart and special and important.

She'd fallen in love with him. Believing that he loved her in return, she had indulged in her forbidden longings and given him everything his kisses demanded.

Three weeks later, he'd left her with nothing but

a note for goodbye, a bleeding, aching heart and three weeks of memories that seemed sordid in light of his defection. She had faced the truth: Gabe Gentry was everything the gossips said he was and more. A liar, a cheat and a womanizer. Oh, certainly he was fun, friendly and he *listened*. And he used each and every one of those traits she'd been so enamored of against her. Sheltered and innocent, she hadn't stood a chance. He'd worked at breaching her defenses until she'd given up and given in.

Like Eve, she'd been lured from the straight path. Overnight, Gabe went from being funny and charming to a handsome rogue endowed with more skill and cunning than any man she'd ever met.

She'd found out the hard way the lessons her parents had tried to instill in her. Sin was so tempting because it came wrapped in such an attractive, alluring package, all tied up with the subtle lie that it was not wrong, that it was all right…really.

Realizing how easily he'd deceived her set her to crying so hard and heavily she'd feared the tears would never stop. Eventually anger replaced her sorrow, anger that burned so hotly that it dried her tears. Anger at Gabe. Anger at herself.

She'd moved through the days, more alone and miserable than before, barely able to concentrate on her schooling. Unable to eat, she'd grown so thin and hollow-eyed that Mrs. Abernathy had urged her to see a physician.

"I regret to inform you that you're expecting a child, Miss Stone," the doctor had said, peering at her over the tops of his spectacles. He didn't bother hiding his disapproval.

Rachel felt her heart plummet. Her already queasy stomach churned. Having a baby? Impossible! Having a baby was supposed to be a joyous occasion, not something that just…happened. And not to unmarried women. Babies were supposed to be the result of…of love.

She must have spoken, because the doctor stood.

"All I can tell you, Miss Stone, is that you are not the first young lady foolish enough to believe a man's lies. I can just hope that you are not so imprudent as to make the mistake a second time."

"B-but what am I going to do? My family…" She paused and swallowed hard.

"Will be devastated, I'm sure," he'd told her, offering her not one iota of help or comfort. "Now, you should try to get as much rest as possible, and eat three healthy meals a day."

She thought she might upchuck at the idea of eating three meals a day. "But I'm so sick, I can't hold anything down."

"Tut-tut!" he'd said, looking at her as if she were a strange organism under a microscope's lens. "My wife was never sick a day during her confinements. I can assure you that you will not rid yourself of this child by vomiting it up. I strongly suggest that you accept your situation and start preparing for some significant changes to your life."

She'd left his office vacillating between despair and fury. The man's bedside manner was nonexistent! He was so uncaring he had no right to hang out his shingle. He was right about one thing, though. She had been very foolish. She'd thrown away her good name, turned her back on a lifetime of teaching and jeopardized her soul. All for three weeks of feeling cherished and loved by a man who'd lied to her about his feelings. Lied to her about everything.

A baby was to be her punishment for loving him.

Ever practical, she supposed it was no more than she deserved. Well, so be it. She pushed aside the panic nibbling at the edges of her composure. Despite her lapses in judgment, she was smart and possessed plenty of grit. She was handling medical school, and she could handle this, too—somehow.

She sat down with pen and paper and considered her options. The doctor had been right when he'd said her parents would be devastated and ashamed of her actions if they found out what she'd done, so she would take measures to see that they didn't find out. That meant returning to Wolf Creek or asking for help from them was out of the question. She couldn't afford to bring up a child and continue with her studies. The small allowance her father sent for her upkeep barely stretched from one month to the next.

Her only recourse was to have the child and put it up for adoption. Only then could she go home and try to put the whole thing behind her. The next months would be torture as she faced the stares and snide smirks she knew she'd receive from her fellow classmates, but it still seemed her best option.

She soon learned that life seldom went as planned. She was in the final month of her pregnancy when Sarah VanSickle, the biggest gossip in Pike County, happened to be visiting her sister in St. Louis and decided to pay Rachel an impromptu visit.

Rachel could still picture the jubilation in Sarah's eyes as she'd swept her up and down with a knowing eye. The loathsome woman had wasted no time scurrying home to recount the news to not only Rachel's parents, but everyone else in town.

It was little wonder that she gave birth to a baby boy the very day her father arrived to confront her about the rumors. Seeing the anguish in his eyes, knowing how deeply she'd disappointed him, she vowed that no amount of persuasion could tempt her to tell him who had fathered her child.

Though he was heartbroken over her actions, Edward Stone was as stubborn as his daughter. From the moment the baby was born, he began to campaign for her to keep him.

After two days of reasoning that sometimes bordered on outright coercion, she'd agreed. She and the son she named Daniel had stayed in St. Louis until she received her medical degree, something made possible when Edward upped his monthly stipend and arranged for Mrs. Abernathy to keep Danny while Rachel was in class. Only then was she forced to summon the courage to go back home and face the music.

Since Sarah had blabbed the news all over town, there was no way Rachel could pretend she'd mar-

ried while she was away, and even if that had been
an option, she wouldn't have added lying to her sins.
Instead, with her well-respected father at her side,
she'd brazened out the whispers and cold shoulders
with the same determination and dedication that
had seen her through her schooling.

A week after arriving home, her mother died,
and Rachel always felt at fault. A short time later,
she'd found the courage to go back to church and
seek God's forgiveness.

Since then, she had worked alongside her father trying to earn back the respect and goodwill
of the townsfolk. When Edward suffered a stroke
two years ago, she'd taken on the bulk of his practice. Though there were a few who still regarded
her as a fallen woman, for the most part she'd been
restored into the town's good graces.

To this day no one—not even her father—knew
the identity of Danny's father.

Now that man lay in her downstairs bedroom and
there was nowhere to run from her past. She'd always believed God had a plan, that things happened
for a reason and that He was in control. When Gabe
had walked out on her after taking her innocence,
she'd wondered what the Lord could possibly have
been thinking by bringing them together. Now she
wondered what on earth He could possibly have in
mind by doing it again.

That afternoon, still weary and upset, Rachel
decided that since sickness and accidents seemed

to be taking a holiday, she would take her mind off of what she'd begun to think of as the *situation* and bake oatmeal cookies with Danny.

She knew she should drive out and tell Caleb his brother was back and seriously injured, but she didn't want to talk about Gabe Gentry, didn't want to waste one single moment even thinking about him. Therein lay the problem. All she'd done since she'd recognized him on the gurney was think about him.

She was reaching for a tea towel to take a batch of cookies from the oven when Danny asked, "Do you know that man, Mama?"

Rachel paused, halfway to the stove. *Take a deep breath and answer him*. After all, he was only exhibiting the natural curiosity of an eight-year-old.

"I knew him a long time ago," she said, choosing her words with care. "But not very well, it seems." It was the truth, after all.

"Pops said he's Mr. Gentry's younger brother."

"That's right." One by one she lifted the hot cookies onto a stoneware platter with the egg turner. Mercifully, before Danny could ask another question, she heard someone knocking. Her father was dozing in his favorite chair, so there was no need to stop. He'd answer the door.

She heard the rumble of masculine voices, and in a matter of minutes Caleb entered the kitchen. "Caleb!" she said, surprised to see him.

"Edward told me it's true," he said, twisting his hat in his big work-roughened hands. His unusual silvery eyes were a dark, stormy gray.

"Yes." Rachel gestured toward a chair at the table. "Have a seat. I'm sorry I didn't come out and tell you, but it was a long morning, and I took a little rest."

"No need," Caleb said, stepping farther into the room but refusing to sit down. "Between Simon and Roland, the Wolf Creek grapevine is in prime working order. Sarah drove out about noon on the pretext of wanting to be the first to see Eli. Of course, she couldn't wait to tell me the news."

"After the way she slandered you and Abby, I can't believe that woman would have the gall to even look you in the eye," Rachel said with a bitter twist of her lips.

Caleb's smile mimicked hers. "I warned her last year not to ever step foot on the place again, but I guess she decided facing my anger was a fair trade for the pleasure of being the first to tell me about Gabe. How bad is he?"

"Bad enough." Rachel listed his injuries and Caleb winced.

"Can I see him?"

"Of course. I should check on him anyway. I've given him some laudanum, so he's unconscious. It's best if I keep him that way for a day or two, until he's past the worst of the pain," she said, preceding Caleb into the bedroom.

As he approached the bed, Rachel heard him draw in a sharp breath. He swallowed hard and looked up at her with an expression of horror. "His face…"

She nodded. "Whoever did this to him intended for him to remember it."

Never one to show emotion, Caleb's response was to turn and walk out of the room. In the hall, he hesitated, almost as if he wanted to say something and didn't know how...or what.

"Would you like a cup of coffee and some cookies?" Rachel asked in a gentle voice. "They're straight from the oven."

"That would be nice," he said. He followed her into the kitchen, where Edward was plopping out spoons full of dough, and pulled out a chair.

Rachel sent her father a silent message and Edward said, "Come on, Danny. It's warmed up some, so let's go outside awhile. I'll sit on the porch while you make a snowman."

Since he'd been begging to go out all day, Danny gave a shout of joy and bounded from the room.

"Bundle up!" Edward shouted to his retreating back, turning his chair and following.

When they were gone, Caleb said simply, "Thank you."

Rachel sat down across from him. "You wanted to tell me something?"

He took a swallow of coffee. "I don't know what I want. When I first heard Gabe was back, I intended to come here and give him a piece of my mind for walking out all those years ago and never once contacting us. That was before I saw how bad he is."

He swallowed hard. A smart, self-educated man

known for his toughness and an unyielding attitude, Caleb had softened a lot since marrying Abby Carter.

"Now I don't know how I feel or what to say to him," he confessed, rubbing a hand down his cheek. "Seeing him like that caught me off guard." He gave another halfhearted smile. "It's hard to summon up a lot of anger when someone is lying there battered and bleeding and can't defend himself."

She gave a half shrug. "True, I suppose, but there's absolutely no excuse for him to not contact you all these years," Rachel said before she could temper her tongue.

Caleb frowned at her animosity.

Realizing she'd let too much of her antagonism show, she took a calming breath. "You never really got along, did you?"

"No." He ran his hand through his shaggy hair. "Well, that's not exactly true. Actually, we never had much to do with each other. He was four years younger than me, and I was always expected to toe the line, get the work done. Lucas mostly let Gabe go his own way, so he never did much of anything that resembled work. When he asked for his inheritance, Lucas just up and gave it to him, and I was left to deal with everything here."

"It must have seemed very unfair."

Caleb's short bark of laughter lacked true mirth. "In more ways than you can imagine. I guess it's pretty obvious that Gabe was always the handsome one, the charming one, the one who could make everyone laugh. I was the drudge, the sensible one, the serious brother. Right or wrong, I always resented him for it."

Caleb pinned her with a hard look. "Maybe I still do. It will be interesting to hear what kind of story he spins when he wakes up. I can't imagine anything he could possibly say to make me feel different toward him, so he needn't expect me to welcome him with open arms. In fact, once he gets better, I won't mind seeing him leave town."

It was quite a speech for the taciturn farmer. Knowing the feelings of her own heart, Rachel kept quiet.

Caleb lifted his gaze to hers. "I know the Bible says I should forgive him and let go of the past, but I don't mind telling you I'm having a real hard time with this."

Rachel offered him a wan smile. "Believe me," she said. "I understand better than you think."

That night, after checking on the patient, Rachel went into Danny's room and sat on the side of the bed. Sweet, innocent little man, she thought, brushing the dark, wavy, too-long hair away from his forehead. Until today, she'd never realized just how much he looked like Gabe, probably because she had taken such pains to bury her memories of him.

With him now beneath her roof, that was impossible. She could only hope and pray that he mended soon so that he could be on his way, preferably, as Caleb suggested, out of town. She didn't want Danny around Gabe any more than necessary.

Brushing her lips against her son's forehead, she rose and went to join her father in the parlor.

"Everyone okay?" he asked, looking up from his book and peering at her over the tops of the glasses that lent his attractively lined face a professorial look.

"Everyone's fine."

Edward laid aside his book, and Rachel sat on the end of the sofa. "What about you?" he asked.

"What do you mean?"

"Are you fine? You don't seem so," he said, tapping into his uncanny ability to see things beyond the surface. "You've been jumpy all day, and angry and…oh, I don't know, maybe even sad. Would you like to tell me why?"

She crossed her arms across her chest. "No."

"Well, then," he said, "do you mind if I hazard a guess?"

Rachel gave him a narrow-eyed look. "Guess away," she said with a nonchalance that did a reasonable job of masking her apprehension.

Edward tented his fingertips and regarded her for a few long seconds. She felt as if he could see into her very heart and soul, and that all the secrets she'd held so close were about to be exposed. He was no fool. Perception and spot-on intuition were two of Edward Stone's greatest assets.

"In all your thirty-one years, I've never seen you the way you've been today. I've tried and tried to figure out what's behind this hostility you have toward Gabe, especially since you never had much truck with him before he left town."

"And have you come up with a reason?" she asked in a voice that, like her hands, trembled the slightest bit.

"I have."

"And?" she asked, regarding him with a steady expression.

"The only thing that makes a woman act the way you have today is rejection. You know, the old 'Hell hath no fury like a woman scorned.'" He looked her squarely in the eye. "I believe Gabe Gentry looked you up when you were in St. Louis. I believe he's Danny's father."

An anguished cry escaped Rachel. How could he have figured it out just from her attitude? She felt a sob claw its way up her throat and pressed a fist to her mouth to hold it back.

"Oh, my dear!" Edward said in a tortured voice, rolling his chair over to her and putting a consoling hand on her shoulder. "How hard it must have been for you to keep that secret all this time."

"I would never have told you," she said as tears slipped down her cheeks. "Never."

"I know that, you hard-headed, silly girl. Would you like to tell me about it? The abridged version, of course," he asked with an awkward attempt at a smile.

Why not? Rachel thought. Perhaps if she told him how it had happened and how she'd felt, it would release some of the guilt and misery that had made her prickly and skeptical and robbed her of so much joy through the years.

"There isn't much to tell," she said almost thoughtfully. She told him how she'd come home from school and found Gabe at her boardinghouse. "I was so lonely and homesick, and it was so good to see a familiar face…" Her voice trailed away. "I invited him in and we had lemonade.

"As he was leaving, he asked me to dinner the next night and we spent every day together after I got home from school," she said, allowing long-suppressed memories their freedom. "He brought me flowers from a street vendor, took me out to eat at fancy restaurants, bought me trinkets and told me all sorts of wonderful, fantastic stories of the places he'd been and hoped to go."

Her tears ran freely as the memories continued to tumble out. "He teased me, and it was—" she gave a huge hiccuping sob "—so nice to laugh. Every evening, he insisted I tell him about what I'd done and what I'd learned. He was just so encouraging, both about my studies and…just everything. I told him all about my dearest hopes and dreams."

She took the handkerchief Edward offered, mopped at her eyes and blew her running nose.

"He made me believe that all of those hopes and dreams could come true. I fell in love with him," she said, summing everything up in those few words. "I'm sure you can figure out the rest."

"I think I understand," Edward said when she

ran out of words. "Your upbringing gave you little or no defense. You had no idea how to guard your heart. So tell me why he left. Did you quarrel?"

Rachel shook her head. "Nothing like that. I thought things were going along just fine. And then I came home from school one day, and he'd left a note with Mrs. Abernathy that said a friend had caught up with him and talked him into taking a paddle wheeler to New Orleans. It was supposed to be great fun, and he'd always wanted to go there. He said the next time he was in town, he'd look me up and we'd go to dinner."

"That's it?" Edward said, with a look of disbelief.

"Oh, no. He said it had been a fun few weeks and that he'd never forget me."

She laughed, but there was no joy in the sound. "I was so ashamed," she said in an anguished whisper. "I'd ruined my whole life. That was bad enough, but when I found out I was going to have a baby, I was terrified. I thought I'd figured out a way that no one would ever find out. Then Sarah showed up and sent all my plans tumbling down."

Tears spilled down Rachel's cheeks. "I know bearing my shame was hard for you and Mother, especially after I came home, and I know my actions are what brought on her death, but I want to thank you for never once throwing it back in my face and for…for making me…k-keep Danny." She choked on another sob.

Edward gave her hand an awkward pat. "Your mother had a heart condition, Rachel. Her health had been going downhill for more than a year. Her passing so soon after you came back was just an unfortunate coincidence. She loved you and she adored Danny."

He smiled. "And as for that young scamp, I hope I didn't *make* you do anything. I hope I just encouraged you to do what you really wanted. I know you well, my precious girl, and I don't believe you'd have been able to live with yourself if you'd given him up. And selfishly, I couldn't bear the thought of strangers bringing up my flesh and blood—or worse, him being put into an orphanage and never knowing the joys of real family. He's a delight, Rachel. I can't imagine life without him."

"Neither can I."

"Besides," he added, "I've never been one to think that two wrongs make a right."

For long moments, the fire popped and crackled while Rachel worked at regaining her composure.

"What do you plan to do now?" Edward asked, at last.

"Do? About what?"

"Gabe. How do you feel about him after all this time?"

"Nothing," she snapped. "I plan to *do* nothing and I *feel* nothing but anger toward him. I hope and pray that he'll leave town again as soon as he's able, which will suit me just fine."

"And if he doesn't? It will certainly be a test, won't it? How long do you think it will take before he figures things out?"

Rachel's face drained of color. "What are you saying?"

There was no compromise in Edward's eyes. "You need to tell Gabe the truth. Danny, too."

Her horrified gaze met his. "I can't!"

"Listen to me, Rachel. You need to tell Danny before someone else sees the resemblance and starts spreading it around town. Believe me, as hard as it may be, he'll be much better off hearing the truth from you than someone else. They both will."

Chapter Two

Christmas Eve morning dawned crisp and cold. Just as dawn was breaking, Rachel rose from the cot beside Gabe's bed and lit the lamp.

He had rested well in his laudanum-induced sleep, but she had not been so blessed. Sleep had eluded her, as thoughts and recollections tumbled round and round in her mind like colorful fragments in a kaleidoscope. Besides a jumble of troubling memories, her mind replayed the conversation with her father again and again.

She couldn't believe how light her heart felt since sharing the secret she'd carried alone for so long. Who would have thought that something that seemed so small could weigh so heavily on a heart? She would be eternally grateful that her father's love and support had not wavered, even after learning the truth.

She knew Edward was right about telling Danny about Gabe, yet the very thought of doing so filled her with dread. How would she find the words? What would Danny say…and think?

She stoked the dying fire and went to see how Gabe was doing, busying herself with changing his bandages and checking his temperature. Her ministering seemed to agitate him, and he began to move about. When she tried to restrain him, he cried out and opened his eyes. Thankfully she saw no recollection there, no wicked, teasing gleam, nothing but agony. The doctor in her wanted him to be pain free and improve under her care; the woman in her shrank from the moment he would open his eyes and look up at her with recognition.

What would he see when he awakened? What would he think when he saw her for the first time in nine years? She turned toward the mirror hanging above the washstand, drawn to it like a June bug to the light. Her reflection wavered in the flickering light of the oil lamp.

She stared at herself for long moments and then, womanlike, rubbed at her forehead with her fingertips as if she could massage away the few slight creases she saw there, lines etched by her deep concern for her patients.

Exposure to the elements in all sorts of weather had tanned her face and hands despite the bonnet she wore, and squinting against the sun had left tiny lines at the corners of her eyes. Despite regular treatments of lemon juice, a faint spattering of freckles dotted her nose.

Age and Danny's birth had added a few pounds,

but according to her father, it was weight she needed. Strangely, her face was thinner than it had been nine years ago, refined by age and life.

She had no illusions. She no longer looked twenty-two. Shouldering the responsibilities that went hand in hand with the demands of her father's practice had taken its toll on her in many ways.

Mirror, mirror on the wall, would Gabe still think her fair at all?

Would he even recognize her? What would he say? What would she? Would he be the shocking flirt she recalled, or would he be filled with contrition?

Telling herself she was a fool for wasting so much as a thought on him, she went back to the bed and dabbed some antiseptic to the cut on Gabe's face.

As she tended to his needs, her mind turned to Caleb's ambivalent feelings about his brother's return. She could relate to them only too well. Like Caleb, and even though she knew that not to pardon Gabe jeopardized her own forgiveness, she couldn't imagine any scenario that would make her feel differently about the man who had taken everything she had to give and walked away as if it meant nothing to him.

Then why are you having such contradictory thoughts about him?

She had no answer for that.

Satisfied that he was fine for the moment, she went to the kitchen, rekindled the fire in the stove and filled the coffeepot. While she waited for the stove to get hot enough to start breakfast, she opened her Bible. Instead of reading, she flipped the pages until she found the pressed petunia she'd placed there. A gift from Gabe, plucked from Mrs. Abernathy's flower bed and tucked behind Rachel's ear when they'd returned from a walk. *"A memento of this evening."*

She could picture the half-light of dusk, could almost hear the sounds of children playing and smell the sweet scent of the petunias dancing in the breeze. Felt again the light brush of his lips against hers. A small, impromptu gesture was so like him. She planned. Gabe lived for the moment.

Impatient with her unruly thoughts, she slammed her Bible shut and began to slice the bacon, placing the strips into the cold cast-iron skillet. Gathering the ingredients for buttermilk biscuits, she measured and mixed flour, salt and leavening and started working the lard into the flour with her fingertips, finding comfort in the simplicity of the everyday task.

Seeing that the stove was hot, she set the skillet of bacon over the heat. After adding just the right amount of buttermilk, she pinched off a biscuit-size piece of dough and deftly rolled the edges under to make it reasonably smooth and round. Placing it into the greased pan, she made a dimple in the center with her knuckle.

Danny, his dark hair standing on end and covering a yawn, came into the kitchen as she was filling the slight indentations with a small dollop of extra lard, just the way her mama had done.

"Good morning," she said, sliding the pan into the oven.

"Morning."

She wiped her hands on a wet cloth and sighed as she watched him pour a splash of coffee into a tin cup and fill it to the brim with milk and two spoons full of sugar. He'd started having morning "coffee milk," as he called it, when Edward had started sharing his own sweetened brew. When she'd questioned the wisdom of the action, Edward had assured her that it was more milk than anything else and maintained it was fine; it hadn't hurt her, had it?

Grandparents! she thought, lifting the crispy strips of bacon onto a platter. If she didn't remain vigilant, no telling how Edward would spoil Danny. But how could she deny him his little indulgences when he had taken on a very special role in Danny's life? Not only was he the child's grandfather, he'd been the closest thing to a father as he was ever likely to know.

Until now.

With her father's words ringing through her mind, Rachel searched her son's face for anything that might give away his paternity. He definitely had Gabe's long, lush eyelashes, as well as the slant of his eyebrows. The dimple in Danny's chin would be a dead giveaway as he grew closer to manhood and his jawline firmed the way his father's had.

His father. Rachel stifled a groan. How could she

not think of him when he lay just down the hall? Resolutely, she opened a jar of red plum jam one of her patients had given her in lieu of payment for stitching up a nasty cut.

"Are you excited about going to the Gentrys' to-morrow?" she asked Danny as she smoothed down the recalcitrant "rooster tail" sticking up from the crown of his dark head.

He nodded, his eyes bright. "I made a present for baby Eli."

"Really? What did you make?"

"Roland gave me some old cedar shingles and helped me drill some holes on one edge so I could put some leather laces through them. I painted Ben's, Betsy's and Laura's names on them with different colors. I made one for Eli yesterday. I thought Miss Abby could hang it on the end of his cradle."

"That was very sweet of you, Danny."

"I made some for the Carruthers kids, too," he said. "I thought they could hang them on the wall above their beds."

"I'm sure everyone will love them," she said, marveling as she often did at what a thoughtful child he was.

Feeling blessed to have him, she peeked at the biscuits. "Almost done," she announced. "How many eggs do you want?"

"Two," he said promptly. "Soft."

"I'll have two, myself," Edward said from the doorway.

"Coming right up," Rachel said, reaching for the

brown crockery bowl that held the eggs she bought from a lady in town.

"I've been thinking about tomorrow," she said, cracking the first egg into the sizzling bacon grease.

As they had the previous year, the Stones had planned to have their Christmas meal with the Gentrys and Caleb's former in-laws, the Emersons. "Why don't I stay here with Gabe and you and Danny go to Abby and Caleb's?"

"Absolutely not!" Edward told her. "You and Danny go, and I'll stay here with Gabe. You can bring me back a plate."

"It will be stone cold in this weather," she argued.

"Then we'll warm it up in the oven. Really, Rachel, you go. It's a special day for Danny, and it's seldom you get much uninterrupted time with him. Besides, it will give you the opportunity to check on Abby and the baby."

He had a point. Rachel put the first two eggs onto a plate and set it in front of him. The hot biscuits and a bowl of fresh-churned butter were placed on the table next to a platter of bacon. She looked from the determination in her father's eyes to the hopeful expression in Danny's. "If you're sure…" she said. "We'll be gone most of the day."

"I'm sure. Gabe is stable, and I think I can handle anything that comes up during that short time. Besides—" he shot a smile toward Danny "—I can read that new book on Italy you're giving me for Christmas."

"Edward Stone!" Rachel cried, her eyes widening in disbelief. "How do you know you got a book about Italy?"

Edward's eyes twinkled. "Never tell an eight-year-old anything you don't want repeated."

Rachel pinned her son with a familiar, narrow-eyed look. "You little rascal!" she said. "Christmas presents are supposed to be a secret."

"I didn't exactly *tell* him," Danny hedged, slathering a biscuit with butter. "He just asked me a buncha questions and sorta guessed."

"Mmm-hmm," Rachel said, trying to fix her father with that same stern look and failing as her mouth began to twitch with the beginnings of a smile. It was no secret that when it came to Christmas and secrecy, Edward Stone was a total failure.

"You're as bad as he is," she charged. "Worse. At least he's just a child."

Stifling a smile, Edward said, "It's settled, then. You and Danny are going. Now don't you need to see to those eggs?"

With the cookies all baked, Rachel spent the day stirring up pumpkin pies and an apple cake liberally laced with raisins and the black walnuts she and Edward had cracked and painstakingly picked out.

Finished with the baking, she and Danny loaded up their goodies and made deliveries to the Carruthers family and a widow or two who had a hard time making ends meet.

By the time their visits were over and they'd finished the evening meal, she was pleasantly weary. The day had been so busy that at times she was able to forget the man lying in the bedroom down the way. Danny helped with the dishes, and they were getting ready to begin their yearly Christmas Eve ritual when an agonized cry came from Gabe's room.

Tossing her dish towel onto the table, Rachel ran toward the sound, throwing the door open against the wall in her haste.

Gabe lay on his back, just as he had been, but as she neared the bed she realized that he was fully awake. His eyes were shadowed with pain that became stunned disbelief as he struggled to raise himself up to his uninjured elbow.

"Rachel?" His voice was deep and husky, as if he were getting over a bad sore throat. Looking to blame him for everything, she'd often thought that his voice was the first weapon he'd used in his insidious assault on her senses. Now, even in her concern, she imagined she heard a hint of wonder in his voice.

"Lie still," she commanded, placing a restraining hand against his shoulder. Offering him no time to formulate a reply, she continued, "What on earth were you thinking trying to get up? You might have injured yourself worse than you already are."

Ever professional even in her irritation, she placed gentle, questing fingers against his bound ribs. "Does it hurt?" she asked, unaware that the question was somewhat silly under the circumstances. She just wanted to get him easy again and steer clear of the feelings churning inside her now that they were face-to-face.

Despite the pain and grogginess reflected in his eyes, he attempted a smile that more resembled a grimace. "Only when I breathe."

Nothing had changed, she thought. Still quick with a smile and a glib reply.

"Do you remember what happened?"

A spasm of pain crossed his features. "A couple of guys jumped me between here and Antoine. How did I get *here?*"

All business, she leaned over him to check the bandage on his head. "Simon Teasdale found you and brought you to me."

She stepped back and allowed her gaze to roam his face. As she had, he'd aged and looked older than the twenty-nine she knew him to be. But, as it seemed with most men, he'd done it better. Maturity had firmed the boyish softness of his jaw and chin as she knew it would Danny's, making it more sharply defined and making his resemblance to Caleb more pronounced, though Gabe would always be the handsomer of the two.

He, too, had a tanned face with crinkly lines at the corners of his eyes, but she knew from past experience that these lines would not have come from worry or the elements but laughter as he pursued countless pleasures. He was still disturbingly handsome and she suspected the inevitable scar he would carry would only add to his aura of mystery and danger. That thought awakened her slumbering anger.

"Did you know them?"

He gave a slight shake of his head. "They had bandannas. I won a lotta…money from a couple guys in a poker game… Little Rock." He made another pitiful attempt to smile. "Guess they wanted it back."

She dabbed at the still-seeping gash on his head with a piece of cotton wool saturated with peroxide. His hiss of pain gave her far more satisfaction than it should have.

"Simon did find your wallet nearby, and it was empty, but if it was someone from Little Rock, why would they wait so long to attack you?"

His eyes looked troubled. "Guess I'm not… thinking straight. Feel like…death warmed over."

"As well you should. You have broken ribs and a dislocated shoulder, which will be pretty painful while it heals. You have a possible concussion. There's a cut on your scalp and another on your cheek that will probably leave a nasty scar."

He attempted a shrug that elicited another grunt of pain.

"You need to go back to sleep," she told him, feeling a sudden, unexpected and annoying rush of sympathy.

"How long have I been here?" he asked, once more speaking through clenched teeth.

"Since yesterday morning."

She could almost see his fuzzy mind trying to calculate what day it was. "So it's…"

"Christmas Eve."

"I'd hoped to be home for Christmas."

The confession surprised her. Home? He'd meant to come back to Wolf Creek?

Of course he was coming home. Why else would he have been between Wolf Creek and Antoine?

"Why? Why now, after all this time?"

Without thinking, she blurted out the question that leaped into her mind, even though she knew that he was in no condition for the battle she felt brewing.

"To try to…fix things…with Caleb."

No wish to try to make amends with her. "Caleb knows you're here, and frankly, he wasn't exactly overjoyed about it." She started to turn away, and his good hand reached out and grabbed hers.

"And you, Rachel?" he asked, as she stared down at the fingers that manacled her wrist. "I know how I left was…wrong. I'm sorry."

So he *did* want to make things right with her. The knowledge gave her no satisfaction; it only stoked her anger. "Why should I believe your contrition is genuine, Gabe? You once told me a lot of things, all of them lies. Why should I believe this sudden change of heart is any different? And your behavior wasn't just wrong. It was contemptible!"

She knew that her tirade was inappropriate and unprofessional, and that the fury consuming her was no doubt reflected in her face and in her voice, which shook as badly as her hands. He was in pain from numerous injuries. It was neither the time nor the place to confront him, but the dam that had held back her pain for so many years had burst, and she could not seem to stop the words that spewed from her like lava from a volcano.

"Did you really think you could just waltz into town and expect everyone to welcome you with open arms? Did you think that maybe Caleb would be so overjoyed by the prodigal's return that he would trot out the fatted calf? Guess what, Gabe, this is real life, not a Bible story, and I don't see any happy endings in sight!"

He looked stricken by her outburst. She didn't care. She *wanted* him to know he had behaved despicably. Wanted him to know the pain *she'd* suffered. She even hoped the knowledge of what he'd done added to his own pain.

His grip relaxed and he allowed her to pull free. She stared at him, but his eyes gave away nothing of what he was feeling.

"Mama?" Danny spoke from the doorway.

Trembling as if she had the ague, she turned. "What is it, Danny?" she asked in a far harsher tone than she'd intended and he was accustomed to.

The child looked from her to the man in the bed, his eyes wide with uncertainty. "Pops wanted me to see if everything is all right."

"Tell him everything's fine," she said in a softer voice.

She kept her gaze studiously on her son, who

looked shocked by the side of his mother he'd never seen. She wished she could call back her heated words. No. Gabe Gentry deserved her anger. She only wished Danny hadn't heard. "Mr. Gentry is just in a lot of pain at the moment."

"But you were mad at him," Danny said, sensing there was more than she was saying. Like his grandfather, he was prone to probe until his curiosity was satisfied.

"Only because he tried to get out of bed," she fibbed, casting a quick glance at Gabe, whose eyes were now shut. "He might have hurt himself worse."

"Oh."

Once more, Danny looked from one adult to the other before backing out the door, leaving Rachel alone with her patient, who stared at her with no visible expression. Why didn't that surprise her? The celebrated Gabriel Gentry would never see his actions as despicable.

"I'll get you some medication," she told him, wanting nothing more than to escape him.

"I don't want it," he said, his jaw set in a stubborn line. "I want…to get up…awhile."

"There's no way you can—"

"It's Christmas Eve," he interrupted, his voice rough with his own anger and something she couldn't put a name to. "Help me to…a chair. I'll be…okay for a while."

"Fine," she snapped. "I'll let you sit up, but only if you let me give you a little something."

He looked as if he would like to argue further,

but nodded. She turned toward the door. "Where are you going?"

"To get Pops's wheelchair."

"Rachel," he said, the sound of his voice stopping her. She turned.

"I had no idea you had a son."

She stiffened but managed a twisted smile. "What did you expect, Gabe? That I would carry a torch for you forever?"

For once in his life, Gabe had no witty comeback.

After a lot of moaning and groaning, Rachel got Gabe into one of her father's robes and settled into the wheelchair with a quilt over his legs. Then she rolled him to the kitchen, where he picked at a bowl of beef stew he didn't want while trying—without much success and despite the small dose of laudanum she'd forced on him—to ignore the various excruciating pains throbbing throughout his body. It irritated him that she'd been right. He should have stayed in bed.

When the simple meal was finished, he was rolled into the parlor, where he sat watching as the Stones went through their Christmas Eve celebration. His muddled thoughts bounced around from one topic to the next.

When he'd awakened, he remembered how he'd come to be in so much agony but had no idea where he was. He'd chosen not to call for help, instead enduring long pain-filled moments as he struggled to sit up with a shoulder that felt on fire and a rib cage that felt as if someone had taken a club to it. No. Not a club. Boots.

When he'd seen Rachel standing beside the bed, he'd thought she was an illusion, and his reaction had been profound pleasure. It hadn't taken long to realize that she was very real and that she did not share his happiness at being reunited.

She was right, he thought as he watched her with her family. He'd treated her worse than terribly. He remembered their short few weeks together as good ones even though she was nothing like the women he usually spent time with.

She was very smart, which was a little intimidating, as was her desire to become a doctor and settle down in Wolf Creek. His greatest goal was to see as much as he could while his money held out. There was plenty of time to worry about what he would do with his life after he finished seeing the world.

It was years before he'd come to grips with the reality that the lifestyle he'd chosen when he left home had lost its luster and that his interest in aimless pursuits had declined dramatically. He'd begun to feel as if he were living in a world of make-believe, while somewhere out there people led real and meaningful lives.

Comprehension led to months of reflection and careful examination of his upbringing and the life he'd tried so hard to leave behind. He'd realized that the void he'd felt in his heart since the day his mother abandoned him and his brother could not be filled with laughter and joking, senseless reveling or meaningless relationships. All attempts to do so had been futile, masking, but never filling, the emptiness.

He'd been left with the sobering realization that his entire life was nothing but an effort to escape the pain that gnawed at him every moment of every day and could not be assuaged by any thrill, pleasure or sinful indulgence known to man. He'd accepted the truth that there was no escaping the past or how it shaped the person you became. At some point you had to come to terms with that, both the good and the bad.

Then one day in Atlanta almost a year ago, he'd been strolling through a park and heard a woman laugh, laughter filled with such undiluted joy that it triggered an unexpected, long-forgotten memory of Rachel. The moment was sharply poignant. In those few out-of-time seconds, he'd been struck with the sudden conviction that he'd had something rare within his grasp and thrown it away.

Over the next few weeks, memories of their time together drifted through his mind with the sweetness of springtime scents on a subtle breeze: Her affirmation that money was not the important thing for happiness, which he'd scoffed at and now knew was true. Her serious, unwavering dedication when mocked for daring to brave entrance to a profession dominated by men. Her willingness to dedicate herself to a life that was not necessarily conducive to her own well-being, but to the well-being of others.

Longing for something he couldn't put into words, he'd begun to wonder if there was redemption for him out there somewhere. If so, he knew he'd have to start in Wolf Creek, the place where his life had first begun to unravel. There, he'd hoped to find new direction and a new purpose for his life, though he had no idea what that might be or how to go about finding it.

Now, sitting in the Stones' parlor while Edward read the story of baby Jesus from the Bible, he wanted to ask Rachel if he could sit in the parlor the next morning and watch the gift opening. Thanks to his mother's leaving and his father's indifference, he and Caleb had never known what these three people shared. Christmas was just another day. Lucas's only concession to the holiday had been a traditional meal because he liked showing off to some of his friends.

Gabe longed just once to experience what a real Christmas should be, but Rachel had made it clear that the less she had to do with him the better, and he had no wish to disrupt their day. The solemn sounds of their prayer, and their happy, laughing voices as they joked and teased each other, brought about a pang of regret so painful that his heart hurt almost as badly as his physical injuries.

The desire to have that kind of love and the knowledge that he had willfully ruined any chance of experiencing it with Rachel was overwhelming in its intensity. The woman he now knew was the most important person to come into his life had made it clear that she had not forgiven him and was not likely to.

He couldn't blame her. She was right. He had used her—not deliberately, perhaps—but she'd been there and they'd both been willing. In his mind she was no different from other girls he'd spent time with. Except, of course, she was very different.

Filled with an incredible sorrow for what he'd tossed away, Gabe blinked back the unmanly sting of tears. Tears were a luxury he had not allowed himself since the day he'd come home and been told that his mother had left for a new life in Boston…a life that was more important to her than her husband or her sons.

Funny how history repeated itself. For all intents and purposes, he'd done to Rachel exactly what his mother had done to him and his brother.

Christmas morning dawned bright and cold. Rachel slipped into Gabe's room to stoke the fire in his fireplace, stunned to find him sitting on the edge of the bed, as upright as possible. A blanket covered his legs. He clutched a shirt in his fists. He was trembling and sweat dripped down his face despite the chill of the room. A basin of soapy water sat on the stand next to the bed. He'd given himself a sponge bath and was trying to get dressed. He looked near to passing out from the effort.

"What do you think you're doing?" She shook her head. Stubborn, stubborn man.

"Getting dressed," he told her in a terse tone.

Knowing how she felt about him, he couldn't bear being near her any longer than was absolutely necessary, so he'd forced himself to the limit to make her believe he was feeling better than he really was.

"Why didn't you ring for help?"

"It wasn't necessary." Despite the medicine still dulling his senses and the pain racking his body, he made his voice as crisp and no-nonsense as hers.

"How do you feel?"

His blue eyes roamed over her, as restless as the wind tossing the tree branches outside the window. "I'll live."

"I certainly hope so," she said, going to the fireplace. She removed the screen and placed a couple of slivers of pine knot and a couple of logs on the bed of coals. He needed to get warm.

"Do you?"

The simple question fell into the silence of the room. Moving with extreme care, she set the screen back in place.

"Of course I do." She went to the bed and set about changing the bandages on his head and face, probing his swollen shoulder and making a swift examination of his bruised chest.

"Can you bring me some hot water?" he asked. "My sponge bath was a bit chilly, and I'd like to shave and clean my teeth. Maybe I'll feel a bit more human."

She pressed her lips together to keep from saying something to antagonize him. It was too soon for him to be doing so much. "I'm not sure you can—"

"I'll manage."

The determined angle of his chin brooked no argument.

When she returned twenty minutes later, Gabe stood at the shaving stand, his mouth set in a grim line of agony. She didn't know how he'd managed to do all he'd done or why he wasn't passed out on the floor. He was dressed in the clean clothes she'd brought him and had somehow buttoned the shirt over the arm that was held against his chest by the sling. The unused sleeve hung loose. He'd shaved what he could of the stubble shadowing his face, but not without leaving a few oozing nicks here and there. He made no comment about the ugly wound that marred his lean cheek.

Placing the straight-edge razor on the stand, he met her gaze in the mirror. "You don't know how badly I hate to ask this of you, but would you mind washing my feet? I couldn't get below the knees."

Her eyes widened. The simple request, one she'd done countless times for other patients, caught her off guard. Taking care of their needs was her duty as a physician and caretaker, but she didn't want to do any more for Gabe Gentry than was absolutely necessary.

As soon as the thought entered her mind, she felt a familiar wave of shame wash over her. Where was her compassion for this man who might well have died if Simon hadn't found him when he had? Where was her Christian charity? She was a good doctor who had never backed away from a challenge or shirked her responsibilities.

Without a word, she picked up the basin of cooling water, placed it on the floor and knelt beside it, going about her task with quick efficiency and reminding herself that serving his needs while he was injured was not only her duty as a physician; it was her duty as a Christian.

As she worked, the story of Jesus, sinless, perfect, washing His apostles' feet slipped into her mind. She concentrated on her task so that Gabe wouldn't see how near she was to tears.

By nature she was a caring person. She knew she couldn't continue to harbor this soul-destroying resentment, but she seemed unable to free herself from it. Could she find a way to set aside the hostility that had taken hold of her the day he'd destroyed her love with his callous dismissal?

She sighed as she pulled a heavy pair of woolen socks onto his feet. She didn't know. But she knew that if she was ever to be the person the Lord expected her to be she had to try a lot harder.

Gabe heard the sigh and watched as she stood and picked up the basin of water to set it on the shaving stand.

"I'll bring you some breakfast a bit later," she told him, gathering the soiled laundry. "Danny will want to open his gifts first."

"That's fine. I'll just rest until then."

He started to lower himself in gradual increments, using his workable arm and clenching his teeth against the pain. Rachel was beside him in an instant, her arms around his shoulders to help ease him to the pillows. She was strong, he thought, as she lifted his legs to the bed and spread a double layer of quilts over him. Stronger than she looked. He didn't know why that should be such a surprise, but it was.

Gabe waited for the screaming pain in his ribs to subside to a dull, throbbing ache. Many things about Rachel surprised him. She was older, but no less beautiful than he remembered. She'd gained some much-needed weight, which only added to the femininity she tried to hide beneath her tailored, no-nonsense wardrobe. The intriguing scent of magnolia blossoms still clung to her.

What surprised him most was that she was no longer the shy woman who'd had trouble carrying on a conversation unless it was a topic she felt passionately about. Her worshipful eyes no longer followed his every move and she certainly didn't hang on to every word he spoke, as she once had.

She was a woman, not a girl. She was a devoted daughter. She was a mother. She was a professional with long-standing ties to the community, successfully crossing the threshold of a field most women were afraid to enter. That alone made her exceptional.

"You must be in terrible pain after moving around so much. Would you like a bit of medication now?"

Was that actual compassion he heard in her voice? He clenched his teeth together and met her gaze steadily. "No, thank you. I've seen too many people get addicted to it. I'll just tough it out."

"I'm only giving you small doses, and I don't think you're in jeopardy of addiction at this point. Toughing it out isn't really a good idea."

Somehow he managed a derisive smile. "A lot of things I've done haven't been good ideas, but that never stopped me, did it?"

Rachel stared at him for several seconds then scooped up the laundry and left him without another word. Let him hurt. It wasn't her problem. Except, of course, that it was. The very thought of the pain he must be suffering went against everything she stood for and left her feeling undeserving of her calling. Unfortunately, some people had to learn the hard way.

As planned, Rachel and Danny went to Caleb and Abby's at midmorning so that Danny could play with the Gentry children and Rachel could help Mary, Caleb's former mother-in-law, with the last-minute meal preparations, since Abby was still confined to bed.

Rachel made the visit double duty, examining mother and baby and concluding they were both fine, at which Abby declared she was able to get up long enough to eat her Christmas meal with the family. Like Gabe, she would not be deterred.

Abby loved the little signs Danny had made.

Caleb tied the leather cords to the end of the crib while Danny watched with pride. The other children, too, were happy with their name signs, and Caleb promised to hang them at the heads of their beds before nightfall. Though he had no talent for building things from wood, he did dabble with whittling and had fashioned a stunning replica of a Colt pistol for his children to give to Danny. Each of them had taken turns putting a coat of shellac on it.

When the dishes were done, Rachel and Mary Emerson put the little ones down for naps. The men went to the parlor, where Rachel suspected there might be as much afternoon dozing as dominoes and conversation. The older children played with their new toys while Mary Emerson supervised, giving Rachel and Abby time for some uninterrupted "woman talk."

Rachel cut two pieces of pumpkin pie, poured two mugs of coffee and went to Abby's bedroom, to find her once again propped up in bed.

"Thank you," she said, as Rachel handed her the pie and set the mug of coffee on a bedside table. "It's been a lovely day, hasn't it?"

"It has," Rachel agreed. "And you got the best Christmas present of all, albeit a couple of days early."

"I did, didn't I?" Abby said with a smile, glancing at the baby all snug in his cradle. She took a bite of pie and washed it down with a sip of coffee.

"What does Caleb think of Eli now that he's here and you're both well?" Rachel asked.

Since Caleb's first wife had died in childbirth the previous winter, Caleb had been terrified when Abby told him she was expecting his child.

"He's beside himself with happiness—and pride," she said with a satisfied grin.

"Well, his fear was certainly understandable," Rachel said.

"I agree."

"You're happy, aren't you, Abby?" Rachel asked, unaware of the wistful note in her voice.

"I am." There was no denying her contentment. "I loved William, but what I felt for him pales in comparison to what I feel for Caleb."

"I'm really happy for you."

Abby reached out a hand to her friend. "Don't look so sad. There's someone out there for you. Don't ever doubt that."

"Do you really think so?"

"I know so." Abby's eyes brightened at a sudden thought. "What about Gabe?"

"What about Gabe?" she asked with a lift of her dark eyebrows.

"As a potential husband, goose! If you married him we'd be sisters-in-law."

Rachel felt the color drain from her face, felt the stiffness in her cheeks as she forced a smile. "Thank you but no thank you," she said. "Gabriel Gentry is not the marrying type."

"You sound very sure of that."

"Haven't you heard the gossip?"

Abby nodded. "Caleb's told me everything about Gabe, but people do change. Caleb is proof of that."

Not everything.

"It must have been hard for both of them growing up," Abby mused. "Caleb told me that until he married Emily, Christmas was just another day."

Rachel registered her friend's comment with a bit of a shock. With the Gentry money, she would have thought Lucas would have seen to it his boys had anything they wanted. What kind of man would deprive children of a bit of happiness once a year?

"Well, Lucas didn't pretend to be anything but who he was," she said. "I don't imagine he was too interested in conforming to society's expectations. Dad says that for all his unreasonableness, Lucas had a reputation for being hardworking. At least he passed that on to Caleb."

"But not Gabe, from what I hear."

"No. Not Gabe."

"Did you know him?" Abby queried, taking another forkful of pie.

"Yes," Rachel said, concentrating on the steam rising from her mug. "Gabe was two years younger than I, though, and we didn't share the same circle of friends."

"Caleb said he was...spoiled." Abby said the word almost apologetically.

"To put it mildly," Rachel said, struggling to suppress the sarcasm in her voice.

"I've heard he's very handsome."

"He's also wild, dangerous and has no sense of decency...from what I hear," Rachel tacked on.

Abby wondered why her friend was so irritated by the topic of Gabriel Gentry. "So I've heard from Caleb. As I said, people do change. I suppose only time will tell if Gabe has."

Rachel took a sip of coffee before answering. "He did tell me he came back to try to make amends."

"That's promising, but I'm here to say that Caleb is struggling with the idea that Gabe is even back after so long. There's been a lot of bad blood between them."

Rachel nodded. "I certainly understand how he feels." Perhaps more than Caleb.

That conversation stayed with Rachel as she drove the buggy back to town. Like Caleb, she was having a hard time accepting Gabe's return. *Because he broke your heart and trampled your woman's pride beneath his fancy handmade boots.*

True enough. That aside, surely she was mature enough to put the past into perspective. As terrible as it had been, she *had* learned from the experience. She was a better person. Stronger and more tolerant of others' mistakes. So why not Gabe's?

No doubt about it, she thought, giving her head a shake. She was a terrible, terrible person! Not forgiving wasn't an option to a Christian, but like Caleb's, her forgiveness of Gabe would come hard.

She prayed he would heal and move on soon. If he chose to stay, she wasn't sure how she would deal with seeing him on a regular basis. *Stop borrowing trouble, Rachel Stone.* No one had any idea what he would do once his injuries healed. Still, there was the remote possibility that he would stay in the area, which meant her father had a point. She had to tell Danny and pray he understood.

But not today.

To her dismay, she and Danny found Edward and Gabe sitting at the kitchen table playing a game of chess. Gabe sat ramrod straight in the chair. He looked awful. He was far too pale, and there was no masking the pain shadowing his sapphire-hued eyes or the challenge in them as he looked at her. He expected her to rail at him for being out of bed, but she was too weary for another battle and kept silent.

"Can I play, Pops?" Danny wheedled, shoving his small body beneath Edward's arm so he could get a better look at the board.

Intent on the game pieces, Edward gave the boy a distracted hug. "Not this game, Danny."

"No one ever wants to play with me," he said, his shoulders slumping.

"That isn't true," Rachel told him, hanging her coat by the door. She turned and took two plates out of the basket she'd carried in. "Pops plays with you all the time."

"Supper?" Edward asked, spying the plates.

"Turkey and all the trimmings," she replied. "I'll stick them in the oven for a bit," she said, doing just that. "They'll be hot in no time."

Finally reaching a decision, Edward moved a piece and then gave his attention to his daughter. "Makes my mouth water just thinking about Mary's dressing."

"I wasn't sure if you liked turkey or not, so I brought ham, too," she said to Gabe. Even as she spoke the words, she regretted showing any concern for his likes or dislikes.

"Either is fine, thank you. And I'll play a game with you sometime, Danny, but I think I'd best get back to bed after I eat."

The unexpected thanks and offer to Danny took Rachel by surprise, though it shouldn't have. Gabe Gentry epitomized charm and grace and friendliness.

What he lacked was integrity and common decency.

Chapter Three

By the time a new year rolled around, the snow was nothing but a pleasant memory, leaving behind a dingy mush that froze at night and thawed during the day. The old year had ended with a rash of croup that kept Rachel running all over town. She had treated no less than seven people on New Year's Eve.

Gabe was still in considerable pain if he moved the wrong way, but his injuries and his strength were improving in slow increments. Despite the sometimes excruciating agony, he was determined to leave the Stone house—and the intolerable tension between him and Rachel—as soon as humanly possible. For both their sakes, he had no desire to prolong the misery.

When he finished shaving shortly after breakfast on New Year's Day, he saw that the gash on his face was healing nicely, though it would leave an ugly scar. He thought about that for a moment and shrugged. There wasn't much he could do about it. Thanks to Simon and Rachel, he was alive.

His once dislocated shoulder was not so tender and his hand was much steadier; he'd only nicked himself in two places. He was congratulating himself on the progress when a knock sounded on his door.

"Come in," he called, glancing up and seeing Danny's reflection in the mirror. He stood in the doorway, staring at Gabe with unconcealed curiosity. "Not too pretty to look at, is it?" Gabe said.

"Must hurt."

"Not much, but the ribs…that's another thing."

When the boy continued to watch him and made no move to say anything, Gabe prompted, "What can I do for you, Danny?"

"Pops said to tell you that Mr. Gentry—Caleb— is here to see you."

Gabe smiled, the action pulling at the stitches closing the wound on his cheek. "Thanks, son."

Danny's eyes widened. He smiled, a smile so bright and wide that Gabe resisted the urge to chuckle.

"Do you need anything?" Danny asked, a look of hope in his eyes. "I can get whatever you want. I'm not doing anything."

"I'm fine, thanks. You can send Caleb in."

"Would you like to play a game of Chinese checkers after he goes?"

The past week, they'd fallen into a habit of playing a game or two in the afternoons. Though Gabe would have preferred to play chess with Edward, he got a lot of satisfaction at how much Danny seemed to enjoy the time they spent together. He also recalled how he'd wished his father was the kind of man who wanted to play with his boys.

"We'll see. I'll probably be ready for a good rest by the time Caleb leaves. Why don't you go get him?"

"Oh. Okay."

Gabe wondered if Danny was as disappointed as he looked. He'd be sure to try to play a game or two with him sometime during the afternoon.

When Caleb came into the bedroom, it was the first time the two brothers had faced each other on a more or less equal footing since Gabe left. Caleb had stopped by on other occasions, but knowing Gabe was still in a lot of pain, they'd postponed any serious discussions.

Though Gabe had wanted this chance to try to make things right and had mentally rehearsed their meeting dozens of times, now that the opportunity was here, he had no idea where to begin.

"How are you feeling?" Caleb asked, taking a chair next to the fireplace. The question was his usual conversational opening. Gabe wiped the shaving soap from his face and eased down into the chair's mate.

"Far from well, but better."

"That's good."

An uncomfortable silence stretched between them. "Rachel mentioned that you got married again last year," Gabe said, hoping to fill the growing silence left by his habitually reticent brother. That hadn't changed.

Caleb nodded. "My first wife, Emily, died during childbirth. I married Abby Carter, a newly widowed woman Rachel suggested I hire for my daughter's wet nurse."

Gabe raised his eyebrows. "That's a bit unconventional, isn't it? Not to mention extreme."

"More than a bit," Caleb agreed. "But we didn't have much choice when Sarah VanSickle started spreading rumors about us, even though I was staying in the bunkhouse with Frank and Leo."

"So Sarah's still doling out misery, is she?" Gabe asked, recalling more than one occasion when she'd caused unnecessary suffering.

"Yep. I keep thinking she'll get her comeuppance, but so far, she just goes along, giving everyone a hard time along the way." There was more silence.

"So tell me about your... Abby. How are things working out?" Gabe asked, in an attempt to keep the struggling conversation going.

"Very well. She's a wonderful person and a great mother."

Gabe saw a gleam in his brother's eyes he'd never seen before. Happiness.

"I love her very much," Caleb added, almost, Gabe thought, as if his brother expected him to make some sort of snide comment about the situation. "We had a son born two days before Christmas."

"A son! You have a son and a daughter?" Caleb nodded and Gabe smiled, unexpectedly pleased for the brother who had borne the brunt of their father's domineering personality. "I envy you."

Caleb looked up to meet Gabe's smiling gaze. "You do?"

"Even I had to grow up eventually, Caleb," Gabe said, poking a bit of fun at himself. He knew what most people thought of him.

"Why have you come back, Gabriel?" Caleb asked, done with idle chitchat.

He shrugged. "I'm not sure I can explain. A while back, I realized that I'd done just about everything and seen all the places I wanted to see, and Lucas Gentry's shadow was still hanging over me. I was as miserable away from Wolf Creek as I had been here.

"Believe it or not, I've given our childhood a lot of thought the past several months, and I came up with some reasons why I felt that way. A few months back, I got the notion to come and see if there was any way for us to make sense of our past. I even hoped that maybe I could make up for the things I've done."

Caleb's eyes reflected his impatience. "Words are fine, Gabe. You were always good with them, but actions speak a lot louder. It's easy to come home when you're down-and-out. It's easy to claim regret and say you're sorry and then saddle up and leave again, convinced you did all you could or should to fix things."

For the first time, Gabe realized just how deep the chasm was between him and his brother. "I know what you're saying is true, and that I've given you plenty of reason to feel the way you do, but I have no intention of leaving."

"What!"

Gabe met his brother's astonished gaze. "I'm staying in Wolf Creek. I'm twenty-nine years old. Wouldn't you say it's time I found a good woman and settled down?"

"What will you do? How will you live with no money?" Caleb asked, unable to hide his shock.

"You're the one who said I was down-and-out, not me. I have a bit stuck by. As for what I'll do, I have no idea." He managed a wry smile. "It'll be a while before I'm able to do much of anything, but when the time is right, something will come along."

Another silence ensued. Finally, Gabe gave a heavy sigh, grimaced in pain and curved his arm around his battered ribs as if to protect them.

"Look, Caleb. I'm truly sorry for the way I acted when we were kids. I think I was trying to get Lucas to notice me, to acknowledge I was alive. If it took acting up to do it, so be it. I'm sorry my behavior left most of the work and responsibility on you. In a strange sort of way, though, I think you actually benefited."

"How do you figure that?" Caleb snapped. "I was the slave who worked and you were the spoiled brat who got by with everything and did next to nothing." His lips tightened with the stubbornness he was known for. "I've hated you for that."

"I can't say that I blame you," Gabe said. He understood Caleb's feelings, but just as Rachel's disgust had been hard to swallow, Caleb's words hurt, far more than Gabe had expected.

"Just think about it a minute. You were the one learning how to work, how to become a productive citizen, while I learned nothing except how to goof off and finagle others into doing my chores. I thought it was funny then, but not now. I cheated myself out of a lot of lessons."

Caleb stared at Gabe as if he'd never seen him before.

"I know it's a lot to ask, and I'll understand if you say no, but I'd like to ask your forgiveness. I'd like the opportunity to get to know you and your family. Believe it or not, I want to be an uncle, and I'd really like it if you and I could find some common ground to build a relationship on."

Rachel returned from a visit with one of her patients just before noon. She found her father sitting at the kitchen table in his wheelchair, slicing a skillet of corn bread into wedges.

"Hey, Pops!" she said, pressing a kiss to the top of his head. "How is everything?"

"Just dandy. How is little Jimmy doing?"

"As well as can be expected."

"Good. Food's ready," he said, indicating a pot of pinto beans and salt pork Rachel had set on the back of the woodstove before she left earlier in that morning. "Will you get Danny and Gabe while I finish up here?"

"Of course."

"Rachel," he said, his voice stopping her.

"Yes?" she said, turning.

"Caleb came to see Gabe this morning. I have no idea what they talked about, but I thought you'd like to know."

"Yes," she said, nodding. "Thank you."

Thoughts of what might have transpired between the brothers filled her mind as she went to fetch Danny. She found him reading one of the books he'd received for Christmas and more than ready to eat, since there were cookies to be had afterward.

Rachel went to Gabe's room, knocked on the door and opened it at his summons.

"Pops has dinner ready," she said, noticing that he was dressed in the extra clothes she'd found in his carpetbag instead of Edward's castoffs. She couldn't help noticing how well they fit his lean, broad-shouldered body. No doubt they'd been tailor-made for him.

"Thank you," he said. "I've been waiting to talk to you."

"Oh?"

He nodded. "I wanted to tell you that I'll be leaving after we eat."

"Leaving?" she echoed, disbelief in her voice. "You're in no condition to be on a horse."

"I don't plan to be. I'm not leaving town, just

checking into the boardinghouse. I think I'm well enough to take care of myself if I don't do anything stupid."

Though she'd wished him gone a hundred times, now that he planned to go she was filled with something that felt far too much like disappointment for her peace of mind.

"And how do you propose to pay for it?" she said, her voice sharper than she'd intended as the nebulous distress vanished in the face of her irritation.

"I had some money stuck in my boot the thieves didn't find," he explained. "It will see me through for a while. Besides, I think you'd agree that I've disrupted your life enough."

Indeed he had, she thought, though she would never admit it. "You have not disrupted my life."

His smile mocked. "Could've fooled me."

Embarrassment flushed her cheeks. "Caring for people is what I do."

"And I'll be the first one to attest to the fact that you're a fine doctor," he said in a gentle voice. "But let's be honest here."

"By all means. If that's possible," she said, unable to mask the sarcasm in her voice.

"Touché." Meeting her irate gaze was one of the hardest things he'd ever done. "Again, I know I treated you badly in St. Louis, and I should have said goodbye in person instead of leaving you that note."

Rachel began to laugh, a terrible parody of the

sound. "You think I'm angry at you because you left me a *note?*" she cried.

"Weren't you?"

"Angry?" She shook her head. "No. Try furious. Or hurt. Or better yet, *devastated.*" She took a deep breath, and feelings and words that had festered far too long erupted from her lips.

"Silly, naive me! I was bound to fall for your smooth-talking ways. I believed everything you told me, and it was all lies. Every single word of it! So tell me, Gabe, where was your honesty back then?"

The vitriol in her voice caused all the color to drain from his face. "I have no excuse, except…"

She made a slashing movement through the air to silence him. "You're right. You have no excuse. Lucky, lucky me! Handsome, worldly Gabe Gentry, the boy every girl in Wolf Creek longed to snare, looked me up."

She gave a bitter laugh. "I can't believe I was so gullible. I actually scoffed at the tales I'd heard about you, because you seemed so kind, and my memories of you were good. So I listened to your lies and fell for your pretty words. I gave you everything I had, Gabe. *Everything.* My love, my—" her voice faltered "—my entire being. You played me for a fool, and when you got what you wanted, you left without a backward glance, off to the next place of interest, the next easy mark."

"I never thought you were an easy—" He tried to interrupt, but again she held up her palm for silence and drew in several deep, steadying breaths.

As quickly as it had come, her anger disappeared. He almost wished it hadn't. The anguish in her eyes was almost his undoing.

"Do you have any idea what you did to me?" she said, her voice breaking. "Do you have any idea how ugly and discarded and *used* I felt?"

Truthfully, he'd never considered that. For the first time he realized how badly his casual treatment had wounded her. There had been other girls, other times, and never once had he considered how his cavalier dismissal might have made them feel. He'd always assumed that they expected no more or less than he was willing to offer. He'd used his God-given looks and charm with utter disregard for anyone's feelings but his own. All his life it had been about him. About what he felt, what he wanted.

The knowledge shamed him.

A glib apology couldn't begin to cover his faults, but still he searched his mind for words to ease her pain, knowing deep in his gut that there were none.

"I think I understand what you felt and why you still feel the way you do."

The harsh laughter was back. "You understand nothing!" she said in a tone of deadly quiet. "Nothing. But you're a man, and men get to walk away. Women are the ones who pay, and I'll pay for my folly the rest of my life."

She swiped at her tears with her fingertips. "Thanks to you, I learned never to trust anything a man says." Empty of words, she felt the heat of anger drain away and turned to leave the room.

Gabe's voice followed her. "You must have trusted at least one man."

She turned back to him with a blank expression.

"You must have trusted one other man," he repeated. "You must have trusted Danny's father."

She paled, and turning left him standing near the fire.

He closed his eyes against the pain.

She'd loved him.

Was it possible that he'd loved her but had been too immature and wrapped up in himself to realize it? He didn't know. All he knew was that staying would have meant putting an end to his roaming ways, and he hadn't been ready to do that. So he had moved on. He had walked away from the one bit of goodness in his sordid past, possibly the best thing to ever happen to him, and, he suspected, the one person who might have saved him from himself.

She'd moved on, too. She'd found someone who wasn't afraid to settle down. Someone who would cherish her enough to make her his wife.

Someone who had fathered her son.

That indisputable fact, more than anything she'd said to him, brought the most grief. The love he'd tossed away so carelessly, another had gained. Staying in Wolf Creek wouldn't be easy, for a lot of reasons.

When Rachel entered the kitchen, she was greeted by two pairs of questioning eyes. She wondered if either of them had heard the actual words of the argument, or if they'd just heard her voice raised in anger.

"He insists on moving to the boardinghouse after lunch," she offered, hoping the statement would be enough of an answer to assuage their curiosity, at least for now.

"Ah," Edward said, but the look in his eyes told her that he knew there was more than she was letting on.

"He isn't well yet," Danny said.

Rachel stifled a sigh. Danny was becoming far too attached to Gabe. Another reason he needed to move on.

"That's what I told him, but he's a grown man and can do as he wishes."

Though he would rather have walked over hot coals barefoot, Gabe went into the kitchen for lunch. The time for running away from his mistakes had passed. Rachel's color was still high, and her full lips were compressed into a tight line of disapproval. From Edward's forced smile and Danny's wary expression, Gabe knew they'd overheard the argument. Just another reason to be gone, he thought, easing himself into the straight-backed chair.

After Edward prayed, and everyone's plate was full, he broke the deafening silence.

"Rachel says you're planning to move to Hattie's this afternoon."

"Yes."

"Of course, it's up to you, but I'm not sure that's wise," Edward told him. "You still have a long way to go to be really out of the woods. Why don't you stay until the weekend—three more days—so that we can monitor your progress a bit longer?"

"I'm not sure that's wise, either," Gabe said cryptically.

"But you can't leave today." Danny's voice was as near a whine as Gabe had ever heard. "You promised to play Chinese checkers with me this afternoon."

Despite telling himself that he wouldn't, Gabe looked at Rachel. It was very possible that she was recalling—as he was—her scathing commentary about his lies, but she was concentrating on buttering a wedge of corn bread and didn't look up except to shoot her son a brief, grim look.

Drat it, he *had* promised! Though he would feel better if he left, was his peace of mind worth breaking a vow to a child? Hadn't he and Rachel just argued about how little his word meant? Hadn't he done enough hedging and misleading? Gabe's fingers tightened around his fork. Making atonement required much more and was far harder than he'd expected, but he wouldn't give her the satisfaction of saying "I told you so."

He forced a tight smile. "That's right," he said. "I did. I'll stay at least tonight, and then we'll see."

After lunch, Danny took Gabe into the parlor and set up the Chinese checkers while Rachel began to clear the table.

"You may as well sit down and tell me what happened," her father said. "You know I won't let up until you do."

Rachel cast him a woebegone look. Edward's persistence in getting to the bottom of things was legend. "I thought it was pretty obvious that Gabe and I had words."

"Indeed. But if I were a wagering man I'd bet it wasn't about his leaving."

"And you would win that wager," she said, turning her back on him.

Edward waited while she washed the glassware and then the flatware. Finally, she turned with a sigh and her signature, narrow-eyed look. "You are the most exasperating man I've ever known."

"That's what your mother used to say," Edward said, holding out his coffee cup for her to refill. "But I would have thought Gabe held that honor."

"You're right. He does. He is." She gave a reluctant, halfhearted smile. "Which makes you the second most irritating man I've ever known."

"So what were the fireworks all about?"

"He said he knew he'd behaved badly and apologized."

"And you yelled at him?"

Rachel's eyes widened. "What was I supposed to do? Tell him all was forgiven?"

"Yes."

Rachel sucked in a shocked breath and stared at him for a few seconds more. Then, with an angry shake of her head, she turned back to her dishes. "You expect too much."

"You've had years to come to terms with what happened, Rachel. Not forgiving isn't like you. You're one of the least judgmental, compassionate people I know, except evidently when it comes to Gabe, and maybe yourself."

"How can I forgive myself?" she asked, scrubbing at a fork with excessive force.

"How can you not when you asked God for His forgiveness and He's given it," Edward countered, his voice gentle.

"I'd like to think so," she said with a sigh. "But how can He?"

"It's what He does."

Again, Rachel stared at her father for long considering moments and went back to her dishes once more.

"Danny is very taken with Gabe," Edward offered.

"I know. It's...concerning."

"He's looking for a father figure."

She whirled to face him. "You're his father figure."

"I'm his grandfather. I do what I can, but it isn't enough. You have to tell him, Rachel."

"I know!" she cried, turning back to her dishes. After a while, she asked without turning to face him, "Does Danny talk to you about Gabe?"

"Sometimes."

"What does he say?" Though she couldn't find

the courage to tell Danny the truth about Gabe, she still wanted to know what her son thought about the man who had fathered him.

Then again, maybe she didn't.

Edward smiled. "He wanted to know if I knew Gabe when he was a boy, and what he was like back then. I told him he was full of himself. Actually, he's asked me that about every unattached man in town."

"He has?" Rachel couldn't hide her surprise. She'd never realized just how much Danny wanted a man—a father—in his life. She'd certainly had no idea he was gathering information about the town's bachelors, no doubt looking for one that fit his own personal criteria for a husband and father.

She would have to have that talk with Danny. Soon. Bringing her thoughts back to the present, she said, "Gabe was rowdy, wasn't he?" Her voice was almost wistful. "But I remember he was always friendly and nice to me."

"Being rowdy doesn't begin to cover it and doesn't mean a person can't be nice as well as rambunctious," Edward said. "Suffice it to say that I told Danny he reminds me a lot of Gabe. It seemed to please him."

"He's nothing like Gabe!" Rachel said, appalled at the very idea.

Edward shrugged. "As I said, Danny is looking for someone he can look up to. He needs that, Rachel."

"And you think he can look up to Gabriel Gentry?" she asked.

"I think that you aren't giving the man enough credit. Whatever he's been and done in the past does not mean he will say or do anything to taint your son, especially while he's living under our roof. And the very fact that he's come back to try to set things straight says a lot."

"I suppose you're right."

"Aren't I always?" Edward deadpanned.

"Right *and* conceited," Rachel said, but she was smiling when she said it. "What about later? When he leaves here? What then?"

"He isn't physically able to leave town for a while, and it's the dead of winter. Once he goes to Hattie's, Danny won't see much of him, and I imagine Gabe will be gone by spring."

Rachel shook her head.

"What?"

"He told me he isn't leaving. He's staying in Wolf Creek."

Edward's gaze met hers over the rim of his coffee cup, his expression thoughtful. "Won't that be interesting?"

Hattie's Hotel and Boardinghouse looked a mile away from Rachel's front porch, where Gabe stood, his carpetbag clutched in his "good" hand. It held nothing but a change of clothes and his shaving gear, but it already felt as if it weighed a hundred pounds. He wished he'd listened to Edward, who had offered to have Roland drive him over.

It was spitting sleet, and the hotel, which sat on the corner just beyond the railroad track, was a blur in the distance. Not that far, really. Getting there shouldn't be too taxing, even with his injuries. He made his way carefully down the steps and the path.

He had given in to Edward's persuasion and stayed the three extra days, spending as much time as possible with Danny, since the boy seemed so needy for a friend. His obvious yearning for male companionship brought back painful memories of that same need. Gabe knew what it was to ache for approval, and how it felt to crave a smile or even a word of scolding that would prove that Lucas realized he existed.

Lucas had never been there for Gabe or Caleb in any meaningful way. The closest anyone came to fulfilling the role he'd abdicated had been Frank, their hired hand.

Edward Stone was a good grandfather, but his stroke had left him unable to share many activities with the boy—especially outdoor activities. Edward had mentioned that Danny liked fishing, and before he realized his intent to do so, Gabe had offered to take him to the creek when the weather grew warmer. The suggestion had brought a wide smile to Danny's face.

He'd seen little of Rachel the past three days except when she came to check his injuries. Strangely, the animosity had all but disappeared, and she now treated him in a far different way. Not friendly, exactly. Civil. It was an improvement.

He found himself longing to have a normal conversation with her, like those they'd shared in St. Louis. He wanted to hear if her hopes and dreams had changed and if her work in Wolf Creek was as fulfilling as she'd expected, but he figured a heart-to-heart talk was way out of the realm of possibility, at least for the time being.

She might be unwilling to forgive him just yet, but clearly she'd forgotten how single-minded he could be when he decided he wanted something. He would do everything in his power to gain her pardon. It was something he had to have if he was to ever move on with his life in any meaningful way.

A frigid wind blew the icy particles against his face, stinging like hundreds of tiny needles. The ground was already covered with a thin layer of the wintry precipitation that made every step treacherous, especially for an injured man.

He turned and looked back at the house. It would be so easy to go back, but something told him it would be easier to gain Rachel's forgiveness, and far easier on both of them if he wasn't around to remind her of the past.

He'd made the break, and nothing but a terrible setback would make him return to Rachel's home.

With her brow furrowed with worry, Rachel stood at the window, the fingertips of her right hand pressed against her mouth, the lace curtain pushed aside so that she could better see Gabe's progress along the treacherous road. He slipped a little. She gasped, and her heart flew to her throat. Ridiculous, irritating man! Exasperation nudged aside her concern. He'd had no business leaving, and he certainly should not be walking in this icy downpour. He'd catch his death of a cold, and then he'd be right back here.

Well, leaving was what he wanted, and she'd never held a patient hostage before. Good riddance to him! She wouldn't have to cook and do laundry for another person and wouldn't have to wait on him hand and foot. No more arguments. No more frustration and anger. Maybe her life could get back to normal now.

She let the curtain fall back into place and turned away, her gaze roaming the empty room. The problem with normal was that it was terribly dreary sometimes.

Chapter Four

Rachel carried an armload of fresh linens into the bedroom Gabe had used. He had been gone a week and thus far she had refused to admit she missed him. All she would admit was that she missed doing things for him. She'd become accustomed to checking on him before she made her daily calls and again when she came in. She missed seeing him at meals, and it seemed that without his clothes, even the laundry seemed lacking somehow.

She placed the sheets and towels into the linen press, closed the doors and turned to lean against them, letting her bleak gaze roam the room. There was no sign he'd ever been there beyond the memory of his dark head against the pillows and the way he watched her with that intense blue gaze as she treated his injuries—a look that, despite all attempts to not respond, made her heart pound, as aware of him as she'd ever been.

Tears burned her eyes. That was the problem.

She might tell herself she was over him. She might claim to despise him, but what she really despised was the fact that she wasn't over him and couldn't rout him from her mind or her heart.

Heaven help her, despite everything, she still loved him.

It made her furious and at the same time miserable. Had she learned nothing nine years ago? Was she deficient of even one ounce of intelligence or self-respect? Was she so weak and lonely that she was willing to ignore the pain and shame of the past and fall willy-nilly into his arms again?

No. She had determined that, no matter what, she would not fall for his flattery and lies a second time. In her orderly, play-by-the-book mind, the fact that she missed him was tantamount to a character flaw. She was no longer the innocent she'd been when she first went to St. Louis.

She'd learned a lot of important lessons through the years. Feelings could be suppressed, ignored and even manipulated if you tried hard enough, and she intended to try very hard to rid herself of the renegade emotions she felt for Gabe.

She would fight them with work and common sense, and if that wasn't enough to keep her from entrusting him with her heart, she would play her trump card: Danny.

Her heart was one thing—Danny's was quite another.

Edward claimed Danny craved a father, so maybe she'd consider trying to give him one. That would drive Gabe Gentry from her mind. She had always expected to marry someday; how could she hope to find love and a father for Danny if she didn't give the single men in town a chance? Maybe it was time for her to start accepting some of the offers of courtship that came her way. Unfortunately, single men were few and far between. She'd had high hopes for Colt Garrett when he'd first come to town as the new sheriff, but there had been no romantic spark between them. Still, she had not abandoned the dream. There was always the off chance of a miracle happening.

She heard Danny's voice in the kitchen. He was more or less himself since Gabe had moved to the hotel, but there were times she caught him staring off into space as if he were miles away, and she knew he was suffering the loss of his new "friend." In retrospect, she was glad she hadn't caved to her father's wishes and her own guilt and told Danny that Gabe was his father. If she had, chances were that he would be even deeper in the doldrums.

Shaking off her dark mood, she pushed away from the linen press and turned toward the door. The Bible promised that these troubled, unsettled feelings Gabe's return had stirred would pass. She wished they would hurry.

As the weeks passed and his body healed, cabin fever almost drove Gabe to insanity. Caleb, his well-read, book-educated brother, had brought him a stack of books and periodicals from his extensive library and Gabe had read until he thought his eyes must surely cross.

Inevitably, his thoughts turned to how he was going to spend the rest of his life. Though he claimed he'd come home to stay, he had no idea how he might make a living. The time he spent re-cuperating gave him ample time to think about his future, but thoughts and dreams could only fill so much of a day, and boredom had not just staked a claim, it had homesteaded.

At the end of January, on one of the unexpected balmy winter days not uncommon to southwest Ar-kansas, Caleb picked up Gabe for Sunday dinner after the morning church service. Though neither of them would claim they were friends, they were trying to put the past behind them and see if there could be more to their relationship than enmity and hard feelings.

Wearing a wide smile, Abby met them at the front door and gave Gabe a hug of welcome. Some-thing close to embarrassment flooded him. Friendly hugs were not something he'd experienced often. The unexpected gesture left him feeling a bit self-conscious.

"None for me?" Caleb asked when Abby turned to hang up Gabe's coat.

A becoming blush crept into her cheeks. "Oh, you!" she said, but grabbed his coat front, pulled him close and pressed a quick kiss to his lips. Gabe noticed how her hands lingered on Caleb's chest and was stunned when his brother dropped another kiss to her mouth.

Gabe was amazed by the obvious love between his brother and Abby. The grave, exacting Caleb whom Gabe recalled from their youth was gone, and in his place was a man satisfied with his lot in life. His brother was happy. Content. Though Gabe was genuinely delighted for him, he admitted to being a tad jealous.

Like forgiveness, he wondered if he would ever experience the love and happiness surrounding his brother or know the kind of satisfaction reflected in his eyes. He knew there were young women around town who thought he was handsome despite the scar on his cheek, but he had no interest in giggling, blushing girls. There was even a widow or two who cast doe eyes at him whenever he passed them on the sidewalk, but no one so far had prompted a smidgen of interest.

Knowing it was foolishness on his part, yet unable to stop, he measured every female against Rachel, and they all came up lacking. Since it was pretty clear that she was unlikely to ever forgive him, he saw his life stretching out into a long, endless expanse of regrets. He was left with the distasteful possibility that if he were to marry, he would be forced to settle for less than his heart's desire.

Abby lost no time introducing "Uncle Gabe" to the children. There was her son, Ben, who was obviously as fond of Caleb as he was the boy, and two-year-old Laura, who vied with her brother for Caleb's attention. Then there was one-year-old Betsy—whose mother had died at her birth, bringing Abby into their lives—and baby Eli, barely a month old.

Frank and Leo showed up to share the meal, and there was much laughter and many reminiscences as they ate. Frank had no compunction about trotting out Gabe's misdemeanors one by one, and Gabe was surprised when everyone, including Caleb, laughed at the reminders of some of his most memorable antics.

He finally begged Frank to be quiet so his less-than-sterling past would not tempt young Ben to follow in his uncle's footsteps. Frank agreed with a throaty laugh, and Gabe was struck by how different this meal was compared to meals when Lucas had presided over the dinner table.

"Just in case things get chaotic later and I forget, I want to ask you to join us at Wolf Creek Church next week," Abby said. "Well, join Caleb, anyway. It's still too cold to get Eli out, so the little ones and I will be staying at home for a bit yet."

Church? Gabe knew from several conversations with Ellie at the café that Abby was a devout Christian and that his brother had rededicated his life the past summer, just one more change Abby Gentry had brought about. But church for himself? Gabe wasn't so sure about that, and he was less sure how the membership would accept him, considering his past.

"I'll think about it."

"See that you do," Abby said in her best school-marm voice, but she tempered the comment with a smile.

When they finished eating, Frank and Leo headed for the bunkhouse, and Caleb started to help with the dishes, another in a growing list of mind-boggling changes time had wrought in his brother.

Abby refused his help, shooing him toward the door. "I'll give you time off since Gabe is here. Why don't you two take your coffee into the parlor and catch up?"

As the two headed for the doorway, she called Caleb's name. When he turned, she smiled and said, "Just so you know, you needn't think I'll make a habit of it."

"No ma'am," Caleb said with a smile. He led the way to the parlor.

The brothers settled into their preferred chairs and spent several minutes talking about the books Gabe had read.

"I know reading can get tiresome," Caleb told him, "but I have plenty more titles I think would interest you. I don't think you'll be ready to look for a job just yet," Caleb said.

"Probably not," Gabe agreed, "and even if I were, I have no idea what I'd be good at or what I might like. How did you know what you wanted to do with your life, and why on earth did you stay with farming after having it crammed down your throat?"

There was little humor in Caleb's laughter. "If

you'll recall, I wasn't given a choice," he said. "You took off and Lucas made it very clear that he expected me to 'step up,' as he put it."

Gabe felt another surge of the guilt that had often beset him since returning to Wolf Creek. No acts of contrition or request for forgiveness would ever be enough to make up for how he'd wronged the people in his past.

"Besides," Caleb continued, "as you pointed out, I knew farming inside and out, and I was pretty good at it. Then one day I realized I actually liked it."

"Thank goodness for that," Gabe said. "I can't say that anything in my background has given me any credentials. Gambling and carousing aren't much as job experience goes."

"I've been thinking about that," Caleb said, after a slight pause. "Abby and I have talked about it."

Gabe waited, uncertain if he liked being the topic of dinnertime conversation, yet knowing that it was inevitable, not just with Caleb and Abby but the whole town.

"You know that when Lucas died, he left everything to me, since you'd already received your inheritance."

Gabe nodded and shrugged. "As was only right and fair."

Caleb took a deep breath. "Maybe so, but nevertheless, I want to offer you a half interest in the farm, if you're willing to do half the work."

Gabe's startled gaze searched his brother's. In his

wildest imaginings he would never have expected such a generous offer. "You aren't serious?"

"I am," Caleb said, reaching for the cup of coffee he'd brought from the kitchen.

"But why?"

"It was Abby's idea," Caleb confessed. "And I'd be less than honest if I didn't tell you that it didn't sit well at first." He drew in another breath. "Then I started thinking about it, and she's right. You're as much Lucas's son as I am, and there's more than enough for the two of us."

Gabe stared at his brother. Just as there was no doubting the sincerity of his confession, there was no doubting the sincerity of the offer. Gabe had to blink back tears. He heard the trembling in his voice as he said, "I can't thank you enough, Caleb. It's a more-than-generous offer, and I realize you're giving me a wonderful opportunity, but it isn't fair to you. I got my part, and I threw it away. This farm is yours, so if it's all the same to you, I'll pass."

Caleb sat up straighter. "Why? I thought you were planning on staying around here."

"I am."

"Well, if you're worried about the cost, let me be clear. I'm not offering to *sell* you part of the farm. I'm *giving* it to you."

"Again, I thank you, but the answer is no."

"Then—"

Gabe held up a silencing hand. "What you've done means more to me than you'll ever know, considering the way things have always been between us, but I won't take you up on your offer because I know in my heart that, unlike you, farming isn't for me. Besides, it's your farm, Caleb. Always will be. You've given it your blood, sweat and tears your whole life. Lucas didn't *give* you anything. You paid for it. Every acre. Every fence post. Every head of livestock."

"But what will you do?" Caleb's expression was troubled.

"I'm not sure, but something will come along," Gabe said. "It always does."

By the end of February, spring was making promises everyone knew she would not keep. Gabe smoothed his shirt collar as a loud rapping sounded at his door. Caleb, no doubt. Abby had been unrelenting in her pleas for Gabe to attend church. Until today, he'd managed to put her off with the excuse that his ribs just weren't up to sitting so long in the hard pews. But with the thrashing he'd received two months past, he was feeling much better, and Abby had declared that his excuse was getting old.

So here he was, dressed up in his Sunday best and waiting to come face-to-face with people who'd known him since birth. People who knew about his many youthful escapades…and indiscretions.

Though the room was a bit chilly, Gabe broke out into a sweat just thinking of the gauntlet he was about to run. He took a steadying breath and flung open the door. If he intended to make a life here, the time for hiding was past.

It was time to face the music.

Time to pay the fiddler.

Gabe followed his brother and Abby into the small church, certain he'd never been more uncomfortable in his life. Expecting censure, he was surprised when a tall, heavy-set man with salt-and-pepper hair and matching beard covering his fleshy cheeks spoke to Caleb and Abby then grabbed Gabe's hand and began to pump it up and down.

"Gabriel Gentry! It's good to have you."

Taken aback by the man's enthusiastic welcome, Gabe barely managed a weak smile. "Thank you."

"You remember me, don't you? Earl Pickens?"

Earl Pickens. Gabe did remember him. "Do you still have the newspaper?"

"I still keep my hand in, but my son, Charles, does most of the work these days."

They talked for a few more minutes, and Abby introduced him to some other couples, people near his and Caleb's age. A few greetings were warmer than others, but no one snubbed him outright. That in itself was gratifying and humbling. Of course, he hadn't seen Sarah VanSickle yet.

"Gabe!"

He turned at the sound of the childish voice. Danny, Rachel and Edward, who was using his canes to get around this morning, were entering the double doors. The boy headed toward Gabe, a wide smile on his face. Rachel reached out to stop him with a hand on his shoulder.

He glanced up at his mother with a questioning look.

"We need to get Pops settled. The service is about to start." Her expression was carefully neutral, and her halfhearted smile did not quite reach her brown eyes when she turned to Gabe. "I didn't expect to see you here."

"You can thank Abby for that," he said, the simple reply challenging her to say anything to her friend. For a moment, she seemed to be searching for a comeback.

Apparently unable to come up with anything pithy, she murmured, "I hope you enjoy the service," and then she followed her father down the aisle.

Gabe could add Rachel's name to the column of folks who were not particularly happy to see him there.

By the time the song leader began the first hymn, voices raised in the a cappella rendition of "The Old Rugged Cross," Gabe had managed to push her cool disapproval from his mind and was able to concentrate on the service.

The minister's sermon was about God's divine providence and how there were lessons to be learned from life's difficulties and bad experiences. He went on to say that problems often enabled us to grow not only as individuals, but in our faith. Always, His goal was for ultimate good, even though many were unable to recognize His plan in the midst of pain and turmoil. People either grew closer to God or turned away when trouble struck.

Gabe wondered what the Lord's plan was for him. He was truly sorry for his past behavior, but he failed to see how Lucas's treatment of him and his brother, his mother's abandonment and his own youthful transgressions could be part of a plan to bring about his betterment or his happiness—or anyone else's, for that matter.

He cast a surreptitious glance at Rachel, who chose that moment to look his way. Her mouth was set in an uncompromising line, and her eyes reflected coolness. It didn't look as if she saw the wisdom of God's providence in his return, either.

Chapter Five

By mid-March, Gabe began to wander to the Emersons' mercantile several times a week in an effort to thwart his boredom. He spent hours talking to Bart and Mary Emerson, catching up on the town's happenings.

He found out who had died, who had married and that there was a growing interest in timber and gravel. He gained insights into his brother's character and details about Caleb's marriage to the Emersons' daughter. He was a bit surprised that they had so wholeheartedly accepted Abby as a mother for their little granddaughter so soon after Emily's death, but then the Emersons were exceptional people.

When he tried to bring the conversation around to Rachel, hoping to learn more about her missing husband, the Emersons, like Caleb, claimed to know nothing. They were not ones to gossip. Since Abby was reasonably new to town, the only thing she knew about Rachel was that she was a good person and a fantastic doctor. Gabe didn't miss the considering expression in his sister-in-law's eyes and wondered if what he thought were casual questions had tipped his hand about his growing feelings for the lady physician.

Some days, he helped unpack new merchandise and rearrange other stock, hoping that the reshuffling would bring attention to product that was slow to sell. Other times, he joined the men whose sole occupation was passing the day by striking up conversations with whoever came through the doors and playing chess or checkers until one of them pulled out a pocket watch and announced that it was "time to get home before Sally/Bessie/Mable/Annie threw out their supper."

At the end of the month, Gabe was surprised when Bart said he wanted to have a talk with him.

"Sure, Bart," Gabe said. "What can I do for you?"

"Mary and I have discussed this, and we decided to talk to you before we do anything else."

"Okay," Gabe said, uncertain where the conversation was headed. There was almost a feeling of déjà vu, as he recalled his talk with Caleb.

"We've decided to sell the store and move to St. Louis."

"Why?" Gabe asked, unable to hide his surprise. "I thought you were happy in Wolf Creek?"

"We are," Bart said, "but we have another daughter and five grandchildren we seldom get to see.

We've been so tied down here that we seldom get away."

"Joanna's children are growing up without us knowing them at all," Mary chimed in. "We've decided that we want to spend more time with them now that Emily is gone."

"What will you do there?"

"Our son-in-law's factory is doing well, and he could use some part-time help in the office. I'd help him a couple of days a week. With our savings and the sale of the store, we should be able to live comfortably enough," Bart told him.

"What about Betsy?" Gabe asked, still trying to take everything in. "You'll miss out on her growing up, too."

"We adore her," Mary said. "Please don't think we don't. We've even talked about taking her with us, if Caleb would let us…"

"…which we both doubt," Bart said.

"But Joanna's hands are full, and we're too old to bring up another child."

"We know that Caleb and Abby will take good care of her," Bart chimed in. "And Caleb *is* her father. Once we move, and I just work part time, we can come back for a visit whenever we want. And we would always welcome Caleb and Abby if they wanted to come visit us."

Gabe saw that they'd given the notion a lot of thought. "Why are you telling me about this?"

"We'd like you to buy the store."

Gabe was sure his mouth fell open. He looked from one to the other. "Me? Why?"

"It was Mary's idea," Bart said. "I know you're trying to decide what to do if you stay here, and this is a good business if it's handled correctly."

"I don't know the first thing about the mercantile business," Gabe said, though the offer had definitely piqued his interest and his mind was already whirling with possibilities.

"Nonsense! You've been a great help to us the past few weeks, and you have some fantastic ideas for new products and promoting sales. Besides, we won't be leaving until early May," Bart said. "It will take that long to make arrangements. If you buy, we could come in every day and work with you... show you the ropes until you get the hang of things."

Gabe's head was spinning. "What about the price?" he asked. "I have a little money stuck back, but I'm sure it isn't enough, and I doubt Mr. Haversham would give me a loan, since I haven't been here long to establish any credit."

"Oh, I figure he might, if I have a talk with him," Bart said. "If not, I'll finance the balance myself."

"You'd do that?" Gabe asked, stunned at the unexpected generosity of the offer. "Why?"

"Because I see you trying to change your life, son," Bart said, clamping a hand on Gabe's shoulder, "and I'm a firm believer that we all deserve a second chance. Nobody gets it right all the time."

Gabe thought it over for a week before deciding to become a retail merchant. Arrangements for the purchase were less trouble than he'd expected. Nathan Haversham might not have agreed with Gabe's previous lifestyle, but like Bart, he liked the idea of a young man who'd seen what was happening in other parts of the country bringing some of those fresh ideas to their town. He was also counting on the fact that Lucas Gentry's blood flowed in Gabe's veins. That alone meant he had a pretty good chance of making the enterprise a success.

While awaiting the arrival of May, Bart and Mary showed him how to take inventory; how many, what kind, how much and when to order; and to whom he should extend credit—as well as to whom he should not. Somewhat surprisingly, he enjoyed the learning process. He liked that no two days were alike. Always gregarious, he liked visiting with the customers, liked hearing their problems and offering his commiseration, even though he had no idea how to fix his own problems.

He'd made a start, though. He'd realized that Rachel might not pardon him, but God could and would, if only Gabe made things right with Him and turned his life around. Feeling the weight of his unworthiness, and humbled by the depth of God's grace, he had become a Christian two weeks earlier. As he'd come up from the still-cold waters of Wolf Creek, he'd felt a sense of peace and responsibility he'd never known before.

Lucas Gentry had not been a God-fearing man in any respect, and the idea of a life built with Christ at its center was an alien one to Gabe; nevertheless, he was committed to doing his best. Since then, he'd worked even harder at trying to be everything he should be, but there were times he knew he failed miserably. That, Abby had assured him with a confident smile, was where grace continued to cleanse.

The morning in late April after he'd signed the papers, he got up before daybreak, dressed and unlocked the front doors before the town was stirring—though he did see a light at the café. Ellie was up making pies and setting her bread to rise. He lit a couple of lamps and walked around the store, looking around, making plans, running his hand over the counter, unable to stop the heady pride of possession that swept through him.

He'd done it! For better or worse, he'd found a way to stay. Now he needed to make himself an accepted member of the community. Whether or not he would be a success was up to him. He *would* be successful. He was smart, willing and, like Nate Haversham, knew he'd inherited enough of Lucas Gentry's business savvy to make a go of things. With just over a week until Bart and Mary left, he needed to soak up every bit of knowledge he could from them.

Folding his arms across his chest, he surveyed the large area, thinking of ways to make his mark on the store. First thing today, he'd order a new sign: GENTRY MERCANTILE. He would choose a day and advertise a grand opening in the newspaper, like the one he'd seen in New York—or was that Boston?—with cookies or cake and punch. He would give away some merchandise as door prizes. People liked that.

He scrutinized the large plate-glass windows and pictured a raised display area built in front of each of them. He could purchase some dress forms to show off the new spring fashions and drape some of his new fabrics over...well, *something* to display their bright hues.

He contemplated the arrangements of the shelving and tables. The chess and checkerboards would be better moved nearer to the potbellied stove. He'd hang a lantern above the tables for better lighting. He could make a pot of coffee every day in one of the blue spatterware coffeepots he sold and keep it warming on the back of the stove. It would be a nice gesture to offer a free coffee to those who came to shop, especially in winter.

He was heading toward the curtain that separated the front of the store from the back room when he heard the bell at the door tinkle. Turning, he saw Rachel poised just inside the entryway.

"You actually did it."

There was no missing the disbelief lacing her voice.

"If you mean buying the Emersons out, then yes, I did it."

"Why?"

Weary of her resentment, Gabe tamped down his own temper. "I told you months ago that I planned on staying."

"So you did," she said with a hollow smile. "I just never thought you really would. How could you do this to me?"

"My staying has nothing to do with you, Rachel," he tried to explain. "It's a choice I made because I believe it's the best course for me. Believe it or not, I didn't set out to ruin your life or decide to stay to make you miserable."

"Well, that's what it feels like." Like him, she was carefully civil.

Feeling the familiar despair sweep through him, he struggled for calmness he was far from feeling. "I'm sorry for that," he said, "but I have tried to make amends."

"You have, but do you really think it's as simple as saying 'I'm sorry'?"

He stepped from behind the counter and advanced on her with a purposeful stride, not stopping until he was within touching distance. If he expected her to retreat as the old Rachel would have, he was disappointed. This Rachel stood her ground.

"Oh, I forgot," he mocked, forgetting that he was supposed to be the peacemaker. "Apologies, even sincere apologies, mean nothing to the upstanding Dr. Stone, epitome of all that is pure and proper."

"No longer pure, thanks to you."

Gabe clenched his fists at his sides, closed his eyes and counted to ten. Then he drew a deep breath, again struggling to find some measure of rationality before speaking. "You're right. Because of me you are no longer innocent, but I wonder if you've forgotten that what happened was by mutual agreement."

Her eyes widened in surprise, and the blood

drained from her face, as if she'd just heard something she'd never thought of before. Her voice quavered with something that sounded like pain. "What I remember is that you left me when you found something that interested you more."

It was an accusation he couldn't deny. Gabe scrubbed a hand over his face. *Dear Lord, help me.*

"You're right. And I have asked for your forgiveness on more than one occasion, which you have denied." The frustration and sorrow inside him was etched on his face. "I can't undo the past, Rachel. So what more would you have me do? Go out on the street wearing sackcloth and ashes? Maybe I should take a cat-o'-nine and flog myself before the whole town. Would that make you happy?"

"I'm not sure I'll ever be truly happy, thanks to you."

"I find that incredibly sad," he said, with a shake of his head, "but I will not allow you to place all the blame for a lifetime of misery on me, when we were equally responsible for what happened.

"The first day I visited church, the preacher said we were given trials because we were expected to grow in faith and to learn from them. One thing I've learned the past nine years—and believe me, everything I've learned has been the hard way—is that we all make mistakes, even the blameless Dr. Stone.

"I've also learned that you were right about us making our own happiness. We can't rely on money or things or other people, because we'll never reach that state until we are satisfied with who and what we are."

"So wise," she said, with a shake of her head. "Tell me, Gabe, are you happy?"

He hesitated no more than a fraction of a second. "I'm getting there." It came as a bit of a surprise to realize it was true.

Speechless, she turned to leave. He reached out and placed his hand on her shoulder. With a gasp, she whirled to face him. "Do you know what *I* remember about those three weeks?" he asked.

She stood mute, trembling beneath his touch.

"I remember a beautiful, shy, incredibly intelligent young woman with a core of determination that awed me." Unable to help himself, he trailed a whisper-soft touch along the curve of her jaw and saw the lingering misery in her eyes dim.

"I remember how delightful she was...." His thumb brushed the fullness of her lower lip, and she sucked in a startled breath. "And I remember how her sweet kisses took away my breath."

He felt the starch go out of her. For perhaps the first time since returning, there was no reproach in the dark gaze that probed his.

"If you felt all that, why did you leave the way you did?"

"Because I was young and unbelievably stupid," he told her.

Their probing gazes clung for long expectant seconds. Then, shrugging free of his hold, she turned and opened the door.

Heaving a sigh of sorrow, he spoke to her back. "The supplies you ordered should be in by week's end. I'll let you know when they arrive."

Without answering, she shut the door behind her and hurried across the street. The bells tinkled merrily as he watched her go, wondering again if she would ever forgive him…wondering if he would ever forgive himself for the way his thoughtless treatment had changed her.

Rachel exited the mercantile, the image of Gabe's contrition, anger and frustration branded into her mind. Ellie was just flipping around the sign to announce she was open for business. Rachel thought about getting a cup of coffee to settle her nerves, but instead turned the other way, heading toward the house, her trembling hands clenched inside her coat pockets, faced with a new reality and an old guilt she could no longer deny.

Until the moment Gabe had brutally reminded her that what happened between them was as much her choice as his, it had been easy to cast herself in the role of the victim, place all the blame on him and take refuge in her anger. That was no longer possible. It was a hard pill to swallow, but he was right. They were both to blame. It was a notion she would have to get used to, just as she would have to get accustomed to the fact that he was not leaving Wolf Creek. She'd pinned all her hopes on his wanderlust, certain that when he was healed, he would take off again.

Since that wasn't to be, either, her immediate problem was what to do about Danny. His welfare was the most important thing in her life, and she was so afraid he was asking for heartbreak if he grew too close to the man who'd fathered him. If only he weren't so infatuated with Gabe!

She recalled the day Danny had come home with a wide smile on his face.

"He's staying, Mama!" he'd crowed, literally jumping up and down.

"Who's staying, Danny?" she'd asked, though she feared she already knew the answer.

"Gabe."

There was no missing the gleam of excitement in her son's eyes or the little leap of her own heart. Both irritated her to no end. How was she expected to keep her treacherous feelings for him from growing if she had to deal with him on a regular basis for the rest of her life?

Up until now, avoiding him had been fairly easy. A polite nod, a perfunctory hello, a pleasant expression when he was around so that no one would suspect what was really in her heart had not been too much of a strain. But there was no way she could ignore him now. She had to have medical supplies and household necessities, and there was nowhere else to get them.

To give Gabe his due, he had become a Christian, and it had not escaped her that he was faithful in his church attendance. For the most part, people around town seemed fine with his attempts to reestablish himself in the community. While both signs were encouraging, she told herself that a few months of good living could not wipe out a lifetime of debauchery.

Except in God's eyes.

The errant thought made her feel ashamed all over again, and she vowed to pray for His forgiveness more vigorously.

"Where did you get that idea?" she'd asked Danny as she locked the glass-front cabinet that held her medical supplies. "I told you he never stays in one place for very long."

"When I went to the mercantile to spend the penny Pops gave me, there was a Sold sign in the window," he'd told her. "I asked Mr. Emerson who bought the store, and he said Gabe. He's going to live upstairs."

Rachel had found herself speechless.

Now, with her early-morning talk with Gabe sitting like curdled milk in her stomach, there was another truth to face. With the recent changes in his life, it was entirely possible that she was borrowing trouble. Maybe Gabe would not hurt Danny at all.

One thing was certain, though. There was no putting off telling Danny about Gabe. It would have to be done. Soon.

At the house, she found her son and father in the kitchen making breakfast. Edward was buttering toast, while Danny stood on a small stool, stirring scrambled eggs with a wooden spoon.

"Good morning," Rachel said, bending to press a

kiss to the top of her father's head. Doing the same to Danny's cheek, she warned, "Be careful."

He cast a surprisingly accurate imitation of her famous "look" over his shoulder. "I am."

"How is Meg?" Edward asked.

Meg Thomerson was a young wife whose husband's main source of pleasure when he was liquored up seemed to be beating her to within an inch of her life. "She's not nearly as bad as the last time, but that isn't saying much."

"Do you think she'll ever leave him?"

"Only in a casket, I'm afraid." Rachel poured herself a cup of coffee. "Elton has her convinced it's her fault he loses control."

"Luther was just like him," Edward said, thoughtfully. "It's a self-perpetuating evil." He shot a severe look at his grandson. "Are you listening, Danny? It's never okay to hit girls."

"I know," he said over his shoulder. "Boys are supposed to take care of girls and keep bad things from happening to them, like I do for Bethany."

Rachel smiled. Bethany was Ellie's eleven-year-old daughter, a Mongoloid who was often the brunt of teasing and practical jokes. "Exactly."

"Is the mercantile opening up today?" Edward asked, peering over the tops of his glasses.

By now, everyone in town knew of the Emersons' sale to Gabe the day before. Unfortunately, Rachel seemed to be the only person who'd felt the necessity to confront him about his reasons. "He's already open."

Danny glanced up from his stirring, eager to hear news about the man he'd taken to so easily.

"I told you," he said.

"So you did. Are those eggs done?" she asked, deftly changing the subject.

"Think so. They aren't runny anymore."

"Good." She scooped the eggs from the skillet and added two sausage patties to each plate before setting them in front of Danny and her father.

They gave thanks for the food and the two guys dug in while Rachel nibbled at her sausage and pushed the eggs around on her plate.

"Anything wrong?" Edward asked.

"Only what you might imagine," she said, offering him a false, sweet smile.

Edward lifted his eyebrows in understanding. "Ah."

That night, Rachel knew she had put off the inevitable as long as possible. She knocked and let herself into Danny's room. He was propped up in bed reading, something he did almost every night before she made him blow out the lamp.

Dreading the next few moments, she sat down on the side of the bed and rested her hand against his soft cheek. "Danny, I have something to tell you." The unsteadiness she heard in her voice confirmed her anxiety.

"Yes, Mama?" The blue eyes so much like Gabe's regarded her solemnly.

Drawing a breath, she plunged. "Do you remember when you asked me about your father, and I told you that he'd gone away before you were born?"

Danny's dark head moved up and down against the pillow. "You said he was young and wasn't ready for the responsibility of a family."

Her mouth lifted in a sad smile. That much was true. But she'd omitted so much more in an effort to keep from telling him an out-and-out lie. "Well, he's come back."

Danny bolted upright. "He has? Can I see him?"

The joy in his eyes was almost her undoing. Tears burned beneath her eyelids and her heart seemed to stop for a beat. "You have seen him," she whispered.

"I have?" he asked with a puzzled frown.

"Danny, Gabe Gentry is your father."

For long moments, he didn't speak, only looked at her while his eight-year-old mind struggled to understand. Finally, he said, "Does he know about me?"

His previous enthusiasm was tempered somewhat by something she couldn't put her finger on. A touch of anxiety? She shook her head. "No. I never told him about you."

"Why not?"

Dear Lord, help me find the words... "There were reasons, Danny, reasons you're too young to understand. Your father and I...we made a mistake. We were a mistake."

"Because he wasn't ready for the responsibility

of a family," he said, repeating by rote what she'd told him before.

"Yes."

"What about now?" he asked. "Will you tell him about me now? I'm eight, so he's older, too, and he's probably ready for a family now, don't you think?"

Rachel's heart turned to ice. How could she have forgotten the second half of the equation? Sooner or later Gabe would have to be told the truth.

"Preferably later," she muttered.

"What?"

"Later, Danny," she told him, forcing a smile. "Be patient for just a little longer. The time to tell someone something like this has to be just right."

And Lord help me, I have to find the courage.

"Do you think he'll be happy, Mama?" Danny asked, his face wreathed in a wide smile. "Do you think he'll be glad I'm his son?"

Rachel pressed her lips together to hold back her tears. How to answer? With Gabe, who could predict? "Oh, Danny!"

She reached out and pulled him into her arms, hugging him close. *Dear God, why does this have to be so hard?* She smoothed his dark hair away from his forehead.

"I know he will," she told him fervently, praying it would be so. "But I still think we should wait to say anything a bit longer."

"Why?" Danny demanded. "Because I'm a mistake?"

A little cry of distress escaped her. How quickly

little minds were able to get to the crux of a matter. Regardless of how it had happened or whose fault it was, she did not regret him. Not for a second.

"Oh, no, Danny! Never believe that. I never thought *you* were a mistake. You're a blessing. The mistake was mine. The mistake was my loving Gabe more than he loved me and for not loving God more than I did Gabe."

"How could Gabe not love you, Mama?" Danny asked. "You're so pretty and so nice."

She smiled a watery smile at his gallant defense. "Thank you. It's sweet of you to say so. But that's the way it was." She paused. "As for telling Gabe about you, I believe it's best if this is our secret, at least for a while. Can you do that?"

Danny's face fell. He nodded. Uncertain if she could take any more of his disappointment, she stood to leave.

"Mama?"

"Yes, Danny?"

"Do you think if he gets to know me, he'd learn to love me enough to take on some responsibility?"

Rachel's heart broke just a little bit more as the uncertainty of the situation settled over her. It terrified her to imagine where the next few weeks might take them. She only hoped that Danny would survive with his happiness and his hope intact. She cradled his freckled face between her palms. "Everyone who knows you loves you."

He thought about that for a moment and asked, "Would you ever leave me?"

"Never! Not for any reason."

The words seemed to reassure him. Then he smiled and she saw a hint of mischief enter his eyes. "Except to go to heaven."

"Well, yes," she said, forcing a reciprocal smile. "Except that. And that would be okay, because one day you'd be right up there beside me."

Once again, she started to go; once again, he stopped her.

"Mama, does Pops know about Gabe?"

"You must call him 'Mr. Gentry,' Danny, not 'Gabe.' And yes, Pops knows."

"Is it okay if I talk to him about it?"

Rachel hesitated and then nodded her approval. She wondered what kinds of questions Danny might come up with for her father and knew that Edward Stone could handle whatever came his way.

Chapter Six

By the time the Emersons left, Gabe was physically back to normal. He worked from daylight until long after dark doing everything possible to improve the store and its contents. Keeping busy was a far better way to spend his time than thinking about Rachel, but even working, his thoughts turned to her as often as not.

He wished there was someone he could talk to about his past and his feelings for her, but no one in town knew about their past, so to say anything would be unthinkable. He couldn't even confide to Caleb, though they were making strides in their efforts at becoming closer.

Spending more time with Caleb showed just how much he had changed. His eyes held happiness based not only on his love for Abby, but on his love of the Lord. It was humbling to see his brother setting the example for his family.

As uplifting as it was to see the changes in Caleb,

it was also a bit disheartening, since Gabe wasn't sure he would ever reach that point of commitment to God, and he despaired of ever finding happiness with Rachel. When he realized there was nothing he could do to change her mind and there was no one to talk to, he resorted to something he'd never done much of before—prayer. He didn't think he was very good at it, but sharing his thoughts and feelings felt so good that he unburdened himself completely, pouring out his sorrow and feelings and frustrations. After all, it wasn't as if God didn't already know what was on his heart. Now there was nothing to do but keep praying and wait for the answer. Yes. No. Or wait awhile.

He was stacking new bolts of fabric onto the table in the dry-goods section, while watching for a glimpse of Rachel through the front window, which now read Gentry Mercantile in bold red and black letters. Earlier, he'd been putting a dress of sunshine-yellow dotted Swiss on one of the dress forms there, hoping it might catch the eye of some lady who needed a new summer frock, when he just happened to catch a glimpse of Rachel and Abby heading toward Ellie's. Abby held Eli, and Rachel had Betsy on her hip, while Laura clung to her mother's skirts. The older boys were nowhere to be seen, since school was in session until the end of the month.

He had watched the two women enter the café, smiling and chatting, caught up in whatever things women talked about when they were together, not,

Gabe supposed, unlike the way the old men who played checkers every day talked about their interests when they congregated. All too soon, the ladies had disappeared inside, and he was left staring at the restaurant's facade and wondering how long it might be before they emerged again. Shaking his head in disgust, he'd started putting out the remainder of the shipment.

Gabe saw Danny often. It seemed that no matter where he went, if school wasn't in session, the child appeared sooner or later. Gabe often caught Danny staring at him in a contemplative way, but whenever he asked what he was thinking about, he'd just smile and say "My father," which set Gabe off on another round of mental torture that left him miserable.

"What a lovely fabric, Gabriel."

The comment came from Sarah VanSickle, who had been back in the shoe section, trying to cram her size eight into a size seven. Now he looked down at the bolt of sea-green seersucker in his hands.

"It is, isn't it?" He picked up a spool of delicate ivory lace. "I thought this might go well with it," he said, trying to make conversation, though everything the woman did grated on his nerves. "What do you think?"

Sarah gave him an arch look, and a smirk intended to pass for a smile lifted the corners of her mouth. "You know women and what they might like *very* well, is what I think."

There was no mistaking the meaning behind the

words. Though Sarah had gone through all the outward motions of happiness the day Gabe became a Christian, there had been a disdainful gleam in her eyes that shouted of her insincerity.

Before he could stop himself, he said, "Perhaps all that riotous living wasn't entirely in vain, right, Mrs. VanSickle?"

Undeterred, Sarah asked, "Wasn't that your sister-in-law and Rachel Stone going into the restaurant a bit ago?"

"I believe it was."

"An interesting situation, that," Sarah said, pretending to sort through a box holding cards of buttons.

"What situation is that?"

"Why, your brother marrying Mrs. Carter, who was a virtual stranger when she moved in with him."

The implication was clear, and the obnoxious woman had left out the important fact that Abby hadn't just *moved in*. She had been hired as Betsy's wet nurse. Caleb had explained how Sarah's vicious gossip had left him and Abby with no recourse but to marry. Control or not, Gabe refused to stand there and have the reputation of one of the most wonderful women he'd ever had the privilege of knowing undermined by the likes of this tacky person. Bestowing his most charming smile on her, he said, "I understand we can thank you for that."

Sarah gasped, and her dark eyes snapped in annoyance. "Whatever do you mean?"

He lifted his shoulders in a nonchalant shrug. "I understand from several people in town that you were the one to play matchmaker to Caleb and Abby."

The portly woman's face turned an unbecoming red, and for once she had no ready comeback.

Mollified, Gabe decided to soften the blow somewhat. His smile grew wider. "They're so ridiculously happy, I'm sure they'll be forever grateful for the little push you gave them."

Knowing she'd met her match, Sarah turned away and pretended to give her attention to the rack of dime novels, while he finished arranging the cloth and sneaked another look out the window. Several children were wandering from the east end of town, which meant that school must have let out for the day. He watched Danny and Ben enter the restaurant.

He was placing canned peaches on the shelf when he saw Danny bound through the open portal, a wide smile on his face. "Hey, Gabe!" he said, running toward the counter.

Before Gabe could reply, Sarah shrilled, "Master Daniel Stone! That is no way to behave in a place of business!"

Danny skidded to a stop and stared at her with wide, frightened eyes.

Gabe set the crate of canned peaches on the counter. He knew what it was like to be full of life and excitement and to have that joy squelched with a few well-chosen words. "Danny."

Danny turned to look at him. "Sir?"

"It's all right. Come get one of the molasses cookies Abby made."

"Mr. Gentry!" Sarah barked as Danny moved to stand next to Gabe. "You do the boy no favors by encouraging him to act like a…a hooligan and then rewarding him for his behavior!"

"Have no fear, Mrs. VanSickle. I hardly think Danny committed any grave social faux pas by running in the store, and I doubt seriously if my…influence will turn him into a hooligan."

Expecting another retort, Gabe was surprised to see a thoughtful expression creep into Sarah's eyes as she stared at him and Danny. He was sure it wouldn't be long before she regrouped and came at him in another verbal assault. She must be a miserable human being.

Gabe gave Danny a cookie and opened a bottle of sarsaparilla for him. If he was going to reward the boy for his bad behavior, he might as well do it up right. "Here you go," he said, lifting Danny onto the counter.

Danny's broad smile was all the thanks Gabe needed. "Wow! Thanks, Gabe."

Gabe gave a sideways glance at Sarah, who looked as if she wanted to say something about Danny's lack of respect by calling Gabe by his given name. Instead, she clenched her jaw and smiled a smile that could only be described as cunning.

While Gabe worked at placing the rest of the peaches on the shelf, he asked Danny if he wanted to go fishing one evening after the store closed. The invitation sparked a smile of such brilliance it was staggering.

"That would be great, thanks. How about Friday?"

"Sounds fine."

Smiling, Danny took another swig from the bottle of sarsaparilla. "Oh! I almost forgot. Mama wanted me to pick up that box of medicine and stuff she ordered."

"Sure thing. It's in the back," Gabe told him. "You finish up here, and I'll get it."

He gathered Rachel's items into a crate and was on his way back to the front of the store when he heard Danny call a greeting to his mother.

Rachel. Gabe paused and took a deep breath before pushing through the curtain that separated the store from the supply room. He hadn't spoken to her face-to-face in more than a week.

"Why, hello there, Rachel, my dear," he heard Sarah say in a sickeningly sweet tone that sent a chill of apprehension down Gabe's spine.

"Good afternoon, Mrs. VanSickle," Rachel said politely.

"I suppose you're aware that Mr. Gentry is spoiling your boy, but I guess that's to be expected... under the circumstances."

"And what circumstances would that be?"

Gabe decided it was time to get in there and explain to Rachel about the cookie and carbonated drink. He didn't want Danny getting into trouble.

He shouldered the curtain aside and met Sarah's spiteful gaze.

She looked from him to Rachel. "There's Mr. Gentry with your order now," she said with artificial pleasantry.

Rachel turned to Gabe, who smiled from the pleasure of just seeing her.

"Hello there. I just went to fetch your supplies."

"Thank you," she said, almost looking nervous. "I started thinking the box might be too heavy for Danny to carry to the wagon."

"It could be," Gabe said, setting the small wooden box on the counter. He gestured toward Danny, who was finishing his drink. "I hope you don't mind that I gave him a little something. I used to be starving when I got out of school."

Rachel shook her head. "That's fine." Her gaze clung to his.

"Danny is such a handsome young man," Sarah commented, her loud voice shattering the sweetness of the moment. "That dark, dark hair, those beautiful blue eyes and that cute little dimple in his chin."

"Thank you," Rachel said, turning to the older woman with a genuine smile. "I think so, too."

Sarah tapped her lips with her finger and let her gaze move from Danny to Gabe and back again. "You know," she said with a little trill of laughter, "it's quite amazing, really."

"What's that?"

"How much Danny and Gabe resemble each other," Sarah said. Speaking over Rachel's gasp of surprise, she added, "Why, they look enough alike to be father and son."

From where Gabe stood, several things seemed to happen at once, and at first none of it made any sense. Danny's horrified gaze flew to Gabe's. Rachel's face drained of color and her panic-stricken look found his for just a moment. Then, with a strangled sound of torment, she snatched Danny from the countertop and set him on the floor. Grabbing his arm, she rushed for the door. Danny cast Gabe a worried look over his shoulder, and the truth exploded inside his mind.

Danny was his.

Rachel's expression and subsequent actions gave the claim all the validity Gabe needed. He suspected that Danny had known and had been afraid of his reaction. If he needed any further proof—which he didn't—it was there on the gossipy woman's triumphant face. She gave him a smug smile, and looking like the cat who'd just come upon a saucer of spilled cream, she turned and began to look through the fabric again.

Gabe turned away from her, his mind racing through a dozen facts and questions. First, the husband he had been so concerned about, the man he thought she'd loved, did not exist and never had. No wonder no one knew anything about him. The notion pleased him more than he could say.

Why hadn't Rachel told him she was expecting his child? Why had she told Danny and not him? And why hadn't *he* suspected the truth long before now?

He felt worse than dim-witted. He possessed above-average intelligence and could add and subtract. In his defense, he had no way of knowing exactly how old Danny was. He was certainly no expert on children, but he did know they could be the result of what he and Rachel had done. His supreme arrogance and unending quest for pleasure had blinded him to the possibility that it could happen to him.

His stomach churned with a sick feeling that rose from his very soul. What a fool he'd been! So many things made perfect sense now—Rachel's anger and bitterness toward him, her unwillingness to forgive. He didn't blame her.

More questions surfaced. Where would the three of them go from here? Would God give him a chance to set things right, or would he be punished for his past? Gabe knew that Abby would tell him that he had been cleansed of his past sins, yet as much as he wanted to believe that and told himself he did, it was a hard concept to comprehend. Nevertheless, he hoped with all his heart that she was right.

First things first. He had to talk to Rachel and make sure she and Danny were okay. He shook his head in disbelief. That was ridiculous. Of course they weren't okay. Still, he had to go and see what, if anything, he could do to make things easier.

Rachel nearly ran to her buggy that was hitched to the rail in front of the restaurant where just moments ago she'd been enjoying the company of her best friends. Clutching Danny's hand, she pulled him along behind her, unaware that he had to run to keep up.

She fought the urge to bawl. No doubt about it, in a few hours her life would be in shambles…again. By dinnertime Sarah would have told half the town Rachel's revealing reaction to the casual comment about Gabe and Danny. She wanted to scream at the unfairness of it, and she wanted to throttle Sarah.

She was afraid to look at Danny to gauge his reaction, and even more afraid of Gabe's, whatever it might be…whenever it might come. But come it would, and there was no longer any hope of escaping or delaying a reckoning.

"Get into the buggy, Danny," she snapped, untying the reins.

"It'll be okay, Mama," Danny said with supreme confidence as he clambered up into the seat. "Gabe likes me. I know he does. He asked me to go fishing with him on Friday."

Rachel looked into the too-serious eyes of her son, realizing for the first time that she and Gabe were not the only ones who would suffer from Sarah's spiteful tongue. Childlike, Danny saw only what his own limited perception perceived. How could she tell him that Gabe's liking had nothing to do with the reality of the situation?

She climbed up next to him, clucked to the horse and took off toward the house at a fast trot.

They were almost home when Danny asked,

"How did Mrs. VanSickle know about me, Mama? I thought just you, me and Pops knew."

An image of Sarah's gloating smile edged into Rachel's thoughts. She ground her teeth together. "Mrs. VanSickle is a very clever woman, Danny," she said, trying her best to hold her fury in check. "I suppose she saw how much alike the two of you look and figured it out."

"Do you think Gabe knew she was right? When I looked back at him, he just sort of stood there with his mouth hanging open."

"Oh, he knew," Rachel said with firm conviction. "Your father is very clever, too." It was the first time she had ever called Gabe Danny's father…at least to his face.

"Well, at least now you won't have to wait for the right time to tell him."

Danny actually looked pleased. She offered him a cynical half smile. "No," she replied with a hint of sarcasm. "I suppose there is that."

Anxious to close the store for an hour so that he could talk to Rachel, Gabe was debating whether or not to lambast Sarah for the misery she'd caused, or at the very least to ask her to leave, when she gave up the pretense of shopping and sashayed to the door, where she turned and gave him another sly smile.

"Well, I must say, Gabriel, this has been a most illuminating afternoon. I've learned so much."

"Yes, it has, Mrs. VanSickle. I've learned a lot,

too, like just because a person goes to church every time the doors are open doesn't mean their hearts are right."

Looking as if she might have a fit of apoplexy, Sarah gave a mighty "humph!" and swept out. Gabe sighed, knowing he shouldn't have given in to his anger but feeling a certain satisfaction nonetheless.

With Sarah gone, he grabbed Rachel's box of supplies, turned the sign in the door to Closed, locked up and headed toward her house. Her buggy wasn't in sight, but Danny and Edward were sitting on the porch, which was edged with purple irises. Two pairs of eyes regarded him with thoughtful guardedness.

Gabe got down from the buggy and carried the box up the steps. "Danny. Edward."

"Hey," Danny said. Seeing the caution in his eyes, Gabe smiled. None of this was Danny's fault, and there was no reason for him to feel fearful or guilty. The tension in the boy's face relaxed.

"Good evening, Gabe. Have a seat," Edward Stone said, indicating the rocker next to his.

"I brought Rachel's supplies. Is she here?"

"No. She said she was going to talk to the preacher." He turned to his grandson. "Why don't you take that box into the office, Danny?"

He complied without a word.

"She told me what happened," Rachel's father said once the child was out of earshot.

"Did you know before?"

Edward nodded. "All these years, she refused to

breathe a word about what happened or with whom, but when Simon brought you in and I saw how she reacted to you, it didn't take a genius to figure out why. My daughter isn't one to be so…hard and unforgiving."

It was Gabe's turn to nod. "Danny knew, too?"

"Yes, but only recently. I told Rachel she should tell him before something like today happened without him being prepared."

That explained a lot about the way he often caught Danny staring at him and the way he hung around wherever Gabe was. What must Danny—his son—be thinking?

His son.

The full impact of that hit him for the first time. Until now, his mind had been filled with his own shock and the embarrassment Danny and Rachel must be feeling.

He had a son. An unexpected and fierce love for the boy flowed through him at the same time the burden of responsibility his new role demanded settled like a stone in his heart. Danny would soon grow into a man, and Gabe's own experience had taught him that the influence he exerted in the boy's life would help determine the kind of man he grew into.

If Rachel let him have any influence in Danny's life.

He plopped down in the rocker next to Edward with the heaviness of an old person. "They must both hate me."

Edward offered a wry smile. "Mind you, Rachel thinks she hates you, but she really doesn't. She's too much of a healer to hate, but I'd be lying if I told you your coming back hasn't taken a toll on her."

In a gesture just like his brother's, Gabe scraped both hands through his hair. "I can only imagine."

"She went through a tough time when she came home after medical school, and it's taken years for her to feel as if she's done enough to make up for her wrongdoings."

Gabe was surprised by Edward's lack of anger. He couldn't begin to imagine what it must have been like to come back to Wolf Creek with a child born out of wedlock. No wonder she'd been so upset when he'd opened his eyes and seen her standing at his bedside. What had seemed like the culmination of a dream to him had been a nightmare to her.

"I'm sorry. I know it isn't enough and never will be, and I have no excuse, except that I wasn't a very good person back then. I think I've changed the past few months. I pray I have."

Edward smiled. "Oh, there's no doubt about that, and Rachel knows it. The forgiveness will come, I promise."

Gabe leaned forward, resting his forearms on his thighs, his hands clasped between his knees. "What about Danny? How did he take the news?"

"A funny thing, that," Edward mused. "Danny has been drawn to you from the first, almost as if he felt a connection between you, or maybe because he could picture you as the father he never had. I don't know. He's been asking questions about you ever since you arrived."

"Like what?" Gabe asked, both pleased and surprised.

"Like what you were like as a boy, what you enjoyed doing, that sort of thing."

Gabe's mouth twisted into a disparaging smile. "And what did you say that made me sound...decent?"

"I told him you were plenty ornery, always getting into things you shouldn't and going places you had no business going...all pretty innocent."

"Thank you." They were silent for a moment before Gabe raked up the courage to say, "And what about you, sir?"

"Me?" Edward looked surprised.

Gabe's eyes met Edward's. "You must hate me for what I did to your daughter."

"Hate? No. I was disappointed. Heartsick. Selfishly, I thought about what people would say about *me* and her mother and how we'd brought her up." A crooked smile claimed Edward's lips. "Human nature, I suppose. If you're looking for someone to cast the first stone, you'll have to look elsewhere. The truth is that no one is perfect. We all make mistakes, some more than others. You and Rachel have made things right with God. If He's forgiven you, how can I do less?"

"Thank you." Gabe heard a noise at the screen door and saw Danny standing there. "Do you mind if I have a minute with Danny?" he asked.

"Certainly." Edward stood with his canes and went to the doorway. "Danny," he called, "your father wants to talk to you."

Wearing an expression that straddled the fence between apprehension and anticipation, Danny came out, held the door open for his grandfather and went to sit on the step. Gabe rose and sat down next to him. Where to start?

Before he could decide on how best to approach the subject, Danny said, "Mrs. VanSickle isn't very nice, is she?"

Gabe shot him a sharp sideways look, a bit surprised by the boy's grasp of the woman's character. Though he would like to say just what he thought about Sarah, he realized this was his first chance to exert a positive influence. "I think Mrs. VanSickle is a very unhappy woman, but you're right—many of the things she says and does are hurtful."

"You're not mad at her?"

"No." Gabe was a bit surprised to realize his heart was filled with so much regret that there was no room for anger.

"What about Mama? Are you mad at her?"

"Why would I be mad at her?" Gabe asked, taken aback by the question.

Danny looked away. "For not telling you about me."

Reaching out, Gabe turned Danny's head back toward him. "I left before she had a chance to tell me, and she didn't know how to find me. The truth is that I shouldn't have left her the way I did. I can't be mad at her for something that wasn't her fault."

"Why did you go? Where did you go when you left her?"

"I went to—" Gabe searched his memory "—to New Orleans, I believe. Why did I go? That's easy. I'd been in St. Louis for a few months, and back then, that was a long time for me to stay in one spot. I was ready to move on to new places and new people. I was always looking for something different back then, Danny. The next fun place, the next good time. I suppose I was looking for happiness."

"Was New Orleans fun?"

"I suppose it was, though I don't recall what I did there or if I was happy."

Danny's forehead furrowed in a frown. "How can you not remember?"

"After a while, what I thought were good times just sort of blended together in a blur of wasted years."

"Wasted?"

Gabe nodded. "The fun I was looking for was often the wrong kind. I hurt your mother, and I did things that God didn't like. I'm not proud of that."

Danny pondered that a moment before asking, "Why did you come back?"

"Because I've been very unhappy the past year or so, and I saw that what I once thought was fun wasn't anymore. I thought maybe if I came back and started over, I could find out what real contentment was like.

"When I was hurt, and I woke up and saw your

mother standing beside the bed, I knew that the only time I was really happy was the time I spent with her." Gabe smiled sadly. "She gave me a lot of love, Danny, and I didn't realize how special that was. All I gave her was heartache."

Danny nodded. "She's got a lot of love inside her," he said with a nod, "and she's been crying a lot since you came."

A knife-sharp pain shot through Gabe's heart. He'd caused her enough suffering. If she'd let him, he'd spend the rest of his life making it up to her.

"She didn't want to tell you about me until we knew you were going to stay here. You are, aren't you?"

"I'm staying."

"And is it all right with you that I'm your son?" Danny's blue eyes were filled with uncertainty.

Slipping his arm around Danny's shoulders, Gabe pulled him close, humbled by his ready acceptance. He marveled at how such a simple thing like Danny relaxing against him in perfect trust could ease so much of the emptiness he'd felt for so many years.

"It's very much all right," he said. "More to the point, I hope you're all right having me for a father. I didn't get off to a good start, but I'll do my best to do better if your mother will let me."

Danny looked up at him and said solemnly, "I think you're doing all right, so far."

For the first time in nine years, Rachel felt the need to unburden herself to someone, only to find that the preacher was visiting a woman who'd just lost her husband. She needed to talk to someone she could trust and who would not be judgmental, someone who might understand the turmoil her emotions had undergone those many years ago. The only person who came to mind was Abby. Rachel headed the phaeton west, out of town.

Abby answered her knock, drying her hands on her apron. "What's wrong?" she blurted, seeing the expression on Rachel's face. "Danny? Edward?"

"They're fine," Rachel said. "At least I think Danny's okay." Her eyes filled with tears. "Do you have a minute to talk?"

Abby took Rachel's arm and pulled her through the door. "I have all the time you need. Come into the kitchen."

Rachel followed her friend through the house to the kitchen, truly the heart of this home. Eli slept in the cradle, and both Laura and Betsy were playing in the square penlike contraption Abby's first husband had constructed. Bread was rising at the back of the stove, and the mouthwatering aroma of chicken boiling escaped the lid of a cast-iron Dutch oven.

Rachel took a seat at the table, and Abby poured two glasses of lemonade before joining her. "Okay, what's happened?"

Rachel's voice was little more than a whisper. "I need to tell you something and ask your advice, but I'm so afraid it will change your opinion of me."

Abby reached out and touched Rachel's hand.

"Nothing you've done or could ever do would make me think any less of you. Surely you know that."

She gave a reluctant nod. "I'll just give you the abridged version."

"However much you feel comfortable telling," Abby said.

Rachel drew in a deep breath. "When I was studying medicine in St. Louis, Gabe looked me up."

"Gabe?" Abby's surprise could not be hidden.

Rachel nodded. "He flattered me and wooed me for a few weeks and then he left with nothing but a note to say goodbye."

Abby raised her eyebrows. "Well, from what I've heard, that doesn't surprise me. A lot of un-suspecting girls have lost their hearts to bounders like Gabe Gentry."

Rachel dropped her gaze to the tabletop. "My heart wasn't the only thing I lost."

The statement fell into the room like the pro-verbial rock.

"I see." Abby tugged one of Rachel's hands free of the glass and clutched it in both of hers. "Look at me, Rachel."

She complied reluctantly.

"You're trying to tell me Danny is Gabe's son."

"Yes."

Uttering the simple word of confession seemed to open a floodgate of emotions. Anger and blame and even shame vanished before a gut-wrenching sorrow. A moan clawed its way up from her battered heart and long-denied tears broke free. It was not a pretty sight and made her crying the night she'd confessed to her father seem like nothing. Abby handed Rachel a clean diaper to mop away the moisture. After long moments, the crying dwindled to a trickle and an occasional shuddering sob.

"Did Gabe know?" Abby asked when Rachel had more or less regained her composure.

She shook her head. "He left before I even knew."

"Have you told him since he's been back?"

"No. But my dad figured things out and told me I should tell Danny before someone else put two and two together. When I found out Gabe was buying the mercantile and staying in town, I had no choice but to tell Danny."

"And what did he say?"

"Actually," Rachel said with a wan smile, "he was thrilled and wanted to know what happened. I told him that I was wrong to put my feelings for Gabe before God and that Gabe wasn't ready to be a father. He wanted to tell Gabe, but I said we should wait until the time was just right. I prayed that he would just leave town, but that didn't happen."

"Nothing's ever that simple, is it?"

"It seems not," Rachel said, swiping the cloth across her still-damp cheeks.

"Obviously, something has happened."

"Sarah—"

Abby leaped to her feet, flinging up her hands in disgust. "I should have guessed that Sarah had something to do with your being in such a state! Tell me what happened."

Rachel sniffed. "Danny went to the mercantile to see if my medical supplies had come in. Evidently Sarah had been there long enough to see some interaction between Gabe and Danny, and when I walked in, she made the oh-so-innocent comment that they looked enough alike to be father and son."

"No!" Abby's eyes were wide with disbelief. "How could she?"

"Quite happily, it seemed."

"What happened then?"

"Gabe and Danny both looked stunned, Sarah looked inordinately pleased with herself, and I corroborated the statement by grabbing Danny and running out." She swiped her fingers across a fresh rush of tears that slipped down her cheeks. "What a mess!"

"I'm sure it seems that way, but all that matters in the end is how the three of you work things out. What did Danny say?"

"He was glad Gabe finally knew the truth. He said that now I wouldn't have to tell him and that it would be okay because Gabe really likes him."

"It will all be okay. I promise."

"How can it be? We'll be the talk of the town."

"Probably. At least until the next bit of gossip comes along. But at least you won't have to carry that burden alone anymore."

"Do you really think that Gabriel Gentry knowing the truth will lighten my load? More than likely he'll deny everything."

"I don't think so," Abby said with a shake of her head. "I've heard the stories about him, so I understand why you'd feel the way you do, especially since his actions with you seemed to confirm the gossip, but I truly believe he's doing his best to change, and both Caleb and I feel that he is taking his new commitments very seriously."

Rachel thought about that. Abby was right. How could she deny Gabe's sincerity when she could not see into his heart and everything she'd heard and seen the past few weeks pointed to a changed man?

"I've put all the blame on him all these years," she confessed. "It was easy. I told myself that he was worldly and knew all the tricks about how to seduce a girl, and I was innocent and shy and he swept me off my feet, but that isn't at all the way I remember it. He was the one who had to remind me that it was a mutual choice."

Abby smiled her gentle smile. "Sometimes it's hard for us to recognize our own part of the blame, but the fact that you have says a lot about how you'll handle things with Gabe from here on out."

"Handle things?"

"You have to talk to him, Rachel."

"I know I will sooner or later."

"The sooner the better," Abby insisted. "The two of you and your father need to stand united—if not for your own sake, for Danny's, because you're correct—there'll be talk aplenty for a while."

Rachel knew Abby was right, but the very idea of discussing the past with Gabe would be like ripping the scab off a partially healed wound. Since coming back to Wolf Creek, she had concentrated on building her reputation both as a physician and a solid, God-fearing citizen. Dredging up the past, both the good and the bad, meant examining every aspect of those three weeks with Gabe. Worse, it would leave her wide open for more heartbreak.

It was dusky dark when Rachel approached the house. She had spent the better part of two hours with Abby and then more time with the preacher. He was not judgmental and told her that her repentance when she'd returned had put her back on the right track. When she asked why Gabe had chosen to come back to stay, the minister told her that no one understood how God worked in our lives, but we had to trust that He had a plan and that every day was within His control. She knew he was right, but she still dreaded her next meeting with Gabe.

Though she knew there were rocky times ahead, the relief she'd felt after telling her father about Gabe was nothing compared to the release she felt knowing that both Danny and Gabe knew the truth. Secrecy was a heavy burden. Now that Gabe knew and she'd accepted her own share of responsibility for their situation, her heart felt lighter than it had been in a very long time…perhaps since the time she'd spent with Gabe in St. Louis.

To her dismay, the first thing she saw when she

crossed the railroad tracks in front of the house was Gabe sitting on the porch steps next to Danny. The tension holding her in its grip the past few hours eased when she saw there was no noticeable strain in either of them, and her heart gave a little lurch of something that wavered suspiciously between joy and hope.

Both of them were resting their elbows on the step behind them. Danny was clearly trying to mimic his father's posture and attitude. His face lit up when he saw her approach, his eyes sparkling with joy. Gabe's expression was unreadable. She wondered if her face reflected her uncertainty and was surprised that the antagonism that usually assaulted her when she saw him was absent. Perhaps her prayers were working. At least it would make dealing with him easier, which was good for Danny's sake. Abby was right. No matter how they felt or what they suffered the next few days and weeks, their main priority must be protecting Danny as much as possible.

As she pulled to a stop at the hitching post, Gabe leaned down and said something to Danny, who got up and went inside. Striding to the buggy with a loose, long-legged gait, Gabe lifted her down without giving her the opportunity to acquiesce or refuse.

His hands were warm at her waist.

Hers gripped his shoulders for balance and also in an effort to resist the almost overwhelming impulse to slide them up to cradle his lean cheeks between her palms. Was it her imagination, or did his hands tighten? Searching for answers, signs, anything to give her a clue as to what he was feeling, she examined his face. He was still unbearably handsome, even with the new bump on his nose and the jagged scar scoring his cheek.

The intensity in his eyes was familiar. When Gabe gave his attention to something, it was complete and undivided. Just now that interest was focused on her. He searched her face, as if he, too, were looking for some way to gauge her frame of mind. Afraid that he would see the vulnerability she was feeling, she broke free and went to sit in one of the rockers.

He followed, crossing his arms over his wide chest and leaning against the porch post. "Why didn't you tell me?"

She'd expected him to broach the subject— though perhaps not quite so soon or in such a direct way. She had not expected the aching tenderness that accompanied the question.

"I didn't know until after you left," she confessed, staring down at the hands clasped in her lap. "And once I did, how was I supposed to find you in New Orleans?"

He had no ready answer.

"Would you have come back to me if you had known?" she asked, glancing upward.

"Yes."

His lack of hesitation surprised her.

"Yes? Are you actually saying you'd have stopped your wandering to be a husband and father?"

"Of course I would have." His expression said that he couldn't believe she'd asked such a thing. "You forget that I know what it's like to be abandoned by a parent. I would never intentionally put a child of mine through that."

Knowing his past and how deep were the scars left by his mother's departure, there was no doubting him. Random thoughts, startling in clarity, raced through her mind, disjointed images of how her life would have been if he'd stayed and they'd brought up Danny together.

Gabe hadn't loved her, had never claimed to. Could her love have held him when restlessness began to creep in? Would what he felt have been enough to keep him at her side when the inevitable trials of life began to edge into their utopia? Could a marriage between them have lasted? Would she have finished medical school or been forced to help support them?

She made a low sound of denial. Now was not the time to indulge in what-might-have-been. "How's Danny?" she asked, curious about both her son's state of mind and how he was handling Sarah's stunning statement.

"He's fine. Perfect."

The enthusiasm in his voice buoyed her spirits. "I wouldn't say he's perfect," she contradicted, "but he's pretty close." The last was said with a proud smile that Gabe returned. The shared moment of parental pride seemed to bind them together somehow.

"From what I've observed, you've done a wonderful job with him," he told her. "I can't begin to imagine what it must have been like to come back here with a child, unmarried, and have the likes of Sarah VanSickle around to lord it over you."

"Actually, Sarah broke the news to the town before I ever came home."

"How on earth did she find out?"

"She made a trip to St. Louis to visit her sister and looked me up. I was almost at the end of the pregnancy when she showed up on my doorstep." Her mouth curved into a derisive smile.

"I can only imagine her glee," Gabe growled.

"She did seem to delight in my embarrassment, and of course, she knew I wasn't married. She couldn't wait to get home and tell everyone."

"I'll be the first to admit that I have more than my share of faults," Gabe said, "but for the life of me I can't imagine how anyone takes so much pleasure from deliberately dealing grief to others."

"I've given up trying to figure it out where she's concerned. At any rate, I hadn't breathed a word to my father about you and never intended to. My plan was to stay away from Wolf Creek until the baby was born, put it up for adoption, finish my schooling and then come home."

"You planned to give up the baby?"

She gave a deep sigh. "Believe me, it wasn't an easy choice. I did a lot of soul-searching and in the end I was convinced that giving him up would be best for everyone.

"What's that they say about the best laid plans of mice and men? When Pops showed up soon after Sarah went home and spilled the beans, he wouldn't hear of my giving up Danny. He said that I might have made a mistake, but that I wasn't going to compound it by giving away my child."

"Thank goodness."

The fervency in his voice sent Rachel's gaze winging to his. His sincerity was as heartfelt as her relief. "Yes. Thank goodness he knows me so well. He knew I'd never forgive myself. So we stayed there until I got my diploma, and I've been trying to make it up to everyone ever since."

"What happened wasn't your fault," Gabe told her. "I took advantage of you."

Rachel looked at him thoughtfully. She'd spent years convincing herself that what he said was true, but now she knew that it had been a mutual longing. Perhaps in the beginning his masculine beauty and charm had played a part, and yes, she was lonely and he had made her feel beautiful and special. But she knew right from wrong and had not been without the tools to withstand his advances if she'd wanted to. She hadn't wanted to, because she'd loved him and believed he loved her.

"No, you were right," she argued. "I was every bit as much to blame as you. I have no excuse except that I loved you and because of that I turned my back on God and everything I'd been taught." Her voice broke, and tears began to slip down her pale cheeks.

Gabe pushed away from the porch railing and

took a step toward her, but she held him back with an upraised hand and a shake of her head. Despite her attempts to keep him away, he knelt next to the rocker. Despite her attempts not to, she couldn't help looking at him. The agony and remorse she'd carried so long darkened her eyes to almost black.

"I've been so angry with you," she whispered. "I loved you so much, and you hurt me so badly."

He reached out and covered the hands twisting in her lap with one of his. "I cared for you, too, Rachel, but—"

"Don't!" she said and then made a deliberate attempt to soften her tone. She was unaware that her fingers had curled around his, that she was holding him at arm's length and yet still keeping him close. "Whatever we shared is all in the past, so just…don't try to woo me with lies and pretty words again," she begged. "Please."

Gabe reached out and lifted her chin with his free hand. "No more lies, Rachel. And no more pretty words unless I truly feel them and think you want to hear them."

The truth of his promise was reflected in his eyes. His fingertips moved gently over her cheek, and his thumb traced the curve of her lower lip as it had the day in the mercantile. "For now, just let me tell you the truth as I've come to know it."

She nodded and waited for him to find the right words.

"Even though I was stupid and self-centered and thoughtless back then, I had enough sense to know you were a very special person. I'm not claiming it was love—I've never had much experience with that emotion, but whatever it was I couldn't deal with it, and so I treated it, and you, with the same casual disregard I did everything."

"Gabe, you don't—"

"Sh," he said, placing a finger against her lips. "I need to say this. I've needed to say it for a very long time."

She pressed her lips together and he continued.

"When I finally came to my senses and realized my life was a shambles and I was no happier than when I left here, I started thinking about you. I dredged up memories of every moment we'd spent together, everything we'd said, done, felt. I knew then that I'd had something special within grasp— maybe my only chance to find real happiness—and I'd tossed it aside.

"I started thinking about my relationship with Caleb, too. We were never close, and as I looked back I began to see that he was the one who got the short end of the stick because I was such a slacker. About a year ago I started playing with the notion of coming back to try to make things right with you and him and anyone else I might have hurt.

"When I woke up and saw you standing at my bedside, I knew beyond a doubt that the time we spent together in St. Louis was the best of my life, and that *you* were the best thing that ever happened to me. I'm truly sorry. For everything. But at the same time, I'm not sorry that I had those few weeks with you, wrong though they were."

Rachel wanted to believe him. She knew he believed what he was saying, that he meant it. But how long before the siren of wanderlust began singing her tempting song in his ear?

She wasn't aware that she'd spoken the words aloud until he smiled and said, "I've heard all her songs and they don't pull at me anymore."

"What if she whispers that Dallas is where you really need to be," Rachel murmured, "or that California has sights you haven't seen?"

"I've been to both of those places and have no desire to go again. At least not alone."

Was he implying he would like to go with her? "How long before some other woman catches your attention, and you begin to wonder what her arms would feel like around you?"

"The only woman whose arms I can even remember is you. Your arms."

How she wanted to believe him, but there was so much at stake. It was time she stopped running on emotion where Gabe was concerned, time she started using her common sense and intellect. She didn't think she could survive if she gave him her heart and he waltzed out of her life a second time. Risking Danny's heart was out of the question. What she could do was grant Gabe forgiveness and move on with her life.

"If it's forgiveness you want, Gabe, you have it." She choked out a breathless sob of laughter. Pressing her hand to her heart, she gave him a tremulous smile. "You don't know what a burden has been lifted just saying those words. I feel so…so free."

"I'm glad."

She sobered suddenly. "This isn't just about you and me and what we felt or may feel now. It's about Danny. It's been about him ever since they laid him in my arms."

"I'm beginning to understand that. Maybe you'll think I'm crazy, but I love him, Rachel. I never had any idea how much you could love a child until he put his arms around me and told me I was doing fine as a father."

Seeing her skepticism, he asked, "Why should women be the only ones who feel that special bond? I want to be part of his life. Please say you'll let me."

She chewed on her bottom lip, her mind racing. How could she deny him this, when his eyes held such earnestness? Yet how could she say yes when she was so afraid?

As if he could read her mind, he said, "There's nothing I can do to undo my wrongs, and I know you have plenty of reason to doubt me, but you can believe me when I tell you that I'm not going anywhere."

She stared at him, wanting to believe, uncertain if the statement was reassuring or distressing.

Chapter Seven

For the next few days gossip around town was worse than a feeding frenzy, and it seemed to Gabe that almost everyone who came into the mercantile sneaked furtive glances at him. Some turned away when he tried to make eye contact. A few regular customers stopped coming by, but he wasn't too worried since he was the only store in town. They'd have to come back sooner or later, unless they wanted to travel to Murfreesboro or Gurdon for supplies.

He figured there was plenty of speculation about him and Rachel at the town's dinner tables, which he supposed was to be expected, but for the most part, his customers treated him as they always had. As he'd overheard one of the old men tell one of his checkers cohorts, it was a rite of passage for young men to sow a few wild oats.

The offhand comment only made Gabe feel worse, especially when the old codger added that he was just a bit surprised that Doc's girl had been involved. That was Gabe's true shame. He deserved everything being said about him, but he was heartsick at the knowledge that Rachel was being talked about.

Besides her and her family, the ones whose opinions meant the most were Caleb and Abby. After Gabe and Rachel talked, he'd rented a buggy and driven to the farm, hoping to break the news to them in his own way. He was flabbergasted to find that Rachel had already confided to Abby, who had told Caleb. Though Gabe expected censure and worse from his brother, he was surprised by his willingness to listen without interruption or reproach.

Gabe told them about his earlier talk with Rachel and ended by confessing, "I don't know what to do to make things right."

"You've already taken the first step," Abby assured him. "You've put your trust and your future in God. You have to turn this over to Him and let Him work this out however it's meant to be."

"She's right. It will all turn out the way He wants it to," Caleb said. "That's one thing Abby taught me. I came up with all sorts of reasons about why I wasn't good enough to make a life with her. I didn't have a relationship with God, I wasn't good husband and father material, I wasn't like William, and I couldn't relate to Ben. The list went on and on, so I did my best to drive her away."

"What!"

Caleb smiled. "That's a story for another day. Let

it suffice for now that, thankfully, God and Abby had other plans. There's something to be said about a woman who has a mind of her own and isn't afraid to speak it. If things between you and Rachel don't turn out the way you want, you'll have to trust that it's the Lord's will, accept it and move on. That will be the hardest part."

Abby smiled. "Caleb's right, but I'm an incurable romantic, and I find it hard to believe that He has brought the two of you to this place after so much time and pain and in such a dramatic way just to tear you apart. Even if you decide you don't suit, I can't believe He doesn't want you to be a part of Danny's life. You do want that, don't you?"

"More than anything," Gabe told her. "Except for Rachel and me to have a life together."

"You love her, then?" Abby asked, smiling her gentle smile.

"I do. But she's made it very clear that she doesn't want to hear anything like that from me and has assured me that I won't play her the fool a second time."

"But if you love her, you wouldn't be."

"I know that, but she doesn't. All she knows is that I walked away from her once." He blew out a deep breath. "The thing is that as good-for-nothing that I was, I'd never have walked out on her if I'd known there was a baby. I'd never do to a child of mine what our mother did to us. I know how badly that hurts and how deep those scars go."

Caleb shot a look to Abby, who nodded.

"What?" Gabe asked, sensing something afoot.

"Frank told me a story about that, and maybe when you hear it, you'll be a bit more sympathetic to our mother."

Gabe gave a disbelieving snort, a bit surprised by Caleb calling Libby "mother." Neither of them had called her anything but her name for years, and their father had always been Lucas.

"I doubt that," he said, "but feel free to enlighten me."

"The way I remember it is that Lucas led us to believe that Mom fell for this guy, wanted to go away with him and just walked away from us," Caleb said.

"That's the way I remember it."

"Frank says that isn't the truth. She wanted to take us to Boston for a visit, but Lucas wouldn't let her. So some visitors came to visit from back East. Lucas claimed she fell for the guy and caught them together in a compromising situation. Frank had a hard time believing that, since he said she'd never been anything but the devoted wife and mother."

"Okay..." Gabe looked at his brother. "So what did happen?"

"By all accounts, Lucas beat the guy up, which Frank says Edward Stone can verify, and told Mom he wanted her gone. She packed up everything, including you, and the wagons were loaded to go to the train station. They were going to pick me up at school when they got to town.

"When they were ready to pull out, Lucas ordered Frank to unload our trunks and bring you to him. He said there was no way Libby was going to take his sons away from him."

Gabe's frowning gaze focused on his brother. "He forced her to leave without us?"

Caleb nodded. "Frank said Mom went a little crazy, trying to grab you back, pleading, crying and yelling that he couldn't do that to her. He told Frank and Micah that if they didn't do what he said, he'd see to it that they never worked around here again. He told her there was no way she could fight him, so for her just to go back East and make herself a new life. He'd see about the divorce. Do you remember any of that?"

Gabe shook his head, though a wisp of memory—a beautiful dark-haired woman cradling his face while tears streamed down hers—drifted through his mind like smoke on a capricious breeze. Was it real or only an image that flashed into his mind as his brother described the day that defined his entire life?

"She said that if she couldn't take us, she wouldn't leave, and Lucas told her that if she didn't go quietly, he'd see to it that she and her family paid."

Gabe regarded Caleb in disbelief. "So she didn't leave us behind because she didn't want us."

Caleb shook his head. "She left because she knew Lucas was right, that there was no way she could win against his money and power. After she was gone, he gathered up everything she'd left behind and burned it. What wouldn't burn he buried out back."

"That place we always thought was an animal grave?" Gabe queried.

"Yep." One corner of Caleb's mouth lifted into a derisive smile. "Sort of puts things into a whole different perspective, doesn't it, little brother?"

"Yes." Gabe frowned. "Do you think that's why Lucas treated us the way he did?"

"Who knows?"

"I wonder if that's why he paid me to leave?"

Caleb and Abby exchanged confused looks. "What do you mean, paid you to leave? You went to him and asked for your inheritance."

"Where did you get that idea?" Gabe asked. "I was so fed up one day that I spouted off to him. Nothing unusual about that, right? I told him I couldn't stand the sight of him, and I couldn't wait for him to die so that I could get my inheritance and put him and Wolf Creek far behind me." He shrugged. "I think I hoped it might hurt him, to pay him back for the way he was always hurting us.

"Whatever I hoped for didn't work. He didn't look like it fazed him one little bit. He stared at me while he chewed on the end of his cheroot. Then he said he was sick to death of the sight of me, too, because every time he looked at me he saw Mama's face. Then he just walked away.

"I figured everything would go back the way it was in a day or two, but the next afternoon he handed me a wad of cash and told me what arrangements he'd made at the bank for me to get the rest of it. Then he told me to pack my bags and get out, the sooner the better, and he specifically told me to never come back as long as he was alive, so I didn't."

Caleb and Abby looked as if they'd just been knocked for a loop. Caleb shook his head. "I had no idea. I knew the two of you were mad at each other, but that was pretty common. I've always thought you asked him for your part."

"Not exactly," Gabe said. "When I looked back later, it was almost as if he was glad to see me go, like it would be a relief to be rid of me. I tried writing a few times, but I figured out pretty quick he had no intention of answering, so I stopped. I'm not going to lie about it. I had a great time for several years. But it gets old."

"What? Traveling?"

"The traveling was great. Seeing all those places was fantastic, though I'm not sure I really appreciated them at the time. What gets old is trying to satisfy every one of your heart's desires. It loses its luster after a while." He smiled at his brother and sister in law. "Like I said before, you were the lucky one. You have everything that's worth anything right here in this house."

Caleb reached out and took Abby's hand. "You're right," he said. "I do."

Rachel entered the parlor, her spirits low, her feet dragging.

"Not much need my asking how your day went,"

Edward said, taking in his daughter's countenance with one quick glance. "Bad, I gather."

"Worse than bad. A couple of ladies actually turned their backs on me when I spoke to them on the street, and Mrs. Taylor canceled the appointment for Sophie's follow-up on her sore throat."

"They'll put aside all that holier-than-thou snobbishness the first time someone gets bad sick and they need a doctor."

"I suppose you're right." Rachel tugged off her bonnet and dropped it onto a chair. "Then, to pile on the agony, I was leaving Ellie's and who should walk in but Sarah herself. To see her face plastered with that smirk of hers while she looked me over with that superior expression, people would never know she'd done her best to ruin three people's lives. She was so sickeningly sweet to me I thought I might upchuck. Dreadful woman!"

Edward laughed. "Pour yourself a cup of coffee, my dear, and settle down. This, too, will pass."

"Do you really think so?"

"I do."

Rachel poured her coffee, added her requisite two spoons of sugar and a dollop of cream and plopped down across the table from her father. "Where's Danny?"

"He wanted to go see Gabe."

"And you let him?" Rachel almost screeched.

"I thought the two of you had agreed that Gabe could be in Danny's life, at least in a limited way."

"We did, but…"

"But someone will see him there and there will be more talk," Edward said, an expression of mock horror on his face. "They probably will, but the die is cast, Rachel. Any harm that's going to happen has already been done, and if Gabe is to be part of Danny's life, it follows that they'll be seen together. Besides, I have a feeling that he and Gabe can handle anyone who gets out of line."

"Do you think so?"

"I know so. When I look at Gabe Gentry now, I see a man who is finally coming into who God meant him to be, and I believe with all my heart that he loves Danny, and that he will protect him as best he can." He smiled. "Besides, I think Danny is pretty good at taking up for himself when he needs to."

"I suppose," she said, but she didn't sound convinced.

The objects of Rachel's concerns, all three of them, were at that moment in the mercantile. Danny was learning the intricacies of chess from old Mr. Jessup. Gabe was putting out a new order of abalone buttons in the dry-goods section, longing for the last hour to pass so he could close the store and take Danny fishing. Sarah was looking through the rack of new spring dresses that had arrived the day before.

Even knowing that she was the creator of the tension that fairly crackled through the air, nothing would alter Sarah's regular excursions to the store, since she couldn't bear the notion that something new might come in and she wouldn't be the first in town to have it. Gabe didn't mind. She was a good customer, and as he'd told Caleb, he could be nice to anyone—well, almost anyone—for an hour or so. No sense cutting off his nose to spite his face, and it gave him a chance to practice forgiveness.

It was hard, but the preacher had told him and Rachel that it was important to perform the outward acts of forgiveness while praying and waiting for God to make them feel it in their hearts. He'd explained that in his experience, only a rare few could be cut to the quick by another and immediately cede pardon to the person responsible for inflicting that pain.

As a reminder to himself and his customers that everything said and done affected others in either a good or bad way, Gabe had bought a big framed slate and wrote a daily scripture on it. He also listed people in town who were in need of prayer for one reason or another.

The day's scripture from Proverbs read: "Pleasant words are a honeycomb sweet to the soul and healing to the bones." As a reminder to do the right thing, he glanced at it often as his gaze followed Sarah's meanderings through the store.

"Hey, Gabe!" Danny called. "Mr. Jessup says I'm gonna make a whale of a chess player one of these days. He says I'm catchin' on faster than anyone he's ever tried to teach."

Before Gabe could respond, Sarah exclaimed,

"Master Daniel Stone! I'm sure you know better than to call an adult by his first name. That is 'Mr. Gentry' to you." She flashed a sly smile toward Gabe. "Or perhaps you should call Mr. Gentry *Father.*"

Uncertain how to answer, Danny's wide-eyed gaze sought Gabe's. Literally grinding his teeth, he winked at the child and cast a quick look at the scripture on the wall. *Please, dear Lord, give me the right words.*

"You know, Mrs. VanSickle, I do believe you're right," he acknowledged in as near-to-pleasant a tone as he could manage. He would love nothing better than for Danny to call him Dad, but before giving him permission to do so, he would have to get Rachel's consent. "By the way, have you seen the new blouse patterns that came in?"

Nonplussed that for once she had failed to draw blood, Sarah swished over to the rack holding the dress patterns. When she brought her purchases to the counter a bit later, Gabe cocked his head to the side and asked, "Did you notice my new sign?"

"I did." She said no more, and Gabe didn't press the matter. He rang up her purchases, took her money and bade her good day, reminding her that he would have a new shipment of Saratoga chips on the next train. The Emersons had told him of Sarah's penchant for the crunchy chip made from deep-frying thinly sliced potatoes, and he tried to keep them in stock for her. Secretly he thought her insatiable consumption of the chips was at least part of the reason for her tendency to portliness.

Mollified somewhat by his remembering her preferences, Sarah left. Gabe heaved a sigh. Finally. He pulled his watch from his pocket and saw that it was almost time to shut down for the day. As he carried the empty crates to the back, he thought about her snide remarks. Something she'd said brought up another issue, albeit unintentionally. She'd called Danny by Stone, when in reality he was a Gentry. Would Rachel consent to Danny calling him Dad and taking the Gentry name?

"You can't be serious!"

She regarded Gabe with patent disbelief.

He stood leaning against the parlor doorframe, dangerously attractive in a faded chambray shirt, denim Levis and a pair of boots that looked as if they had more than a brief acquaintance with work. His arms were folded across the impressive expanse of his chest.

"I can't be serious about what? Letting Danny call me Dad, wanting him to have the Gentry name, or you going fishing with us?"

"All of them!" Rachel snapped, whirling toward the kitchen doorway to escape the teasing glint in his eyes. It had far too powerful an effect on her for her comfort.

She never heard him cross the large braided rug covering the floor, but the weight of his hands on her shoulders stopped her midstride. She took a deep breath and wished she hadn't when the scent of his spicy cologne began its subtle assault on her senses. Her eyes drifted shut.

"Did anyone ever tell you that those little curls at the nape of your neck make it look extremely kissable?"

She sucked in a shallow breath and stood very still, her hands fisted at her sides, fighting the impulse to tip her head forward the slightest bit.... Common sense returned in a flash. She'd taken that path once and look what had happened.

"You've told me," she said with feigned patience. "Often. And you promised me you wouldn't say things like that."

"I promised not to say it if I didn't mean it, and I do." He blew out a frustrated breath. "Okay. Back to the problem at hand. What would it hurt for Danny to call me Dad? We'd both like it."

His voice held a gentle persuasion, and it sounded closer. She imagined she felt the soft whisper of his breath stirring loose tendrils of her hair. *Had* he leaned nearer?

"Everyone would..." Determined to regain her composure, she turned to face him and made the mistake of looking into his eyes. She immediately forgot what it was she meant to say. Like Danny, he had the most outrageously long eyelashes.

"Know?" Gabe said, picking up her thought. "Guess what, pretty girl, they already do. Let's not try to hide anything else. By taking control and doing what we think is right for us and for Danny, we keep the busybodies from manipulating the situation. Let everyone think what they want. They will anyway."

It was true. "It's just that we'd be confirming things."

"I can't see how we can do anything else, can you?"

The news was already out, so... "No. Not really."

One battle won, Gabe thought. "About the Gentry name. I don't—"

"Stop it, Gabe," she commanded, glaring at him. "Don't push your luck. I am not changing Danny's name. He will be Danny Stone until such time as I marry, if I do. Then he can take that man's name, if that's what they both want."

He nodded, very serious. "I see," he said with a nod. "Angling for a proposal, now, are you?"

"What!" she cried, marveling at the sheer audacity of the man. Then, seeing the familiar teasing twinkle in his eyes, she narrowed her own to angry slits. "Wretched, wretched man!" She brushed past him.

"But you still think I'm handsome."

She heard the laughter in his voice, and a dozen memories rushed through her mind, only to be squelched by reality. "I think you're incredibly conceited and full of yourself," she said over her shoulder and suppressed a shiver when she felt his fingers against her neck as he toyed with one of the errant curls.

"Does that mean you won't go fishing with us?"

She stopped in her tracks. Heaven help her. There

seemed no escape from his determination, and that, she admitted with a sigh, was what worried her. Gabe Gentry with a goal was hard to deny. Worse, the more time she spent with him, she was becoming less and less certain that she wanted to resist.

I wonder what he'd have said if you'd told him that you were pressing for a proposal? How fast and how far do you think he'd have run? She shoved the thought aside and said over her shoulder, "It's my night to cook. I have to fix dinner for Pops."

"I'll have Ellie send over something from the café, and while I'm at it, she can make us up a picnic supper. And will you please turn around to talk to me. I'd much rather talk to your pretty face than your back. Besides, your neck is too much of a temptation to resist much longer."

That sent her whirling around. His smile was broad, mischievous and as endearing as Danny's. He *was* very, very handsome. And charming. And he knew it.

Which was extremely maddening.

She gnawed at her bottom lip in indecision. It had been a terrible few days, and fishing was not her favorite pastime. She had agreed to let Danny spend time with Gabe, and even though she was convinced he loved Danny, she was still concerned about letting him spend too much time with him. So didn't it make a strange sort of sense to go fishing with them and see to it that Wolf Creek's prodigal didn't corrupt her son?

Pushing aside the little voice that whispered she

was lying to herself and that she was really going so she could spend time with Gabe herself, she said, "All right. I'll go."

"Well, you don't have to sound so thrilled about it," Gabe said matter-of-factly. "You might turn my head."

Wolf Creek was running high from all the spring rains. From the whoops of laughter and excited shouts, Danny and Gabe were having a marvelous time. Never a fan of threading worms on hooks just to watch them drown, Rachel lay on her stomach on a quilt she'd brought, reading the latest installment of a serial she'd been following in *Frank Leslie's Popular Monthly.*

Finished with the story, she closed the magazine and set it aside, resting her chin on her palms and watching the two males connecting over the "manly" pursuit as sons and fathers had been doing since the beginning of time.

As she watched, Danny jerked another fish, his third, onto the bank. Gabe helped put it on the forked stick they were using as a stringer, and Danny raked through the bucket with grimy hands, looking for another of the huge worms they'd found hiding in the fertile soil beneath the damp leaves.

"Hey, Mom!" he cried. "You're gonna cook these for me tomorrow, aren't you?" They were small perch, and there wouldn't be much left when they were cleaned, but he was so precious with his hair standing on end and his eyes alight with excitement

over catching them, there was no way she could refuse. He was every bit as hard to resist as his father.

"If you clean them, I'll cook them," she promised. Tossing Gabe an innocent look, she said, "Unless I'm mistaken, cleaning fish falls into the father
department."

As soon as she spoke the words, she longed to
call them back. Why had she deliberately made
reference to the situation in a way that only reinforced it?

"Yes, ma'am, it is," he said with a pleased smile.

Irritated with herself for being so susceptible to
his magnetism, irritated with Danny for being so
happy when she was so miserable, irritated with
Gabe for...well, for being Gabe, she stifled a groan
and rolled to her back, flinging her forearm across
her eyes to block the late-afternoon sunlight that
sifted through the canopy of new green leaves.

Why was he still able to make her heart pound
and her pulse race with nothing but that teasing
smile of his? She'd hated him for so long, blamed
him for everything, but once she'd seen him hurt
and bleeding, her resentment had begun to dissipate. As if that weren't bad enough, she found that
the tender feelings she'd buried so painstakingly beneath layers of loathing and disgust were reemerg-
ing slowly, like the brave crocuses that pushed their
tender heads up toward the sun despite the discour-
agement of being buried beneath layers of leaves
and snow.

Just because he'd explained why he'd walked

away from her and she accepted and believed him didn't mean that she was ready to give him a second chance. He had proved lethal to both her emotional and spiritual well-being. He'd hurt her so badly she hadn't been certain she would ever recover. She'd known she would probably never find the courage to trust her heart to another man and doubted she would ever find one whose touch stirred her as Gabe's did.

But she'd had Danny, and through him she had a part of Gabe, maybe the best part. She was thankful for that. Even though he seemed a changed man, she could not let Gabe Gentry wear down her defenses again. To do so would be insanity. So why was the notion so very tempting?

Chapter Eight

Gabe was taking cash from the register to pay Claudia Fremont for a basket filled with dozens of large brown eggs he would resell when Artie Baker, one of his chess and checkers "regulars," burst through the doors.

"Slow down there, Artie," Gabe said with a smile. "What are you in such an all-fired hurry about?"

"I was just checkin' to see if you'd heard the news. Figured if you hadn't you ought to."

Willing to humor the old man, Gabe said, "I heard that Paul Gillespie's milk cow died."

"Naw," Artie said, with a shake of his grizzled head. "That's old news."

"Guess I haven't heard it, then."

"Joe Carpenter over at the telegraph station said yer mama's comin' in on the nine-o'clock train in the morning."

Gabe felt as if someone had landed a hard right

to his gut. "My mother?" He wondered if the question was actually as stupid as it sounded.

"If Libby Gentry is yer mama, then that's who I'm talkin' about," Artie said as if Gabe was more than a bit dim. "Hattie's all atwitter about it. Says she got a letter just yesterday from Libby saying she was coming and would need rooms for two other people she was bringing with her. Hattie figures they're Libby's kids."

Kids. His mother had other children. He wasn't sure why that came as a shock. If she and Lucas had divorced, there was no reason she would not have married again and started another family. Still, that notion was as alien as the fact that the mother he'd resented most of his life was actually coming back after all these years and that he would have to face her.

Another fact slammed into him. If the young couple were his mother's children, they would be his and Caleb's brothers or sisters. How would he and his new siblings react to each other? Half-formed visions of what might transpire the next few days began to race through his mind. What would he say to the woman who had birthed him? Even knowing that he'd been wrong about so much of their past, he wondered what she could possibly have to say to him and Caleb.

Gabe's stomach churned. He and Rachel were already the talk of the town, and Libby's coming would only be more grist for the gossip mill. Between them, he and Caleb had contributed more

than their fair share of natter for the rumormon-
gers the past year or so. There was no doubt that his
brother and Abby would be affected by the news.
Danny, too. Coming on the heels of Sarah's bomb-
shell, it was too much.

He was vaguely aware that Artie and Claudia
were looking at him expectantly, waiting for him
to make some sort of response. He wasn't aware
that he'd mumbled something under his breath
until Artie cupped a hand around his ear and asked,
"What's that?"

Knowing he was expected to treat this mind-
boggling news with his usual easygoing composure, Gabe forced a smile. "It looks like the Gentry
family will be providing some more chin-wag for
the gossipmongers."

He wondered if Caleb had heard the news yet. As
soon as he could close up, he'd ride out and tell him.

Seeing that they weren't likely to get much more
response from Gabe, both Artie and Claudia took
their leave, no doubt to spread the word that Wolf
Creek's most notorious resident was coming back
for a visit.

Gabe was sitting on a stool behind the counter,
nursing a cup of rancid coffee and trying to figure
out who he could get to watch the store so he could
ride out to Caleb's, when his brother walked through
the door. His intense gaze zeroed in on Gabe.

"You've heard." They spoke the words almost
in tandem.

Gabe nodded and watched Caleb take a blue spatterware mug and pour himself a cup of the sludge from the coffeepot. Gabe raised his eyebrows and grimaced. "I can't recommend that."

Caleb's mouth quirked into something that, with a lot of stretching, might pass as a smile. "Since marrying Abby, I've discovered I like living dangerously. Besides, misery loves company, right?"

"You bet." Gabe joined his brother at the table where the old-timers played their games. He chose to postpone the serious talk for a bit and frowned at Caleb instead. "How can you imply that marriage to an angel like Abby is dangerous?"

"You ever try shoeing a horse after spending most of the night walking the floor with a colicky baby? Or getting all dressed up for church and having an infant spew all over your clean shirt?"

Gabe bit back a smile. "Can't say I have."

No matter how much he grumbled, Gabe knew Caleb loved his life. They stared at their coffee in silence for a few moments before Caleb took a sip. He shuddered, got up and added three spoonfuls of sugar to his before taking another tentative sip. Frowning, he asked, "You got any of that condensed milk?"

"I do." The thick, sweetened milk was a favorite of his brother's.

"How about we break out a can? Add it to my bill."

Gabe got the milk and punched a couple of holes in the top with his pocketknife. They doctored their coffees and settled into the ladder-back chairs, their long legs stretched out in front of them.

"How did you find out?" Gabe asked.

"I was about to order lunch at the café when Pete Chalmers came in and asked if we'd heard the news. I canceled lunch and came straight over here." His stomach growled.

Without a word, Gabe got up, cut two small wedges of red rind cheese, ripped a length of brown paper off of a large roll and scooped a handful of crackers from the barrel. Then he snagged a jar of Mrs. Pritchard's homemade sweet pickles from the shelf. They ate in silence for a while, chewing on more than their impromptu lunch. They were both aware that this was the first time in years—maybe ever—that they had shared a common problem.

"Why do you suppose she's coming back?" Gabe asked at last, taking a bite of cracker and cheese and washing it down with a swig of coffee.

"Maybe because Abby wrote to her," Caleb offered, concentrating on spearing a pickle.

"She what!" Gabe yelled, jerking upright and sloshing coffee all over the checkerboard he'd neglected to move. "That interfering little brat!" he muttered, wiping at the spill with a pristine white hankie he fished from his pocket.

Caleb cast him a mocking sideways look. "A minute ago, she was an angel."

"I've changed my mind," Gabe grumbled. "She's a menace. Worse than a dog with a bone when she gets one of her notions."

"Tell me something I don't know," Caleb said, putting another chunk of cheese on a cracker.

"You're serious about this? She actually did write to Libby?"

Caleb stared at the cracker and cheese as if it held the secrets of the universe. "I'm not sure, but I suspect as much. She kept after me to do it, and I kept saying no. Knowing my wife, I expect she did it for me."

"Why would she do that?"

Caleb shrugged. "Come to dinner this evening. We'll ask her."

"I did it because it's high time the two of you got rid of all those hard feelings you've been carrying around all your lives," Abby confessed that evening as they sat down to eat. "I just wrote introducing myself and telling her about Emily and Betsy and my marriage to Caleb." Seeing the irritation in Caleb's eyes, she added tartly, "Well, if my daughter-in-law had died and I had a grandchild, I'd want to know about it."

"So when did you write this letter?" Caleb asked.

"Last spring sometime," Abby told them. "I thought there was a chance she'd answer, but she never did. Then when Eli came along, I sent another telling her about him, but I certainly never expected her to come, since she didn't bother to write back after the first letter." She sighed. "Are you really so furious with me?"

Caleb's scowl eased. "Not furious," he said.

"Maybe mildly irritated. I was hoping to get more of a rise out of you, though."

Abby's shoulders slumped in relief. She looked from him to Gabe. "For some strange reason, he—" she cut her eyes toward Caleb "—gets a kick out of making me angry." With her forefinger extended, she made circles near her ear, as if to indicate her husband was a bit crazy.

Gabe laughed. That was one of the strangest things he'd ever heard.

"Seriously," Abby said, "you both need to see her, look her in the eye and ask her about her side of things."

Gabe thought of Rachel confessing how easy it had been to put all the blame on him until he'd come back and she was forced to face him. As she'd said, it was easier to stoke the fires of bitterness and hard feelings from a distance.

"Frank told us the truth, so we know that she didn't leave us out of selfish reasons, like we'd always thought. Gabe and I can live with that," Caleb said.

"With all due respect to Frank, he only knows what he saw the day she left and what was being bandied all over town." Again she looked from one brother to the other. "You owe it to yourselves to hear what she has to say. And you owe it to your children to give them a chance to know their grandmother."

Grandmother. Danny. Gabe didn't relish the idea of telling Rachel and Danny about Libby's return.

Of course, by now, they'd no doubt heard the news. What would Rachel think about telling Danny he had a brand-new grandmother when he'd just learned he had a father? What would Danny think?

He sighed. He suspected Abby was right, but it didn't make the idea of meeting Libby any less disturbing. What did you say to a mother you hadn't set eyes on in nearly a quarter of a century?

Danny was all agog with excitement when Rachel walked into the house from making her rounds out in the country.

"I have a grandma!" he cried, his smile so wide it threatened to split his freckled face.

Weary, unsuspecting, Rachel set her bag onto the seat of the hall tree and wandered toward the kitchen, where she knew she'd find her father working on supper. "Really?" she said, riffling Danny's hair as he skipped along beside her. "Just where did this grandma come from?"

"Boston, I think, but she's not here yet. She's coming on the train in the morning."

Rachel shot a confused look at her father, who was peeling potatoes at the table. His smile was overly bright.

"Danny, do you mind playing outside for a few minutes? I need to talk to Pops."

Danny opened his mouth as if to argue, but she gave him the look, and he mumbled, "Yes, ma'am," and then he headed for the door.

Feeling the beginnings of a headache coming

on, Rachel sat down across from her father. "What was that all about?"

"This, dear readers," Edward intoned melodramatically, "is the next installment of our serial, 'The Trials and Tribulations of Dr. Rachel Stone.'"

"What now?" she asked, resting her elbows on the table and massaging her temples.

"It appears that Libby Gentry Granville and two companions will be arriving in our fair city on the morning train from Boston."

"Libby Gentry Gran…" Rachel's eyes widened with recognition.

"Exactly," Edward said. "Caleb and Gabe's long-lost mother. The one who allegedly left them for another man."

"Allegedly?" Rachel parroted with raised eyebrows.

"Innocent until proven guilty, my dear," Edward reminded her. "I never took Libby for a woman who would betray her wedding vows. Of course, it might have been because I was half in love with her myself at the time."

Rachel's face turned scarlet. "Daddy! What about Mama?"

"Your mother and I weren't an item when Libby first came to town, and I think all the young bucks were smitten with her to some degree. As soon as it became apparent that she had eyes only for Lucas—or rather, that he intended to land her—I zeroed in on your mother."

Rachel smiled. "Thank goodness."

"Yes," Edward agreed with a smile, "thank goodness."

"Why do you think she's coming back?"

"To try to make things right with her sons, I would imagine."

"It seems there's a lot of that going around these days."

"As well there should be. Life is too short for grudges and hard feelings. I believe God wants us to make amends whenever we can."

"You're right," she agreed with a nod. "Who are these 'companions' she's bringing with her?"

Edward shrugged. "Speculation around town ranges from her other children to a couple of high-toned Boston attorneys come to *wrest* the Gentry farm from Caleb." Edward's theatrical tone had returned. He sobered suddenly. "My guess would be her children."

Frowning, Rachel chewed on her lower lip. "Do you think she'll want to meet Danny?"

"Of course she will, once she learns about him."

Rachel swallowed a lump in her throat. "One more person to hear about my ill-fated relationship with Gabe."

One more person to judge her. Gabe's mother, no less! How would she ever be able to face Libby Gentry Granville? Even her name sounded intimidating.

She must have spoken her fears aloud, because Edward replied, "Intimidating? Libby?" He laughed. "Believe me, she was never an ogre, my dear. I actually remember her being very nice. Put yourself in her shoes. It can't be easy for *her* to come back to a town that has thought of her as an adulterer for two decades and face the children she abandoned."

Rachel sat up straighter. "I never thought of it that way. I'm sure you're right. How do you think Gabe and Caleb are taking the news?"

"I'm sure they're both as upset about it as you are, and no matter how it turns out, I give Libby high marks for having the courage to do it."

Rachel caught her lower lip between her teeth and considered that. Here she was, worried about more gossip, a rather insignificant problem compared to what Gabe and Caleb were facing. How were they feeling knowing that the mother who'd walked out of their lives was about to return? Did she realize that her arrival would dredge up all the old anguish?

"What do you mean, 'no matter how it turns out'?"

Edward shrugged. "Caleb and Gabe might refuse to see her or forgive her."

Concerned only with her own feelings, she hadn't thought of that, either. Would Gabe listen to what his mother had to say? She hoped he would at least hear her out. She knew firsthand how much better she'd felt after they had cleared the air and put their feelings aside to do what was right for Danny.

She glanced at the watch hanging from the chain around her neck. Almost closing time for the mercantile. She looked at her father. "Do you think I should go over and talk to him?"

"It can't hurt," Edward said. "And while you're at it, why not invite him to supper? There's plenty."

Rachel paused. The suggestion seemed almost as if Edward were giving his stamp of approval to her forming a more intimate relationship with Gabe.

"You wouldn't be trying to play matchmaker, would you?"

"There's no need. Even when you're fighting him tooth and nail, a blind man could see that the two of you still have feelings for each other…that whatever it was that you felt isn't over." Seeing that she was about to object, he continued. "Whether you like it or not."

"I don't like it." There was no reason to deny what he'd said. Edward was too smart, and he knew her far too well. She sighed. "I suppose you think I'm completely barmy to feel anything for him after the way he used and abandoned me," she said, her voice a shamed whisper.

"I've never been a big believer in coincidence," he said, a thoughtful expression on his still-attractive face. "So what I think is that God is working in both your lives and that He has given you a second chance."

Her dark eyes held query and a tiny smidgen of hope. "And Gabe? You…you really think he feels something for me?"

Edward winked at her. "If I were a gambling man, I'd make book on it."

* * *

Edward's words followed Rachel as she made her way across the railroad tracks, past the hotel to Antioch Street. Was her father right? Did Gabe really care for her? Oh, she knew he was attracted to her and held a certain fondness for her, but was he only being nice so that she would grant him greater access to their son? She didn't think so. He seemed to enjoy the time they spent together with Danny— more and more time the past couple of weeks, and though he sometimes flirted, never once had he done or said anything inappropriate.

Recalling his peppermint-scented breath against her nape that day in the store and the huskiness of his voice when he'd told her it looked kissable, she felt a little shiver scamper down her spine. She was an educated woman, certainly smart enough to know *that* was not love, but was it possible that her father was right and Gabe did still care? Was that caring love? The possibility was both thrilling and alarming.

She was just approaching the store when the object of her thoughts stepped through the aperture, key in hand. He smiled, the automatic action bringing the pleasing crinkles at the corners of his eyes into play. "Hello there!" he said. "I was just on my way to your place. Do you need something? I can let you in."

Rachel took a steadying breath and rammed her hands into the pockets of her dark blue skirt. "No. I just wanted to talk to you."

He raised his eyebrows. "It must be serious if you're looking for me."

"Serious enough," she said. "What did you need to see me about?"

Did she imagine the shadow that flickered across his face? "Something's come up. Would you like to go to Ellie's and get a cup of coffee or a glass of lemonade?"

Where everyone would see them together. That would just add more fuel to the fire! "No, thank you," she said. "Actually, Pops wanted to know if you'd like to join us for supper."

Gabe couldn't hide his surprise, or miss the reluctance in her voice. "Supper doesn't include a hefty dose of arsenic, does it? Or maybe hemlock?"

"I don't find that in the least bit funny."

"I can see that," he said somberly. "I'll make a note in my book of Rachel Stone observations." He turned his palm up and pretended to write with his finger. "Don't try to tease the great Dr. Stone, since clearly she has no funny bone." He glanced up, his eyebrows raised in sham surprise. "My, my, I do believe I have the start of a poem."

"Are you ever serious?"

"Do you ever have fun?" he countered. "The Bible says there are times to laugh, Rachel—remember?"

"I remember. Are you coming or not?"

"Of course I'm coming. How can I turn down such a gracious invitation?" he mocked. "What time?"

"Come now. We need to talk."

"So you said. About?"

"Something's come up," she said cryptically, tossing his own answer back at him. She turned to walk away, and after making sure the door was locked, Gabe followed. His loose, long-legged stride soon brought him to her side, and they walked down the street together, both with their hands stuffed into their pockets.

At the corner, they passed Mrs. Carmody and her brood of six. The frazzled housewife looked from Rachel to Gabe and actually pulled her skirt aside as if she would somehow be contaminated if she allowed the fabric to brush against Rachel. She did speak, though her mouth was pinched with disapproval, and only after Gabe made it a point to greet her and her children with his customary good manners.

They were in front of the hotel when Meg Thomerson came out, balancing a basket filled with soiled linens on her hip.

"Let me get that, Meg," Gabe said, taking the basket from the woman whose husband treated her as a sparring partner.

"Thank you, Mr. Gentry," she said, pushing a stray strand of hair from her astonishing green eyes. "And thank you again for letting me have some more time on my bill at the store."

"That's not a problem," he said gruffly.

What a wonderful thing to do, Rachel thought, trying to meet his eyes. Everyone in town knew that

Elton Thomerson was a deadbeat, and there were few people willing to extend him credit. It was up to Meg to take up the slack.

Three years and two children ago, she was considered more than pretty, but the time with Elton had taken its toll. There were premature lines at the corners of her eyes, and barely three months past her latest delivery, she looked far too thin. Even so, her smile seemed never far from the surface.

She beamed at Rachel with her usual friendliness while Gabe deposited the basket into the bed of the buggy alongside three others. Rachel knew she would deliver the sheets and towels the following afternoon all clean and ironed wrinkle free. She didn't know how the petite woman managed to stay so positive, except that she never failed to make a church service unless she or one of the children was ailing.

"I should have part of my bill when I finish up Millie's laundry," she told Gabe before looking at Rachel. "And I should be able to pay off Seth's sore-throat bill next week."

"Don't worry about it, Meg. I'm not hurting for it."

The woman's eyes filled with tears. "Thank you, Dr. Rachel. I don't know what this town would do without you." She looked from Rachel to Gabe. "And I think it's so wonderful that the two of you have found each other again after all these years."

Rachel cast a sideways glance at Gabe, who was rearranging the baskets and giving a good impression of being deaf. She offered Meg a weak smile. Wondering how to reply, she settled for a simple "Thank you."

Gabe helped Meg into her buggy and they watched her make a left turn at the corner and disappear. Wisely, he chose not to comment and fell into step beside Rachel.

"Giving Meg time to pay her bill is very nice of you."

"Yep," he quipped, making light of it. "No doubt they're casting a bronze statue of me even as we speak."

"Well, it isn't that big a thing," she teased.

"She needs help," he said, suddenly serious. "I feel sorry for her. And we all need a hand at some time in our lives."

Knowing that was all he'd say, they walked in silence for a moment. "What's come up?" Rachel asked finally, tilting her head to look at him. The heat of the late-afternoon sun coaxed out the red tones hiding in her dark hair.

"Ladies first."

Looking askance at him, she drew a fortifying breath and plunged. "I hear your mother is coming to town tomorrow."

"I hear the same thing." A wry half smile lifted one side of his mouth.

"And?"

"And it's a bit disconcerting to say the least."

"You didn't know she was coming?"

"No. Neither did Caleb."

"Hmm." Rachel shot him a frowning glance. "I wonder why she decided to come after so many years."

"Probably because Abby wrote to her after she married Caleb to tell her about Emily, Betsy and her own marriage to Caleb."

Rachel lifted a hand to shield her eyes. "Abby knew she was coming, then?"

"Actually, she didn't," he said, switching sides with her so he could block her from the sun's rays. "She never heard a word back, but she wrote Libby again when Eli was born, and it seems that for some reason, Libby has now decided to pay a visit."

"You call your mother Libby?"

"Caleb and I stopped calling her Mother after she left us."

There was no need to ask why. "How do you feel about her coming?"

"I have mixed emotions," he confessed. "Both Caleb and I grew up believing she left us with no backward glance, but we recently found out that Lucas wouldn't let her take us. That puts a different slant on things, at least for me." He sighed. "As for how I feel about it, I keep coming back to the notion that maybe I'm feeling a little like Danny must have felt when he found out about me."

Rachel considered that and thought he could be right. She recalled Danny's excitement as well as his trepidation and curiosity. As he had, Gabe was no doubt wondering what Libby Gentry Granville would think of the person he'd become. He would be wondering if she loved him, and if they could ever forge a meaningful relationship. Yes, it was easy to see that Gabe and Danny would share parallel feelings.

"And Caleb?"

"You know Caleb. He doesn't give away much about what he's feeling."

"Will you tell her about... Danny?"

Gabe turned toward her, completely blocking out the sun. He studied her face before answering. "Yes, Rachel, I'll tell her about Danny. And you. And how I managed to mess up the best thing that ever happened to me."

Rachel ducked her head and started walking again, before he noticed the tears that sprang into her eyes. The frankness of the statement tugged at her heart in a way that threatened to set her bawling her eyes out. Of all the things he'd said to her about their past...explanations, apologies or whatever else, there was no doubt that those simply spoken words and the emotions driving them were genuine.

They'd reached the whitewashed arbor that sat at the end of the path leading to the front of her house. Covered with clusters of pale yellow roses, it stood near the road, its delicate curve inviting people in. As she started to step through, he grasped her arm in a gentle grip.

Releasing his hold on her, he framed her face with his hands, the pads of his thumbs riding the crests of her cheekbones, his spread fingers cradling her head. She didn't try to pull free, wasn't sure she could have if she wanted to. Tipping back her head, he met her troubled gaze.

"You're worried about Danny meeting her."

She nodded.

"Danny is her grandson. They have the right to meet each other. What happens beyond that is up to them, just as what happens between me and Danny is up to us. That's fair, don't you think?"

"Yes," she said with reluctant acquiescence.

Leaning forward a bit, he rested his forehead against hers. Their noses bumped. The scent of the ever-present peppermint he seemed so attached to mingled with the masculine aroma of his aftershave, something that reminded her of far-off lands.

Her eyes drifted shut.

He took a deep breath and straightened. His hands slid to her shoulders. "What else?" he asked, showing an astonishing insight into her thoughts and emotions, an insight she'd noticed during their time in St. Louis.

"Ah," he said after a moment. "You're worried about what she'll think of you, right?"

"Yes," she admitted, allowing him access to even more of her feelings.

Holding herself very still, she breathed in the scent of him and fought the onslaught of memories that swept through her. It would be so easy to let her arms slide around his hard middle and lean into him. So tempting to rest her head against that broad chest and let him support her for a while.

"The whole town has believed for twenty-plus

ycars that she was unfaithful to my father. I have no idea what really happened, but whether she's a vamp or a victim, I can't picture her as the kind of person to judge others."

Rachel stepped back. There was no teasing about him now, nothing but the intensity she remembered. Never mind that he had been irresponsible, thoughtless and selfish nine years ago. At that moment, all that mattered was that he understood exactly how she felt and was doing his best to ease her mind.

It worked until he lowered his head and kissed her.

Chapter Nine

The kiss was the softest whisper of his lips against hers, as delicate as the brush of a butterfly wing, as insubstantial as the beat of a hummingbird heart. There was no persuasive technique involved. No insistence or demand. Instead there was hesitation and promise. It was nothing at all how she remembered his kisses.

If there was any last lingering resentment, it faded to nothingness, and the last remnant of her resolve melted away. She knew there would be no more manipulating her feelings, no pretending or trying to deny them by pushing them aside. She gave in and gave up to the love she felt, and it felt so very good. And scary.

Just when she feared she might somehow give herself away, he stepped back with a last almost-as-if-he-couldn't-help-himself stroke of his thumb against her lower lip, a tender gesture that was fast becoming familiar.

"Why did you do that?" she asked, hearing the breathlessness in her voice.

That he was dead serious at that moment was undeniable. He was not teasing or testing her. She did see a hint of remorse, as if he were torn between wanting to kiss her and being sorry he had.

He lifted his shoulders in a halfhearted shrug. "I couldn't seem to help myself. I'm sorry if I offended you."

"You didn't." Was it her imagination, or did her denial surprise him? He might have said something else, but Danny burst through the front door, raced down the steps and launched himself at Gabe, who knelt and caught the child up in a tight embrace. Rachel felt her heart constrict in sudden painful perception. Danny adored Gabe. Gabe adored Danny.

"Is it true?" Danny asked, resting his hands on his father's shoulders and leaning back to look at him. "Do I really have a grandma?"

"It seems you do," Gabe said, smiling.

"Tell me all about her."

"I don't know much about her," Gabe confessed. "She...left when I was just a little boy, younger than you."

Danny stared at Gabe for long moments, giving the statement serious thought. Then Gabe stood, and Danny moved between his parents. He turned to face them, grabbed one of Gabe's hands and one of Rachel's in his and tugged them along the path to the house, confident that even though he could not see where he was going, they would not let him fall.

"It'll be okay, Dad," he said with a tone of grave certainty. "I 'spect she left because she just wasn't ready for the responsibility of a family, the way you weren't ready back then."

Rachel's face flamed at hearing the words she'd spoken to Danny repeated to Gabe. She glanced at him and saw him looking at her with a thoughtful expression that soon turned to one of gratitude. At that moment she knew that he realized what she'd done and appreciated the fact that she had not painted him the villain of their particular story.

"She's been gone a long time and growed up a bunch I'll bet," Danny said, offering a child's simplistic reasoning to the situation. "I 'spect that once she gets to know and love you, she'll be ready to settle down and be a mom. I just hope she likes me, too."

"How could she not?" Gabe said with a laugh, delighted with his son's logic. The joyous sound and Danny's answering smile filled Rachel's heart with joy. An image of them together around the table—a family—slipped like a will-o'-the-wisp into her mind.

Pipe dreams.

Though she admitted to loving him, she was no longer the shy innocent of her youth, and she was certainly no worldly sophisticate, nothing like the kind of woman Gabe was accustomed to. She was not charming, playful or clever. On the contrary, she was often considered too plainspoken and stuffy, and she had the added disadvantage of possessing above-average intelligence, something most men did not appreciate in a woman.

She was just Dr. Rachel, pretty enough she supposed, but still a small-town girl whose biggest goal was to heal those she could, and to be the best person she could be. No matter how much Gabe might have changed, she was just too afraid of disappointing him, too afraid of being hurt a second time to trust him with her heart. If that happened, she knew that she would never recover.

After a supper of ham, boiled potatoes with butter, buttermilk biscuits and fresh green beans, everyone pitched in to clean the kitchen.

Afterward, Edward challenged Danny to a game of dominoes while Rachel and Gabe retired to the front porch. They sat side by side in matching rockers that overlooked the front yard and the buildings across the railroad tracks. The corner of the hotel was in plain view, and beyond that, they could hear the occasional rattle of a wagon on Antioch Street.

Neither spoke, content to sit and listen to the serenade of tree frogs and insect songs that were punctuated by the strident, plagiarized melodies of a mockingbird ensconced on the rose trellis.

"I hear the box lunch is coming up next weekend," Gabe said at last. "Are you taking part?"

"I always do. It's more or less expected that everyone do something. It's mandatory if you're an unattached woman." She offered an ironic smile.

"It's supposed to be an unobtrusive way to bring un-married folk together. Not that it works very often."

"I imagine the bids on your boxes are high," he commented with a questioning lift of his eyebrows.

"I do all right."

"You're bound to be the prettiest single lady in town."

She laughed. "Actually, Ellie and I are considered the town's spinsters, even though everyone says we're pretty enough for *mature* ladies."

"Mature, hmm?"

"Yes." She actually laughed, a sound that sounded awfully close to a giggle. "I believe that's a creative way of saying we're over the hill."

Gabe threw back his head and laughed, too, amused at the thought that two of the prettiest women in town were considered past their prime.

"Believe me, it's no laughing matter. The men who bid on my boxes are usually the more *mature* gentlemen." This was said with a definite hint of amusement in her brown eyes. "Most of them are widowers looking for someone to take care of them in their old age. Who better than the town doctor?"

Gabe chuckled again. "Well, I'll be sure to give them a run for their money this year."

It sounded like a promise. Her mind moved ahead to that day and the possibilities it might bring. Quiet between them returned. She recalled that even in St. Louis, when he was taking her around to show her the many sights, they'd had the ability to share time together with no need to fill the silence with meaningless conversation. It had surprised her then, and still did.

"I'd like to thank you for what you told Danny."

Even though they were attuned at the moment, she was so lost in thought that she didn't immediately grasp what he was referring to.

"What he said about my mother not being ready to take on a family," he explained. "I know you must have said the exact thing to him about me."

She answered with her customary directness. "I told him what I felt was the truth."

That took him by surprise. "Well, I appreciate it, especially since it's clear that you held a lot of resentment toward me. You could have said a lot of things to prejudice him against me."

"I would never do that, no matter how I felt. As you reminded me, I'm hardly without fault in the matter, and as you also said, whatever develops between two people should be just that—between them. It's not my way to force my opinion on someone else."

"Has it changed?" he asked, his voice as soft as the gathering shadows.

"What?"

"Your opinion of me."

Instead of answering, she stared at him for long seconds. "I'm still observing," she said at last.

"Fair enough." He looked at the buildings across the way, their edges softened by the gathering shadows. "I'd best get back before it gets too dark to put one foot in front of the other."

She stood, and he followed suit. "Thank you for the supper. It was delicious."

"You're welcome." She wondered if he would try to kiss her again and wondered what she would do if he did. Instead, he reached out and trailed a finger down her cheek, smiled a bit ruefully and went down the steps.

She watched him go through the rose arbor. "Gabe!" she called.

He turned.

"Will you let me know how things go…with Libby, so I'll know what to expect for Danny?"

He gave her a wave of acknowledgment she could barely make out and strode toward buildings across the way.

Libby Gentry Granville had arrived.

According to the gossip—and there were plenty of folks eager to keep Gabe in the loop—The Southwest Arkansas and Indian Territory train chugged into town from Gurdon at precisely nine o'clock, belching black smoke and spitting sparks as the wheels ground to a stop.

Moments later, a magnificently dressed older woman had descended the train, followed by a younger woman who looked to be in her early twenties and a man whose age was somewhere in between. At exactly 9:05, two people burst through the door of the mercantile, almost knocking each other over in their haste to deliver the news.

Gabe thanked them and sent them on their way.

He was certain that his seeming disinterest would be added to the mix of reports as word spread around town.

He wondered who the man could be. Rumor had it he looked about Caleb's age, so he couldn't be another brother, though the young woman must be his sister. Funny. He was just getting used to having a relationship with his estranged brother and now there would be another sibling to get to know…if he were so inclined.

A grim smile hiked one corner of his mouth. It was highly unlikely that Libby would come all this way and not insist on spending some time together. The reality was that his mother's unannounced visit could not have come at a worse time. He was still adjusting to meeting Rachel after so many years and reeling from the knowledge that he had a child. All that while learning how to establish a new business and trying to carve out a place in a town that considered him a dissolute wastrel.

Caleb, bowing to the wishes of his headstrong and tenderhearted wife, had come by earlier to see if Gabe would like to go to the station to meet the train with him and his family.

"I don't think so," Gabe told him, still uncertain how he felt about the whole thing and what he could possibly say to the visitors, knowing there would be dozens of pairs of eyes watching the whole she-bang. "I don't think I can find anyone to run the store on such short notice."

"I understand," Caleb said. "I've been fighting

Abby on this since yesterday, but she finally wore me down."

Abby wins again, Gabe thought with a smile. She was doing a bang-up job of transforming her husband into a more social human being.

"You're not getting cold feet, are you?"

Drat it! Caleb was far too astute to fool for long. "I suppose you could call it that," Gabe hedged. "It's just that I've had more than my share of notoriety, and I have no desire for more. I don't want our first meeting to be discussed over the dinner table. Whatever happens between us at our first meeting should be relatively private."

"Then at least come out to the farm for dinner," Caleb pressed. "Abby is planning a huge family feast."

Seeing the familiar tightening of his brother's jaw, Gabe figured he'd better accept.

"Sure," he said. "That would be great. You know I never turn down Abby's cooking."

"Wonderful!" Caleb's rare smile made a brief appearance. "Make sure you rent a nicely sprung buggy so they'll be comfortable for the drive out."

"Whoa! What do you mean 'they'?" Gabe asked, though the question was completely unnecessary.

Caleb gave a nonchalant lift of his shoulders. "Since you're coming, it seems logical for you to collect everyone and drive them to the farm, since they have no idea how to get there." He portrayed an excellent impression of innocence.

Duped and manipulated and no way out of the

situation! "Fine," he told Caleb ungraciously. "I'll do that." Gabe pointed a finger at Caleb. "But you owe me, big brother, and don't you forget it."

Caleb had only laughed and left.

Now, as he worked about the store, he wondered how the reunion was going. Caleb claimed he no longer harbored any hard feelings toward their mother, but as mellow as he'd become, good Christian that he was trying to be, and as much as he claimed to have forgiven her, Gabe couldn't see his brother welcoming Libby with open arms.

At least he had guts enough to go meet her, while you're here hiding behind a pitiful excuse.

True.

He supposed that Libby would want to meet before he picked them up to go to the country, but he never dreamed she would walk through the doors of the mercantile.

His back was to the door and he was arranging a new shipment of chambray shirts by size when he heard a woman speak his name.

As soon as the weather permitted, he'd started opening both doors to let in the springtime breeze, which meant there was no jangle of bells to announce a customer. He'd compensated by adding a bell on the counter, like the one Hattie had at the hotel, so that he would know someone needed help if he was working in the storeroom.

Hearing his name, he froze, his hands smoothing a collar. Though it seemed inconceivable, he immediately recognized the soft, melodious voice.

He remembered hearing her laugh—though rarely, it seemed now. A hazy recollection of her crooning a lullaby to him and Caleb as she sat on the edge of their bed at night swirled through his mind like a wisp of smoke. He recalled that clear sweet voice explaining that his father wasn't angry at him; he was just angry…or worried, or whatever feeble reason she could think of to distract him from his tears and Caleb from his gradual retreat into stoic solitude.

Wondering if the rest of her was as he remembered, Gabe turned. She stood just inside the door, flanked on either side by her companions. The young woman wore a celery-green dress with a tiered lace overlay and three-quarter-length sleeves ending with a double lace frill.

The man was clad in the latest fashion—charcoal flannel trousers topped with a burgundy waistcoat beneath a casual jacket of muted black, gray and burgundy plaid. The girl was looking at Gabe with wide, uncertain eyes while the man regarded him with a careful scrutiny, almost as if Gabe were a prime example of horseflesh he was thinking to purchase.

From what Gabe could tell from the distance separating them, his mother was little changed. She was still the tall, slender, elegantly beautiful woman of his faded memories and still bore herself with a straight, upright carriage. Out of the blue he remembered her admonishing him and Caleb not to slump.

Instead of the everyday cotton dresses he recalled her wearing, she was gowned in a day dress of some royal-blue fabric with a knife-pleated skirt, a small bustle, a fitted bodice with set-in sleeves and a high stand collar. A waterfall of delicate lace cascaded down the front. The trio exemplified big-city wealth.

While he was recovering from his shock and trying to sort out how he was feeling, Libby murmured, "Oh, Gabe!" and crossed the room, weaving between the aisles and displays, her steps impatient, an eager smile on her face.

Something akin to panic gripped him. It felt as if his heart seized up and he found it hard to breathe. She must have sensed something was amiss, because she stopped a few feet from him, her smile dying a slow death. Her eyes, as blue as his own, roamed over his face, as if she were trying to assess the changes the years had made while also trying to judge his mood. Even from where she stood, he detected the faintest, well-remembered smell of her favorite scent, lilac.

All the love he'd felt as a child came rushing back, and he suddenly wanted to hug her, to feel the comfort and peace he'd always felt when enfolded in the warmth of her embrace. Fast following that was the memory of him crying himself to sleep after he and Caleb were told she'd left them. He could almost hear the sound of his sobbing in the silence of their darkened bedroom, could almost see Caleb lying stiffly next to him, his face turned to the wall, as if to block out the world.

The tenuous tenderness passed. The quiet grew near unbearable as they stood there staring at each other. He should say something, but what? At a total loss for perhaps the first time in his life, he extended his hand to shake hers. The stilted action was the height of formality. "Hello, Mother. I trust your trip was comfortable."

The anguish in her eyes was palpable, and he felt like a cad for causing it. He might have hurt people in the past, but never with it as a goal.

Hearing the tonal inflection in his voice seemed to settle something in her mind. She fixed a bright smile on her face and, still clinging to his hand, pulled him toward the couple standing near the door, both of whom were regarding him with less-than-friendly expressions.

"Gabe, this is your sister, Blythe, and my stepson, Winston Granville. Blythe, Win, this is my younger son, Gabe."

Blythe extended a small, lace-gloved hand. "How do you do, Mr. Gentry," she said, her voice tinted with the same formality as his own.

Dismay filled him. He knew she was miffed that he was treating her mother with obvious coolness. He didn't blame her. He didn't want there to be conflict between him and his half sister, or conflict between him and his mother, for that matter. He'd had enough discord and anger to last a lifetime.

Hoping to ease the awkwardness, he said to his sister, "I'm doing quite well, thank you, but I'd do a lot better if you called me Gabe."

A blush spread up her throat to her face. It seemed his little sister was a shy one.

Then he turned to the man, who regarded him with the supreme composure that seemed to accompany being born with money. Gabe was somewhat surprised that Win seemed very protective of his stepmother. Gabe liked that. He extended a hand, which was met with a firm grip. "Win. It was good of you to accompany Mother." As he spoke, he realized he meant the words.

"I'm always glad to help Mother however I can. And this is one trip I wouldn't have missed," Granville said, a hint of steel both in his tone and his tawny eyes.

Strangely it wasn't the veiled antagonism that rankled. It was Win Granville calling Libby "Mother." Of course, truth to tell, she had spent far more time being a mother to this man than she had her own sons. Gabe was the real outsider, not Win Granville.

Striving for a bit of normalcy in an unconventional situation, Gabe said, "I understand I'm to drive us all out to Caleb's for supper."

"Yes," Libby said, adding, "if it isn't too much of an imposition."

He managed a smile. "None at all. Actually, you're in for a treat. Abby is not only a wonderful wife and mother, she's an excellent cook."

"My first impression was that she is very sweet and genuine," Libby said. "It's good to have my opinion reinforced." Her almost wistful gaze met his. "Caleb seems happy."

Even though they'd been apart most of his life, spending time with Rachel and Danny had taught him just how much a mother was invested in the happiness of her children. "I believe he's very happy, thanks to Abby."

"And you've never married?" Libby asked.

"No."

But I have a son. He'd have to tell her soon, he supposed, otherwise someone else would beat him to the punch, just as they would with the sordid details of his life while he was away.

"Hard to please?" she asked with a smile.

"Too self-indulgent for too many years," he corrected and plunged in. "I may as well tell you, since if you haven't heard, you will. I've been away the past nine years and my behavior during that time was—" he expelled a harsh breath "—less than sterling, I'm afraid."

He watched as they tried to absorb what he'd said. His mother looked troubled by his confession. Win seemed speculative. Blythe was clearly scandalized. He could almost see her innocent mind trying to visualize what that behavior might have included. It was easy to see there would be no hero worship of her big brother. At least not this one.

Lew Jessup strolled through the doors, bypassing the checkers tables and heading toward the new shirts, casting a curious glance at the foursome. Gabe wasn't the least surprised at his timing. When

Artie Baker followed in a matter of seconds, Gabe stifled a groan. The two must have been sent as spies for the rest of the town.

Unlike Sarah, though, there would be no maliciousness connected to their reporting on the actions of the newcomers. Still, Gabe would rather have any meaningful conversations with his mother and siblings conducted in private.

He offered his extended family a dry smile and gave a slight jerk of his chin toward the two men. "Now doesn't seem the best time to discuss this since it seems business is picking up."

Win understood perfectly.

"Hattie at the hotel serves a light lunch, and Ellie at the café across the street is open from daylight until dusk. I can personally recommend either place. I'll pick you up for Caleb's after I close—say about six?"

Gabe was aware that he was rambling, but he really just wanted them to leave before some other disaster occurred.

The thought had no more than crossed his mind when a denim-clad tornado burst through the doors. All eyes turned toward the sound of bare feet slapping against the wooden floor. Gabe's heart stopped. Danny. His dark hair stood on end, and a smudge of dirt smeared his right cheek and the bib of his overalls. His hands and feet were as filthy as the tin can he clutched. His gaze zipped past the visitors and zeroed in on Gabe. A wide smile echoed the excitement sparkling in his eyes.

"You oughta see the big ol' worms I found, Dad. I thought maybe Grandma would like to go fishin' with us while she's here."

Three pairs of eyes turned toward Gabe. He wasn't sure whether he should laugh or cry. No doubt about it, God had a fantastic sense of timing, as well as an incredible sense of humor. Gabe motioned Danny closer. As he passed the trio, he looked up, his eyes growing wide with comprehension. He stopped in front of Gabe, who rested his hands on Danny's shoulders. He swiveled his head back and up and whispered loudly. "Is that her?"

Gabe nodded and let his own gaze move from his mother to his sister and stepbrother. "Mother, Blythe, Win...this is Danny. My son."

With his uncanny aptitude to size up a situation in nothing flat, Danny instinctively realized he needed to make a good impression. He set the can on the floor, scrubbed his hands down his thighs and finger-combed his hair to smooth it, succeeding only in adding a smudge of dirt to his forehead.

Win's expression was unreadable. Blythe's eyes were as large as silver dollars, and the shock on his mother's face transitioned to a smile as she watched Danny's impromptu toilette.

"Pleased to meet you," Danny said, extending a grubby hand. Seeing how dirty it was, he quickly withdrew it and offered his grandmother a blinding smile instead.

To Gabe's surprise, the well-dressed Mrs. Granville sat back on her heels in front of Danny, putting them at eye level. He couldn't tell if the sheen in her eyes was pleasure or tears. She held out her own hand, and Danny cast an inquiring look at Gabe. When he gave a single slight nod, the boy thrust out his hand once more.

Libby cradled the dirty hand in both of hers. "I'm very pleased to meet you as well, Danny," she said, clearly captivated with the child. "And I would love to go fishing with you. Perhaps tomorrow afternoon after I have time to rest up from my trip?"

"That'd be great," Danny said, "but it will have to be after church and the box lunch."

"Box lunch?" Win queried.

"It's an annual event," Libby explained. "They auction off box lunches the ladies have made, and the money is used to help people around town. After everyone eats, there will be games and just a general good time."

"Some of us are gonna sneak off and go fishing," Danny offered. "It's a lot of fun." He looked up at Blythe and Win. "I don't know who you are, but if you're with my grandma, I guess you can come, too, if you want." He gave Win a considering look. "You might want to bid on my mom's box. She's making fried chicken, and next to Ellie's, it's the best in town."

"Maybe I'll do that," Win said, his expression giving away nothing of what was going on inside his head. "And as for who we are, since I am a brother of sorts to your father, it appears that I am your uncle Win."

Danny looked at Gabe. "Caleb is your brother. Is he my uncle, too?"

The subject of how everyone was related hadn't yet come up in all the hubbub of the gossip. "Yes."

"So Abby is my aunt."

"Right."

Danny scrunched up his short freckled nose and squinted, trying to work out the familial ties. "So me and Ben are *cousins.*"

"'Ben and I are cousins,'" Gabe corrected automatically.

"No, Dad," Danny said, all seriousness. "You can't be Ben's cousin. If Caleb is my uncle, then you're Ben's uncle."

The trio of new relatives laughed, clearly delighted with the child. As well they should be, Gabe thought with a surge of fatherly pride.

Win smiled at Danny. "I'd be happy to go with you and your grandma fishing. It promises to be an entertaining time. Blythe?"

Her gaze traveled from one person to the next. "Well, uh, certainly," she said, almost managing to suppress a delicate shudder. "I'd be happy to go along. I'm your aunt Blythe, by the way."

That settled to his satisfaction, Danny narrowed his eyes in perfect mimicry of his mother. "I'll bet you need someone to put your worms on the hook, don't you, Aunt Blythe?"

"I… I'm afraid so," she confessed, turning a pretty hue of pink.

Danny shrugged and shook his head in typical male disgust. "Girls."

It was Win who, seeing the curious onlookers, ended the fiasco. He held out his hand to help Libby to her feet. "I think we should go back to the hotel and rest a bit before lunch. It's been quite an eventful morning. We'll have plenty of time to...discuss things."

"True," Libby said, rising. "It isn't every day a woman acquires five wonderful grandchildren." She ran her hand lovingly over Danny's sweaty head, but she was looking at Gabe as she spoke, her way of saying that whatever the situation, it would be all right.

"I'll expect the whole story later, Gabriel." She placed a finger beneath Danny's chin, tilting his face upward. Her voice trembled as she looked at Gabe and said, "He's so much like you it's amazing."

Then, regarding Danny thoughtfully, she asked, "Do you have any other grandparents?"

"Just Pops, my mom's dad. My mom's the doctor."

Libby regarded Gabe with a lift of her eyebrows. Clearly Danny had piqued her interest with the announcement about his mother. "I thought Edward Stone was the doctor."

"He used to be," Danny offered. "But now my mom is."

Libby looked thoughtful, working out more family ties. Then, as if the conversation had not taken a brief turn, she said, "So you call Edward Pops. I like that. Instead of Grandma, do you think you could call me Pip?"

Gabe couldn't imagine a less likely name for a woman of such elegance and refinement. A memory surfaced. He could almost see Grandpa Harcourt looking at his daughter, his eyes alight with love and pride as he said, *"Isn't she a real pip?"*

"Sure," Danny said, "but it's a really funny name."

"Maybe so," Libby said, "but my father called me that, and it's been such a long time since anyone else has used it, I think I would like it very much if you and the other children did."

"Pip and Pops. I like it," Danny said, offering another of those wide smiles.

That settled, Libby gave the grubby child a hug, not a bit concerned that he would ruin her beautiful walking dress. The trio started toward the door, Gabe promising again to pick them up at six. They had almost made the opening when Sarah swept through. It seemed God wasn't finished with him yet.

"Why, hello, Libby," she gushed. "I heard you were in town."

"I imagine you did," Gabe's mother said. "Sarah, I'd like you to meet my daughter, Blythe, and my stepson, Win. Children, Sarah VanSickle."

The Granvilles made the polite, appropriate responses, but Sarah hardly noticed. She was too busy looking around the room to see who was present.

"I see you met your grandson," she said with a

triumphant smile. If she was hoping to hear something negative about Gabe's conduct or Danny, she was disappointed.

"I did," Libby said, her features schooled to serenity. "Isn't he the cutest thing?" She brushed past Sarah as if she were something distasteful. "If you'll excuse me, we really must run."

"How long will you be in town?" Sarah called after her.

"As long as it takes."

"To do what?" Sarah pressed. "I was hoping we could get together."

Just outside the doorway, Libby turned. Gabe could almost see his mother biting her tongue. It was an expression he'd seen often enough on his brother's face.

"Oh, we will, Sarah," she said in a pleasant voice. "But when we do, I want us to have a nice private conversation." With that, she turned and started down the sidewalk as if she hadn't a care in the world, Blythe and Win trailing behind.

Gabe's gaze shifted to Sarah, who looked as if she were about to suffer a fit of apoplexy. What beef could his mother possibly have with Sarah Van-Sickle that she was intent on discussing? Whatever it might be, it was clear that Libby was wise to the viperous woman's tricks and had no intention of allowing Sarah to make the past, and whatever dicey tidbits it entailed, a public spectacle.

Chapter Ten

Gabe made it through the rest of the day and the gauntlet of questions thrown at him by almost everyone who came to make a purchase. Somehow he managed to deflect or ignore most of them with generic answers or the pretext of needing to help another customer.

Danny had returned to the mercantile after going home to tell Edward that he'd met his grandmother and informed Gabe that Rachel was out in the country checking on a patient. He drew a sigh of relief. He'd been granted a brief reprieve before facing Rachel to tell her that Danny had spilled the beans about who his mother was.

He was about to close when he saw Rachel coming down the sidewalk. She looked tired, frazzled and troubled. He wanted to pull her into his arms and tell her that everything would be all right, that his mother was not the least bit intimidating and that whatever happened he would be right beside her so she would not have to bear this newest crisis alone. But even though there had been a definite softening in her attitude lately, she'd made it clear that Danny was her primary concern. The rare times he'd felt they were connecting on a more personal level, he had been so afraid of her returning to her former scornful attitude that he'd backed down, afraid to push too hard.

He waited until she got inside before locking the doors and turning the sign to Closed.

"Danny told me he met his grandmother," she said without preamble.

"Quite by accident, but yes, he did."

"He also told me she really liked him and said something about an aunt and uncle and everyone going fishing tomorrow."

"All true."

Rachel's expression seesawed between relief and disbelief. "Do you mind giving me your version? Our son is a master at glossing over anything he feels might upset me or that might put him in a bad light. Somehow, I can't believe it—" she waved her hands through the air in a vague gesture "—was the happy occasion he portrayed."

"Actually, it was," Gabe said. "More or less." He gave her a condensed version of everything that had transpired, including Sarah's contribution to the drama. He finished with, "Libby asked him to call her Pip, which was her father's pet name for her."

"And she seemed to accept Danny, no questions asked?"

Gabe smiled. "Oh, there will be plenty of questions. Count on it. But there was no hiding the fact that she was quite taken with him, even though he was absolutely filthy."

Rachel's dismay was unmistakable. "I wanted him to be nice and clean and on his best behavior when they met for the first time," she wailed. Then she asked, "How dirty was he?"

"Extremely," Gabe said, a smile surfacing at the memory of Danny's grimy condition.

Seeing how the corners of his mouth hiked up in amusement, she said, "This is not funny, Gabriel Gentry, though I can see how someone like you might see the humor in it."

He refused to take offense at a statement he realized was rooted in some sort of motherly embarrassment.

"Danny had been digging worms," he explained, "and he'd brought them with him. However, he *was* on his best behavior. Quite the young gentleman, in fact."

"Really?" She still looked somewhat distressed, but her whole posture was more relaxed.

"You should have seen him, Rachel," he said with a soft laugh. "It was very funny. He smoothed his hair." Gabe mimicked the action. "And smeared more dirt on his face in the process, and when he started to shake her hand and saw how dirty it was, he stuck it behind his back instead."

"Oh, no!"

He reached and took her hands in his, drawing

her closer. For once she didn't resist. "She adored him, Rachel," he told her, his eyes smiling into hers. "Who wouldn't?"

He brought her hands to his lips and pressed kisses to her palms. "Trust me when I say that everything will be fine." He released his hold on her and drew his watch out of his pocket. "Unfortunately, I have to run you off right now because I'm supposed to take everyone to Caleb's for dinner."

"What about you and Libby?"

He shrugged and gave her hands a squeeze. "We didn't really have a chance to talk. There were too many curiosity seekers milling about. I'll have a better grasp of things after tonight, and you and I will talk tomorrow, while we share your box lunch."

"You seem very confident that you'll be the highest bidder," she said, almost playfully

"Confident enough."

Libby was enchanted by Caleb and Abby's brood. She spent time talking to Ben about his trapping, telling him how much Caleb had liked it as a boy, and cuddling Laura—both were Abby's children from her marriage to William Carter.

After Abby put the children to bed, the adults retired to the parlor to enjoy coffee and a slice of Abby's buttermilk pie so that Libby could tell her side of the story, which was, she insisted, one of the reasons she'd come back to Wolf Creek. As it turned out, Frank *had* been correct in setting the story straight as far as he knew the truth. Libby filled in the blanks.

"I fell for Lucas Gentry the first time I saw him," she said, a reminiscent smile on her face. "With my very different…upbringing, he was the antithesis of everything familiar, which I found quite exciting. He wasn't a handsome man in the traditional sense, but he was ruggedly good-looking, and there was an attractive brashness and self-confidence about him that drew me, at least in the beginning."

A pensive smile softened her features. "I loved it here, too. I'd been brought up a city girl, but there was something about the rolling hills and the fresh air and the close-knit community I found appealing."

"A blessing and a curse," Abby volunteered.

Libby's smile held a touch of irony. "You're right, of course. I had no idea in the beginning that that closeness could also be a detriment, since it was next to impossible to keep a secret for long."

She looked at Caleb. "When I came to town, Sarah Davis—Sarah VanSickle now—and Lucas were expected to marry, though there had been no formal announcement."

Gabe and Caleb shared a look of disbelief.

"When it became apparent that he was interested in me, she was furious," Libby said. "He ended things with her, and for the remainder of my visit, he pursued me rather intensely."

"I don't doubt that," Caleb said with barely concealed hostility. "Once he got hold of an idea, he didn't let it go."

"No," Libby said, "he didn't. The night before we were to go back to Boston, he proposed, and I said yes. My parents were unhappy that things had moved so fast, and my father was…oh, I don't know… There was something about Lucas he just didn't trust. But I was marrying age, so they agreed. They delayed their return for two weeks until we could put together a small wedding that was fancy enough to satisfy my mother."

She drew in a deep breath. "Lucas was like a chameleon, able to adapt to a situation with very little effort. He became whatever he needed to be to get what he wanted, and then he changed into something…someone else. Once he had me, it was off to the next item on his list. At first he was generous with everything but his time, but it didn't take long for me to realize how he used his generosity for control."

She looked from one of her boys to the other. "I know what you're wondering, but he was never abusive, at least not in the beginning."

Caleb's face looked like a thundercloud. "Are you saying he hit you?"

She reached out and patted his hand. "No, nothing like that. But abuse can take many forms. You came along ten months after the wedding and Gabe four years after that. You boys gave me a reason to get up every morning. You helped fill the lonely hours that being alone so much created.

"Lucas was too busy making a name to have time for us. He was either working or off trying to buy more cattle or land—anything to make more money or gain an edge. He thrived on the power it afforded him. When I look back now, I see that his being away so much was really a blessing of sorts."

"He did like having people in his debt and kow-towing to him," Caleb said. "I remember that."

"Yes," Libby said. "He took us to Boston for a visit once, but he refused to go again, saying that he could have bought another parcel of land for what the visit cost. He wouldn't let me go alone with you boys, claiming it would be too hard on me.

"He became quite miserly, too. The three of us dressed like peasants except when he wanted to show us off, and he went around on a prize stallion decked out in the latest and finest so that he would look more impressive for his wheeling and dealing."

"Did Grandmother and Grandfather Harcourt know how things were?" Blythe asked her mother, clearly stunned by her mother's confession.

"I never told them, but I think they suspected. They came as often as they could, but it wasn't enough. I have to say the church was a big support, but I'd been taught not to air my dirty laundry, and besides, it was too embarrassing. I didn't want any-one suspecting what my life was really like, and I don't think Lucas would have taken kindly to my exposing his true colors to the world."

"He sounds like a terrible person," Abby said, scooting closer to Caleb and taking his hand.

"It sounds as if *terrible* doesn't begin to cover it," Win added.

"All I can say is that money and power became

his gods." She sniffed and continued. "One autumn when you boys were three and seven my parents came to visit and brought along my older brother, Tad, his wife, Ada, and her brother, who just happened to be Sam Granville."

A collective gasp filled the room, and Libby offered a wan smile. "Sam's wife had died a couple of years earlier, and he was left with his two boys, Win and Philip. Sam was handsome and funny, and he made me laugh…."

Gabe and Caleb exchanged troubled looks but did not interrupt. Blythe's face wore a reminiscent smile, no doubt remembering her father.

"Lucas was jealous, though I'm not sure why, since by this time, our marriage was over in every way that mattered. The old dog-in-a-manger adage, I suppose. We lived in the same house. I cooked, took care of everyone, and he made more money and gathered more…of everything.

"One night Tad, Ada, Sam and I went for a walk down by the creek while my parents kept an eye on you boys. Lucas had gone somewhere and hadn't bothered returning for supper. We were walking back, and it was getting chilly. Tad and Ada hurried home, but Sam and I dragged behind, talking about plays and art and music…"

Her voice trailed away and she looked at her sons again. "As much as I loved you, it was nice to have a bit of time free of responsibility and to be able to carry on a conversation about things outside this house, this town. When I mentioned being chilly, he took off his jacket and put it around me, and there was one of those moments that seem—" she shrugged "—suspended in time."

A muscle in Gabe's cheek worked. He wanted to ask if Sam Granville had kissed her, but before he could say anything, Libby's control broke and tears began to slide down her cheeks.

"At precisely that moment, your father came thundering out of the woods on that demon horse of his. The timing was so perfect I always wondered if he'd been watching and waiting for just a moment like that.

"I want you to know that Sam didn't kiss me. I took my marriage vows too seriously. I would never have let him even if Lucas hadn't arrived when he did." She swiped at her eyes and blinked fast. "Of course, Lucas was furious. He got off the horse and...said a lot of terrible things to me and to Sam...accusing us of things I would never do. And then he hit him and hit him and—"

"Enough!" Gabe commanded. His stomach churned at the images filling his mind. He didn't need to hear any more. Frank had told Caleb that Lucas had almost killed the man he'd suspected his wife of cheating with. There was no need for a blow-by-blow description.

She nodded. "It was months before he healed," Libby said, "and even then, he never walked quite the same. Some injury to his spine, I suspect. His last few years were spent in a wheelchair."

Despite the pain of what he'd thought was her

rejection, despite the troubled years, Gabe believed her, and if the expression on Caleb's face was anything to go by, so did his brother. But whether or not he believed her, Gabe's behavior left him in no position to cast stones.

His mother had wanted to make things up to him and Caleb, just as he'd wanted to make things right with Caleb and Rachel. She'd taken that all-important first step, and it was up to him to meet her halfway.

Standing, he reached out and drew her to her feet and into his arms in an awkward gesture of comfort. He heard her sob and felt her arms close around his middle, felt her press her cheek against his shirtfront and her tears wet the fabric.

Fighting the emotion thickening his own throat, he whispered senseless, meaningless words of comfort and crooned soft soothing sounds. It was a language universal in origin, one that God Himself had designed for the hearts and minds and lips of mothers. They were tender words and gentle murmurs passed down from generation to generation, a distinctive means of communication that some few men—those who did not consider themselves too manly for such nonsense—might awkwardly adopt for just such an occasion.

Blindly, Libby reached out an arm to Caleb, who rose and allowed her to draw him close. Gabe, who had never seen his brother shed a tear during their growing-up years, thought Caleb's eyes looked overbright.

After a few moments, she pulled back, gathering herself and her emotions. He remembered that about her, too. Libby Gentry seldom got emotional, but when she did, she masked it as soon as possible. At one time or another they'd all learned that showing Lucas any weakness only made it easier for him to inflict more pain.

Taking the handkerchief Gabe offered, Libby wiped her eyes and waved them back to their chairs. "Sit please," she urged. "There's more."

Rachel dressed for church, her stomach filling with butterflies at the thought of meeting Gabe's mother for the first time. Facing a woman who had conversed with the child whose existence was proof of your disreputable past was not only nerve-racking, it filled Rachel with renewed shame.

She regarded herself in the mirror, her gaze fixed on the woman who stared back from its silvery depths. She wore a pale lavender dress with a white piqué V-shaped insert trimmed with purple piping. White cuffs and collar similarly trimmed finished the simple tailored dress that she felt befitted her station in town. She looked every bit the country doctor and nothing at all like the woman Libby Granville no doubt thought she was.

How her life had changed since she'd gone to Simon's wagon and discovered her past lying bleeding inside! Until then, her days had been uncomplicated and fulfilling, though perhaps a bit uneventful. She'd seldom shared time with a man and often wondered if anyone would ever come along to town to capture her interest. When the sheriff arrived, she'd gotten her hopes up, but it hadn't taken long for them to realize that there was not one spark of excitement when they were together.

Unlike the way the air fairly crackled when she was with Gabe.

He had only to enter a room and her lonely heart refused to listen to the sensible warnings of her head. She could not fault his behavior. He was everything a woman dreamed of in a man. Attentive. Caring. Helpful. Danny loved him with every fiber of his being, which should have been a consolation but in actuality frightened her for her son.

Gabe said he wasn't going anywhere, but what if his business venture failed and he had to go somewhere else to make a living? What if he found no one in town to love and went to another city to find a bride? What if that wife didn't care for Danny, or was jealous of their relationship? What if this unknown woman refused to live in the same town as the scarlet woman who would be a constant reminder of his past? Gabe might have to move, and Danny...

She shook her head in despair. It was an impossible situation, and she had no idea what to do about it. She'd asked God for His guidance, but He had given her no visible sign of what to do.

Sufficient unto the day is the evil thereof.

The words from the sixth chapter of Matthew echoed in her head, derailing the troubling turn of her thoughts. She paused in the act of stabbing the filigreed hatpin through her hat and into her upswept hair, thinking about the real meaning of the familiar passage. It was one she often quoted—sometimes almost flippantly—when day-to-day concerns seemed to be piling up to insurmountable heights.

There *was* no reason to worry about the future, since no one had a guarantee of what the next moment might bring, as Caleb had found out when what should have been the joyous occasion of his daughter's birth was mitigated by his wife's death.

Rachel told herself that she believed the Lord was with her no matter what, but she wondered if her life reflected that belief. Strong-willed and fond of being in control, she found it hard to surrender her will to Him, often trying to solve problems herself without waiting to see what He had in mind.

It all came down to whether or not she believed that God was working His plan in her life, taking her down the road He wanted despite the times she wandered off track or willfully chose to walk away from Him, determined to do it her way. Did she believe He was all-powerful, able to make adjustments to counteract her wrong moves?

If she didn't, she should.

She closed her eyes, a prayer of sorrow and supplication for a greater understanding and a stronger faith filling her mind. When she was finished, she had accepted that no amount of worry would change His plan. The best way to deal with the evils of life was one day at a time.

As soon as Rachel stepped through the doorway of the church, Gabe took her by the elbow. "I need to talk to you."

The weariness she saw in his eyes spoke of a sleepless night and suggested he'd learned something about his mother's leaving he hadn't known before, something he was having trouble coming to terms with even twelve hours later.

"Danny, will you please help Pops get settled?" she asked, not wanting little ears to hear whatever it was Gabe needed to tell her. When they'd gone, she looked around at the stream of arrivals.

"It's getting pretty crowded in here," she whispered, looking around at the knots of people mingling around them. "And since you're so sure you'll be the top bidder for my box lunch, we can talk while we eat."

Seeing his surprise, she realized that his thoughts were centered on something completely different. "Don't tell me you forgot one of the biggest events of the year?"

"It's been a peculiar couple of days," he murmured, "and last night was…very enlightening to say the least, but it did fill in a lot of blanks for both me and Caleb."

"What is it?" she asked sotto voce, intrigued in spite of herself.

Gabe lowered his voice. "Libby didn't have the affair—Lucas did."

With her mind still reeling from Gabe's pronouncement, Rachel passed down the aisle and took her seat in the pew next to her father. She'd been there no more than a moment when a soft hum rippled through the gathering, and heads began to turn toward the back of the room.

Despite her reluctance to meet her, Rachel felt a surge of sympathy for Libby Granville. Perhaps more than anyone else, Rachel understood what Libby must be suffering. She recalled her own experience—the thudding heart, trembling hands and nausea that had churned inside her, the same nausea that was no doubt roiling inside Gabe's mother as she made her way toward the pew where her family was seated.

The service passed by in a haze and was over before Rachel knew it. There was a mass exodus as everyone hurried to fetch their boxes or baskets before heading to Jacksons' Grove. Rachel saw to it that Danny and Edward and his chair were settled in the preacher's wagon before driving to the house and collecting her own basket.

There was plenty of time for catching up with friends and neighbors and lots of lemonade and fruit punch to drink during the time it took for everyone to arrive. The air was filled with the shouts and laughter of happy children and the hum of dozens of conversations. At day's end, everyone would go home filled with good food and new memories.

The auction might be a way to pair up the single people, but the boxes made up by the married women fetched good prices, too, since good-natured bidding often broke out between a husband and his brothers or brothers-in-law.

The older women kept the children entertained and provided food for them and those too old to be interested in the bidding, while the adults drifted away to share their meals. The afternoon would be whiled away with games of horseshoes, baseball and tag, while others meandered to the creek or found a quiet spot beneath the shade of a tree and indulged in a nap.

Rachel and Danny were wandering through the crowd, speaking to people she knew while he chatted with his friends. She saw him give a handful of wildflowers to eleven-year-old Bethany Carpenter, Ellie's daughter. He always went out of his way to show her some kindness. She saw a smiling Sheriff Garrett talking to Ellie, and a strained-looking Meg Thomerson, the baby in her arms and little Seth clinging to her skirts. Elton stood next to her, looking surly and already three sheets to the wind. Rachel said a quick prayer that he would not lose control again.

She glanced over to her father's vantage point beneath a large oak from which he had chosen to observe the festivities. It was close enough to the action of the bidding to observe what was happening but far enough away to be out of the throng.

He was smiling with pleasure; problems did not seem to be the insurmountable obstacles for him they did for Rachel.

She was about to turn back to check on Danny when she saw Libby Granville approach Edward's wheelchair. As Rachel watched, Libby smiled at Edward and extended both hands in greeting. Their mutual pleasure was evident, and the faint sounds of their laughter drifted across the meadow, along with the buzz of friendly chatter, squealing children and birdsong.

Rachel watched as Gabe and two strangers joined the pair. The siblings made an attractive trio. Blythe was dressed in a pretty summer frock of rose-hued organdy. With his dark blond hair and golden eyes, Win was as handsome as Gabe, but in an entirely different way. Elegant and self-possessed, he was the epitome of Boston fashion in a pale gray pinstripe suit.

Gabe said something and Rachel saw her father give a shrug and a vague wave. Gabe turned to scan the throng and spied her in the midst of the crowd. His serious expression transformed into the amazing smile that never failed to cause her heart to flutter. Despite the scar that grew fainter every day, he was a gorgeous man and would still be handsome when he was her father's age.

Day by day she was learning that there was more to him than a pretty face and inborn charm. She'd noticed many of them all those years ago, but when he left her, she'd thought he only pretended to have those qualities she'd fallen in love with.

He was kind and generous and blessed with patience and a dry sense of humor that popped up when she least expected it. He truly liked interacting with people, especially women. He paid close attention to their opinions, which she believed was the reason the new line of ladies' clothing he'd added to his inventory was so successful. He'd been blessed beyond most. It just wasn't fair.

"What isn't fair?"

The sound of his voice pulled her from her day-dreams. She must have been deep in thought if she hadn't seen him coming. As he stood there smiling down at her as if neither had a care in the world, she suddenly felt nothing like a successful physician who dealt in life and death, and more like a gauche miss just out of the schoolroom. But then, she'd always felt that way around Gabe.

"It's nothing."

"You didn't look as if it were nothing. You looked…dismayed."

"Can you blame me with everything that's going on?" she asked, hoping to switch the conversation from one unacceptable topic to another.

"Hey!" He chucked her beneath the chin. "It's not that bad. We all had a very revealing talk last night, and Caleb and I know exactly what happened. My mother said she didn't have an affair."

"And you believe her?"

"I do. So does Caleb. I'll tell you all about it later. Right now, why don't you come and meet her. I took all the blame for what happened between us, and she was more than happy to let me."

"You talked to her about us?" Rachel cried in a scandalized whisper.

"I told you I would, and you know it had to be said. There was no way around it."

She turned her face away. "I imagine she thinks I am some sort of hussy who—"

"She most certainly does not. Now stop trying to see the bad in this and look at the good."

"What good?" she asked, turning to face him again.

Before he could answer, Danny raced up and grabbed Gabe around the waist. "Dad, can Ben and Caleb go fishing with us when we go?"

"Certainly," Gabe said, "but it will be later, after we all have our picnic."

"Okay," he said, already off and running toward his friends.

Gabe's face wore a smile of complete satisfaction. "There went the good."

He meant it. He didn't see Danny as a burden or something to be ashamed of. He was truly thrilled about being a father, thrilled to be Danny's father. That much *was* good. In fact, it was wonderful.

He held out his elbow for her to take. "Ready?"

"I suppose we might as well get this over with," she said crossly, tucking her hand into the crook of his arm.

He laughed at her distinct lack of enthusiasm and gave her hand a pat. "That's the spirit!"

The laughter drew attention to them, though it seemed that they'd attracted a gaggle of gawkers just by standing there.

"Excuse me for not being too keen on the idea, but it's more than a bit humiliating."

"Don't I know it? Don't forget that it's an experience I was subjected to when I had to face your father. Thankfully he didn't shoot me, and I promise that my mother won't attack you, either."

Rachel glowered at him.

"She isn't going away any time soon, sweet-heart," he said, smiling that easy smile. "Come on. We'll face the music together."

She was hardly aware of their progress across the green field with its patches of yellow and pur-ple wildflowers. She was too rattled by his casual use of the endearment. *Sweetheart.*

If only I were his sweetheart.

Where had that come from? she thought irrita-bly. It was one thing to vow to be kinder and more forgiving. She could even love him, as long as he didn't suspect how she felt. That would be disas-trous, something she had to remind herself of sev-eral times a day.

Everyone in the group surrounding her father was laughing, but they turned as one as Rachel and Gabe drew nearer. Expressions ranged from pleas-ant inquiry to guardedness to thoughtful. Emotions that fit the circumstance, depending on one's per-spective, Rachel thought. To her surprise, it was her father who spoke up instead of Gabe.

"Rachel, this is Libby Granville, Gabe's mother—which I'm sure you know," he added with a cheerful grin. "Libby, this is my daughter, Rachel, Danny's mother."

Rachel offered her hand and Libby took it in a light grasp. "I'm so pleased to meet you, Rachel. Gabe has told me a lot about you, and you've cer-tainly done a fine job with Danny."

Rachel wondered if her face blanched at the wom-an's directness. Clearly Libby Granville was not one to beat around the bush. Having that frankness focused on her, she found, was a bit disconcerting.

"Thank you, Mrs. Granville. He's a wonderful little boy, but he can be a handful sometimes."

"He wouldn't be his father's son if he wasn't a handful," Libby said with a rueful smile. "And please call me Libby. Mrs. Granville was my mother-in-law." She gestured toward the couple standing nearby. "This is my stepson, Win, and my daughter, Blythe."

Blythe shook her hand somewhat awkwardly. Win's grasp was warm and firm, and she wondered if it was her imagination that he held her hand a tad longer than necessary. His tawny eyes brimmed with good humor. "My pleasure, Dr. Stone."

"Thank you. And everyone please call me Rachel. We don't stand on ceremony in Wolf Creek."

"Rachel, then," he said.

Rachel's glance encompassed them all. "So how are you finding our town so far? I'm sure it's quite a change from Boston."

"It is very different," Win agreed, "but it does have its points of interest. Mother has been excited about coming ever since Abby wrote to her more than a year ago."

"I wanted to come so badly then, but Sam was very ill, and there was no way I could leave him," Libby explained. Her eyes darkened with sorrow. "He passed away just after Christmas, and when Abby wrote telling me about Eli, I told Win and Blythe I simply had to come back. They both wanted to meet Gabe and Caleb, so here we are."

The conversation fizzled for a moment, and Rachel scoured her mind for something else to say. Unfortunately, her brain appeared to have turned to mush.

Gabe came to the rescue. "Everyone is going fishing with Danny after the auction and picnic," he said, coming to her rescue. "Would you and Edward like to join us?"

She was about to open her mouth to say that she had things to do when Edward spoke up.

"We'd love to."

"Are you sure you'll be up to it?" Rachel hedged, appalled at the thought of spending any significant time with the Granvilles. "It will make a long day."

"But a good one," Edward assured her. "Libby and I have a lot of catching up to do. I'll be fine, I promise."

He did spend too much time inside, she thought. Mostly because she wasn't always there to see to it that he got out and about as he should. And he was also tied down with watching Danny and being responsible for starting the evening meal. She shouldn't begrudge him this short time with a friend, even if she knew she would be miserable.

She mustered a smile. "If you're sure we won't be intruding, we'd be glad to join you."

As everyone was expressing their pleasure, someone rang a dinner bell and announced that the auction was about to begin. Mayor Talbot had been designated as the auctioneer, and bidding on the first basket started with a description of what was in it and who'd contributed it. Offers flew briskly, and cheers went up when Abe Caldwell had to pay three dollars for his wife's box.

Abby's was up next, and to everyone's surprise, Win got into the spirit of the day and joined in the battle, raising Caleb's every bid so that he was forced to pay seven dollars to share lunch with his wife. Gabe and Win were laughing so hard they could hardly catch their breath.

Caleb's face looked like a thundercloud as he paid the money, but Abby turned toward Win and gave him a wide smile and a wave. She was still laughing as she and Caleb sauntered off to find a spot down by the creek.

"It isn't like he can't afford it," Gabe offered, pulling out a monogrammed handkerchief and wiping his eyes.

Three more boxes sold, and then Rachel's came up.

"This basket was donated by Dr. Rachel Stone." Homer Talbot lifted the blue-patterned feed-sack dish towel and peeked inside. "Looks like fried chicken, homemade biscuits, pickled beets, a jar of slaw, some of Edward's famous lime pickles and pound cake with— What's this, Rachel?" he asked, holding up a pint jar.

"It's called 'lemon curd.' Something I haven't tried before."

"Looks dee-licious!" the mayor said. "Some gentleman out there is going to have a real treat." He looked directly at Gabe. "Who'll start the bidding at fifty cents?"

Gabe raised his hand, and someone across the way raised him a dime. Then, from behind Rachel, a voice said calmly but firmly, "Five."

The crowd gasped, and Rachel and Gabe both turned to see Win standing leaning against a tree, his eyes alight with mischief.

"What do you think you're doing?" Gabe snapped.

"Bidding on the lady's basket," he said. "It all sounds delicious, and I haven't had any lemon curd since I was in London a few months ago."

"Let's keep things moving," Homer said. "Do I hear five-fifty?"

Glaring at his stepbrother, Gabe held up his hand. "Eight," he said over the murmur of the crowd.

Win's gaze locked with Gabe's. "Ten."

Gabe's face was as red as the jar of beets in the basket. "This isn't funny. What kind of game do you think you're playing, *brother?*"

"You thought it was funny when Caleb had to pay, *brother,*" Win reminded him. "And it's no game. It's just that when I see something I want, I go after it."

Chapter Eleven

❧

Gabe bid twelve dollars and Win relented with a shrug. The crowd was abuzz over the spirited bidding rivalry and curious about what it might mean to Dr. Stone and Gabe's relationship.

It was a ridiculously high price to pay, but there was no way Gabe was going to let the aristocratic Bostonian share a lunch with Rachel. Who did that blue-blooded upstart think he was, anyway? Just because the Granvilles were somebody back in Boston didn't mean Win could come into Gabe's neck of the woods and try to snatch the woman he loved out from under his nose. If Win was entertaining some half-cocked notion to "go after" Rachel, he'd soon find out that he'd have another battle on his hands!

Gabe pulled the cash from his wallet and went to pay the fee to Ruby Talbot. Collecting the basket of food amid a chorus of good-natured ribbing, he stalked toward the group gathered beneath the trees.

A sudden thought struck him. Was it possible Win was thinking of spending more time in Wolf Creek than he let on?

The previous evening, his stepbrother's conversation seemed centered around the town. He appeared to have looked things over since arriving and had asked a lot of questions about businesses or storefronts for sale, about what the town needed and what possible avenues for growth there might be not only in Wolf Creek, but in the surrounding area.

At the time, Gabe had assumed Win was just making conversation and had listened but offered little to the discussion. Caleb had lived here his whole life and had his fingers on the pulse of what was happening. He'd answered Win's questions without reserve, discussing several possibilities for new businesses.

Now that Win had all but come out and announced his interest in Rachel, Gabe wondered if he'd misjudged the older man. Was he attracted to her enough to be a true rival? Enough to relocate his business?

Stalking along toward the group beneath the trees, Gabe's stomach twisted beneath the reality of the situation. Maybe she would rather have someone like the upstanding Granville heir than a ne'er-do-well who'd done everything in his power to mess up his life. And hers.

He approached the gathering, automatically looking for the outsider. Win was still lounging against the tree, regarding him with an amused expression.

Though he'd seemed okay at first, Gabe wasn't sure he liked his stepbrother overmuch. He was sure of one thing, though. His plan had been to take things slow and not pressure Rachel, but with Win in the picture, maybe it was time to move things along. He was going to ask her to marry him. Soon. The worst that could happen was that she would say no.

Rachel picked up a quilt she'd brought and her wary gaze moved from one man to the other. "Will you make sure Danny gets something to eat, Dad?" she asked Edward.

"Of course I will."

"Don't worry about a thing. Your father and I have it well in hand," Libby said. "I'll even fix Edward a plate." She gave a shooing wave of her hands. "You two go on now and enjoy your meal."

"Thank you," Rachel said and hurried to catch up with Gabe, who evidently had no qualms about leaving her behind.

"What was that all about?" she asked, as she fell into step with the irritating man.

His face held wide-eyed innocence. "What was what all about?"

"Don't pretend you don't know what I mean, Gabriel Gentry. What was that between you and Win?"

Gabe shot her an irritated look. "You heard him. When he sees something he wants, he goes after it. Meaning you, of course."

The notion that Win Granville might be interested in her was stunning. He was too self-confi=

dent, too sophisticated, too everything she would not be interested in. She laughed. "He was just stirring up a bit of controversy for the fun of it—he does seem to have a wicked sense of humor—or he was just helping out the town by bidding up the price of the baskets."

Gabe stopped and turned to her. "That's a very generous observation, and one anyone who knows you would expect you to make, but don't be naive," he said. "You must know that you're a very beautiful woman, even though you make me want to bang my head against the wall most of the time."

She stared at him, uncertain whether to laugh at his frustration, thank him for thinking she was beautiful or smack him for saying that she drove him crazy. Then she saw the uncertainty in his eyes.

She pressed a palm to her heart that gave a ridiculous little flip of joy. Oh, my! It would be easier to believe that the world would stop turning before believing she would ever see what her eyes were telling her now.

He was jealous.

More than that, for perhaps the first time in his life, he was unsure of himself. Her heart thudded beneath her hand. He'd kissed her and told her he cared and she'd believed him as far as it went, but was it possible that he really truly cared for her? The thought was almost overwhelming.

"You're imagining things," she said, willing her voice to steadiness. "And I may be naive, but I'm not silly enough to fall for the likes of Win Granville.

The man is as handsome as sin, but he definitely has heartbreak written all over him."

Pressing his lips together as if he were afraid he might say something to add to the volatility of the conversation, Gabe turned and started walking. Rachel followed, searching for a topic that might restore some harmony for the next hour or so. After a moment or two, he stopped beneath the spreading branches of a huge oak tree. The nearby creek gurgled and bubbled and rushed headlong over the rocky bottom.

"How's this?" he asked, frowning at her.

"Perfect." She unfurled the red, white and blue quilt she'd brought along. "You were right. Your mother isn't at all judgmental. I like her."

Gabe put down the basket and lowered himself Indian style. Rachel sank down on her knees, her skirt billowing out around her. Their gazes locked as she waited for him to respond.

"I like her, too," he admitted. "And I didn't expect to."

There was no need for him to explain, and she was thankful to see that his grumpiness had disappeared. "You said earlier that Libby didn't have an affair—Lucas did."

"Right." While she set out the lunch, he told her everything that had transpired the evening before. "You'll never in a million years guess who he was seeing."

"I can't imagine…"

"Sarah VanSickle."

They'd reached the dessert portion of the meal, and dropping that bit of news into the conversation almost caused the piece of pound cake Rachel had just sliced to slip from her fingers.

"Sarah VanSickle?" she echoed, putting the cake onto a delicate saucer trimmed with clusters of forget-me-nots. She thrust the plate at him.

"It surprised me, too, although knowing her as I do, I'm not sure why," Gabe admitted. He held out the cake while Rachel added a dollop of the lemon curd.

She fumed as she fixed her own dessert. How could anyone deliberately come between a husband and wife? How could anyone destroy a family through sheer malice? No one should have to suffer what Libby and her boys had gone through, all because of one man's ego and one woman's vindictiveness.

That any of them had come out of it with as few scars as they had was nothing short of a miracle. She saw God's hand in sending Frank, the only person to offer two young boys what comfort and love they'd received during their youth. Frank had done what he could to counteract Lucas's callousness, somehow managing to instill good old-fashioned decency in them.

She saw God's plan in the way He'd brought Caleb and Abby together, and how through Abby, He'd worked to reunite a mother to her sons and grandchildren. It was so easy to see and trust Him working in the lives of others, but did she dare trust that He was working in hers and Gabe's? Had it been God's plan for Gabe to be attacked on his journey home last December? Had Simon been sent just so he could bring Gabe to her doorstep? Was it His intent for them to work through their troubled past and become a family?

"What are you thinking?" Gabe asked, bringing her convoluted thoughts back to the present.

She lifted her gaze to his. "I'm thinking that life is very complicated. It's unfair and often downright ugly, and only by the grace of God do we manage to come through it relatively unscathed."

He frowned. "Those are pretty weighty observations."

"Well," she said with a self-deprecating smile, "as you well know, I am not a featherbrain by reputation."

She took her first bite of cake. Gabe had finished his while she was woolgathering. "Do you think Libby will confront Sarah now that there's no one around to stop her?" she asked.

"Oh, you can count on it."

She finished her cake and busied herself with gathering and wrapping the soiled plates and flatware in a plain dish towel to transport them back home.

"Do you know what really infuriates me?" he asked, pitching the dregs of his lemonade into the grass and handing her the glass.

From her perspective it was all infuriating. "What?"

"That Sarah can go around and deliberately pick people's lives to pieces when she's guilty of far worse than most of them."

"Maybe she's asked for forgiveness for what she did to your family," Rachel said, striving for fairness.

He made a scoffing sound. "If so, I'm sure she got it, but what about the things she's done since?"

"We all sin, and most of us commit the same sins over and over," Rachel said. "At least I do. Seventy times seven, remember?"

"I understand that, but there's a difference. When we ask for forgiveness and mean it, we may inadvertently fall back into that old sin. The difference is when you ask for forgiveness all the while *intending* to go out and do the same thing at the next opportunity."

Rachel thought of how Sarah's wicked tongue had forced Caleb and Abby into marriage, and how her spitefulness had caused her to spread the news about Danny's paternity to the four corners of the county. How many other lives had she ruined through the years? Would she ever stop her campaign of malice?

That question triggered another, troubling idea about her life. She had almost let her anger and animosity devour her. If Gabe had not returned, would she have become like Sarah? The thought was sobering, frightening. Like Sarah, she attended services regularly, but by harboring hostility toward Gabe, wasn't she just as wrong?

"You're right," she told him, searching for the right words for Gabe. "What she does is wrong, but instead of lowering ourselves to her level and maligning her, we should—"

"—pray for her," he said in disgust. "I know."

"Yes," Rachel said, unable to hide a smile. "But you really should have a better attitude when you do."

Seeing the mirth in her eyes and knowing she was right, he offered her a halfhearted smile in return. "I know you're right, but I have a way to go with this Christianity thing."

Rachel sobered, knowing that she, too, had a long way to go. "Coming from someone with years of firsthand experience, I can promise you that we'll never get it right, and it isn't always easy. The thing that matters is that we keep giving it our best, which I haven't always done, even though I should know better."

"What are you talking about? You're one of the best people I know."

"I wasn't very Christ-like when you came to town, was I?"

Gabe's expression held no condemnation. "You had reason to...hate me."

"I didn't hate you, but every time I looked at you, it all came back to me. The shame and guilt and how alone I was when you left me with nothing but an offhand goodbye." She drew in a shaky breath. "And as much as I tried, as much as I *wanted* to, I didn't really hate you. I don't."

Gabe's eyes held an indefinable tenderness that she had opened up to him. He was sorry to have been the one to cause her so much pain. "What do you feel, Rachel?" he whispered, leaning toward her.

Their gazes met and held. "I don't know." She shook her head. "That isn't true. I think I do know, but I'm afraid."

The trembling words came straight from the heart.

He moved closer, and as he had the day outside her house, he rested his forehead against hers. Her eyes drifted shut.

"Don't be afraid, Rachel," he said. "I do know what I feel, and it's as real and true as the sunrise, because that's what you are. Real. True. Back in St. Louis I wasn't thinking about anyone but Gabe Gentry, but this time everything's different. What I feel isn't going away, and neither am I. We have all the time in the world."

"How can you be sure it won't go away?"

He dropped a quick kiss to the tip of her nose.

"Because my heart is involved this time. Because Danny's heart is involved. I pray yours is. And because this feels so right that it scares *me* to death sometimes. I ran from what you made me feel once. Not again."

He was scared? She drew back to get a better look at him. "Why would you be scared?"

"I'm scared that despite everything I do and no matter how hard I try, that when I finally do ask you to spend the rest of your life with me—and I will ask you—that you'll say no."

Rachel couldn't speak for the knot of emotion in her throat. It was what she'd dreamed of nine years ago. But time and circumstances had changed. They had both changed. When he asked, what would she say?

"Stop trying to figure out what you'll do," he said, almost as if he could read her mind. "I'm not asking you for anything today. And I promise you that whatever your answer is, I will do everything in my power to never cause you that kind of pain again."

"The woman is impossible!" Libby said, stalking across Caleb's parlor. Another week had passed and they were all congregated at the farm to share another meal. This time Rachel, Edward and Danny were in attendance, even though Rachel felt like an outsider.

With the meal over, the dishes washed and put away, and the little ones down for an afternoon nap, the grownups were gathered to hear the details of Libby's confrontation with Sarah the evening before.

"Be specific, Mother." Win sprawled in a wingback chair, his long legs crossed at the ankles, regarding the contrasting tips of his shining shoes. He glanced up. "Surely she listened to what you had to say."

"Oh, she listened," Libby said, whirling around

to face her family. "I told her that I'd always known about her and Lucas. She had the gall to tell me that if I'd been the right kind of wife, he would never have strayed."

"That's interesting." Edward said. "Especially since it's common knowledge that he broke off with Sarah and took up with a woman from Murfreesboro not a month after you left."

Rachel and Gabe exchanged surprised looks. This was new information and said even more about what a rogue Lucas Gentry had been.

"Serves her right," Libby snapped, clearly in a huff. "Then when I confronted her with starting the gossip about Caleb and Abby even though her accusations were groundless, she informed me that we were supposed to 'abstain from all *appearance* of evil,' and she felt it was her Christian duty to bring awareness to the situation, so that it could be set straight."

Caleb's jaw clenched, and he opened his mouth to say something, but Abby stopped him with a hand on his arm. "And here we are," she said, meeting his heated gaze with a smiling one. "As happy as two fat cats in the sunshine."

"It could have turned out far differently," Caleb groused.

"Could have, but didn't."

Rachel saw that Libby looked at her new daughter-in-law with unabashed affection.

"All's well that ends well, then," Blythe said. Though she seemed painfully shy, as her time in

Wolf Creek had passed and she got to know her brothers and their families better, she seemed more comfortable contributing to the conversations.

"I don't mind telling you that I was furious," Libby continued. "She was totally unrepentant about anything she'd done. When I brought up Rachel and Gabe and told her she had no right to blather her suspicions about Danny to everyone in town, she just laughed. 'Your sins will find you out,' she said, to which I replied that she was twisting scripture and what she had done was motivated by pure meanness—not goodness. Then I reminded her that we are to 'keep our tongue from evil.'"

"And?" Gabe asked, fighting the urge to smile as he listened to his mother go on about her confrontation with her archenemy.

"She told me not to preach to her and stalked away. I realized then that I was casting pearls before swine and—"

Edward's sudden hoot of laughter silenced her in midsentence. Planting her hands on her slender hips, Libby glared at him, but then when she realized how ridiculous the idea of her and Sarah tossing scripture back and forth in the heat of an argument must sound, she joined him.

"You can't reason with unreasonable people, my dear," he told her. "I'm afraid that unless something drastic happens to make Sarah see the error of her ways, she'll never change. It's a reality you'll have to deal with if you do decide to move here."

Caleb, Abby and Gabe looked as shocked by the

casual comment as Rachel felt. The animation on Blythe's pretty face vanished, and her hands tightened in her lap. As usual, Win's expression gave away little, but Rachel thought he seemed watchful beneath the nonchalance, as if he were inordinately interested in everyone's response.

Frowning, Caleb addressed Win. "I know we talked about this some, but I thought you were just making conversation, showing interest in town. Are you really considering a move from Boston?"

Win gestured toward Libby, who sat down in a chair next to Edward's.

"Well, I am. At least for part of the year. With Sam gone, there's no reason I can't go where I wish. So why not? Win is perfectly capable of overseeing the family businesses."

"Which are?" Gabe asked.

"Actually, Win worked with his father's newspaper and printing endeavor, and Sam handled the furniture-manufacturing facility," she said. "Since he died, Win has taken it on, too. Along with Philip's help, of course. He's an attorney."

Gabe was impressed in spite of himself.

"Win and Blythe have had me for more than twenty years, and I feel I have so much to make up for with you two boys and the grandchildren here. I would miss Win and Blythe terribly, of course, which is why I'm considering equal time at both places."

"Unless Blythe and I decide to come, too," Win added, casting a quick glance at Gabe, who felt a sudden urge to smash his fist into his stepbrother's aristocratic nose.

"I don't want to move," Blythe said, her lips forming a pout that made her look younger than her twenty-two years. "Wolf Creek is a nice little town, but after living in the city all my life, I can't imagine being happy with no theaters, museums or parks and no eating establishments but the hotel and Ellie's café."

"The choices are a bit limited," Win said, "but I think that's exactly why this might be a good place to branch out. It seems to me that the area could use a new business or two. What about an attorney? There are bound to be legal issues that crop up, even with so few people."

"Are you saying your brother might move, too, if the rest of you come?"

"Not Philip!" Win said with an emphatic shake of his head.

"I agree," Libby added. "I can't see him ever leaving the city, but some young lawyer out there will settle here one day."

"So it's really all still up in the air," Caleb said. "What would you do with your days, Mother? As Blythe said, we don't have much to do in the way of activities, and there isn't much of a social scene. I don't see that changing any time soon."

"I'm not sure. I'll be somewhat limited being gone half the year, but I'll think of something. Maybe Ellie would let me help her part of the day."

"You'd work in a café?" Rachel asked, astounded

at the thought that the stylish woman sitting across from her would lower herself to work in an eating establishment.

"Well, I'm a pretty fair cook, and I had a lot of practice before I went to Boston. I'm certainly not above it, just because my husband left me with a lot of money," she said with a shrug. "It doesn't matter what we do. It matters that we do something and that we're happy doing it. I happen to like being busy and I love to cook and bake."

"I don't know, Mother," Win kidded her. "I'm not sure your piecrust is up to Ellie's standards. Her food is pretty wonderful. Not to mention she's a real stunner. What I can't figure out is why someone hasn't snatched her up."

"Sheriff Garrett is working on it," Gabe said, giving Win a pointed look. "They've hit a bump or two lately, but it's nothing they can't resolve, I'm sure."

"What kind of bumps?"

Abby looked around the room. "Well, I don't want to gossip…"

"For pity's sake, Abby!" Caleb said. "Just tell the truth. Colt is a good man, but his children are wretched little brats."

"I can vouch for that," Gabe said. "I actually shudder when I see them come through the doors at the store."

"They are a handful," Rachel added. "But that isn't the biggest problem."

Everyone looked at her expectantly.

"Ellie's daughter, Beth, is a Mongoloid. Ellie's husband took one look at her and disappeared. She hasn't seen him since, so Ellie isn't divorced, and she isn't a widow. Until her husband is located or declared dead, she couldn't marry again if she wanted to."

Over the next few days, every moment Rachel was not treating someone's ailment, she was thinking about her conversation with Gabe and his mother's announcement that she might return to Wolf Creek. She wasn't sure how she felt about that, but she understood the older woman's need to reconnect with her sons and establish relationships with her grandchildren. She would think less of Libby had she not felt the way she did.

As for everyone else, they were fine with the idea. Neither Danny nor Ben was accustomed to having a grandmother around and were ecstatic about the notion. No doubt the younger children would be just as happy once they figured out exactly what having a grandmother meant.

Two days before the Granvilles were scheduled to return to Boston, Edward asked them to the house for dinner. Win and Blythe declined, stating that Ellie was having chicken and dumplings at the café, a dish they hadn't tried before coming to the South and one they declared was so good as to be "positively sinful." Though they might be right about how good it was, Rachel suspected there was something more behind their refusal. She also suspected that that something more was Libby wanting to spend some special time with Danny before she left.

But it wasn't only Danny Libby wanted to spend time with. When the supper dishes were done and put away, Edward challenged Danny to a game of checkers and Libby suggested that she and Rachel sit on the porch. Nervous, though she wasn't sure why, Rachel acquiesced.

"I wanted a chance to talk to you alone before I leave," Libby said.

"I understand."

Libby smiled. "I'm not sure you do. I imagine there are all sorts of things running through your mind, including wondering what I really think of you." She reached out and patted the hands Rachel clutched in her lap.

"I've talked to Gabe, and he told me about St. Louis. After hearing about his antics through the years, I was a bit surprised that he took the entire blame for what happened."

"You kept up with him and Caleb?" Rachel asked, surprised.

"Some," she said with a nod. "Enough to know that Caleb was turning into a sour recluse and Gabe was running amok. When he left here, I lost track of him except for what few things made the papers back East. I never heard a word about you and Danny, though."

"There's no way anyone could have known about me and Danny until Sarah spoke up." Rachel said.

"I never even told my father who Danny's father was."

"So Edward said."

"Who kept you informed? Surely not Lucas."

"No, not Lucas," Libby said with a laugh. "It was Frank, actually, but I only heard from him a time or two a year, since reading and writing aren't his strong suits. And when there was some medical problem, your dad would drop me a line through Frank. It was all very hush-hush. I couldn't have Lucas finding out that I was keeping up with them."

Rachel liked Libby even more, knowing she'd done what she could to keep up with her sons' development.

"Do Caleb and Gabe know?"

"Yes."

"I appreciate your openness, Libby, and I especially appreciate your acceptance of Danny. It was very gentlemanly of Gabe to take sole responsibility for what happened. For years I told myself that he was the only one responsible, but the truth is that I was as much in the wrong as he was." She took a deep breath and met Libby's gaze. "Suffice it to say that he's very hard to withstand when he puts his mind to something—not that that is an excuse."

"He always was hard to resist," Libby agreed with a gentle smile. "When Caleb got into trouble, he got all serious and helpful and did any and everything to get back in my good graces. Gabe turned on the charm and wooed me back into a good mood by entertaining me with some sort of foolishness or another."

Rachel had no problem envisioning that, since Danny was pretty adept at the same thing.

"Since coming back and hearing about how truly appalling their time with Lucas was, I'm ashamed of not having tried harder to do something to get them back. Sam had money. I should have found a good attorney and…done something."

"Lucas Gentry was a powerful man," Rachel said, wanting to ease the pain reflected in the older woman's eyes. "Even more daunting than his fortune is the fact that he was very politically connected, from local attorneys to the governor. He wouldn't have hesitated to use that influence against you."

"Thank you for pointing that out. I know you're right. It's just that I hate what happened to them, and I worry about how it affected them as they grew up."

"Lucas's behavior had a profound effect on everyone's life, including yours," Rachel reminded her. "Thank God you've come through it, stronger. You've made a wonderful new life and have Win and Blythe. Caleb is like a new man since Abby came along, and I truly believe Gabe is on his way to happiness, so stop worrying. Dad always says that worry is like a rocking chair. You can rock all day and never get anywhere. One thing I've realized is that we can't undo the past. All we can do is take the lessons we learn from our mistakes and apply them to future situations."

"As you've done."

She shrugged. "As tough as Caleb and Gabe's life was, it has made them the men they are. Imperfect, certainly, but basically good men. That goodness had to come from you, from the memories of you they never let go."

Libby's eyes shimmered with tears. "He loves you, you know, and the longer I'm here, the more I understand why."

Rachel's breath caught. "He loves Danny."

"Don't sell yourself short, my dear."

Rachel felt her own eyes fill with tears. "How can you be so nice to me?" she whispered. "When you know…"

"I'm not here to cast stones," Libby said. "We all fall short, and no matter how much we'd like there to be, there are no little sins and big sins. Just sins.

"She may never acknowledge it, but Sarah's gossiping tongue is just as bad as what happened between you and Gabe. The two of you have learned from your mistakes and have made things right with God. You're trying to live good lives. It's a heart thing, something Sarah just doesn't get."

"So you've forgiven her?" Rachel asked.

"I'm working on it," Libby said with another of those dry smiles. "So!" She swiped her fingertips beneath her eyes and her voice took on brisk purpose. "Now that we have that cleared up, do you have any objections to my moving here?"

"What I think has no bearing on your decision," Rachel said, surprised that Libby would seek her approval.

"Of course it does. I'll have a lot of contact not only with Caleb and Gabe, but with the children. How do you feel about my being part of Danny's life?"

Touched that she cared about her feelings, Rachel said, "I think it would be wonderful for him to have a grandmother. As long as you don't spoil him too much," she added.

Libby's eyes widened and she placed a palm against her chest as if the comment had inflicted a mortal wound. "But spoiling is what grandmothers are for, and I have so much catching up to do."

Seeing the genuine dismay in Rachel's eyes, Libby laughed and leaned forward to give her a quick hug. "I'll try."

Knowing she was fighting a losing battle, Rachel gave in to the inevitable. She would now not only have to share Danny with Gabe but with his mother, and possibly Win and Blythe.

Not necessarily a bad thing.

Reluctantly, she agreed with the little voice whispering inside her.

Chapter Twelve

Libby was long gone and everyone else in the house was sleeping soundly. A shaft of moonlight slanted across Rachel's bed, and a whisper of air drifted through the partially open window, causing the lace curtains to ripple gently. She lay there thinking of her conversation with Gabe's mother and conjuring up images of what it would be like with Libby Granville in town. In her life.

Libby claimed Gabe loved her, and with those words running through her mind, Rachel began to dream of re-creating some of the funny, tender moments she and Gabe had once shared and building a life with their son. Would it ever happen? She'd begun to nurture the tiny, tentative hope that it might.

She often thought of Gabe's statement on the day of the box-lunch picnic. He was going to ask her to marry him. When? What would she say if he did? According to his mother and her father, Gabe loved her. Could she trust it was true? Could she trust *him* again?

She heard the sudden patter of raindrops and sighed in pleasure. She loved hearing rain against the rooftop. Then, realizing that the window was half-open, she scrambled to a sitting position and swung her legs over the side of the bed. She'd almost reached the window when she heard another soft clatter and realized it wasn't rain at all. Someone was throwing gravel.

Grabbing the shawl that was draped over the back of a nearby chair, she flung it around her shoulders and poked her head out the window. Gabe stood near her mama's rosebush with his hands on his hips, his head tipped back watching to see if she would answer his summons.

"What are you doing here?" she screeched in a loud whisper. She was appalled by his presence yet unaccountably pleased to see him. What a scandal it would be if anyone else saw him! Thank goodness Danny, not her father, had the room next to hers. Unlike Edward, Danny slept like the dead.

"I haven't seen you all day, and I wanted to tell you that I…"

Her breath hung suspended and her heart seemed to stop midbeat.

"…I miss you."

"Gabe," she all but groaned. Then, pushing aside a ridiculous rush of pleasure, she summoned her most professional tone. "Go home. I'll see you tomorrow."

"Did anyone ever tell you that you're a heartless woman, Rachel Stone? Where will I see you tomorrow? At the store or between the times before you hurry off to see a patient? Where's the romance in that?"

"Romance?" She croaked the single word in a low, stunned voice.

"Yes, romance. Obviously you've never been courted before."

The insidious, ridiculous pleasure blossomed inside her. "Really? What was St. Louis?"

"That doesn't count because I didn't know what I was doing or why," he said in a low undertone. "This—" he spread his arms wide "—is the real thing. I told you."

She chewed on her lower lip. Uncertainty lent stridency to her voice. "If someone sees you here, it won't be pleasant."

"What can they do? Talk about us?" he challenged.

She resisted the urge to giggle. "Go home, Gabe."

"So practical," he said with a low chuckle and a shake of his head. "We need to work on that." He took a step backward. "Tomorrow, then. I have to take a load of grain out to Mr. Connor after I close, but when I come back, I'm going to ask you to walk with me down by the creek and I'm going to ask you a very important question, so you'd better be ready. Preferably with the answer I want to hear." He pivoted to leave.

"Gabe!"

He turned.

"What if you don't get the answer you want?"

"Then I'll try harder." She saw the flash of his smile in the moonlight. "I'd like tomorrow better than next month or next year, but I'm learning that I can be a very patient man, and I have it on good authority that women can't resist me, so it's only a matter of time."

She smiled at the teasing tone of his voice, her heart light with promise.

"You're a very conceited man," she told him, but there was no real condemnation in the words.

"I prefer to think of it as confidence. And it's part of why you love me. You do, you know."

He sketched a jaunty salute, turned and left her dangling out the window, her mouth hanging open. She watched him disappear into the trees behind the house, knowing he was right, drat him. She was even starting to believe that her love was returned, but neither fact altered the nagging fear of whether or not she was ready to trust that love enough to take a second chance.

The sun was still plenty high in the western sky when Gabe drove his wagon back toward Wolf Creek the next day. He'd told Rachel he wouldn't rush her, but he wanted her to know how he felt. As anxious as he was to have the upcoming conversation with her, he'd needed the extra couple of hours to settle his nerves. He couldn't recall ever feeling so scared about what a woman would say.

She well knew that he was no innocent. She might be more inclined to say yes if he were blameless and they had no past to come between them, but no matter what she said, he didn't regret that time. It had taken him years to realize that if he hadn't looked her up in St. Louis, he might have gone on with his aimless life indefinitely.

She was like no woman he'd ever met. Serious and still somewhat shy, yet decisive and professional. She was dedicated to her goals. Intelligent and innately good. After all these years, he understood why he had turned his back on her. Once she had given him her heart, she had given him everything else she possessed with utmost trust. Even as self-serving as he'd been, he was smart enough to realize how special that was. What did a man like him do with love like that? How was he to return it? His only knowledge of love was the vague memories of his mother, who had left him. And so he'd panicked, written her a note and disappeared.

What a fool he'd been! But when he'd awakened with her name on his lips and his eyes wet with tears long after she should have been nothing but a hazy memory, he'd realized what an impact she'd had on him. That was when he'd gathered the courage to come home.

And here they were, almost six months later. If he thought it had taken courage for him to return, he couldn't imagine how brave she'd been to come home with an illegitimate child. Yet she had endured the whispers and speculation. She had restored her good name and was well respected in the community. Did he have the right to jeopardize that by asking her to share his life? Maybe not, but he intended to anyway.

The sound of shouting and neighing horses up ahead jolted him back to the present. He thought he heard a woman scream. What was going on? he wondered, slapping the reins against his horse's back, urging it to speed up.

The road curved, and as he rounded the slight bend, he saw that a surrey had been forced off the side of the road. Two horsemen with bandannas pulled up over their faces had dismounted and were yelling at a stout woman, but he was too far away to make out what they were saying.

He recognized the buggy at the same time one of the men reached out and tugged an earbob from one of the woman's ears. Sarah VanSickle! And it looked as if she was being robbed. Even as the thoughts came together, Gabe saw her knock her attacker's hand away from her other ear. When the man grabbed at her reticule, she stepped backward and received a couple of blows for her effort.

Recalling his own encounter with bandits on this very stretch of road—possibly these same two—he urged the gelding to a tooth-rattling pace that launched him up from the bench seat every time the wheels hit a bump. As he neared the scene and pulled his horse to a stop, Sarah recognized him.

"Gabe! Help! Please!" She was holding her abdomen, and her lip was bleeding.

When he leaped to the ground, the thief who was watching Sarah's abuse at the hands of his co-hort turned to face him. The familiar coal-black eyes above the bandanna's edge were filled with a chilling malevolence. "Well, well, well. Back for more, are you?"

The eyes and the gravelly voice breached the entrance to a memory Gabe had slammed the door on. These were definitely the same men. Even if the robber hadn't uttered the telling statement, he would never forget that voice.

"Yeah," he said. "And I'm not hungover this time."

Lunging forward, he hit the outlaw's midsec-tion with his shoulder, wrapping his arms around him and using his forward momentum to bring him down. The men hit the ground with loud grunts. They wrestled, rolling over and over, one on top and then the other, exchanging blow for blow. During the struggle, the stranger's kerchief slipped down, but Gabe didn't recognize him. He looked Indian, though.

He paid for his lack of attention with a particu-larly hard punch to the kidney and another to the eye. With blood running down his face, he hauled back and landed a well-aimed strike to his oppo-nent's face. The man's grip loosened, and with his lungs heaving, Gabe struggled to regain his footing. He swiped at the blood dripping off his chin and faced the man who held a handful of Sarah's ruffled bodice in one hand and a bowie knife in the other.

"Give him your reticule, Sarah," Gabe told her, angling closer. From the corner of his eyes, he saw the man he'd fought roll to his knees and draw his Colt. "Give them what they want."

Sarah looked at him as if he'd grown two heads. "Don't be ridiculous, Gabriel! I'll do nothing of the sort."

"It's only jewelry. It can be replaced."

"Jewelry Randolph worked long hours to pay for," she snapped.

The man jerked suddenly and she went careening forward. The action was accompanied by the sound of rending cloth. As she staggered to regain her footing, the big man's hand came away with a handful of fabric.

"My brooch!" With no thought of the knife in his hand, she leaped forward, her hands curled into claws. She meant to scratch out his eyes, Gabe thought. Unfortunately, she only managed to drag the handkerchief down. She gasped when she saw who it was. Another blow sent her sprawling onto the ground.

The man Gabe had fought let go a string of curses. "They've seen us, Elton."

"So they have, and that's no good at all."

From the look in his eyes, there was no telling what he'd do. Unaware that they were both near death, Sarah struggled to her feet and rushed her assailant once more, swinging her reticule like a lasso.

"Give me my earrings!"

Gabe cast a quick look at the other desperado

and saw that he'd turned his weapon toward Sarah. Gabe sprang forward, hoping to knock her out of the line of fire.

Several things seemed to happen simultaneously. Two loud *boom*s shattered the evening air. Sarah screamed and then just…disappeared. Something seared his side. Almost simultaneously an intense pain blossomed in his head. He heard both men yelling and cursing. He knew he needed to help Sarah but was having a hard time battling back the shadows stealing over at him. As the all-consuming pain and blessed darkness carried him away, he thought he heard Sarah screaming and the clatter of hooves pounding down the gravel road.

"Gabriel!"

The sharp voice sounded familiar. He didn't like it. Something stung his face, and he forced his eyes open a crack. A grotesque face stared down at him. Pale. A bruised eye. Mouth swollen to twice its size. Scraggly hair. A fancy hat sitting at a cockeyed angle on her head. A ridiculous pheasant feather dangling down.

He must be in the middle of a nightmare. If he didn't know better he would say it was Sarah Van-Sickle leaning over him, calling his name in sharp, demanding tones and slapping his cheeks, insisting that he get up.

He heard her. Trouble was, he couldn't. He hurt too badly, and the shadows were pulling at him again.

* * *

It was just before candle lighting, and there was no sign of Gabe. Rachel was sitting in the parlor, pretending to read the newest copy of *Woman's Home Journal* while a tedious refrain chased through her mind: *He's changed his mind. He's changed his mind...changed his mind...*

The sounds of half a dozen yelling voices interrupted the litany, followed by the loud clatter of wagon wheels rumbling across the railroad tracks. More crying out ensued, shouts that were accompanied by the sound of a whip cracking through the air and hoofbeats thundering toward the rear of the house.

Someone was making quite a ruckus, which meant that whatever it was must be serious. Leaping to her feet and calling for her father, she headed for the office. All thoughts of Gabe vanished as she mentally prepared herself to deal with this newest crisis. Patients arrived at all hours of the day and night, and she needed to be clearheaded to attend them.

No amount of preparation could have equipped her for what she saw when she flung open the door. The wagon Gabe used to make deliveries sat there, but it was Sarah VanSickle who held the reins. Her tear-streaked face was battered and bruised and smeared with blood. Her expensive hat was askew, and one feather dangled by her ear.

"Sarah!" Rachel said, rushing forward. "What on earth happened?"

"Robbed outside Antoine," she said, sobbing as her tenuous hold on her dwindling stamina slipped away.

"Robbed?" Edward said from the doorway. "Who…?"

"Elton Thomerson!" she cried. "I didn't know the other one."

Elton Thomerson? Meg's husband? Stunned by the information, Rachel had no time to dwell on it. "Let me help you down," she said.

"I can't walk," Sarah said with a shake of her head. "I think I broke my ankle when I went over the side of the gully. It's Gabe you need to help. He's been shot."

Blood drained from Rachel's head and she swayed with sudden dizziness.

"Rachel!" The sharpness of her father's voice dissipated the gathering fog. "Go check on him. I'll get the stretcher."

Thank God for her father, she thought. He always seemed to be there when she needed him most. She spied Danny in the doorway next to his grandfather. His frightened eyes were wide and glittered with unshed tears. She knew what must be going through his mind. He had just found his father. Was he about to lose him? He needed a task that would divert his mind from the news that Gabe had been shot.

"Danny!" She heard the same brisk command in her voice that she'd heard in her father's. Like a true Stone, Danny's head snapped up and he gave her his full attention.

"Run get Roland. I need someone to help me get your father inside. Then go tell your grandmother and the others. They need to know what's happened. Run like the wind."

Danny took off, passing Roland, who was just rounding the corner of the house. If there had been time, Rachel would have hugged him in relief.

"I heard all the commotion and headed this direction. Figured you might need some help," he said, already moving toward the rear of the wagon. "There's a passel of folks headed this way to see what's going on."

Grabbing her skirt in one hand, she hurried to join him. When Roland saw who it was, he raised his troubled gaze to hers. She knew he was remembering the other time a beaten, bloody Gabe had been brought for her to patch up.

Edward returned, dragging the stretcher behind him. Rachel slid it into the wagon bed and Roland climbed in, lifting Gabe's upper torso while Rachel took his feet. Every molecule of her body was telling her to hurry, yet common sense urged her to take care.

A quick visual once-over told her that he'd been in another fight— were there more broken ribs?— and confirmed that he had indeed been shot. Twice. One bullet had struck him low in the side. The other had grazed his skull just above his left eyebrow. It had bled profusely, which was normal for a scalp wound. The bleeding had slowed to a sluggish ooze. She didn't want to think that if it had been an inch over he would be dead. She didn't want to think of possible brain trauma.

Together, she and Roland got Gabe into the surgery and onto the table. She gave Roland a quick smile of thanks. "Go get Mrs. VanSickle and take her into the bedroom. She thinks she's broken her ankle. Dad will have to handle that while I take care of Gabe. Then stay close in case we need you."

Knowing Roland would do her bidding, she gave Gabe a whiff of ether to keep him from waking while she treated him, then scrubbed her hands. She cut away his shirt and vest and pushed the fabric aside to examine the wound on his side. Luckily the bullet had entered the soft tissue near his waist. She rounded the table and heaved him to his side. Spotting the exit wound, she knew the bullet had traveled straight through. She was cleaning the injury when her father came into the room.

"How about some help?"

"That would be great, but what about Sarah's ankle?"

Edward was already scrubbing his hands. "It isn't broken, just a really nasty sprain. I gave her a little laudanum to ease the pain, so she'll be fine until we get to her. From the looks of things, Gabe needs us worse than she does."

"He does," Rachel said, probing with sterile tweezers for any bits of fabric that might have been drawn into the cavity by the expansion and contraction of the surrounding flesh.

While she worked on the soft-tissue wound, Edward irrigated the head injury and probed the area with his finger. "I'm pretty sure there's no fracture or bone splinters," he said. "And the bullet missed all the big vessels. He'll have a massive headache when he wakes up, but barring infection, he should be fine with a few stitches."

Still as white as a sheet, Rachel looked up from her own work and flashed him an uneasy smile. *Barring infection...* The unknown element that doctors always worried about. But Gabe was strong and healthy, and she'd done a thorough job of cleaning his wound, as she knew Edward had. *Please, God...*

When she finished bandaging Gabe's side, she determined that besides a few bruises on his face, he had no other injuries. Then she poured some fresh water, fetched a clean cloth and began to wash away the blood.

Her touch was as gentle as if he were a newborn, as she cleansed the reminder of the ordeal and revealed the face she loved so much. She smoothed the cloth over a cheekbone, trailing it over his eyebrows and the grooves in his cheeks.

"Rachel."

She looked up to see her father's smiling face.

"Maybe you ought to marry the boy so you can keep an eye on him. We can't have this happening every six months."

"What makes you think he wants to marry me?" she asked, amazed by the breathlessness she heard in her voice and surprised that her father had brought up what she'd supposed would be a touchy subject.

"Because he's already asked me if I'd mind."

Rachel had no time to think about what her father had said. After they checked Sarah over and treated her cuts and scrapes, Rachel immobilized the swollen ankle. Sarah would spend a miserable few days, but her injuries were not serious, and Rachel released the groggy female into the care of her husband and son, telling them that if they needed her in the night, not to hesitate coming for her.

Secure in the knowledge that she and her father had done all they could for their patients, she cleaned and straightened the bedroom and treatment room. Rock steady and able to rely on her skill and knowledge in a crisis, she was less professional if the patient was someone she cared about, often assaulted by a ridiculous panic and shakiness once the emergency had passed. Mundane tasks helped steady her.

After peeping in on Gabe once more, she and her father went into the parlor, where the Granvilles and the preacher sat waiting for news of his condition. Someone had made coffee and served the leftover peach cobbler she'd made for supper.

Libby, who was cuddling Danny on her lap, looked up as soon as she spied them in the doorway. Worry added years to her pretty face. Danny, too, looked anxious. Thank goodness his grandmother had been here to comfort him.

"How is he?" Libby demanded. "Danny said he'd been shot."

"Yes."

"Who would do such a thing?"

"Sarah said it was Elton Thomerson and another man."

"A local, I assume?" Win asked.

"Yes. Sarah told Dad she was being robbed and Gabe came to help, but that's all we know at the moment. There was no time to ask too many questions since he needed immediate attention. We'll have to wait until one of them is lucid enough to tell us more."

Weary from standing so long, Edward, who had traded his canes for his wheelchair, rolled himself over to Libby and gave her hand a reassuring squeeze. "Barring infection or trauma to the brain, he should be fine."

"Trauma to the brain?" Win echoed. For the first time since meeting him, Rachel saw a breach in his supreme self-possession.

"He sustained a gunshot wound to his side." Rachel put her hand on her own side to indicate the approximate location. "The bullet went all the way through. I cleaned it as best I could and removed a few cloth fragments. But infection is always a concern.

"It appears the second bullet grazed his scalp." Again, she pointed out the spot. "Dad didn't detect any bone fragments, and we don't expect any other damage at this point, but we can't be completely sure. Unfortunately, we have no way of looking beneath the skull to assess any other injury."

"Is he gonna be all right?"

The question was asked by Danny, who looked at her with the fearful expression of someone who realized that his world had been turned upside down and he had no way to set it aright.

Rachel crossed over to him and squatted down. Danny catapulted from his grandmother's lap into his mother's embrace, flinging his arms around her neck.

"I hope so, Danny," she said, holding him close and inhaling the little-boy scent of him. Dirt and sweat. A smell she could breathe in all day. One Libby had been robbed of by Lucas Gentry. She blinked back the sudden sting of tears. "You know Pops and I will do everything we can to make him better, but it's in God's hands."

He pulled back to look at her. "Then we should pray, shouldn't we?"

"We have been," Blythe offered. "But we can certainly pray now if you like." She looked at the minister. "Brother McAdams, would you lead us, please?"

"I'd be glad to."

The preacher led the request to God, praying for returned health for both Gabe and Sarah, for the capture of the men who'd caused the injuries and for strength for the families and protection for the community from further incidents. When he'd finished, Danny seemed comforted and asked if he could see Gabe.

"Of course you can," Rachel said, standing and taking Danny's hand. "I'll go with you."

"If it's okay with you, I think Pip should go," he said and gave a shrug. "I mean, Dad is her little boy, and I know she's worried about him."

"You're right, of course," Rachel told him, meeting Libby's gaze. Like Danny, Libby had just found Gabe. If her heart was aching half as much as Rachel's, she was in a lot of pain.

Rachel followed Libby and Danny to the room where Roland had put Gabe after Sarah was taken home. She stopped in the aperture and leaned against the doorframe. Libby went straight to the bed and reached out to brush back an errant lock of Gabe's hair. Danny stood in the doorway watching, almost as if he were gathering the courage to face Gabe's injuries.

Finally he took a tentative step and then another. Libby held out her hand to him and pulled him to her side. Rachel watched as he looked from the bandage wrapped around Gabe's head, over his bruised face to the one circling his middle. He swallowed hard.

"He looks really sick, doesn't he, Pip?" he asked in a low, trembling voice.

"He does," she agreed, pulling up the sheet to hide the disturbing picture from Danny.

Rachel approved of the answer and gesture. There was no sense denying the obvious.

"Do you think he'll be all right?" he asked in a quavering voice.

"I do." The statement held firm conviction. "His father was as tough as nails, and I come from sturdy New England stock, and your mother and grandpa are very good doctors. Besides he's already come through one round with those robbers, so I can't imagine him letting this get him down, can you? He has too much to look forward to."

Danny angled his head and looked up at her. "Like what?"

"Like being a father to you, for one thing. I know it's in God's hands, but I just can't believe that He would bring your father back to his family and not allow you to have a life together."

"Like God sent him back here on purpose?"

"I really think so," she said, brushing Danny's hair away from his forehead as she'd done for Gabe. "God works in our lives, Danny, even when we don't do what He wants. He says, 'You didn't do what I wanted, and now look what a mess you've made of things! But don't worry, I can fix it if you'll only trust me and let me have control of your life.'"

She smoothed his hair again. "People usually understand things better and change as they grow older. Often they try to fix their mistakes by doing the right thing. I believe that when they do, it's God working in their lives."

He nodded. "Is that what He's doing with Mom and Dad? Mom said they made a mistake a long time ago. Do you think God is trying to help them fix it?"

Rachel blinked and swallowed the lump that suddenly clogged her throat. From across the room, Libby's eyes met hers.

"I do," she said with the same conviction she'd used earlier. "I really do."

Chapter Thirteen

It was almost midnight when Rachel finally convinced the Granvilles that Gabe was stable and they all should go back to the hotel for some sleep since they would be leaving for Boston the following day. When he arrived, Caleb joined her in trying to convince his mother. Libby finally agreed to get some rest but vowed that nothing could persuade her to leave town until she knew for certain that Gabe was on the road to recovery. Understanding the maternal mind-set, Rachel offered no further argument.

Once she had donned her gown and robe, she went into Gabe's room and made another thorough check of him. His pulse was steady, and both injuries had all but stopped bleeding. He stirred as she listened to his chest.

"Lie still," she said, gently pressing a hand to his shoulder.

At the sound of her voice, he opened his eyes,

glassy with pain and dulled by the anesthesia she'd given him. "Rachel."

His voice sounded as if he'd swallowed gravel.

"Don't talk."

"Not going anywhere."

"Not for a while," she said, removing the earpieces and looping the stethoscope around her neck. She started to turn away, and his hand moved with surprising speed to grasp her wrist.

"Don't go."

"I'll be right here," she said.

"Promise."

"I promise." The vow seemed to satisfy him, and he closed his eyes. She slipped from his loose grasp, and convinced that he was holding his own, she lay down on the cot.

Drawing a deep breath, she forced the hands fisted at her sides to unclench and folded them over her middle. Using a technique her father had taught her, she started at her toes and willed every part of her body to relax, releasing her not only from the tension, but also the "doctor mode." Once she was filled with calmness instead of cool objectivity, she could try to process the past few hours and all they meant. One thing stood out above all else.

Gabe might have been killed.

She wasn't aware that the tears she'd imprisoned behind a facade of professionalism had escaped and were running down her temples. She had waffled over her feelings for weeks now, knowing she loved him but telling herself she wasn't sure she could trust him or that love, feeling he had to prove that he had changed and that he intended to stay no matter what, so that she and Danny would not get hurt.

What a cockamamy notion! She either loved him or she didn't. Real love didn't set rules. It didn't depend on stipulations: *Promise you will never do anything to make me angry or hurt me. Prove that you won't repeat the same transgressions so that I can trust that you mean what you say. Do all these things and I'll love you.*

Ridiculous and naive.

Love just *was*.

Loving someone and sharing a life was fraught with pitfalls that guaranteed pain. Whether it was sudden and passionate, tender and gentle, or based on the solid bedrock of respect and mutual liking learned through the years, love was an indefinable emotion that crept up and took root in the heart, often when you were not looking for it and least expected it.

Love bloomed indiscriminately and for reasons no one understood, often striking two people who were totally unsuited or were in disparate places in their lives—like Caleb and Abby.

It was near impossible to imagine two people less likely to suit, yet despite that, and despite not knowing it at the time, they had each seen something in the other they needed to be whole.

She began to think it was the same with her and Gabe, and yet she had almost let her stubborn pride and resentment blind her to the truth. She would make no excuses for him or herself or their past. The truth was that even back then she'd recognized something in him that she lacked and yearned to possess.

He was interested in almost everything and she was single-minded. He was curious and she was cautious. He was spontaneous; she was structured.

Yet she'd been drawn to something else about him. She sensed there was a hunger gnawing at him, but she had not been able to pinpoint what it was. Only in the past few weeks had she realized that his happy-go-lucky persona was nothing but a veneer to hide his loneliness, and his years of defying convention had been a quest for some indefinable something to fill the void in his life and his heart.

An emptiness left by a dearth of love.

Lying immobile, trying to keep the noise of her crying as quiet as possible, her aching heart threatened to break as she tried to imagine what it must have been like to grow up with Lucas Gentry as a father in a house that was not a home. With no one to comfort, to encourage, to love. She could not reconcile the image with her own loving upbringing.

She imagined what it must have been like to grow to young adulthood with Lucas setting the standard. There had been no one to teach Gabe and Caleb decent values, respect for women or the difference between love and desire. That he would grow up to be a scoundrel was not so surprising. The surprise was that he'd grown up to be decent in spite of his upbringing…or lack of it. Libby's goodness and integrity surely ran through his veins.

Rachel could almost imagine Gabe's thoughts as he wandered aimlessly over the country seeking the next city, the next amusement, the next woman. Maybe *here* would be the place, *this* would be the diversion, *she* would be the woman, only to realize that they were not.

She was positive of one thing now. He was not the same man she'd fallen for nine years ago. She couldn't imagine that Gabe throwing himself between a bullet and a woman who had wronged him so badly. This Gabe had made great strides in becoming a different person. This Gabe was a man she could love and trust, and yet it had taken the prospect of losing him to make her realize it.

If he did die—and that still was not outside the realm of possibility—he would never know she loved him or that she would say yes if he did ask her to marry him. Faced with the possibility of losing him, she was certain she wanted nothing more than to spend the rest of her life with him, teaching and showing him all about the love he'd never known.

She would let him teach her about the things she lacked and so desperately needed—like spontaneity and seeing the unexpected humor in the commonplace and what it was that made him so fascinated with so many areas of life. She wanted to wade in the creek, to fly kites, to go off for a weekend without a plan.…

She prayed, asking God to spare Gabe, for her

sake and Danny's. Prayed for another chance to get things right. Even knowing that her requests might not be answered in the way she wished, when she whispered "Amen" she was at peace.

She had done everything in her power to restore him to health. He was fine for the moment. It was enough. Like Libby, Rachel believed that God indeed had had a plan when He brought them all together again. They would just have to wait to see what it was.

The following morning dawned sunny and full of promise. Gabe had slept soundly through the night. If he was able, she would have him sit up today.

After a quick breakfast and a single cup of coffee, she left her father in charge of the patient and headed across town to see how Sarah was doing. She hoped the woman was enough recovered to tell her exactly what had happened.

She found Sheriff Garrett there with the same goal in mind. They exchanged smiles and greetings.

Sarah was propped up in bed and was having a light breakfast, though she said she wasn't the least bit hungry. She was still groggy from the laudanum and had trouble keeping her thoughts corralled, but she managed to give a reasonable account of what had happened on the Antoine road.

"I'd gone out to the Allen place to take Nita some supplies. She's been having a hard time of it since Yancy was killed."

Nita was an Indian who, to the consternation of

many in town, had married an Irish logger some thirty-three years before. Not only had they held it against her, they'd looked down on her son, until he'd left to make his own way in the world.

"The boy is back from prison now, you know," Sarah said. "Though someone well over thirty isn't a boy, is he? He's quite a menacing-looking individual," she said with a shudder. "Big and mean looking. He never said a word or cracked a smile while I was there. Nita said he—"

"Begging your pardon, Sarah, but can you tell us what happened to you and Gabe yesterday evening?" Colt asked, sensing that a gossip session was about to begin. "You said you'd taken them some supplies."

"Yes, just basic things. It's our Christian duty to help others, you know, even if they are savages."

Colt's mouth tightened. "Right. So what happened on your way home?"

"These two masked ruffians ambushed me! They came riding out of the woods and forced me to pull over. Then one of them dragged me from the buggy and ripped off my earrings. Thank the good Lord my ears aren't pierced," she exclaimed. "Ears bleed a lot, don't they, Rachel?"

Not waiting for her to answer, Sarah forged ahead. "About the time they demanded my reticule and other valuables, Gabe came along and told me to give them what they wanted. Well, I told him, told the others, too, that I had no intention of handing anything over. I like my jewelry, and

Randolph worked hard to buy it for me. You understand, don't you, Rachel? How a woman feels about her pretties?"

"Of course," she replied, eager for Sarah to move along with the story. She was more than a bit amazed by Sarah's tenacity and willingness to fight.

"Gabe and the other man wrestled around and his bandanna fell down, but I didn't recognize him. I was trying to scratch out the other hooligan's eyes, and he lost his mask, too. You can't imagine how shocked I was to see that it was that no-good Thomerson scoundrel."

"So it *was* Meg's husband?" Rachel asked, forgetting that she was not the one asking the questions.

"I told you that last night," Sarah complained. "You should pay better attention. At any rate, one of them said that we'd seen their faces. The other one pulled his gun, and I could see by the cold meanness in his eyes that he had every intention of using it. He swung it toward me and told Gabe to stay back. I flung myself into the gully, figuring any harm that might come of it would be better than being shot. As I was going over the edge, Gabe threw himself between me and Thomerson.

"He could have been killed," she said, dabbing at her eyes with a snowy-white napkin, "but he stepped between me and those bullets."

The sheriff and Rachel looked at each other, shocked by the display of emotion. Maybe Sarah had a heart after all.

Colt asked her a few more questions and said if he needed to know anything more, he'd come back when she was feeling better.

After he left, Rachel examined Sarah from head to toe. Satisfied that she, too, was doing well and cautioning her to stay in bed for the remainder of the day, Rachel promised to be back before supper and headed to Ellie's.

She stepped into the cozy café with its cheerful yellow gingham curtains and blue crockery displayed on the shelves. The air was redolent with the mingled scents of frying ham and fresh-brewed coffee, teasing her taste buds even though she'd eaten with her father.

She was surprised to see Win sitting at a table near the window. Ellie was nowhere to be seen, probably in the kitchen. Bethany was standing at the pass-through to the kitchen, waiting for an order. Her hair, strawberry blond instead of dark auburn like her mother's, rippled down her back in loose waves. She turned and recognized Rachel. The smile that bloomed on her face shone in her slanted brown eyes.

"Coffee, Miss Doctor Rachel?"

Her words were not enunciated clearly because of the extra length of her tongue, but you could still understand what she was saying.

"That's right, Beth. And will you add some of that condensed milk if you have it?"

"Yes, ma'am."

Rachel took the seat across from Win. "Eating alone?"

"Everyone else was still asleep, and I needed my coffee," he told her with that easy smile of his. "Of course, the ham smelled so good I decided on breakfast, too. May I buy you some?"

"Thank you, but I ate with Dad."

"How's Gabe?"

"He had a good night. Everything seems fine this morning. I don't suppose you know if your mother rested or not."

"No. Have you found out anything else?"

"Sheriff Garrett was at Sarah's when I went to check on her."

Bethany arrived with the coffee and set it down carefully. "Thank you," Rachel said, smiling at the young girl. "You look very pretty in that blue dress."

"Thank you, Miss Doctor Rachel." She turned to go back to wait for the order.

"What a shame," Win said, watching her go. "If it weren't for the Mongolism, she'd be a beautiful child."

Rachel speared him with a disapproving look. "She's a beautiful child just as she is," she informed him in a tart tone. "And actually very smart in her own way."

"Forgive me," he said, seeing that he had ruffled Rachel's feathers. "I mean no disrespect, merely that it is a sadness."

"I'm sure you didn't, but please don't waste any

time on pity. Neither Bethany nor Ellie would appreciate it, I can assure you."

Ellie chose that moment to step through the swinging door, Win's breakfast in her hands. His relief was palpable. Instead of handing it to her daughter, she said, "Will you please bring that little bowl with Mr. Granville's gravy, Beth?"

"Yes, Mama."

The smile Ellie bestowed on her daughter lingered as she turned back to Win. "Here you go," she said, setting down the plate filled with fried ham, biscuits and three eggs over easy.

Win looked at the spread with combined pleasure and dismay. "You wouldn't want to marry me, would you?" he asked, his tawny-brown eyes gleaming with that wicked, teasing twinkle.

Ellie's face flooded with color, and Rachel thought she saw a bit of panic in her brown eyes. Though she could hold her own with the old-timers who often tormented her about one ridiculous thing or another, she was unaccustomed to casual banter from handsome strangers. Certainly the upright sheriff didn't tease this way. He was far too serious.

Quick to recognize that he'd overstepped some invisible boundary, Win held up a hand to stay whatever she was about to say. "Forget I asked," he quipped with another of those ready grins. "You'd be the death of me."

"I beg your pardon," Ellie said with a frown.

"I'd weigh a ton if I ate like this every day," he told her with a rueful smile. "Die of a heart attack."

The tension in Ellie's shoulders eased, and she turned her attention to Rachel in an attempt to take the conversation another direction. "What did you find out from Sarah? I know Colt went out with a posse, but no one has heard who they're looking for yet."

"Elton Thomerson," Rachel said and proceeded to recount Sarah's tale.

"Too bad Colt didn't get the information last night. He might have been able to arrest him before he left the country," Ellie said.

She was right, but there was no way Sarah would have been coherent enough to tell her story the night before. "Whether he's picked up and tossed into prison or took off for parts unknown, Meg will be left to fend for herself," Rachel said.

They discussed Meg's situation for a few more minutes. Rachel told them that Nita Allen's son, Ace, was out of prison, and Win informed them that they planned to stay in Wolf Creek at least another week to monitor Gabe's progress. Eventually, the conversation returned to the robbery and Sarah's tearful championing of Gabe.

"So Gabe took a bullet for her," Win said, spearing up another bite of ham.

"That's what she said."

Three more customers came in, taking Ellie away from their benign gossip session. Rachel left Win to finish his breakfast and went back home to see about Gabe and tell her father what she'd learned about the robbery.

* * *

Consciousness returned with a stomach-churning wave of pain. Gabe gave a groan and tried to sit up, which only cranked up the anguish a notch. His hands went to his head, though it seemed as if he were moving them through molasses.

Immediately, he felt cool fingers wrap around his wrists to force them back to his sides. He opened his eyes and saw Rachel standing there. She placed the back of her hand against his forehead and then his cheek.

"Do you know who I am?"

He frowned. "What kind of stupid question is that?" he asked, feeling as if he were speaking around a mouth full of cotton wool.

Her lips twitched as she fought to suppress a smile.

"Do you know who you are?"

He squinted in irritation and pain. "A better question might be who are you and what did you do with the mother of my son?" he mumbled somewhat testily.

Joy bubbled through her. Thank God there didn't seem to be any damage to the brain. He would be fine if they could keep the infection and fever away. She did laugh then. His dry sense of humor was one of the things she loved about him.

"What's so funny?"

"You are."

He scowled. "May I have some water, please?

My mouth feels like I've walked ten miles through the desert."

"Just a little," she said, pouring an inch into a cup. "If you think your head hurts now, you don't want to find out how it would feel if you start vomiting."

"What's wrong with me this time?" he asked.

She explained his injuries as she slipped her arm beneath his shoulders and eased him upright while he pushed against the mattress. She held the cup to his lips and he sipped slowly, savoring every drop. "Thank you."

"Do you feel like being propped up awhile? I'm going to give you something for the pain."

"Maybe for a while," he said. "But no pain medication."

"We've been through this before, Gabriel," she said in a firm tone as she placed a couple more pillows behind his upper torso. He groaned and grumbled the whole time she eased him to a sitting position.

She crossed her arms over her chest. "I rest my case. Just let me give you enough to take off the edge during the day and help you sleep through the night. Please."

"You're a tyrant."

"And you're a hardhead. You'll heal better if we can stay on top of the pain," she wheedled.

"Fine," he said, his face gray with agony. "I do feel like I've been rowed up Salt River."

She measured a small amount of laudanum.

"Well, you *were* in a fistfight, besides being shot. Can you tell me what happened?"

"Rachel. Is there any possibility that you've been in Pete Chalmers's hard cider?"

"Humor me."

"Sarah was being robbed. I went to help. The guy, someone I should know but don't remember, was going to shoot her, and I tried to stop him, so it seems I was the one who got shot."

"Very good," she said, giving him an irritating, patronizing pat on the hand. She wet a cloth with cool water and began to bathe the perspiration from his face.

"Is Sarah all right?" he asked.

"It seems she bailed off into the ravine while you took the bullets. She has a sprained ankle."

"She's lucky she didn't break her neck. I remember her trying to help me stand up and us leaning against each other as we hobbled to the surrey. She was crying and saying that I would *not* die. That she might have been responsible for my misery, but she absolutely refused to be responsible for my death."

"That sounds like Sarah," Rachel said, putting the washcloth back into the basin of water. "Now go to sleep."

"Are you going to be this bossy when we get married?" he grumbled.

"Probably."

At the end of a week, Gabe was still suffering from headaches, but he was feeling well enough to sit out on the front porch with her father or Danny and enjoy the late-spring breeze. Thankfully, there had been no sign of infection. Rachel credited it to her thorough cleaning of the wounds.

Sunday afternoon found him sitting with his eyes closed, and his head leaned against the tall back of a rocking chair while Danny played a game of checkers with Ben. Caleb and his family and all the Granvilles were there. They had shared a final meal together before Pip and the others headed back to Boston. Rachel knew his interaction with the company had tired him, but he refused to rest since it was their last time together for several months.

A desultory breeze tickled the leaves of the rose-bushes and sent the yellow heads of the coreopsis bouncing to an unheard rhythm. Stomachs filled, eyelids heavy, the conversation was as aimless as the gentle wind drifting over them.

Rachel couldn't recall when she'd felt so at peace. After she had foolishly replied to Gabe's question about marriage with a facetious answer that could only be construed as a "yes," she'd been waiting for him to bring up the subject again. So far, he'd said nothing. She wasn't certain whether to be disappointed or relieved.

Though it was almost every woman's dream to find the right man and marry, the thought of committing to a lifetime with someone raised all sorts of worrisome questions for a woman set in her ways. She wondered where they would live and if Gabe would tire of her racing off into the night at the beck and call of the people in town. Would he really be happy in Wolf Creek, and perhaps most importantly, would he want to have more children? He doted on Danny, but what would he be like as they traveled through the ups and downs of a pregnancy together?

Wonderful.

Somehow she knew that as well as she knew her own name. She was lost in thoughts of a little girl who looked a lot like Danny when she saw a surrey headed toward them, trailing a cloud of dust.

"That's Sarah's rig," Edward said. And indeed it was. Her husband, Randolph, who everyone thought deserved far better than what he had for a wife, was driving.

"What on earth can she possibly want?" Libby said. "Hasn't she caused enough trouble?"

They didn't have to wait long to find out. Randolph pulled to a stop near the rose-laden arch, helped his wife down from the buggy and handed her a set of crutches.

"Hello there, Randolph," Edward said. "Come and join us. We have a couple of extra chairs."

So far, Sarah had not said a word or made eye contact with anyone. All her attention was focused on maneuvering the stone pathway.

"Thank you, Edward," Randolph said. "It's a lovely afternoon, isn't it?"

"Indeed it is."

Sensing that the adults might not want children present, Blythe took it upon herself to herd them into the house for a lemonade while Sarah hobbled up the steps and sat down next to Rachel.

"I'll wait in the buggy," Randolph said.

"Thank you, my dear," she replied with a smile of genuine gratitude. "And thank you for understanding."

He nodded and strode out toward the road.

"I'm so glad you're all here," she said. "It will make this easier."

Her gaze moved around the group, all people whose lives she had complicated with her unbridled tongue. "That ordeal last week opened my eyes to a lot of things," she said, jumping right into the subject. "Staring down the barrel of a Colt puts things into perspective really fast. I realized in that moment that I have been a Christian in name only. Oh, I've spouted scripture with the best of them and helped the needy, but it was all more something to do than something I really felt in my heart. It will take some time, but I mean to change that."

She inhaled deeply, as if she were fortifying herself for a battle. "The first thing I wanted to do was to come and thank you, Gabriel." Her voice quavered with emotion, and there was no hint of her usual smug superiority. "If you hadn't come along when you did, I might have been found in that ravine dead."

"No need to thank me, Sarah," Gabe told her. "Anyone would have done the same."

"If you believe that, you're more naive than I've been led to believe," she said with a touch of asperity. Again, she let her gaze rove around the gathering. Her eyes were overbright.

"I have hurt all of you deeply by spreading rumors and gossiping and stirring up all sorts of trouble. A lot of folks in this town who'd been treated like that would have just driven by without so much as a fare-thee-well. And I honestly can't say I'd blame them."

"Maybe you aren't giving the people in town enough credit," Abby said. "Yes, you have hurt all of us, but everything has come to rights, and I feel that I speak for us all when I say that we've forgiven you." She gave Caleb a sharp look.

He nodded.

"Gabe? Edward? Rachel?" Sarah queried and received three nods in tandem.

"Well, Elisabeth," Sarah said, pinning Libby with a pointed look. "What about you? Can you forgive me for... Lucas?"

Libby was silent for long moments. Finally, she looked at Sarah. "Knowing you weren't the only one, Sarah, makes it easier. Certainly I can. While no one wants a marriage to break up for any reason, and I was devastated when mine did, I'm certain I was much happier with Sam than I ever could have been with Lucas. Forgiving you for your part in my losing my boys will be harder, but with God's help, I'll manage that, too, in time."

"Thank you. I don't deserve it, but thank you all." Tears spilled down Sarah's cheeks. She grabbed her crutches and heaved herself to her feet.

Rachel's eyes felt prickly, as well. As furious as

she'd been at the woman, as much as she had detested Sarah's behavior, she felt a sudden sorrow and even pity. She hoped that Sarah had truly repented for her wrongs and would turn her life around.

At the bottom of the steps, she turned and looked from Gabe to Rachel and back to Gabe. When she spoke, there was a hint of the old Sarah in her tone. "No doubt you'll think me pushy when I say this, Gabriel, but you really should marry Rachel. That boy of yours needs the security of knowing both his parents are together."

Gabe turned to look at Rachel, but his words were directed to Sarah. "For once, I think you're exactly right, Sarah." One corner of his mouth lifted in a teasing half smile. "In fact, she's already said yes—more or less."

"I don't recall your asking me to marry you," Rachel denied. "I believe you asked me if I would be so bossy when we were married."

"And you said 'yes.'"

"I said 'probably,'" she countered. "I didn't think you knew what you were saying since you were under the influence of a painkiller at the time."

"I knew, and I meant it."

Smiling, Rachel leaned toward him and whispered, "So did I."

And then she kissed him, the imperfect man who had stolen her heart. Danny's prodigal father, finally come to a place filled with love. Home.

* * * * *

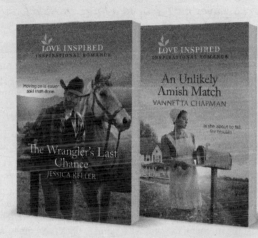

"Get back!"

Definitely a female voice, from the other side of the barn. He walked around the barn. If someone had asked him to guess what he might find there, he wouldn't in a hundred years have guessed correctly.

A young Amish woman—Plain dress, apron, *kapp*—was holding a feed bucket in one hand and a rake in the other, attempting to fend off a rooster. At the moment, the bird was trying to peck the woman's feet.

"What did you do to him?" Daniel asked.

Her eyes widened. The rooster made a swipe at her left foot. The woman once again thrust the feed bucket toward the rooster. "Don't just stand there. This beast won't let me pass."

Daniel knew better than to laugh. He'd been raised with four sisters and a strong-willed mother. So he snatched the rooster up from behind, pinning its wings down with his right arm.

"Where do you want him?"

"His name is Carl, and I want him in the oven if you must know the truth." She dropped the feed bucket and swiped at the golden-blond hair that was spilling out of her *kapp*. "Over there. In the pen."

Daniel dropped the rooster inside and turned to face the woman. She was probably five and a half feet tall, and looked to be around twenty years old. Blue eyes the color of forget-me-nots assessed him.

She was also beautiful in the way of Plain women, without adornment. The sight of her reminded him of yet another reason why he'd left Pennsylvania. Why couldn't his neighbors have been an old couple in their nineties?

"You must be the new neighbor. I'm Becca Schwartz—not Rebecca, just Becca, because my *mamm* decided to do things alphabetically. We thought you might introduce yourself, but I guess you've been busy. Mamm would want me to invite you to dinner, but I warn you, I have seven younger siblings, so it's usually a somewhat chaotic affair."

Becca not Rebecca stepped closer.

"Didn't catch your name."

"Daniel...Daniel Glick."

"We didn't even know the place had sold until last week. Most people are leery of farms where the fields are covered with rocks and the house is falling down. I see you haven't done anything to remedy either of those situations."

"I only moved in yesterday."

"Had time to get a horse, though. Get it from Old Tim?"

Before he could answer, a dinner bell rang. "Sounds like dinner's ready. Care to meet the folks?"

"Another time. I have some...um...unpacking to do."

Becca shrugged her shoulders. "Guess I'll be seeing you, then."

"Yeah, I guess."

He'd hoped for peace and solitude.

Instead, he had half a barn, a cantankerous rooster and a pretty neighbor who was a little nosy.

He'd come to Indiana to forget women and to lose himself in making something good from something that was broken.

He'd moved to Indiana because he wanted to be left alone.

Don't miss
The Amish Christmas Secret *by Vannetta Chapman,*
available October 2020 wherever
Love Inspired books and ebooks are sold.

LoveInspired.com

*Before he testifies in an important case, businessman
Michael "Mikey" Fiore hides out in Jacobsville, Texas,
and crosses paths with softly beautiful Bernadette, who
seems burdened with her own secrets. Their bond grows
into passion...until shocking truths surface.*

Read on for a sneak peek at
Texas Proud,
the latest book in
#1 New York Times *bestselling author Diana Palmer's*
Long, Tall Texans series!

Mikey's fingers contracted. "Suppose I told you that the
hotel I own is actually a casino," he said slowly, "and it's
in Las Vegas?"

Bernie's eyes widened. "You own a casino in Las
Vegas?" she exclaimed "Wow!"

He laughed, surprised at her easy acceptance. "I run it
legit, too," he added. "No fixes, no hidden switches, no
cheating. Drives the feds nuts, because they can't find
anything to pin on me there."

"The feds?" she asked.

He drew in a breath. "I told you, I'm a bad man." He
felt guilty about it, dirty. His fingers caressed hers as they

neared Graylings, the huge mansion where his cousin lived with the heir to the Grayling racehorse stables.

Her fingers curled trustingly around his. "And I told you that the past doesn't matter," she said stubbornly. Her heart was running wild. "Not at all. I don't care how bad you've been."

His own heart stopped and then ran away. His teeth clenched. "I don't even think you're real, Bernie," he whispered. "I think I dreamed you."

She flushed and smiled. "Thanks."

He glanced in the rearview mirror. "What I'd give for just five minutes alone with you right now," he said tautly. "Fat chance," he added as he noticed the sedan tailing casually behind them.

She felt all aglow inside. She wanted that, too. Maybe they could find a quiet place to be alone, even for just a few minutes. She wanted to kiss him until her mouth hurt.

Don't miss
Texas Proud *by Diana Palmer,*
available October 2020 wherever
Harlequin Special Edition books and ebooks are sold.

Harlequin.com

HSEEXP0920